# Defensive

# HEARTS

## ALLEY CIZ

# DEFENSIVE HEARTS

# ALSO BY ALLEY CIZ

.

.

.

.

.

## Stay Connected With Alley

**Amazon**

FB Reader Group

**Website**

# BLURB

### Chance

The day I saw Gemma Steele's delicious body wearing nothing but a few scraps of lace, I knew being traded was the *least* of my problems.

Her sexy text may not have been meant for me, but that image is not something a warm-blooded man could *ever* forget—no matter how badly he wants to. I've tried to resist her, but I can't seem to escape Little Miss Suzy Sunshine. Every interaction is rife with tension and animosity, until it boils over, and we cross the point of no return.

That's when I know I'm screwed, because now when I look at her, all I think is: *Mine.*

Who knew a simple selfie could be such a recipe for disaster?

### Gemma

The first time I met Chance Jenson, I was into the whole broody-bad-boy thing.

But then he opened his mouth and I quickly realized he's not just a little moody—he's the grumpiest jerk to ever lace up a pair of hockey skates. I wasn't having any part of it. I agreed to cook for his dogs, but promised myself that the only thing *he* would ever eat are his words.

I spent more than a year doing my best to hate him, but when Chance's lips land on mine, I feel...*conflicted.*
I don't want to want the jackass.
I certainly don't want to have *feelings* for him.
Unfortunately for me, my heart seems to have other plans.

### What the hell am I going to do?

*\*\*DEFENSIVE HEARTS is an enemies-to-lovers romcom filled with hella sexual tension featuring a sunshiny personal chef, a grumpy hockey player who's jealous his dogs get all her love, and a sexy selfie that pushes this possessive alphahole over the edge. While this hilarious romance stands alone with its HEA, you won't go wrong catching up with the best girl gang around—The Covenettes—in the rest of the BTU Alumni series.\*\**

Defensive Hearts (BTU Alumni, Book 7) Paperback

Alley Ciz

Paperback ISBN: 978-1-950884-98-8

Copyright © 2023 by House of Crazy Publishing, LLC

Copyright © 2023 by House of Crazy Publishing, LLC

Cover Designer: Julia Cabrera at Jersey Girl Designs

Cover Photographer: Wander Book Club Photography

Cover Models: Soj M & Yesi

Editing: Jessica Snyder Edits, C. Marie

Proofreading: Chaotic Creatives; My Brother's Editor

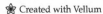 Created with Vellum

# DEDICATION

*This book is dedicated to the jerks I call my friends who refused to let me retire in 2022 like I tried to.*
*#LoveYouBishes*

# AUTHOR NOTE

Dear Reader,

Defensive Hearts can be read as a stand-alone but it is interconnected in the BTU Alumni world. You do not need to read the others first but they do show you a more in-depth history and might help you keep track of the crazy cast of characters as large as The Coven and their guys.

Now for those of you who have been asking for Gemma and Chance's story since the first time they were all tension-y in Sweet Victory...get ready to watch these two battle it out for their happily-ever-after.

XOXO

Alley

BTU3- Sweet Victory (Vince and Holly)
BTU4- Puck Performance (Jase and Melody)
BTU5- Writing Dirty (Maddey and Dex)
BTU6- Scoring Beauty (Ryan and Amara)
BTU7- Defensive Hearts (Gemma and Chance)

# TEXT HANDLES

<u>Gemma</u>
**PRECIOUS GEM:** In Chance's Phone
**PROTEIN PRINCESS:** To The Coven

**Chance:** DICKHEAD DADDY (In Gemma's phone)

<u>The Coven</u>
**Maddey:** QUEEN OF SMUT
**Jordan:** MOTHER OF DRAGONS
**Skye:** MAKES BOYS CRY
**Rocky:** ALPHABET SOUP
**Becky:** YOU KNOW YOU WANNA
**Gemma:** PROTEIN PRINCESS
**Beth:** THE OG PITA
**Holly:** SANTA'S COOKIE SUPPLIER
**Melody:** BROADWAY BABY
**Amara:** MAKE ME OVER GOOSE
**Zoey:** DANCING QUEEN
**Ella:** FIDDLER ON THE ROOF
**(Honorary) Sammy:** THE SPIN DOCTOR

# PLAYLIST

- "River"- Bishop Briggs
- "Can't Be Tamed"- Miley Cyrus
- "One, Two Step"- Ciara and Missy Elliott
- "What's Your Fantasy"- Ludacris
- "Last Night"- Keyshia Cole and Diddy
- "Invisible"- Hunter Hayes
- "You Make Me Wanna"- Usher
- "I Need a Girl (Pt. 1)"- Diddy, Loon, and Usher
- "My Way"- Usher
- "So Sick"- Ne-Yo
- "Let Me Love You"- Mario
- "Gangsta's Paradise"- Coolio and L.V.
- "California Love"- 2Pac, Roger, and Dr. Dre
- "Sexy Can I"- Ray J
- "Nice & Slow"- Usher
- "Baby"- Brandy
- "I Can Love You Like That"- All-4-One
- "U Remind Me"- Usher
- "My Boo"- Usher and Alicia Keys
- "U Got It Bad"- Usher
- "Shake Ya Tailfeather"- Murphy Lee, Nelly, and Diddy
- "Come to Me"- Diddy and Nicole Scherzinger
- "Pass The Courvoisier Part II"- Busta Rhymes, Diddy, and Pharrell Williams
- "Me & U (Remix)- Cassie, Diddy, and Yung Joc

- "Tell Me"- Diddy and Christina Aguilera
- "Gossip Folks"- Missy Elliot and Ludacris
- "Changes"- 2Pac, Talent
- "Keep Ya Head Up"- 2Pac
- "The Next Episode"- Dr. Dre and Snoop Dogg
- "Forgot About Dre"- Dr. Dre and Eminem
- "No Diggity"- Blackstreet, Dr. Dre, and Queen Pen
- "'Till I Collapse"- Eminem and Nate Dogg
- "Lose Yourself"- Eminem
- "River"- Eminem and Ed Sheeran
- "Just Lose It"- Eminem
- "Candy Shop"- 50 Cent and Olivia
- "How We Do"- The Game and 50 Cent
- "P.I.M.P."- 50 Cent
- "Disco Inferno"- 50 Cent
- "If I Can't"- 50 Cent
- "Remember The Name"- Ed Sheeran, Eminem, and 50 Cent
- "The Boy Is Mine"- Brandy and Monica
- "I Wanna Be Down"- Brandy
- "Top of the World"- Brandy and Mase
- "I Swear"- All-4-One
- "Motownphilly"- Boyz II Men
- "Pony"- Ginuwine
- "This Is How We Do It"- Montell Jordan and Wino
- "Doo Top (That Thing)"- Ms. Lauryn Hill
- "Real Love"- Mary J. Blige
- "Family Affair"- Mary J. Blige
- "He Wasn't Man Enough"- Toni Braxton
- "No More Drama"- Mary J. Blige
- "Honey"- Mariah Carey
- "Fantasy (Remix)"- Mariah Carey and Ol' Dirty Bastard
- "You Don't Know My Name"- Alicia Keys
- "Do It To It"- Cherish and Sean Paul
- "Killing Me Softly With His Song"- Fugees
- "No Woman, No Cry"- Fugees
- "I'm Goin' Down"- Mary J. Blige
- "Still D.R.E."- Dr. Dre and Snoop Dogg
- "Nasty"- Janet Jackson

- "No Scrubs"- TLC
- "Snoop"- Salt-N-Pepa
- "Creep"- TLC
- "Red Light Special"- TLC
- "Don't Let Go (Love)"- En Vogue
- "My Lovin' (You're Never Gonna Get It)"- En Vogue
- "All My Life"- K-Ci & JoJo
- "Crazy"- K-Ci & JoJo
- "Tell Me It's Real"- K-Ci & JoJo
- "Here Comes the Hotstepper"- Ini Kamoze
- "It's Tricky"- Run-D.M.C.
- "Bump n'Grind"- R. Kelly
- "Too Close"- Next
- "Enemy"- Imagine Dragons and JID
- "I Shot Cupid"- Stela Cole
- "Dirty Thoughts"- Chloe Adams
- "F U Anthem"- Leah Kate
- "Victoria's Secret"- Jax
- "Frustrated"- R.LUM.R
- Spotify Playlist

# CHAPTER 1

## Chance

*One year ago*

"Didn't your mother ever warn you your face could freeze that way?" I pull up short, my steps halting on the stairs as I swing my gaze over to the blonde cocooned in her husband's arms, bouncing her hazel eyes over my features.

Holy…shit.

When I went upstairs to unpack, there was one Donnelly in the kitchen. Now there are three, plus the Donovan who married into their family. This is way more people-ly than I'm used to in my downtime.

All I wanted was a drink after being buried in moving boxes for the last hour. But, instead of finding a beverage to quench my thirst, I'm greeted with an assessment that has me wishing I kept a jockstrap on me when I finished unpacking. I know the woman is a mom, but *damn* it takes talent to make a grown man wish for ball protection with a single facial expression. Also…what the hell is it about kitchens that cause people to gather like it's a freaking waterhole in the Serengeti?

I force the muscles in my face to relax, smoothing out the scowl currently being critiqued before it leads to more commentary. It's one thing dealing with criticism from the talking heads about my performance on the ice. However, coming face-to-face with a similar analysis in my free time is not a situation I have experience with.

*Shit.*

On a good day, nobody would ever mistake me for Stanley Sunshine, Suzy Sunshine's hotter older brother, but even I can agree my attitude lately leaves a lot to be desired. And snapping at this woman? Yeah…that would be detrimental to my health. Or worse—my career.

Why? Well, that clean-cut white guy she must be standing on tiptoe to see over is both her older brother and my new team captain, Ryan Donnelly.

Captains…

Ugh. I can't seem to escape them.

"I'd apologize for my sister"—Ryan waves a hand at the blonde who has switched her scrutiny to him in an epic side-eye —"but it'll probably be easier if you just get used to her."

He makes a good point.

She may not be as recognizable as the athletes she manages PR for, but anyone who is *anyone* in the sports world *knows* who Jordan Donovan—formerly Donnelly—is. And for those of you in the back of the class who may not know, the chick has bigger *cajones* than anyone in the locker rooms she frequents.

"That's a motherfucking fact." The booming amused statement comes from Jase Donnelly swiveling to and fro on the barstool next to Ryan.

I'd question why he's here since he doesn't even play for our team—in fact, he plays for our rivals, the New York Storm—but as Ryan's younger brother and Jordan's Hemsworth-looking twin, I guess it makes sense, though I can only make that assumption based on what I've seen in the movies or on TV because that is certainly not a family dynamic I have dealt with firsthand.

As if sensing I need the prompting—because they are vastly more intelligent than me—two massive skulls press against the backs of my thighs until my knees buckle and my feet move. I shuffle the rest of the way into the kitchen thanks to my own personal manners patrol—my two Great Danes, Pebbles and Bamm-Bamm— and join this impromptu Donnelly family gathering.

"Shut up, Jase." Jordan scowls at her twin.

"What'd I do?" He shrugs, holding his hands up as if to say, *I'm innocent.*

Jordan shifts onto her forearms, her long ponytail swinging forward onto the countertop. "Why are you even here? I thought Gemma was coming over."

Jase shifts in his chair, pulling his phone out of his pocket. "Sh-she is," he stutters, setting his phone down on the counter.

The corner of Jordan's mouth rises, her cheekbone twitching with the movement. Whatever expression she's making while typing on her phone has Jase scrambling to appease her.

"Have I told you I love you today, wombmate?"

"Suck-up," Ryan cough-says into his fist, causing Jordan to jerk her attention back to him.

"Don't act all innocent, Ry. You keep talking smack and watch what happens."

Ryan pales under his summer tan, Adam's apple bobbing slowly as if to confirm: *See, everything you've heard about her is true.*

"Your wife is a menace, Donovan," Ryan complains to the man once again cocooning the woman in question.

Jake Donovan, the goalie for the Blizzards and another one of my new teammates, laughs at his brother-in-law before glancing my way. It doesn't matter that he's dressed in a faded *Blizzards Hockey* tee, gym shorts, and a backward navy ball cap; the man is just as formidable without the bulk of his goalie gear and skates as he is with it.

But...him winking at me with one of those twinkling green eyes, including me in this insanity, is...weird, as is Jase jumping up and shouting "FACT" as he throws *booyah* arms.

*What the fuck is this?*

Is this what a typical Donnelly family powwow is like? And do they regularly have them on Tuesday afternoons?

Nothing, absolutely *nothing* about this scenario looks like my life from a mere week ago, but for some unexplainable reason, that tiny eye movement has a strange sense of camaraderie pumping through my veins.

I shake off the sensation and focus back on the conversation playing out in front of me. It feels like I should be taking notes, so it's probably best I pay attention and don't miss anything.

"Don't try pinning this on me, Cap," Jake challenges. "*Your* sister is a product of her upbringing."

"Yet you still married her, Brick," Ryan challenges back, his posture improving as his confidence returns.

This time Jase's "FACT" is a bellowing cheer.

"Yes, he did," Jordan retorts, utterly undeterred by her brothers' comments. I'd even go as far as to say there's an air of smugness to her statement. "So don't force me into having my husband kick your ass, Ry."

Jase loses it, his body sliding off his chair like water off a duck's back.

Completely unfazed by his brother's antics and his sister's threat, Ryan leans back onto his elbows. "Never gonna happen, Jor." He swivels his head around lazily and hooks a thumb at his chest. "I'm his captain."

"Mmm, is that so?" Jordan angles her body to face Jake's before walking her fingers up his chest. The moony eyes he stares down at her with have me tempted to call my dentist to check for cavities.

*What in the—*

First, I stumbled into this confounding conversation. Now... this? Am I high on dust? Were my moving boxes coated in some type of psychotropic drug? I swear that has to be it. It's either that, or I've somehow entered an alternate reality.

This is not the same Jake Donovan I know from the ice. My experience with the over-six-foot wall of a man—aptly nicknamed The Brick Wall to our fellow puck heads—is of him fiercely and systematically blocking my shots on goal. This version has me wondering if I somehow stepped onto the set of some cheesy romantic comedy.

This is *so* not my scene. Accepting Ryan's offer to live with him until I sort out my housing issues was difficult enough for...reasons.

But...this? Being tossed into what is obviously a ridiculously tightly knit and *way too* hunky-dory happy group is as fun as sitting in an ice bath after a brutal practice.

I know it makes me an asshole of the highest order, but the way they seamlessly and effortlessly include me in... well...*any*thing is tripping me the hell up. Is this some sort of new age hazing I've never heard of? I get that I'm the new guy, the rookie who was traded midpreseason under...complicated circumstances—but why the fuck are they treating me as if I've been part of their squad since college like the rest of them have?

What's their angle?

And Ryan? Nobody is actually *this* nice, are they? Experience tells me it can't be possible. He has to be hiding some epic assholery behind his "nice guy" persona.

Fuck me. I know why trust is such a hard thing for me to give, but none of this makes it feel like any less of a double-edged sword.

"Sorry to tell you this, Cap, but…"

The smile blooming across Jordan's face is just this side of evil, effectively snapping me out of my suspicious musings. The hairs on the back of my neck rise as she lets her incomplete sentence linger.

Holy shit. What is it about this woman that constantly makes my balls want to retreat inside my body like a turtle seeks shelter inside his shell?

"Pussy outranks pucks every time," Jordan finally finishes.

Who is this woman? It makes me sound like a stereotyping patriarchal douche, but women who look like her don't typically bro around like one of the guys. It's…weirdly refreshing. Though again, I feel that slice of sharpened steel against my psyche.

Ryan's body folds in two, Pebbles and Bamm-Bamm taking advantage of his bent position to lick all over his face, long tongues slipping into his open mouth as he mock-gags to the soundtrack of Jordan's cackle.

My muscles seize, ready and waiting for Ryan's rebuke.

It's coming.

I know it.

How dare the great and powerful captain be violated by the lowly rookie's dogs with drive-by French kisses.

Except…instead of evicting me from his home, Ryan laughs. Like full-on belly laughs, complete with an arm banded around his middle, shoulders bouncing like a too-warm puck ready to be swapped out, a palm slapping the granite countertop with skin-ringing force.

"Well, hello to you too." Ryan gives each of my pups a hearty scratch between their floppy ears before smoothing his hand around to cup them under glistening, slobber-filled jowls. "That's the most action I've gotten in a while." He plops a smooch on Pebbles's black nose.

"*Eww.*" Jordan sticks a finger in her mouth with a dry heave. "TMI, bro."

"Says the girl boinking our best friend," Jase chortles.

"Boinking?" Jordan's brows smash together. "Really, Jase?"

I knew...*knew* Ryan's offer to live with him was too good to be true.

This is precisely the type of situation that makes my skin crawl. And now, all because the Blizzards' organization struggled to find temporary housing that allowed Pebbles and Bamm-Bamm, there's no escape from this group of inappropriate over-sharers.

Awesome.

"All settled in?" Ryan dodges Jordan's attempt to ruffle his hair, bobbing and weaving on his barstool.

My answer to the polite and completely genuine question is more grunt than actual English. My pups huff as they take their places beside me, leaning against me as I instinctually spread my feet apart to brace myself for their familiar weight. My shoulders fall, my whole body deflating at the sound. There is nothing like being judged by your dogs to put a man in his place.

I have to dig for it, but I eventually find the gratitude these people deserve. They may have me completely off balance with their openness and generosity, but I should know better than to hold others' actions against them.

Still...it's harder than it should be because fuck me, I'm triggered.

Three words.

*Fuck.*

These days that's all it takes to trigger me faster than the goal lamp after a slap shot, and this conversation has been littered with sentences comprised of them.

It's amazing, really, how such tiny things can have the capability to upend a person's entire existence, how such simple, short sentences can alter life to nearly unrecognizable proportions. They say bad things come in threes, and that certainly seems to be the case as of late.

"Alright." Jordan presses up on her toes to kiss the underside of Jake's jaw before pushing him away from her. "You three"—

she circles a finger around to include her husband and brothers—
"go play *Mario Kart* or something. Lord knows you could use the
practice."

"I'm pretty sure it was *my* Yoshi owning *your* Rosalina's ass
on Rainbow Road last night," Jase boasts, moonwalking away
from her. I swear the only thing bigger than his probably Viking-
somewhere-in-the-Donnelly-lineage looks is his over-the-top
personality.

"Keep talking shit, wombmate, and watch what happens."

Jase hisses, making a cross with his fingers. "Devil woman."

"Word to the wise." Ryan steps up to my side while Jordan
chases Jase out of the kitchen. "My sister is going to mama bear
the crap out of you since you're one of the new guys *and* because
she's a sucker for fur babies, but she also has a twisted sense of
revenge should you mess with her."

"Duly noted." I nod, reaching down to pet Bamm-Bamm,
who's still by my side, unlike his sister, who's prancing around
with Jase.

"Good luck." Ryan claps me on the back, and I'm about to ask
*With what?* when I notice Jordan has come around to our side of
the island counter and perched on top of it.

And now I'm back to wishing for my jockstrap. Scratch that—
I'll take *all* my hockey pads to guard against the serious expression now gracing Jordan's pretty face.

"Talk to me about *why* you thought it was a good idea to
punch Stanton." Jordan laces her fingers together, folding her
hands over her knee.

"Why? Worried I'm going to do the same thing to Ryan?"

"First off…" Jordan slices a finger through the air. "Lose the
attitude. I'm not the enemy here. In fact, if you let me, I can help
you."

"I don't need your charity." I grab the back of my neck,
pacing in a small circle.

"Charity?" She barks out a laugh. "Oh, honey, no. You would
be paying me."

"Then why?" I spin back to face her. "Are you really worried
my aversion to captains will extend to your brother and I'll go
after Ryan?"

"Please." Jordan rolls her eyes. "I don't know what things
were like in Minnesota, but if you even *tried* going after Ryan,

the *entire* Blizzards roster would have your very fine broody ass."

An unexpected laugh bursts from my lips. "Are you allowed to talk about my ass like that? You're married."

Jordan smashes her lips together like she's trying to restrain a laugh of her own before calling out to her husband. "Babe, Jenson here is concerned about me complimenting his ass."

Jake doesn't even bother to pause his *Mario Kart* as he answers, "I don't care where you get your appetite, baby, as long as you eat at home."

"Gross," Jase shouts.

"Not cool, bro," Ryan adds.

I scrub a hand over my face. What rabbit hole have I fallen into?

"Thanks, babe." Jordan returns her attention to me. "Now spill."

Yeah...that would be a no. Because the *why* behind me punching my old captain in the face is not really something I like to think about.

*Chance, I'm pregnant.*

Oof, hearing those three words was like having Freddy Krueger himself jump out of my dreams to deliver that bombshell like a living nightmare.

"There's nothing to spill," I mutter.

"Mm-hmm." If the expression on Jordan's face is anything to go by, she doesn't believe a single word I'm saying. "Because sending fists flying at people's faces *screams* nothing to spill."

"Are you sarcastic like this with all your clients?"

"Aww." Jordan claps her hands with a happy shrug. "I *love* how easily you've accepted that I'll be your publicist."

"And the answer is yes," Jase calls out, obviously eavesdropping on my conversation with his twin, though I shouldn't be surprised given what I witnessed earlier. "Sarcasm is the love language of the Covenettes."

"Covenettes?" I ask, arching a brow.

"It's what my idiot brother calls my girl gang. Don't mind him." Jordan waves him off. "Tell me about what happened with Stanton."

"I don't know." I smack my hands against my thighs. "I don't typically condone violence off the ice, but the jackass needed to learn that actions have consequences."

"You mean kinda like how karma served you up three of the worst words a hockey player—hell, *any* athlete—can hear?"

Oof. Talking about hitting the nail on the head and triggering a person.

*You've been traded.*

Not my finest hour, that's for sure.

"Be nice, baby," Jake cautions, sending me an *I'm sorry my wife believes in brutal honesty* glance over his shoulder.

"Looks like I'm not the only one who doesn't pull their punches," I say in an effort to change the subject.

"Don't worry." Jordan hops down from the counter. "You'll learn to love that about me." She pats me on the chest. "We'll talk more later," she threatens before flouncing away and climbing onto her husband's lap.

Finally, after doing my damnedest to avoid purging my guts, I'm blessedly alone in the kitchen and can get that drink I initially came down for. Unscrewing the cap on a Gatorade bottle, I chug back half its contents then one of the phones on the counter lights up with a text. I glance at it out of habit and damn near swallow my tongue.

On the screen is a selfie of one of the most fuck-hot women I have *ever* seen in a set of gray lingerie that should be *illegal* to send over a text message.

My jaw drops as I take in her curves and her long dark locks spilling around her shoulders, curling around the cleavage spilling over her bra. A surge of heat ignites between my legs as my eyes wander lower to her full lips and captivating gray eyes twinkling with playful promise.

I gape at the photo like some kind of ticking time bomb waiting to go off any second, torn between the temptation of this beautiful woman and the urge to close my eyes to shut out the memory of who she reminds me of.

I don't know who she is, but she's *clearly* trying to get someone's attention. When her next text comes through, the *who* she's trying to reach becomes obvious.

PROTEIN PRINCESS: Would this make you show me your hockey stick?

Fuck me.

She's a bunny.

Of course she's a bunny. Women don't send text messages like *that* to people like Jase Donnelly unless they are a puck bunny thirsty for hockey dick.

I should know. I've had my share of experience with the type.

But I've learned my lesson: no more puck bunnies. They only come with drama.

Drama and lies.

Drama that ends up with you getting traded from your hockey team.

And lies about being pregnant with your child.

# CHAPTER 2

*Gemma*

M s. Mary J. Blige croons about the importance of real love
through my AirPods as I heft the reusable totes from the
back hatch of my SUV.

One, two—*oomph*—seven bags hang on my shoulders as I
prepare to carry my body weight in groceries in a single haul.
Because really, who wants to ever make more than one trip? Not
this girl.

*Er.* Lift

*Ugh.* Shift.

*Oof.* Untwist.

Wait…

Umm…

Okay…

YES!

There it is. So much better.

Man, that strap was making it its personal mission to become
one with my body by burrowing into my skin.

Finally settled, I reach out for the plastic to-go cup of iced
coffee waiting for me to reclaim it, quickly wrapping my lips
around the straw for a hearty, life-affirming sip. *Ahh, that's the
stuff.*

Look at me go. If grocery hauling ever became an Olympic
sport, I'd be able to join that elite club many of my clients are in
because I'd win all the freaking medals.

Bopping along to the music, I type in the code for the front door, letting myself into Ryan's home while mentally sifting through the meals I'll be preparing to meet his culinary needs. Giddiness pumps through my veins the closer I get to the kitchen. Just the thought of all those stainless steel appliances and miles of granite countertops fills me wi—

*Eep.*

My feet slip on the tile…

*Urmpf.*

One of my flip-flops goes sailing through the air as my legs go all akimbo—*ohnoohnoohno.* The epic load of groceries I was bragging about handling like a boss minutes ago prevents my arms from pinwheeling for balance…

*Squeak.*

Like Jesus, gravity takes the wheel, and I plummet toward the floor.

*Oof.* This is *so* not what Snoop meant by *drop it like it's hot.*

A deluge of liquid hits me before I can process the pain radiating through my back. *Son of a broccoli, that's cold.* Then the gentle clatter of bouncing plastic…

*Grunt.*

Something slams into me.

*What in the—*

Drenched in twenty-four ounces of iced coffee goodness, I whimper at the loss of my pecan pie-flavored favorite, shivering thanks to the aforementioned java, and slowly take stock of my person.

Flat on my back, legs cocked like they're ready to be sketched into one of those crime scene chalk outlines, arms pinned out to my sides by tote bags like an ineffectual scarecrow, I'm sticky as all hell—though I smell *ah-may-zing*, thanks to my fallen comrade —and I…

Can't…

Breathe.

Something…is…

Crushing…me.

*Schwick!*

I guess I can add dog slobber to the list of liquids coating my skin.

Wait…when did Ryan get a dog?

*Woof.*

I whip my head around to the right. Scratch that—two dogs?

With a whole lot of grunting and absolutely zero grace, I wiggle and maneuver until I'm free from my reusable, environmentally friendly shackles. Once liberated, I reach up to scratch the chest of my new furry friend. A quick check of the tags on the collar tells me we finally have our first four-legged Covenette.

"I'm all for an enthusiastic greeting, Pebbles, babe." That earns me a quick lick across the tip of my nose. "But could you maybe help a girl out and shift a bit?"

She gives me a head tilt punctuated by a dollop of drool on my chin before springing off of me. She immediately drops onto her haunches, massive paws spread on the tile floor, head dipped low, ass lifted high, long tail circling with so much propeller-like abundance of enthusiasm I worry she might take flight.

I think I may have just met my actual spirit animal.

I may question if I'm a "real" professional more often than not despite the degree I earned in nutritional science from Brighton Tynes University, but a day like this, when my favorite *One day I'll make the onions cry* tee is covered in the coffee my brain desperately needs to function, is not one of those times.

Nope, today is a day when I am supremely grateful that the clients—at least that's what I call them when I wanna feel official —I'm a personal chef to are made up of my friends and family. Because if Ryan Donnelly, captain for the New Jersey Blizzards, Prince Charming—or, as we've dubbed him, Captain America— of the NHL, wasn't practically family, I'd *never* have had the brussels sprouts to walk into his room and help myself to a replacement shirt while he showers. Thankfully boundaries are something that quickly gets left at the door when you become a member of our squad.

Ryan lets out a far-too-girlish-for-a-man-his-size squeal when I call out a quick hello on my way to his closet. That little sound more than makes up for the loss of my coffee companion.

I'm still giggling as I peel the sticky cotton doing its best impersonation of cling wrap from my damp skin, shimmy out of the soiled tee, and drop it to the floor with a wet *plop*.

"Any particular reason why you're stealing my favorite shirt?" Ryan asks as I'm tugging a well-worn *Property of BTU Athletics* T-shirt over my head.

Now I'm the one squeaking like a rusty hinge in need of WD-40 while he chuckles, pleased to have turned the tables on me.

"Make a little noise when you walk, would ya?" I complain, tugging the shirt until I pop through the collar like a prairie dog peeking out of its burrow, my messy bun automatically listing to the side. Damn his athletic prowess, making him all graceful and shit.

"Not as fun being the startle-ee as it is the startler, hmm?" Arms folded over his broad chest, one foot crossed lazily in front of the other, Ryan leans against the doorjamb of the walk-in, paying no mind to the water droplets trailing down his tan skin or the fact that he's standing in front of me in nothing but a towel.

Nope, there's zero shame in his game. I guess I'm considered small potatoes when one spends most of one's days around two dozen men in some form of undress.

"I figured it was only fair." I bend, hooking a finger inside the damp collar of my soiled tee, grimacing at the wet spot left on the hardwood.

Ryan's eyes flare wide before his brows dip as he stares at the mess dangling from my finger. "Damn, Gem." He smooths a hand across his mouth in an attempt to smother his amusement, but I'm too caffeine deprived to appreciate the effort. "Looks like the twins aren't the only ones who need sippy cups."

My jaw unhinges at being compared to our—no shared blood is needed to claim relation—toddler-aged nieces, and any restraint Ryan may have had bursts free in an echoing bellow.

The jerk.

"The nice Donnelly, my ass," I grumble, stalking past the snickering man who is damn lucky I feel professional enough not to poison his food.

"Aww, Gem…" Ryan falls into step with me, draping an arm over my shoulders and tucking me in tight to his bare side. "You know I love you."

"Mm-hmm." I ignore his cajoling, focusing all my attention on knotting his borrowed shirt at my middle.

"Hey." I'm pulled to a stop, a finger notching under my chin, tilting my face up until I meet concern-filled baby blues.

*Dammit.* Now I feel like a bitch for overreacting. PMS and lack of caffeine are *far* from a love match.

"Sorry," I say, dropping my forehead to Ryan's rib cage.

"Nothing to apologize for." He squeezes my upper arm, nudging me to start walking again. "We all have our days. Now, if you were to put laxatives in my food or something…" The side of his mouth ticks up into that smirk that can make a puck bunny sigh at a thousand paces. "Then we'd have a problem."

Now I'm the one giggling through a declaration of love. Oh, how well he knows me.

"I would *never*." I flatten a hand to my chest in mock offense. "I'm a *professional*, Mr. Donnelly."

"Cut the *Mr. Donnelly* crap." He rolls his eyes. "But you're right."

I preen. I mean…what woman doesn't like to be told she's right? *points to self with two thumbs* Not this one.

"That does sound more like my sister than you."

That's a fact. My girl Jordan certainly has a reputation when it comes to revenge pranks. Thankfully, she only uses her powers for good…*mostly*.

"No need to tempt fate, though," Ryan muses. "Let's go make you a fresh cup of coffee."

I stop at the threshold of the room, spinning on my heel and placing a palm between his defined pecs, shooting a pointed glance at his pebbled nips looking at me like a set of spaced-out googly eyes. "Do you maybe want to get dressed first?"

He waves a hand up and down his fit body. "Are you saying you don't like what you see?"

No. The man is the definition of eye candy. Of course I like it, but…while I may have read *Flowers in the Attic* at far too young an age, and we aren't technically related, that is *not* the type of sibling affection I feel for these Donnelly men.

With so many over-the-top personalities in our group, it's easy to forget the nice guy cinnamon rolls like Ryan also have the cocky gene that seems par for the course with professional athletes. Though, I guess it's hard to fault them for it when they've achieved things so few are capable of. But if you tell my cousin Vince I said that I'll cut you. That man-child's head is already so big it barely fits through most doorways. Lord help us when he finally wins the UFC's Light Heavyweight belt. Seriously...pray for us.

"Are we fishing for compliments this morning?" I mime casting a line and reeling it in.

"Who doesn't like to be told they look good?"

I snort. "And the dozen or so trending hashtags dedicated to your devilish handsomeness and manly prowess aren't enough to boost that self-esteem of yours?" An endearing blush blooms on his cheeks, and I exaggeratedly coo, "You, Ryan Donnelly, are the sexiest thing on skates." I clutch my hands in prayer, shrugging my shoulders and tilting my head for good measure. "Not even your brother can compare."

Dancing backward, I toss my arms out wide with my last declaration, my hand smacking something with an "Oof."

"*Ohmigod.*" I whirl around, jumping back until my back is pressed to Ryan's front.

A deep chuckle rings in my ear, but Ryan isn't the reason shivers are rippling down my spine. No, that honor goes to Mr. Tall Dark and Broody.

*Holy cannoli.*

His obsidian eyes are currently shooting daggers at me from across the narrow hallway, the dark brows above them cutting a harsh line across his olive-toned forehead when his gaze drops to take in the arm Ryan wraps around my middle to prevent me from being one with the floor for the second time this morning.

My skin grows tighter as if too small for my body, and my heart beats against my rib cage like it's trying to escape.

*What in the watermelon?*

"The look on your face was priceless, Gem." Ryan chuckles.

"Yeah, I bet it was a real Kodak moment, Cap," I reply dryly. "Jesus." I turn and poke him. "Warn a girl next time."

"What? That you were about to smack my roommate?" That damn smirk of his returns.

"Umm..." I wave my arms wildly, gesticulating like a penguin trying to take flight despite being a flightless bird.

Damn, looks like I didn't learn my lesson about exuberant bodily movement.

"Or *maybe* how you even have a roommate in the *first* place."

There is so much sarcasm in my tone that Ryan could practically use it like paint to redecorate with.

"Don't play like this doesn't make you downright giddy." Ryan bounces a finger between him and Mr. Could Murder a Person With His Eyeballs across the way. "You know you love cooking breakfast for hockey players."

There's a scoff, and would you look at that, the homicidal vibes radiating my way have suddenly quadrupled.

Oh-kay.

What.

The.

Fuck?

I love a broody bad boy as much as the next girl, and the hottie over there? With his short, messy, inky waves, equally dark eyes, close-cropped beard, and tattoos peeking out from under the collar and short sleeves of his T-shirt and running down his arms...

Yeah, let's just say he will have my girl Maddey itching for her notebook and pen when they meet. If ever *anyone* was tortured hero goals for the book boyfriend in her next bestseller, it's this guy.

But for me? I prefer my grumpy heroes on the pages of Maddey's romance novels. I don't have time for that kind of negative energy in my real life.

Clapping my hands, I bounce on the balls of my bare feet. "You are right about that, my fine sir." Unable to resist any longer, I flick one of Ryan's googly-eyed nips, mildly disappointed the pebbled flesh doesn't actually have a little black disk to spin around.

"Ouch," Ryan barks, slapping his hand over his abused flesh.

"Don't look at me like that." I shrug at his narrow-eyed glare. If only he knew his glower has *nothing* on Murder Eyes over yonder. "You're the one keeping the nips on display."

"*You* stole my shirt," he challenges.

"You have a whole closetful of them." I gesticulate toward the bedroom behind him.

"Since when did breakfast turn into a *No shirt, no shoes, no service* type of affair?"

"Mmm..." I pinch my bottom lip between my fingers. "Never. Eye candy is one-hundred-percent nutritionist-approved. But pants?" I flick my gaze to the towel slipping dangerously low on his Adonis belt. "They might be a good idea." I tap the tucked knot holding the terry cloth together. "Unless you're planning on going full-on *Magic Mike*." I shimmy my shoulders, sticking out my tongue playfully. "Now that's what I'd call dinner—or in this case, breakfast—and a show."

Ryan gives a resigned shake of his head. "Why can I already imagine The Coven Conversation that would take place if I did?"

His mock shudder has me giggling. It's hilarious how scared a group of grown-ass men are of a simple group chat. But then again, my besties who fill that particular text thread are some of the baddest boss bishes around.

The atmosphere shifts the millisecond Ryan disappears inside his bedroom, a thick, cloying cloud of animosity filling the hallway like sludge.

Blowing out a breath, I fight against the weird negativity and turn to introduce myself to Ryan's new roommate. "Hi." I give Mr. Doom and Gloom my sunniest smile, hoping maybe I can beam some optimism into him like I'm freaking Cheer Bear from the *Care Bears*.

Spoiler alert: it doesn't work.

Instead, his jaw clenches, the bone popping out so harshly I worry it'll break through the skin. Damn, somebody needs fiber in their diet because an expression like that has to mean the dude is constipated as fuck.

"I'm Gemma." I stretch out a hand, but the gesture seems to be for naught since he doesn't reciprocate the greeting. Instead, he recoils like I'm contagious.

"Yeah"—he rolls his eyes at my hand—"no thanks."

"Huh?"

"I'm not interested in what you're selling, sweetheart." His hands go up as he takes two steps away from me.

"Selling?" I ask, utterly confused.

"Yup." He runs his gaze over my body, condescension coating my skin like vegetable oil, only to boil over when it locks onto where I have Ryan's shirt knotted. "I may have unwittingly shared in my captain's sloppy seconds before, but I have *zero* desire for a repeat performance."

"*Excuse me?!*" I screech, offense and confusion warring inside my chest.

"I know, shocking, right?" His patronizing tone grates on every one of my coffee-needing nerves. "I'm confident you'll survive without my dick seeing as you're already bouncing between the Donnellys." His cheeks puff out with an audible exhale. "Talk about brotherly love, am I right?"

What in the—

Who does he think—

Heat fills my cheeks, and I sputter, my mind struggling to formulate a response.

"Aww...don't be embarrassed." His derision grates. "You should be proud."

"Proud?" I parrot ineffectually.

"*Yup.*" He pops the P and arches a brow. If his attitude hadn't already unlocked the achievement of making me want to punch him in the nose, that single facial expression certainly would have done it. Call it a character flaw, but I've always found myself jealous of those able to lift a single brow. I can't; it's always both or none at all.

"Oh yeah?" I fold my arms across my chest to keep from actually punching him. It's too early in the day to be racking up broken bones. "And why is that?"

"You're not just spreading your legs for any ol' puck head. Nope—you bagged the golden boy of the NHL." He slow-claps. This motherfucker SLOW. CLAPS. "Congratulations, Princess."

Flashbacks from high school assault me and almost knock me to my knees. *Fuck.* I may have done my best to reclaim the power of that nickname with my text handle, but I hate when it's used against me like this jackhole is doing.

"Don't call me that," I mutter through clenched teeth. There's only one nickname I *loathe* more than that one.

"Why?" That infuriating brow goes up again. "Ryan is pretty much hockey royalty."

"*So?*"

"Sooo..." he drawls. "When royalty plays with your pussy, your puck bunny status gets bumped to puck *prin-cess*." He mimes placing a crown on my head, all while clearly refraining from touching me.

"Fuck you," I growl. How fucking dare he. I don't even know

this asshat's name, and he's over here insulting me. Seriously, who the fuck does he think he is?

He clucks his tongue. "I thought we already went over this. It doesn't matter how thirsty you are for hockey dick, *mine* won't be one you'll be getting wet."

The flipping ego on this guy. Who the frankfurter does he think he is? Where does he get off talking to me this way? He didn't even bother to introduce himself. We're talking bare minimum effort here, people.

It's a shame he chose to jump to conclusions instead of getting to know me. If he had, he would have discovered I have a reputation for being the sweet one of the group. Whether I feel professional or not, I know I'm the best damn chef to ever cook in their kitchens. Too bad, so sad for him he'll *never* find out. The only thing this asshole will ever eat when it comes to me are his words.

# CHAPTER 3

## *Chance*

*Present day*

The door to the garage slams shut behind me, but not even the cacophony of noise is enough to summon my beasts. So much for man's best friend.

I shake my head, resigned to the fact that I'm nothing more than second best whenever there's a blue SUV parked in the driveway.

Gemma Steele, the bane of my fucking existence since the moment I saw her picture on Jase Donnelly's cell phone over a year ago. Though, if the infuriating woman knew I'd seen her like *that*, she certainly would have murdered me and found a way to train my dogs to help her get rid of my body.

The familiar soundtrack of '90s R&B, tinkling giggles, and staccato howls echo down the hall and filter into the mudroom. Sounds like they're having a grand ol' time without me...again. What else is new?

Dumping my gear bag on the shelf, I place my keys on their hook and scrub my hands over my face.

*Fuck me.* Why did Gemma have to go and prove to be so much more than I assumed she was? Maybe if she wasn't way too good for the likes of me, I would have stood a chance at correcting how I acted when we first met. Instead, it's just easier to keep her at arm's length by being a dick.

How did I get here?

How did finding professional heaven land me in personal purgatory?

*Shit.*

Driving my hands into my hair, I tug at the short strands until my scalp stings, banishing those kinds of thoughts before they can evolve into something far more dangerous for my mental health.

"Don't do it, Pebs," Gemma warns with a teasing lilt to her tone.

My tenacious pup responds with a *wop-wop* howl.

I creep down the hall, stopping before reaching the entrance to the kitchen and press my back to the wall, eavesdropping.

I don't know what's worse: the fact that Gemma Steele regards me with the same affinity as the dumps Pebbles and Bamm-Bamm litter the backyard with—and isn't afraid to make that known—or that I have spied on the woman interacting with my dogs enough to acquire the skills of a grade-A stalker.

"Don't act like I can't see you, girl," Gemma cautions.

*Wop-wop-wop.*

"You know I'd never size shame you, honey, but you aren't exactly considered tiny."

Pebbles gives a sharp bark, followed by one of her disgruntled growls. Gemma quickly coos with affectionate reassurance, the throaty sound traveling down my spine, settling in my balls, and bringing my cock to life.

*Fuck.* Chubbing up because of Gemma Steele is a frustratingly frequent occurrence. I'm like one of Pavlov's subjects, except instead of a bell, it's the distinctive purr, that gentle rolling in the back of her throat that sets me off.

*There's also the memory of that picture.*

Fuck me with my hockey stick—sans lube.

I shut that thought down *immediately*. Who the hell knew a simple selfie could be a recipe for disaster?

From that very first day when we bumped into each other— quite literally—outside of Ryan's bedroom, our interactions have been wrought with animosity, the tension between us palpable. I never considered myself a masochist until I met Gemma Steele. What else could explain how I could make sweeping declarations about never sinking my dick inside her, only to have said dick perk up and practically wave for her attention moments later, all because she used that motherfucking coo loving up on my fur babies.

It's been over a god*damn* year—shouldn't I be immune to her by now? Is there no end to this affliction?

"I'm just saying…" Lips smack in an exaggerated kiss, and there I go being jealous of my dog—again. "It's hard to be stealthy when you're taller than me, babes."

The heavy *thump-thump-thump* of Pebbles's strong tail beats against the floor with one of her excited wags.

"Oh no you don't."

An instinctive grin pushes at the corners of my mouth. I know what's about to happen.

I hear the clinking *snick* of Gemma placing her beloved chef's knife down on the counter.

Good—this is good. It's best to avoid Gemma when she's holding something she could easily flay me with. It's a feat in and of itself, given the reason for her presence in my home.

"Oof."

Gemma grunts.

"Pebs…"

Pebbles pants merrily.

"See?" I imagine Gemma tilting her head, that messy bun she's partial to flopping over with the action as she engages in a staring contest with the OG stubborn female in my life. "You have model height."

Rounding the corner, I stay at the perimeter of the kitchen and stare at the scene in front of me.

Gemma stands, legs spread, feet braced a little more than hip-width apart to support the added weight of Pebbles's massive frame. And, sure enough, my best girl stands a few inches taller, her giant paws resting on Gemma's shoulders.

Would you look at that? I was correct: Gemma's bun is crooked, the bright yellow of her scrunchie peeking through the dark strands every time it sways as she adjusts her stance.

"Careful, Princess." Gemma's head whips around at the sound of my voice, her gray eyes narrowing with her usual contempt. "You're sounding a bit jealous."

"Oh great." Gemma gives me one of her signature eye rolls before returning her attention to Pebbles. "Dickhead Daddy is home."

I've never had a daddy kink—not that there's anything wrong with those who do, I'd never yuck on another dude's yum—but hearing those two syllables roll off Gemma's tongue…

Yeah, that's just as bad as hearing her fucking coo.

Thankfully, my dogs finally deem me worthy of their attention, both barreling toward me in their typical bull-in-a-china-shop manner. Their small horse-sized bodies easily conceal what the athletic shorts I changed into after morning skate do not.

"You make it sound like I'm not welcome here." My feet are stepped on and tails beat against my thighs, but I barely notice as I vigorously scratch my babies' furry butts.

"I mean…" Gemma shrugs, shoulders and hands rising, palms splayed toward the ceiling.

As if choreographed—a feat I wouldn't put past Gemma, given her disdain for me—my pups abandon me and take up like sentries at her sides. Gemma's gaze flicks from them to me, long lashes fluttering. The grin she gives me is taunting, a pleased tease. It's stunning, near blinding in its beauty. As is she. It's fucking annoying as hell.

Why couldn't she be ugly?

Instead, she's all tempting curves my hands itch to grab as I pound into her until we reach mutual orgasmic bliss. Her lips are pouty to the point of insanity, my lizard brain having imagined putting an end to some of our more heated arguments by guiding her to wrap them around my cock.

Then there are her damn Disney princess–big eyes. Those mercurial irises have a way of hitting me harder than a slap shot to the gut.

All in all, she's this enticing combination of sultry siren and girl-next-door innocence.

Do you know what's worse? She's just as god*damn* beautiful on the inside—her attitude toward me notwithstanding. Though, it's that attitude that keeps me safe from doing something exponentially stupid.

I seem to be the only exception when it comes to the sweet Gemma Steele I constantly hear so much about. It's why, as dazzling as her smile is, it holds none of the sunshiny goodness I've witnessed directed at others. I blame the hard check I took to the boards during practice for the pang in my ribs and not irritation caused by the fact that she gifts it to literally *any*one who isn't me.

"You're not done yet?" I snap, my vexation at how much she continues to consume my thoughts bubbling over, and I gesture jerkily to the kitchen island covered in various stages of meal prep.

"I wasn't aware I was on a time clock." She smacks the counter, and I instinctively take a step back when her long fingers wrap around the stainless steel handle of the chef's knife, her chopping erratic.

"Yeah..." I fidget, my gaze bouncing around the kitchen. "Well..." How the fuck does she manage to make me uncomfortable in my own home? "Maybe if you spent more time *actually* preparing the dogs' meals instead of playing with them, you'd accomplish what you're being paid for." I scoff. "And you call yourself a professional."

Gemma's knuckles turn white, the ridges of the metacarpals darkening in stark relief as her hand tightens around the cutlery, her chest heaving with controlled breaths.

Oh...look...

My dogs aren't the only traitorous bastards in the room. My eyes want to join in on the fun, my gaze dropping to the generous cleavage swelling inside the V-neck collar of her shirt and spilling over the top of the *Your opinion is not part of the recipe* apron wrapped around her torso. I can't help but think she only wears that particular gem at my house.

"Oh my god, Pebs." Gemma barks out a humorless laugh, the hairs on the back of my neck rising at the harsh sound. "Did you hear that?"

A familiar prickle simmers beneath the surface of my skin at the purposeful shift of Gemma's attention, her body leaning over until she's nose to snout with my dog. Pebbles basks in it, dancing in place, floppy ears flapping, hindquarters wagging faster with every *What did I miss? whopping* howl.

"The rookie who was ousted by his last team because he had a temper tantrum is trying to school me on professionalism."

The annoyance from her ignoring me quickly boils over, begging to be set free. I want to lash out. I'm *desperate* for it, my hands balling into fists as I resist the urge. No matter the compulsion, I lock onto the last tendrils of control and rein it in.

"It wasn't a temper tantrum," I argue, but it's halfhearted at best because I can't entirely deny her claim. My intentions may have been noble...ish, but my execution sure left a whole lot to be desired, my actions in the past tainting my present.

Gemma purses her lips, her attention finally shifting to me, though the epic side-eye she's leveling me with isn't much of a win.

"You say potato; I say vodka." Her hand flounces around in the air before she easily goes back to pretending I don't exist, brushing me off without a single fuck given.

I stab my fingers through my hair again, my molars grinding until the scrape of enamel echoes inside my skull. This woman will be the death of me.

With frustration serving as my only guide, I round the island, stepping over a lying Bamm-Bamm, until I'm on the same side of the counter as Gemma. Hands balled into fists, knuckles serving as a shelf, I place them on either side of her hips. She sucks in a stuttered breath, her back expanding against my chest as I cage her against the cool granite.

"I love watching you play at being tough." I bend, the tangy-sweet scent of lemons overtaking any common sense I may have retained, causing my lips to trail down the fluttering pulse in her neck. "But how tough could you *really* be if you have to borrow your cousin's catchphrase to make your point?" I hum to empha-size *my* point. Gemma's hips oscillate the slightest fraction, brushing the delicious fullness of her ass along every inch of hardness I haven't managed to wrangle since that first *fucking* coo.

She freezes, her entire body going rigid like a hockey stick, tension building until...

A wet nose intrudes, shattering the moment. Seems two minutes is far too long for Pebbles to feel neglected without making herself known.

Gemma's head falls back onto my chest, the wiry hairs escaping her bun getting stuck to my scruff.

"Hey, Chance?" Gemma's voice turns breathy, and if it weren't damn near impossible, I'd say it's growing close to a coo.

I swallow thickly. "Yeah?" My eyelids start to drift closed at the feel of her warm breath ghosting along my jawline.

"Remember the day we met?"

Yes—vividly.

Unfortunately.

She spins in my hold, back arching, breasts pillowing against my chest.

She places a hand on my stomach, my abdominals contracting under the touch. It's subtle, but there's no missing the slight flex of her fingertips when she feels the movement of my hard-earned muscles.

Slowly, achingly so, her hand drifts downward, the distance toward the waistband of my shorts decreasing as the tent inside them increases. I can deny it all I want, but there's no disguising how Gemma Steele affects me.

The blunt edge of her nail skims the head of my dick through the mesh material of my shorts. Did she reach for me, or did my overeager anatomy do the reaching?

"Mmm," Gemma purrs, my mind blaring warnings my body refuses to heed in its aroused state. "Feels like *your* hockey *dick* is thirsty." She circles her finger, my toes curling inside my Nikes. "Too bad you weren't the only one who made a promise that day."

"A promise?" I croak. What promise? What is she talking about?

"*Mm-hmm.*"

*Fuck.* Does she have to hum like that? The way the sound vibrates through me makes it impossible to concentrate.

Gemma rises up on her toes, the drag of her budded nipples pulling a guttural groan from my throat.

"I promised I'd make you eat your words, but...just like how the only appetites I satiate with my cooking are your *dogs'*...I won't *ever* be the one to quench your *thirst.*"

With that, she shoves me away, my feet tripping over Pebbles, sending me crashing into the countertop behind me, my elbow catching the beveled edge.

I wait for a beat, cupping the aching joint and rubbing away the tingling pain while watching Gemma. She pays me no mind, just chop, chop, chopping away in her meal prep for my dogs.

I push away from the counter, refusing to stand there stewing in my thoughts and irrational growing regret. Stomping out of the room, I pointedly ignore the fact that neither of my dogs follows.

# CHAPTER 4

## *Gemma*

The sense of calm I've lacked since my little...*moment* with the most infuriating man in existence washes over me the second I step inside my family's gym, The Steele Maker. I inhale a breath, luxuriating in the cool kiss of air conditioning on my cheeks, gaze roaming over the place, marveling as I always do at how much it's changed.

There's a glassed-in room for classes, and the gym area now boasts both the classics like treadmills and free weights as well as the more hard-core stations of battle ropes and tire flipping.

Gone are the lonely set of speed bags and the handful of duct-taped punching bags. Instead, two rows of shiny black beauties line the far wall of floor-to-ceiling windows.

We still have artistic black-and-white action portraits hanging on the walls; there are just more athletes represented in them now. My favorite addition to the decor is the magnificent painted mural filling the entire middle wall of the gym depicting the American flag and Olympic rings.

Then there's the heart and soul of The Steele Maker: the boxing ring and MMA octagon. They may have been replaced by state-of-the-art versions, but the octagon will always be what Dad and Uncle Vic used as a playpen when they would bring me and my cousins, Rocky and Vince, to the gym as kids.

This place may have changed through the years, expanding and evolving along with the business and Steele reputation, but it doesn't matter if it's the cramped building it used to be or this two-story, half-block, glass-and-steel structure. The Steele Maker will always be my second home.

"Hey, boo." The singsonged greeting has me shifting my attention to the gorgeous redheaded gym manager, Becky Reese, seated in her designated position of power behind the large half-circle reception desk.

"I take it someone misbehaved?" I point to my ear then circle my finger at the *NSYNC song playing through the gym. It's a well-known fact that if boy band music is pumping through the sound system, one of the guys fucked up. Becky rules the roost with an iron fist.

"Eh." She shrugs. "A part of me thinks they do it on purpose."

I nod in agreement. "Knowing my cousin, he probably does."

Searching the black-and-gray-matted floors, I scan the fighters paired off to spar and find the man himself, not at all surprised to see Vince sporting matching Superman-printed gym shorts and hand wraps.

"Sooo." My shoulders bunch at the teasing gleam entering Becky's bright-green eyes. One doesn't need psychic abilities to know what's about to happen. "Did we have fun at Chance's today?"

*Sonofa*—

Sure, sure, sure...when I first told my girls about the day I met Chance Jenson, about when he *charmingly* dubbed me nothing more than the human equivalent of chocolate left on a hockey player's pillow, they had my back. They said all the appropriate things, but since then and seeing what they call "tension" between us, well...the dickhead has pretty much made me the low-hanging fruit for my friends' fodder.

Guess that's what happens when talking smack and teasing are your squad's love language.

"We?" I lay my forearms across the counter, adopting an unaffected lean when I'm anything but. "Why is it always *we* when you ask? Is *some*one trying to live vicariously?"

I attempt to arch a brow at the fighters—well, one in particular—scattered around the gym, but instead of only one going up, both stubborn bastards wing up my forehead. This is one of those moments I wish I could lift a single brow like Chance because it would *really* help emphasize my point, and—

*Sonofabitch!*

WHY THE FUCK AM I THINKING ABOUT CHANCE JENSON?!

*Oh-ho-ho, look at you pretending you haven't been thinking about him since he was all pokey pokey with his penis against your backside.* That devil on my shoulder taunting me sounds suspiciously like the freckle-faced redhead still eyeing me speculatively from across the reception desk.

*Oh shit.*

The knots in my shoulders radiate through my entire body at the saccharine smile stretching the corners of Becky's mouth. If growing up with Becky Reese has taught me anything, it's to gird my loins anytime she exhibits an expression like that.

*Whoops. Not today, Trouble.*

Nope. I don't need to hear about the merits of a good hate fuck. And trust me, I've heard them all. It's truly a testament to my friends' creativity that they continue to invent new ones. I blame the romance author of the bunch. Maddey can wield a thesaurus like a weapon.

"Oh, would you look at that? Rocky brought baby Ronnie with her," I say, desperately latching on to a change of subject.

Avoidance. Yup, avoidance is the name of my game, and there ain't no shame in it.

Shoving away from the front desk, I make a beeline for the baby strapped to his mom's chest in his octopus-printed carrier. Look at me seeking sanctuary in a three-month-old whose only form of communication is adorable nonsensical babble.

"Hey, Gem." Gray eyes our entire generation shares courtesy of our fathers flick to me before they return to the two men grappling on the mats. A smirk pulls at the corner of Rocky's mouth when her husband, Gage, pins her brother with an armbar. "Nice, Champ."

"You sound like you doubted me, Blue." Gage's tone is dry and not at all out of breath like he should be after being all roly-poly athlete with my cousin.

"*Never*," Rocky taunts, and I press my lips together to restrain a laugh. You know the saying *Don't poke the bear?* Well...that's even better advice for a Kraken, at least when he's the current reigning UFC Heavyweight Champ.

With an agility you wouldn't expect from a man of his hulking stature, Gage bounds to his feet, the playful smile he typically only reserves for his wife gracing his sweaty face as he stalks in her direction.

*Holy jalapeño.*

I'm shocked, utterly *shocked* Rocky's matching athleisure wear hasn't singed off her entire body thanks to the fire blazing in Gage's crayon-blue eyes before he hooks an arm around her middle and hauls her in for a kiss.

*Yeeeeah,* Ronnie isn't going to be an only child for long.

"You might want to pass off my nephew before you try making him a sibling," Vince heckles, and my laugh finally bursts free at how in sync our thought process is.

Rocky flips us the bird without ever breaking the kiss.

A sweaty arm drapes around my shoulders, enveloping me in way too much man stench as Vince tugs me in, placing a kiss on my temple. "'Sup, cuz."

Wiping away the moisture transferred from his skin to mine, I shoot an elbow at his ribs. "Gag, you stink."

"Did you just verbally gag?"

I nod, pinching the smelly limb between the very tips of my fingers, wiggling free. "That's how bad it is."

Vince pouts, but I was vaccinated against his puppy-dog eyes years ago. "Does Chance make you gag too?"

"Wh-what?" I sputter as the memory of tantalizing fresh soap invades my brain before I can stop it.

*Dammit, Dickhead. Why do you have to shower and smell so good when you get home from the rink?*

I shake my head to rid myself of the intrusive thoughts.

"She'd have to give in to their sexual tension to gag," Rocky retorts, and I almost give myself whiplash bouncing my gaze from one cousin to the other.

"Ew." Vince throws his hands up, shuffling away from the TMI convo he inadvertently waded into.

"Blue," Gage groans and follows Vince when Rocky gives him a *What are you gonna do?* shrug. At least this time I'm spared the usual tongue-poking-against-the-cheek simulation to go with the taunt.

"And on that note…" I slide to the left, my rubber flip-flops gliding across the padded flooring with ease. "I've got work to do in my office."

"Chickenshit," Rocky quips, falling into step with me as I make my retreat.

"Aren't you guys bored with this yet?" I feign nonchalance, waving back to my dad inside the boxing ring when he holds up a mitt-covered hand. "It's been over a year."

"I never knew denial was genetic," Rocky muses knowingly.

I side-eye her, communicating with my peepers how unamused I am. This is not that. Her denials about Gage when he first started training at The Steele Maker are nothing like whatever the hell it is I do whenever the topic of one Chance Jenson comes up.

My sigh is heavy. While the teasing is an ever-present, ever-continuous occurrence, it always seems to worsen every—and I mean *every* damn time—I cook at Chance's.

I don't get it. I know cooking is part of my job description, but feeding people? That's my passion. It's totally my jam. *He-he. I made a food pun*

Anyway…the point I was trying to make is that with Chance being the only person I refuse to add to my roster, *especially* since I cook for his dogs, you would think that would clearly indicate how much I loathe him.

Rocky laughs, utterly unconcerned with my ire. Instead, she stalks around my white-painted desk, settling into the purple leather chair behind it, feet kicked up and crossed at the ankles, hands systematically patting circles along Ronnie's back.

*Damn…*

I could easily hate her for her easy confidence, but I love her too damn much.

"All kidding aside…" Rocky's gaze rises to meet mine, eyeing me in a quick up-and-down pass. "You good, Gem?"

The utter sincerity behind the question has any defensiveness bunched in my muscles sliding off like condensation down a glass, my knees giving out along with it. I yelp, the cool leather of the yellow love seat pushed against the wall hitting the expanse of thigh exposed under the cuffed hem of my shorts.

*Dammit.* This is what happens when your family members are

also your closest friends. They can pick up on all the things you keep buried deep, deep down.

"It's nothing like that." I wave off her concern. I'm only the baby of the family by a couple of years, but Rocky and Vince have always been protective of me. That only intensified after the high school experience I had following their graduations.

"Like that?" Rocky shifts, her hand stilling on Ronnie's back, her brows crashing together as she assesses me like one of the fighters she works with.

Oh no, this isn't good.

"Wait…"

Yup, *definitely* not good.

"Does that mean something *else* happened?"

No.

Nope.

Nothing happened.

That shiver sliding down my spine is from the screech of the chair's wheels as Rocky scoots in closer, not from the memory of how Chance's body felt pressed against mine.

The goose bumps sprouting on my skin are from the intensity of Rocky's stare down—she's all elbows propped on the edge of my desk, fingers laced together, chin resting on the shelf they create—not from the ghostlike brush of lips on my neck.

Then there was—

Nope. Not a flipping *chance* I'll be thinking about that.

I play dumb. "I don't know what you're talking about, Rock."

The narrowing of her eyes and the flat press of her lips tell me she's not buying what I'm selling. *Dammit.*

"*Suurrrre* you don't." Rocky shifts to leaning in the chair again, rocking gently as she runs through what I'm sure are countless scenarios. "And here I thought I needed to worry that Beck's teasing picked at an old wound when in reality, you were just holding out on your favorite cousin."

"Don't let Vin hear you call yourself that." I drop my chin to glance over my shoulder like I have X-ray vision and can see the gym through multiple layers of sheetrock.

"Puh-lease." Rocky makes a fart noise with her mouth that has a sleepy Ronnie lifting his head toward his mama. "I live for making that fool feel jelly."

I giggle at the accuracy of that statement. I've witnessed more than one rock, paper, scissors challenge between my cousins for the right to claim the number one spot as one of our group's favorites. For years it was mostly me and Jase Donnelly they fought over, but with the growth of our squad's next generation, those battles have steadily increased.

"Enough chitchat." I push up from the couch and head for the giant clear dry-erase board situated against one of the walls, wheeling it out to the center of the room. "I need to know which of the guys our dads have scheduled to fight next."

There's always a rolling schedule with the number of fighters on our roster, but the titleholders typically have longer camps and considerable—understandably so—more requirements.

I move over to the blank half of the board, a pink dry-erase marker suspended in the air. "I want to get a jump on the revised meal plans now that hockey is back in full swing."

Officially I'm The Steele Maker's resident culinary nutrition-ist, but the moonlighting I do for the handful of my professional hockey-playing friends—and one enemy's dogs—are all baby steps toward my ultimate goal of running my own boutique agency. That goal may feel like more of a pipe dream than anything else most days, but I'm completely confident in my role here at the gym.

Rocky swivels around to glance at my two-year wall calendar, humming softly like she does anytime she calculates timeframes. "Gage just defended his title this summer, but Vin…hmm…I'll schedule a meeting with Jordan and Skye because he's coming due."

I nod my agreement, switching to the red marker I've desig-nated for him, already jotting down some of my cousin's favorite training-approved meals. Planning is always easier when All Things Sports, the sports public relations firm run by two of our fellow Covenettes, is involved. The work ATS does for us may be significantly more intensive for our title bouts, but we utilize their services for all our fighters. Gotta love those bestie perks.

"What about the others?" I ask, and we spend the next hour breaking down the individual needs of those who make up Team Steele Maker.

After we're done and Ronnie has gotten his fill from his mama's tatas, I secure the baby in his car seat and bring him back to The Hightower—the apartment building the majority of The

Steele Maker peeps call home—with me. I still have hours of meal planning and grocery orders left to do for my clients, but nothing beats working from the comfort of home while a cheesy romantic comedy plays in the background. Plus, taking the little man with me will help distract me from those pesky thoughts of another more annoying man I can't seem to shut up.

# CHAPTER 5

## Chance

Digging the edge of my skate's blade into the ice, I use it as a pivot point, changing my trajectory on a dime and stopping the puck from making it to our offensive zone, effectively breaking up the opposing side's dump and chase play.

"Nice, Jenson," Coach Watson bellows, giving a sharp blast of his whistle. "Again."

Sweat streams down the sides of my face, hitting the ice in steamy *plop-plop-plop*s as I get into position to repeat the same drill for the dozenth time, my lips spreading into a smile around my mouth guard at being recognized for a job well done. With my contract up at the end of the season, the pressure was already on to prove myself, but the change in head coach this season makes it feel like I'm starting over from scratch.

"Ten says you can't do it again, Rook," chirps Parsons, a giant freckled-face Irishman, from across the ice.

"I got twenty that says not only does he do it again, he gets the assist on the beauty I'm about to slip past Brick." Ryan extends a gloved hand for me to bump but jackknifes up, wheeling around to level the full weight of his captain intensity onto Jake standing between the pipes. "Don't even start."

"What'd I do?" Goalie mask lifted to rest at his temples, Jake feigns innocence, but it's a poor attempt at best, given the shit-eating grin splitting his face. The dude is cheesing so hard I can make out the divots of his dimples from all the way over here.

"You married my sister," Ryan accuses, directing that captain glare my way when I chuckle at their brotherly banter.

"*Yeah*, I did," Jake boasts, doubling down on the insinuation with a Pony-style air hump. His movements are far more clunky than seductive, but still an impressive feat with all the goalie gear he's sporting.

The shrill tweet of a whistle has Jake freezing midthrust.

"Oh, I'm sorry." Coach Watson's sarcasm is thicker than the snow clinging to Ryan's practice uniform as he skids to a stop in front of our captain. "Is my hockey practice getting in the way of your girl talk?"

A wave of titters echoes across the ice before the entire team automatically choruses, "Sorry, Coach," and then gets into position.

Outside of the respect Coach automatically gets given that he is, in fact, Coach, he's also an intimidating presence on the ice. A stocky white man in his early fifties, he hasn't lost much of the bulk he earned in his playing days. No one messes with Coach.

With a shake of his head, he places his whistle between his teeth, hunching slightly before lifting his shrewd and, shockingly enough, amused gaze my way. "Alright, boys"—he holds out the puck, readying it to drop—"money's on the line. Show me what you've got."

I spring into action the second the puck is in play, weaving through my teammates who are playing as the opposition. Determination pumps through my veins as I chase down the puck to break up the play and get into the perfect position for an assist to Ryan. Sweat continues to stream down my body, my muscles straining to their limits with every inch of ice covered.

I need to make this play.

And, no, it isn't about the money.

Well…not in the sense you're thinking. Ryan wouldn't blink at losing twenty bucks to Parsons. Hell, he'd pay the guy and then treat the entire team to lunch.

No, winning this bet is about proving myself as a valuable asset to the Blizzards' organization. I desperately want to stay in New Jersey. The circumstances behind my arrival last year may have been less than ideal, but miracle of miracles, I found a home and, more unexpectedly, a family here. I never knew I wanted or needed either, but now that I have them, I'll do everything in my power to hold on to both.

*Might want to work on being a little bit nicer to Gemma then, hmm?*

That inappropriately intrusive thought from my conscience almost has me bobbling the puck when I pivot and deke around Parsons. Thank Christ for muscle memory kicking in and making it possible to hold on to the play, allowing Ryan to score with his predetermined beauty of a top-cheddar goal.

Fucking infuriating woman. No matter what I do, I can't seem to escape her. Our every interaction is rife with tension and animosity. Granted…it's mostly the consequence of how I handled things when we first met, but if *ever* I was triggered during that tumultuous time, it was the morning I came face-to-face with Gemma Steele for the first time.

Wanna know the fuck of it all? If she ever, I mean fucking *ever*, found out *what* triggered me toward her, she really would flay me with her trusty chef's knife. Shit…she'd probably manage the feat with a plastic spork.

I never meant to invade her privacy. I swear on Lord Stanley's cup that was *never* my intention, but…*fuck*. I doubt even Mr. Good Guy Ryan himself would be able to look away from the sight of Gemma in that boner-inducing set of gray lingerie.

Her breasts spilling over the scalloped lace edges.

The generous swells pressed together into the most enticing cleavage, making my dick beg to fit itself inside the tight space.

The shadowed peekaboo of areola taunting me, drawing my gaze to the bullseye of nipple pebbled against the delicate fabric.

A handful of seconds is all it took to have the image burned into my brain over four hundred days later.

"Good hustle out there today, boys." Coach Watson compliments us as the team files into the visitor locker room. "Bring that same intensity tonight, and Tampa won't stand a chance."

A rebel yell echoes off the walls, chorusing with the clatter of pads and skates being discarded.

"Ew, gross," Ryan complains seconds before a mitt ricochets

off Jake, nailing me in the head then falling to the floor with a thud. I glance from it to Jake tossing his arms wide with a "The fuck" before finally lifting my gaze to the thrower.

"Just because you wifed up my sister doesn't mean I want to be subjected to your sexting."

"I'm not sexting," Jake challenges, but the return of those deep dimples on display gives away his lie.

"Bullshit."

I duck, narrowly missing being hit by the second glove Ryan chucks. Note to self: *Hey, self, stop choosing a locker between brothers-in-law.*

Even as I have the thought, I know I'm not going to heed the sage advice. I've learned being accepted enough to occasionally get caught in the cross fire of Donnelly-Donovan family squabbles is the highest compliment one could get.

"*Ooo*, look out," I singsong. "Cap is cursing."

"Stuff it, Jenson." There's zero heat in Ryan's tone. He's more than used to us teasing him for his uncharacteristically clean—at least when it comes to professional athletes' standards—mouth.

"What's the saying?" Jake arches a brow. "Pot meet kettle?" He waves a hand from his phone to the one in Ryan's hands.

It takes an extended beat, but Ryan's face contorts in disgust. "What the hell? I'm not sexting Carlee. That's...that's..." He sputters as if so flabbergasted the words are more impossible to find than Waldo. "That's fucking gross."

Carlee, Jake's sister, is only nine years old, so yeah, I agree—the mere insinuation is most definitely gross.

"And, you know...illegal," I add unhelpfully, biting the inside of my cheek to restrain a smile.

Not Jake, though. Nope, the dude is bent over, arms banded across his bare torso, skated feet practically tap-dancing, howling in laughter at Ryan's revolted indignation.

Can't say I blame Jake. Our poor captain looks like he shoved an entire box of Sour Patch Kids in his mouth while being tased in the balls. And if you're wondering what a grown man looks like getting tased in the nads, make sure to ask our friend Maddey to tell you the story about when her now husband was asked to help with her stalker issue over the summer.

"You know what..." Ryan trails off, lifting his phone to his ear instead. "On a scale of putting itching powder in my underwear to glitter bombing my house, how mad would you be if I made you a widow?"

"*Ooh shiiiit.*" I cup a hand over my mouth, falling backward into my cubical, my back hitting the wood with a thump. "He called Mommy on you, Brick," I whisper-shout.

"Don't call my sister Mommy," Ryan cautions, angling the phone away from his mouth.

"But she calls me Daddy." Jake puckers his lips in a series of kiss-kiss kisses, dancing away from Ryan's halfhearted grapple.

With my hands braced on the bench seat, I hoist my body up, extracting myself from the situation before inadvertently becoming a witness to fratricide, and head for the showers.

After pulling on my boxer briefs and adjusting the elastic band, I unlock the cubby holding my phone and curse at the old text notifications on the screen. "Fuck me."

"Sorry, man. I'm taken." I barely register Jake wiggling the fingers of his left hand under my nose as I work through the ramifications of my dog sitter's text.

I drop to the bench, not even acknowledging Jake's joke. A weird sense of panic starts to flow through my veins as I try to figure out what to do.

"Dude?"

I clutch my phone, not loosening my grip until the hard edges dig into my skin.

*Shit.*

*Shit.*

*Shit.*

My head hangs heavily, my shoulders slumping as an angry growl of frustration works its way up my throat.

"Chance? You okay?" Jake's hand cupping my shoulder in a squeeze finally snaps me out of my mini spiral.

"Huh?" I blink, the room slowly coming back into focus. *Whoa.* Talk about an overreaction. "Yeah, I'm fine. My dog sitter had to bail. Family emergency."

"Shit." Jake rakes a hand through his hair. "Want me to see if Jordan can bring them to our place?"

I'm shaking my head no before he finishes asking the question. "I appreciate it, man, but I couldn't ask that of her." Jake and his wife already have two dogs of their own, both Labradors, plus twin two-and-a-half-year-old girls and a six-month-old baby boy. There'd have to be no one, I mean absolutely *no one* else I could ask before I asked them to add my two beasts to the mix.

Jake ignores my refusal, his fingers already typing a message to Jordan as we finish dressing. Resigned, I fall silent, mentally running through any other possible options to take care of my babies until I'm back in Jersey next week.

All around me, the locker room empties as my teammates make their way to the team bus waiting to take us back to the hotel. That familiar sense of belonging hits me as they call out various invitations for how to spend our downtime.

The dynamics of the Blizzards are unlike anything I've experienced with any other team I've played on. But, unfortunately, that found-family bond won't help me now. Can't ask them to watch my dogs when they're traveling with me.

"And that, folks, is why my wife's the de facto leader of The Coven." Jake mimes dropping a mic before clearing his throat to read, "Why doesn't Chance just ask Gemma to stay with them? One, she loves those fur babies, and two, she's already at his house cooking for them. And"—he adopts an exaggerated falsetto, phonetically reading out *oh-em-gee*—"I still think it's *hilarious* Gem doesn't *actually* cook for Chance. But anyway... yeah, he should totally ask her."

Damn. I would have bet good money he dropped the subject and was back to sexting with Jordan based on the goofy grin he was sporting. Not so much.

"Leave it to JD to work in a dig whilst being helpful," Ryan says with a brotherly *Little sisters are a pain in the ass* headshake.

"Bro." Jake bounds up the bus's steps, chuckling. "I can't believe you said *whilst*. You are *so* old."

Ryan may not say the words, but his face is screaming, *The fuck?*

I clap him on the back in solidarity, shooting a quick elbow back at Jake.

"Good looks." Ryan extends a fist to bump when Jake doubles over with an *oof*.

I tap my knuckles to his. "I got you." After all, it is my job to defend my captain, even if it's when his brother-in-law is being ageist about their one-year age difference.

"So..." Jake leans around his seatback. "You texting Gem or what?"

*Shit.*

I don't *want* to. Texting Gemma always feels like a slippery slope. It opens up a vein of communication that seems too familiar, too intimate. It makes me want things I have no business wanting.

But...

I don't see any other option.

Ugh.

Removing my phone from my pocket, I juggle it between my hands, mentally vacillating back and forth. *Dammit.* Talk about a Sophie's choice.

I lift my gaze to Jake, who's typing away and laughing at his conversation with his wife. I stare holes through his profile as if considering asking them doesn't make me the most selfish person on the planet. I'm an asshole, but am I *that* much of an asshole?

*The pups love Gemma.*

It's that thought that finally shuts down the selfish insanity playing devil on my shoulder. Because, yes, Gemma may hate me, but she doesn't hate them. She loves up on them with an intensity that rivals mine.

*Sonofabitch.*

Here goes nothing.

> ME: Hi

Lame, I know, but texting with Gemma Steele always feels like a delicate situation to me. And I don't mean delicate like a particular set of lingerie I can't get off my mind, but like a bomb —ready to explode in my face at the first mistype.

> PRECIOUS GEM: New phone. Who dis?

I gnash my teeth at her infuriating response. Of course she goes with sarcasm. Why did I expect her to be anything less than sarcastic with me?

> ME: Can we cut the sarcasm, Princess?

PRECIOUS GEM: But it's my favorite ingredient in life.

*Jesus Christ. This woman.*

PRECIOUS GEM: And don't call me Princess.

ME: But that's what you are. The precious, precious little Protein Princess of the Covenettes.

I snort, catching Ryan eyeing me curiously in my peripheral. "You've never heard the phrase *You catch more flies with honey,* have you?" he asks.

I shrug, but my nonchalance is ruined by the barking laugh Gemma's next text pulls out of me.

PRECIOUS GEM: You're such a fucking dickhead.

If only she knew how I altered her Protein Princess text handle on my phone.

ME: The mouth on you, Princess.

Ryan, still reading over my shoulder, hisses through his teeth. "I'll ask JD to come up with some nice things to say at your funeral."

"Umm, who are you, and what did you do with the nice Ryan Donnelly I used to live with?"

Jake pauses in his texting long enough to chime in, "The good guy persona is on hiatus while he's dating Coach's daughter."

"Puck heads who once secretly dated their teammates' sister should *really* keep their opinions on others' dating lives to themselves," Ryan deadpans, his cheeks pinking at being called out.

"*Pfft.*" Jake thrusts his left arm high, showing off his silicone wedding band by flipping the bird with his ring finger.

The buzz of my phone pulls my attention away from their bickering over the merits of bro code.

> PRECIOUS GEM: Eww *green nauseous emoji* Don't be flirty. It's gross *puke emoji*

*Flirty? What the hell is she talking about?*

> ME: Listen...I know you have a thing for hockey dick, but news flash \*\*news flash GIF\*\* not every player flirts with every puck bunny they come across.

I regret the message as soon as I hit send, instantly typing an apology, but Gemma's response is faster.

> PRECIOUS GEM: FUCK YOU VERY MUCH, DICKHEAD.

And damn, is she furious.

> ME: Shit.

> ME: I'm sorry.

She says nothing.

> ME: Can we start over?

Still nothing. Not a blinking dot to be found.

> ME: Please?

"Tried to warn you." It's the nicest, most old-Ryan type *I told you so*. The fact that he was right fucking grates. Even worse is how I couldn't help myself. *Why do I always insist on poking the bear where Gemma's concerned?*

The bus is pulling into the hotel by the time those dancing dots finally appear. Sweat coats my skin under my tailored suit, my after-practice shower officially having gone to waste.

PRECIOUS GEM: DAMMIT! Pebbles just guilted me into texting you with the cutest head tilt ever. I swear, it's like she knows I'm ignoring her daddy.

My girl coming in clutch.

ME: The kids don't like it when Mommy and Daddy fight.

PRECIOUS GEM: OMG! I just threw up in my mouth a little bit. Don't EVER refer to us as a unit AGAIN.

ME: You can't blame me for that one. It was your cousin who did last week at book club.

PRECIOUS GEM: Yeah...

PRECIOUS GEM: Well...

PRECIOUS GEM: Vince will be getting laxatives in his venison chili this week just for that.

My mouth waters at the mention of the famous chili recipe.

ME: You can't desecrate such a sacred dish like that.

PRECIOUS GEM: I love how you act like you know anything about it. Too bad, so sad for you; you've never had the pleasure. Though...sacred is an apt adjective. The guys have said eating it is practically a religious experience. Hell...Deck proposes EVERY TIME I make it.

My jaw clenches. I've witnessed quite a few of said proposals, and I've hated every single one—hell if I know why.

ME: Despite your best efforts, Princess, I have had the pleasure. Ryan and I polished off the last batch you made him while we watched game film before we left.

> PRECIOUS GEM: SONOFABITCH! *string of expletive-faced emojis*

I can't help but chuckle at her flustered typing, my laughter only growing with the flurry of typo-filled messages that follow.

> ME: Look...I need a...

I hit send without saying what I actually need. It's as if my reluctance has made it physically impossible for my fingers to type out the letters to spell favor.

> PRECIOUS GEM: A what?

> PRECIOUS GEM: A clue?

> PRECIOUS GEM: A brain?

> PRECIOUS GEM: Ooo, I know—a soul.

> ME: A FAVOR.

My capitalized text must cut off her next sarcastic comeback because I'm subjected to another agonizing delay of dancing dots.

> PRECIOUS GEM: You know...usually when people need a favor, they ask nicely. But I guess the shouty caps are on brand for you.

I scrub a hand over my face. *Jesus Christ.* I knew this wasn't going to go well, but this is *far* worse than I could ever have anticipated.

Shit, at this point, I'd rather play tonight's game without my cup than have to ask Gemma for a favor. And if it were any other favor except *this* one, I would say fuck it. I'd put my phone on DND and pretend this whole experience was nothing but a bad dream during my pregame nap.

> ME: I'm sure you noticed Amanda isn't there.

PRECIOUS GEM: Why, yes, I am in possession of a working set of peepers and can, in fact, see that Amanda is not currently in residence.

ME: OH MY FUCK! I didn't mean right this second. I know she has class.

PRECIOUS GEM: Oh, I'm sorry. Did you or did you not bring up the subject of Amanda's whereabouts? *screenshot of earlier text* Was this supposed to be a read-between-the-lines-type situation?

ME: Jesus Christ, woman! Can I fucking ask you for a favor already?

PRECIOUS GEM: Only if you start switching out those swear words for magic ones.

*The fuck?!*

I yank at my tie, banging my forehead against my still-closed hotel room door.

"Told you you should have been nicer." Ryan jerks his chin toward my phone, eyeing me from the open doorway to his room.

Grumbling out a "Yeah, yeah, yeah," I switch over to the mobile key app and stalk inside my room, stripping off my suit jacket and tossing it into the ether.

ME: Please, would it be at all possible for you to please do me a favor until we get back from our road trip this weekend, please?

PRECIOUS GEM: Aww...look at all those pleases. *clapping emoji* Much better.

ME: Thank you.

PRECIOUS GEM: OMG! First, a plethora of pleases, now a thank you from Mr. Grumpy Gus himself? I feel like I should run out and buy a lotto ticket.

> ME: GEMMA.

> PRECIOUS GEM: Oh, rein back in those shouty caps. What is it you need? Because if it's a kidney, I'm kind of partial to having my matching set.

*What in the world is she going on about?*

> ME: Do I even wanna know how my needing a kidney entered the realm of possibilities?

> PRECIOUS GEM: That was a hell of a hit you took to the boards last night in third.

I can't help but grin at her admitting she watched the game. Sure, our friends get together for most of our games—the Donnelly-Donovan families have a box at The Ice Box, the Blizzards' home arena—but my chest puffs out with pride at her noticing—and *complimenting*—my gameplay.

> ME: I knew you liked me. Were you wearing my jersey while you watched too?

> PRECIOUS GEM: In your dreams, Canada.

As much as it pains me, specifically in the below-the-belt region, I do dream about her, but the Gemma Steele who visits me in dreamland is never covered by the shapeless sack of a hockey sweater. Nope, she's *always* rocking that lingerie set from the thing that will not be named.

Though I must admit the idea of my name stretched across her back has officially taken root in the primal part of my brain an—*Fuck! Cut that shit out right now.*

Gemma Steele abhors me. Any fantasies of her being mine are futile and can only lead to ratcheting up the already volatile tension between us. I may have been accepted into their little BTU Alumni squad thanks to my position on the Blizzards, but I'm smart enough to know if things escalate to a breaking point, *I'm* the one getting ousted from the group.

This has *bad idea* written all over it.

ME: Can you dog sit the pups until we're back from our road trip? Amanda had a family emergency come up.

PRECIOUS GEM: OMG, that's what you wanted to ask me? Hang out with my favorite canines for days on end? That doesn't sound like a favor. That sounds like heaven.

I blink.

And blink again.

That's her answer?

Tossing my phone, I flop face forward onto the bed, bouncing as I land on the mattress.

I can't believe it was that easy of an ask.

Coverette

# CHAPTER 6

# Coven CONVERSATIONS

From the Group Message Thread of The Coven

> YOU KNOW YOU WANNA (Becky): Gemmy, Gem, Gem.

> YOU KNOW YOU WANNA: We miss you at home.

> YOU KNOW YOU WANNA: **picture of a Swiffer with Gemma's picture on it**

> SANTA'S COOKIE SUPPLIER (Holly): FYI, she's been moving Swiffer Gem all around the apartment.

> YOU KNOW YOU WANNA: But, alas, no matter how many times I put her in the kitchen, she still hasn't made me a sandwich.

> MAKES BOYS CRY (Skye): Careful, Beck, your patriarchal conditioning is showing.

> SANTA'S COOKIE SUPPLIER: DOWN WITH THE PATRIARCHY!

> QUEEN OF SMUT (Maddey): **Maleficent matriarchy GIF**

ALPHABET SOUP (Rocky): Why do you think we had Gage cook dinner last night?

MOTHER OF DRAGONS (Jordan): **Well played GIF**

PROTEIN PRINCESS (Gemma): 1. Why doesn't it surprise me that there is a Swiffer Gem? 2. What did Gage make? And 3. I don't care how rough and tough Mr. UFC Heavyweight Champ is; if he scratched my pans, I'm coming for him. Those things are my babies.

BROADWAY BABY (Melody): I'm more surprised Beck hasn't made one before now.

MAKES BOYS CRY: True. It does feel like an oversight.

BROADWAY BABY: OMG **facepalm emoji** Why did I show the picture of Swiffer Gem to Jase?

MOTHER OF DRAGONS: Rookie mistake, Mels.

ALPHABET SOUP: Let me guess—he's trying to come up with his own version?

BROADWAY BABY: Yup! He's currently debating whether he should make Hockey Stick Gem or OH MY G—

QUEEN OF SMUT: Uh-oh. A cutoff text is NOT a good sign.

MAKES BOYS CRY: You might want to start auditioning a new potential SIL, Jor.

MAKES BOYS CRY: ^^See what I did there? **Barney Stinson self-five GIF**

YOU KNOW YOU WANNA: **Jim and Pam air high five GIF**

MOTHER OF DRAGONS: We really need to get Amara added to the chat. She's at least dating my sane brother.

THE OG PITA (Beth): Yeah, but she and Ryan only just started dating. You might scare her off with all this SIL talk.

ALPHABET SOUP: ^^My cousin-in-law makes a good point.

QUEEN OF SMUT: Don't worry. I've got the next gen helping us lock down our newest Covenette behind the scenes. **I got you, boo GIF**

DANCING QUEEN (Zoey): I feel like that's the least you could do since you abdicated the role of Jordan's SIL to marry your brothers' best friend instead of her brother.

FIDDLER ON THE ROOF (Ella): Umm, you've seen her husband—can you blame her? That man looks fiiine in his uniform.

PROTEIN PRINCESS: **crying laughing emoji** Abdicating? That's for monarchies. It isn't a sister-in-lawship like some dukedom.

YOU KNOW YOU WANNA: I don't know…Cap certainly seems like he has a throne a girl could sit on.

MOTHER OF DRAGONS: Eww. **puke emoji** I just threw up in my mouth a little.

QUEEN OF SMUT: **No comment GIF**

PROTEIN PRINCESS: Umm…Madz? **link for Maddey's Belle Willis Amazon Author Page**

SANTA'S COOKIE SUPPLIER: Look at all those cinnamon rolls and best friend's brother books you've written. I would say you've had ALL the comments.

MOTHER OF DRAGONS: LA LA LA LA *sticks fingers in ears* I CAN'T HEAR YOU.

MAKES BOYS CRY: Says the woman who has all of Maddey's audiobooks.

YOU KNOW YOU WANNA: Oh snap! Called out by the bestie.

BROADWAY BABY: Sorry, I'm back. Oh damn, you ladies were chatty.

FIDDLER ON THE ROOF: Where'd you go?

DANCING QUEEN: You might want to tell Loverboy there is such a thing as TOO quick for a quickie.

MOTHER OF DRAGONS: **Jordan has left the conversation**

MAKES BOYS CRY: Bish, stop playing. I see you glued to your phone **Work wife GIF**

BROADWAY BABY: Lol, Zo. Sadly, that's not what he was doing, but don't you worry, Jase has a thing about hat tricking me when he fucks me.

QUEEN OF SMUT: OMG. I'm putting that in a book.

MOTHER OF DRAGONS: I hate you guys.

YOU KNOW YOU WANNA: No, you don't.

MOTHER OF DRAGONS: I feel like I'm going to regret asking, but what was my wombmate doing?

BROADWAY BABY: He was digging through my wigs so he could make his "Gemma" more authentic. **eye roll emoji**

ALPHABET SOUP: Pics or it didn't happen.

BROADWAY BABY: Don't encourage him.

MOTHER OF DRAGONS: I'm so happy he's not my problem anymore **Freedom! GIF**

BROADWAY BABY: Can I return him?

MAKES BOYS CRY: Not without a receipt.

BROADWAY BABY: Dammit!

PROTEIN PRINCESS: Speaking of receipts, look at this awesomeness I got on Etsy. **picture of Pebbles wearing a dog collar with the same witch hat as The Coven's matching tattoo printed on it**

ALPHABET SOUP: Is that our tattoo?

QUEEN OF SMUT: Shut up! That's the cutest.

SANTA'S COOKIE SUPPLIER: Did you get Bamm-Bamm anything?

PROTEIN PRINCESS: Duh. Couldn't leave my guy hanging. Check out this beauty. **picture of Bamm-Bamm wearing a Gemma is my favorite hooman dog collar**

YOU KNOW YOU WANNA: **Oh snap GIF**

YOU KNOW YOU WANNA: Chance is not gonna like that.

PROTEIN PRINCESS: No one cares what Dickhead Daddy has to say.

QUEEN OF SMUT: **spits out water GIF**
Umm…EXCUSE ME, but when did Chance's
nickname evolve from Dickhead to Dickhead
DADDY? YOU GUYS ARE SUPPOSED TO GIVE
ME THE CLIFNOTES UPDATE WHEN I COME
OUT OF THE WRITING CAVE. SOMETHING
LIKE THIS IS VITAL INFORMATION!!!

MAKES BOYS CRY: Oh no. Madz busted out the
shouty caps. We're in trouble.

DANCING QUEEN: Not to go against girl code,
but who cares about Madz at a time like this?
Gem calls Chance Daddy? **Minion WHAAAT
GIF**

ALPHABET SOUP: We're gonna need details
STAT.

SANTA'S COOKIE SUPPLIER: OMG, Beck is
making popcorn.

MOTHER OF DRAGONS: Ahh yes, finally
someone not boning one of my brothers. I am
here for ALL the details.

YOU KNOW YOU WANNA: OMG OMG OMG.

YOU KNOW YOU WANNA: Please, please,
PLEASE tell me this is your foreplay, and he's
gonna spank you for trying to claim favorite
when he gets home.

THE OG PITA: **This GIF**

BROADWAY BABY: **Shaq shoulder shimmy
GIF**

FIDDLER ON THE ROOF: **air spank GIF**

QUEEN OF SMUT: **Tinkerbell getting butt-
tapped GIF**

PROTEIN PRINCESS: Umm **scratches head GIF** How did we get from me showing you my Etsy purchases to Chance Jenson spanking me?

YOU KNOW YOU WANNA: Don't look at us.

YOU KNOW YOU WANNA: You're the one who calls him Daddy.

DANCING QUEEN: I'm gonna need more details. I'm talking about all the dirty ones.

QUEEN OF SMUT: Same. And don't worry…I have my notebook; I'm ready. **Elle Woods notetaking GIF**

MOTHER OF DRAGONS: Don't underestimate a good spanking. Remember that one Julia Wolf book we read for book club?

SANTA'S COOKIE SUPPLIER: Ooo, Through the Ashes. Yeah, Julia writes top-tier sexy times.

MAKES BOYS CRY: What I really wanna know is, does he leave your underwear on, or is it a bare-bottom spanking?

ALPHABET SOUP: Oh, good question. She does have the BEST lingerie collection out of any of us.

**PROTEIN PRINCESS HAS NOTIFICATIONS SILENCED**

BROADWAY BABY: Oh my god. Did Gem just put us on DND?

YOU KNOW YOU WANNA: **Stephanie Tanner "How Rude" GIF**

SANTA'S COOKIE SUPPLIER: As a person speaking from experience, she can run all she wants, but she can't hide.

# CHAPTER 7

*Gemma*

L isten…I know food is my thing and cooking is my life, but holy guacamole, this was not a life achievement I needed unlocked. Not once when little five-year-old Gemma was asked in kindergarten what she wanted to be when she grew up did I respond with, *I want to be a sardine.* Nope, that wasn't on the short list. Hell, it wasn't even on the *long* list.

Yet…here I am, stuffed between my two furry charges like the meat in some *Flintstone*-tribute sandwich.

Tiny, silky hairs poke their way into my nasal passages as I crane my neck around Pebbles, glancing to my left, marveling longingly at the vast space available for lounging. I'm talking miles of cushions, plump gray micro weave stretching out as far as the eye can see—totally unoccupied, other than my notebook filled with jotted-down ideas for my business.

It amazes me how despite their massive size and the equally impressive real estate of this far too comfortable to be owned by such a prickly person sectional, Pebbles and Bamm-Bamm seem to be in some silent *Who can be closer to Gemma?* battle.

*Oof.* Can't a girl get some space for her lungs to fully expand? Is that honestly too much to ask for?

Bamm-Bamm, to his credit, isn't affecting my lung capacity. His black-and-white, cowish-speckled body is curled into a sort of a ball shape, only his head resting on my lap—though his giant skull overtakes the entirety of my thigh, and I'm not so much a fan of the way his slimy jowl keeps fluttering and clinging to my bare skin with every peaceful exhalation he snores. I swear it's making this sound like the playing card Vince used to put in his bicycle spokes when he wanted to pretend he was Batman racing down the street on his Batcycle. And yes, before you ask, that comic-loving man-child did so while donning the pointy-eared mask and black cape.

Pebbles, on the other hand? She gives negative fucks about my personal space. My girl is sitting in my lap—literally. My left leg has been asleep for the better part of an hour, thanks to her bony ass digging into it. Not to mention, whenever she panics, thinking I may have somehow left her as if I apparated away like the Weasley baby Ronnie is named after, she blocks my view of all things—specifically the television broadcasting the Blizzards game.

"Oh, come on." I toss my arms up at the badly missed tripping call by the refs. "Are you blind?"

A wet tongue coats the entire side of my face in slobber, and I give Pebbles a good head scratch for her show of sister solidarity. While some people may judge me for my enthusiastic couch coaching, these pups would never. They even joined in, adding a round of booming, albeit lazy, barks to my cheers during Chance's fight in the second period, though Bamm-Bamm did give me a confused head tilt at hearing me issue words of encouragement toward his dad.

Now before you start with the questions, I feel like it's important to point out that hockey—more specifically, my fandom of the New Jersey Blizzards—outweighs any hatred toward certain players hailing from the Great White North.

The game has been intense, with both teams trading shots on goal without successfully slipping the puck past the other's goalie. I've lost count of the number of *That's my man* GIFs Jordan has sent to the group chat with each save.

The intensity of the game only grows the closer the game clock ticks to the end of regulation. The players' determination is palpable, radiating through the high-definition screen mounted on the wall and increasing my pulse until I'm fidgeting on the couch with every pass of the puck.

One minute left, and there's a line change. Ryan, Chance, and Parsons dart across the ice weaving between Seattle players like they are practice cones, their movements choreographed in the kind of graceful precision reserved for professional athletes.

Seattle double-teams Ryan like they've been doing all game, cornering him against the boards. Not until Chance comes racing by does it dawn on them that they've made a tactical error. Realizing their mistake, the Seattle players spring into action, but it's too late. Chance releases the puck in a blur of black, passing it to Ryan with jaw-dropping ease, then pivots to block the overcorrecting Seattle defenseman, checking him off his skates and onto his ass.

My blood pumps faster through my veins as the scene unfolds on the ice, the hair down my arms standing on end. Enthralled, I attempt to shift closer to the action, only to be propelled backward because of Pebbles still in my lap, my body ricocheting off the cushions the same way the puck flies off the net as Ryan slips a beauty of a goal right into the Seattle goalie's five-hole.

The buzzer blares, the light above the goal glowing bright red as the announcers recap Ryan's already impressive stats for the season. Just like that, the Blizzards add another *W* to their win column, and damn if I don't dissolve into a puddle of relieved goo.

Jeez. If I get this invested in watching a game as a fan, how the hell do coaches handle it? This shit is stressful.

I'm passively watching an episode of *Chopped* when my phone buzzes with a text an indeterminate amount of time later.

> DICKHEAD DADDY: You up?

I stare at the message notification on my phone like it's challenged me to a staring contest. The adrenaline high from the game must have short-circuited the few remaining brain cells in Chance's dumb jock brain.

Oh-kay, that was bitchy of me, but the sting from how our earlier conversation ended hasn't entirely faded.

> ME: **Gemma's phone only accepts messages after midnight from people who DON'T have a giant hockey stick up their butt**

DICKHEAD DADDY: Fuck! I said I was sorry.

If "foot in mouth" was an actual disease, Chance Jenson would be patient zero.

ME: Actually…you didn't.

DICKHEAD DADDY: I'm sorry.

Stubbornness pumps through my veins, my eyes narrowing into a glare so fierce I'm thankful I can't shoot laser beams out of my eyeballs. The last thing I want to do is accept this apology.
But…
The utter lack of delay in Chance correcting his mistake pulls my maturity to the forefront.

ME: Okay. Thanks.

DICKHEAD DADDY: Am I allowed to text you now?

ME: As long as it's not for a booty call.

DICKHEAD DADDY: WTF?

DICKHEAD DADDY: Must you be sarcastic right now?

ME: But it's my greatest joy in life.

DICKHEAD DADDY: I don't doubt that at all.

ME: Aww…you're not as dumb as you look.

DICKHEAD DADDY: Damn. Here I thought we kissed and made up.

ME: I will NEVER kiss you.

DICKHEAD DADDY: Famous last words, Princess.

I hate it when he calls me Princess.

> ME: Not even if you turned into a frog.
> Actually…frog Chance might be preferable.

> DICKHEAD DADDY: Shit. Note to self: Gemma is
> salty at 2 in the morning. Just so you know, the
> tequila's in the cabinet next to the fridge.

> ME: Not to point out the obvious, but if I'm not
> down with the late-night booty call, what makes
> you think I'm a smexy selfies sender?

There's a delay before Chance's next text this time, and I wonder if my smartassery finally has him throwing in the towel.

> DICKHEAD DADDY: Why do I always feel like
> we're having two different conversations?

> ME: That sounds like a YOU problem. But I feel
> like it's my duty to let you know that tequila
> doesn't make my clothes fall off—that's my
> cousin.

> DICKHEAD DADDY: Oh…I'm well aware of that
> fact.

The laugh that barrels its way out of my chest is so unexpected I startle both dogs awake. I can't help it because I, too, am sadly in possession of the knowledge of what tequila does to Vince's clothes. There is not enough brain bleach in the world to erase the memory of him tossing his clothes like Oprah does car keys and dancing around the support pole in Deck's basement like a stripper featured on the main stage. My mom would tell you that was karma's way of punishing me for drinking underage. Oh well.

> ME: Aww…did you and Vince compare
> manscaping techniques?

> DICKHEAD DADDY: **GIF of waxing scene
> in The 40-Year-Old Virgin**

ME: Umm...is this Jake? I have to be talking to Jake, right?

DICKHEAD DADDY: Why the hell would Jake be texting you from MY phone?

ME: I don't know. *shrug emoji* It's the only thing that made sense to me.

DICKHEAD DADDY: Again...I do not see the connection.

ME: Well...this conversation has been mildly entertaining, dare I say borderline fun. Unless I actually am asleep like I probably should be at this hour and this is just a dreamish-nightmare scenario reminiscent of NyQuil-induced insanity, it only makes sense that it would be Jake or somebody else.

DICKHEAD DADDY: I'm still not seeing why.

ME: Because... **Michelle Tanner eye roll GIF** The sender of these messages is funny, almost downright lighthearted, and the Chance Jenson I have experience with? Yeaaaaah, not how I would describe him. Ergo, ipso facto, this couldn't possibly be Chance Jenson messaging me.

ME: Unless...

DICKHEAD DADDY: I have a feeling whatever you are about to say is going to officially make me regret initiating this endeavor.

Chance's message has me giggling while still thumbing out my own. This whole exchange is beyond strange. I'm used to him putting me at risk of wrinkles from frowning. Laugh lines from smiling? Yeah, not so much.

And why am I drawn to *this* version of him?

> ME: Is your assholeness a curse from a fairy godmother? Like it wears off at the stroke of midnight?

> DICKHEAD DADDY: *blinks* ...

> ME: Just saying, I think this is the first time I've ever talked to you this late. Is that the special sauce? The secret ingredient? Man, I always thought your Disney reference was Beast. I never thought to use Cinderella. *mind-blown emoji*

Snapping a quick screenshot of our convo, I shoot it to Maddey. She's the only person who will truly appreciate my wittiness, and she certainly doesn't disappoint.

> QUEEN OF SMUT: Top-notch Disney references **clapping, "Well done" GIF**

> PROTEIN PRINCESS: **Elvis "Thank you, thank you very much" GIF**

I'm still mumbling out a bad Elvis impersonation when I tap over to read Chance's next volley.

> DICKHEAD DADDY: Anyway...moving on...

Is it wrong I feel disappointed? Because...I kinda do.

*What is wrong with me?*

Sleep. I should totally go to sleep because exhaustion is the only thing I can think of to excuse the feeling.

*And what about the rest of this past week?*

That voice inside my head is wholly annoying and respectfully needs to shut the fuck up. The last thing I need reminding of is how much fun I've had sparring with Chance through text this week, or how much I've looked forward to each of his texts. I will go to my grave denying it.

> DICKHEAD DADDY: How about we get to the real reason I texted you this late—how are my pups?

*Gah!* Why is it that even when I want to hate him because he's the biggest dick to ever dick, a question like that makes me cheese more than a platter of nachos?

> ME: They're the best. Are you sure you're their owner?

> DICKHEAD DADDY: What? Of course I am. Why the hell would you ask me that?

> ME: Are you sure? Like, really, really sure? Absolutely positive and all that jazz?

> DICKHEAD DADDY: THE FUCK, Gem?

We're going to pretend him calling me Gem doesn't send a thrill through my system, pretend my nipples aren't perking up like puck bunnies whenever our squad goes out to Rookies, the sports bar we've been frequenting since college. Nope, the response those hussies in my over-the-shoulder boulder holders are having to him will be our little secret, mmkay?

> ME: I don't know, but I feel pretty confident that you dognapped them from somebody because they are WAY too nice to have been raised by you.

> DICKHEAD DADDY: Not to sound like a broken record, but I'm not sure I see the connection.

Oh, he makes it *too* easy.

> ME: Well, you, sir...

> ME: Are not nice.

> DICKHEAD DADDY: I'm nice.

> ME: Yeah...on Opposite Day.

Three little dots appear, then disappear, only to repeat the process four more times.

DICKHEAD DADDY: I don't even know how to respond to that.

ME: Let me guess...

ME: It's physically painful for you to admit I'm right about something.

DICKHEAD DADDY: You'd have to actually be right for me to admit it.

ME: Pfft. **rolls eyes** You're such a liar.

ME: Tell me...is it a physical manifestation? Like, does it burn when you pee? Do you get hives on your nutsack?

DICKHEAD DADDY: Wow...I didn't realize you had such an obsession with my junk, but this is the second time you've referenced it. First, it was inquiring about my manscaping habits, and now this. Is this your sly way of getting me to send you a dick pic?

ME: **gag GIF** Nobody wants to see that.

DICKHEAD DADDY: Now who's the liar?

ME: Puh-lease. **unimpressed little girl GIF** Besides...I'd need to hella zoom in to be able to see your micropeen **magnifying glass "Where is it?" GIF**

DICKHEAD DADDY: Fucking hell, you're infuriating. Why did I even text you?

ME: I've had that exact thought every day this week.

I chuckle, delighting probably a bit *too* much in how easily Chance makes it to torture him. He really should work on it.

Bamm-Bamm shifts, his icy-blue eyes hitting me with a *Be nice to my daddy* look. Dammit, that long puppy-dog stare hits a girl right in the solar plexus and knocks the sass down a few pegs.

Guilt has me wiggling to stretch an arm out and snap a selfie of me still snuggled in my doggy cocoon.

Minutes pass. Every second that goes by grows more *excruciating* than the last. The worst part? The hell if I know why.

I do my best to shift my attention back to the television, forcibly putting my focus on the cotton candy the *Chopped* contestants somehow need to incorporate into their main dish challenge instead of on my unbuzzing phone.

Spoiler alert—it doesn't work. Nor does absentmindedly rubbing Bamm-Bamm's silky ear between my fingertips.

Nope.

Instead, my skin grows tighter, pulling against my bones like cling wrap on leftovers, not to mention my belly is churning like I ate gas station sushi. Seriously, do yourself a favor and never buy gas station sushi. I don't care how appetizing it looks, don't do it—trust me.

> DICKHEAD DADDY: Do you routinely hang out with my dogs in your underwear?

What?

What is he—

*Oh shit.*

"This is all your fault," I grumble to the furry, heated blankets responsible for raising my body temperature to clothing-removal levels. "You're lucky this bralette is cute."

I'm never going to hear the end of it when I tell the girls I accidentally sent Chance a picture of me in my newest Victoria's Secret.

> ME: I find it hard to believe you don't sit on your couch with your hand down your tighty-whities Al Bundy-style whenever you're home.

> DICKHEAD DADDY: Again with a reference to my below-the-belt region. Remember, Princess, there are 26 letters in the alphabet.

Did I mention how much I *hate* when he calls me Princess?

ME: Why are you giving me a lesson on the ABCs?

DICKHEAD DADDY: Because…you only seem to be focused on the D—my D.

ME: If I wasn't riding the adrenaline high from watching you playing Seattle, I would swear you were in Chicago right now because that line sounds like you've been hanging out with Tucker.

DICKHEAD DADDY: And for the record…I DON'T wear tighty-whities.

I fumble my phone like it's suddenly become a hot potato, bounce, bounce, bouncing it between my palms before it lands on the floor with a resounding *smack*. It doesn't matter that my phone is now face down on the area rug; the image of a shirtless Chance, six perfectly defined abdominals on display like a freaking pack of King's Hawaiian rolls front and center, a dark-haired happy trail directing my gaze lower to the thumb hooked in the band of his black boxer briefs, the tight material strained from the—yup, *definitely* not a micropeen—bulge beneath it.

*Sonofabitch!*

Chance Jenson has officially been added to my pole vault. What the past life karmic retribution is this crap?

# CHAPTER 8

## *Chance*

There's a crick in my neck, and my muscles feel the pull of the shower calling like a siren luring sailors to shore. But have I moved?

Nope.

Instead, I've been sitting in my car for the past fifteen minutes, my gaze pinging between the door leading into the house, Gemma's SUV still parked in the extra space, and my phone. More specifically, the picture saved to my camera roll.

Why did I save it? Why didn't I leave it to get lost in the abyss of the continuous message thread?

For over a year, I lived—more like suffered—with the memory of what Gemma looks like in nothing but ball-churning lingerie. Now that memory feels like nothing more than a hazy déjà vu compared to this high-definition image.

*And I went and made sure it was saved for posterity.*

Whatever. I've given up any hope of forgetting about it. If over eight hours and almost three thousand miles traveled on buses and airplanes didn't do it, nothing, *nothing* will.

The few hours of sleep I got on the team's cross-country flight home were fitful, rife with the memory of it. Hell, it was only years spent conditioning myself to catch some Zs wherever or whenever I am that meant I managed to get any at all.

Not like I had a respite—not even dreamland was safe from the only thing on my mind: that selfie. It's really fucking annoying, let me tell you.

I need something, *anything*, to put an end to this endless thought spiral.

With considerable effort, soundtracked by a cacophony of groans, I haul my weary body out of my vehicle, feeling *all* the effects of the team's week-long road trip. The first thing I notice when I step inside the mudroom is the absence of music. It's so strange I do a double take, abandoning my bags in the middle of the room, and step back into the garage.

Yup, there it is—Gemma's SUV.

Could she be outside with the pups?

Except...

When she's done so in the past, playing with them while letting their food cook, I've never known her to not have some type of music on. The perpetual soundtrack of '90s hip-hop and R&B is a facet of Gemma Steele's vivacious personality.

So....

Why then...

Is my house...quiet?

The soles of my sneakers squeak unnaturally loudly against the silence as I step through the shadows cast by the skylights overhead.

Wait...why are there no lights on?

I have to force myself not to double back to the garage again and confirm that exhaustion didn't have my eyes playing tricks on me, that there *was* a blue SUV parked in the spare bay.

My chest deflates, my breath rushing out of me in relief when I spot Gemma in her usual spot at the kitchen island. Her hair isn't up in its typical messy bun; instead, those chestnut-brown locks are down around her shoulders, just as perfectly messy as they were in *the* picture. Slap my ass and call me Sally if the visual doesn't have those earlier thoughts rushing back to the surface. The urge to grab those waves and wrap them around my fist is visceral, my fingers twitching to touch, the command for her to drop to her knees crawling up my throat. I'm nanoseconds away from saying fuck it all to do just that, but...

Gemma seems...off.

There's a pinch to her brow, and I'm not talking about the small V-shaped I-hate-Chance-Jenson creases she typically has in my presence; these grooves are deeper than the Grand Canyon. She's also being...quiet. Like the missing music, she's not jabbering away, carrying on a conversation with the dogs like she's fluent in canine.

Bamm-Bamm is the first to notice my arrival, lumbering out of his regal perch to greet me. Having missed my guy, I crouch low, kicking one leg out behind me for leverage as he presses his weight into me, his slobbery jaw brushing drool along my cheek before he rests his heavy head on my shoulder. I don't bother wiping it away, more than familiar with the "snail trails" they leave on my skin and clothes—it's their love language.

Bamms groans contently at my deep collar-jingling neck scratch, and since my being is tuned to all things Gemma Steele despite my violent efforts not to be, I catch her wincing in my peripheral.

That sense of something being off hums again and I'm about to question if she's alright, but the writing on Bamm-Bamm's collar finally registers.

*Gemma is my favorite hooman.*

What the?

"Really, Princess?" I arch a brow, getting a face full of dog tongue.

Gemma's wince gets wincier.

Okay...something is definitely not right here.

I'm on my feet, rounding the island within seconds, a primal beat pulsing through me with each step I take.

"What's wrong?"

"Nothing," Gemma claims, and maybe if she weren't staring blankly at the countertop, I might believe her.

"Bullshit," I bark, raking a hand through my hair at her deflection.

Gemma slams her eyes shut, crinkles forming at the corners, and I instinctively close the last of the space between us.

And...

That was a mistake. Gemma's body heat bleeds into mine, the sweet scent of lemons wafting my way and taunting me, drawing me closer.

*Fuck me.*

This is why I usually do everything in my power to keep as much physical distance as possible—at a minimum, two small horse-sized dogs—between us. Gemma Steele is temptation incarnate from afar. Up close? My resolve starts to crumble like Superman near kryptonite.

Shaking off her allure like Bamm-Bamm drying off after a bath, I intentionally soften my voice. "Gemma."

Nothing. No sarcastic comment. No witty quip.

Just...no response.

Okay, I'm officially worried. I don't care what she's saying— or in this case, not saying. Something is not right here.

Risking life and limb, I shift until my chest brushes against Gemma's arm. Tipping my head to the side, I run my gaze over her, starting with that pinched expression, then across the ashy pallor that's replaced her usual olive complexion. Each anomaly I pass only ratchets up the swirliness in my gut.

My mission stalls after I pass the jut of her clenched jaw, my eyes locking and homing in on the movement of her throat as she swallows. I'm pretty sure the thoughts that simple bodily function provokes are illegal here in the States, or at least in a few of them.

The clang of Gemma's chef knife has my gaze snapping down to the hands she now has splayed on the countertop, noting how the color has leached from her fingertips due to her grip on the granite.

"Gemma?"

The dogs swarm around us, bumping and pressing against our legs. Gemma blinks, glancing down to give Pebbles a reassuring head scratch before finally lifting those mercurial eyes of hers to meet mine.

"Ever hear of a thing called personal space?" Her gaze flicks to where the cotton of my T-shirt is curling around the feminine curve of her biceps.

"Ever learn that it's polite to answer someone when they call your name?"

Ooo, *somebody* didn't like the manners lesson.

The narrowing of her eyes should have warning bells clanging inside my head, especially with how close her trusty chef's knife is, but she's invading my senses, from the press of her body against mine to her understated sweet aroma, causing my signals to cross.

The pink tip of her tongue peeks out, wetting her lips, and I bite the inside of my cheek hard enough to draw blood.

Must.
Resist.
The.
Urge.
To.
Follow.
Its.
Path.
With.
My.
Own.
*Oh shit.*

Despite the slow mental cautioning, the primal dumbass taking up residency in my brain drowns out my common sense with his chant of *Kiss me, lick me, fuck me. Mine. Mine. Mine.* I've moved close enough to feel the warmth of Gemma's breath blow across my lips when she calls out, "Hey, Siri, what's the definition of personal space?"

A male Australian-accented voice responds, "The physical space immediately surrounding someone, into which any encroachment feels threatening to or uncomfortable for them."

An unexpected chuckle escapes me because of course her Siri is set to sound like a Hemsworth. That is undoubtedly a bloodline the Covenettes are obsessed with.

"You feel threatened by me, Princess?" I ask, not for a second believing that to be true, a fact confirmed by the return of Silent Gem.

Sliding my foot behind her adorably bare feet, I shift to my right, keeping my chest in contact with her body, letting it brush along her back, reveling in the stuttered breath she inhales.

"Though, I gotta say…" I dip my head to her neck, humming against her soft skin. "I *can* see that the uncomfortable part is true."

I nip the vein fluttering with her erratic pulse, my lips pulling into a grin at her almost-inaudible gasp.

"W-wow." The breathy stutter takes all the snark out of Gemma's retort, and she requires two attempts at clearing her throat before she can speak. "I didn't think disdain was something a person could see with the naked eye."

"I don't know about disdain"—I drag my fingertips across the generous curve of her hip, forcing my palm flat on the counter and caging her in instead of gripping that enticing swell—"but I'd have to be blind to miss how hard your nipples are for me right now."

Though neither of us would need to know braille to make out how rock fucking hard I am as the erection to end all erections nestles into the swell of her ass when she rolls her hips.

Gemma glances down as if to confirm if what I said was true.

It is.

Her nipples are tight little dime-sized points testing the limits of her thin cotton shirt, poking out proudly, fully on display, practically *begging* for my attention.

*Shit.*

No amount of denial can withstand how I *yearn* for her. I have to admit I'm a bald-faced liar and I *want* her. I'm *desperate* for her. All I want to do at this moment is spin her around, hoist her onto this counter, rip her shirt off, bury my face in her chest, pull her nipples into my mouth, and bite, lave, and suck on them until she comes, my name spilling from those tempting lips.

"Tell me something, Princess." I smirk at her cute little growl. "Are you wet too?"

Her back expands against my chest, and my hand rises from the countertop as if it has a mind of its own, finding its way to Gemma's stomach. My fingers drift beneath the hem of her shirt, flexing at the feel of her smooth flesh.

"If I were to slip my hand inside these leggings"—I toy with the band bisecting her midsection—"would I find you *drenched* for me?"

Gemma smacks my hand away and shoves me backward. She reaches for a bowl of ground venison across the counter, but when she spins to stalk away from me, she sways, jerking an arm up and pressing a palm to her head.

I don't get the chance to ask what's wrong. Instead, I'm springing into action, grateful to all the years I've spent playing hockey for honing my reflexes to athletic perfection, enabling me to catch Gemma as her body collapses toward the floor.

Sadly the same can't be said for the bowl. It falls with her—or, more accurately, onto her, spilling ground meat all over.

Except…she's too busy being fucking unconscious to notice.

*Holy shit.* Gemma just passed out. What am I supposed to do?

Bracing her with an arm along her back, I bend my knees and gently lower her to lie on the meat-littered tile. I sweep my free arm out wide, shooing both curious dogs away.

*Shit.*

*Shit.*

*Shit.*

What the *fuck* am I supposed to do? Do I call 911? Do you call 911 for somebody passing out? Is that an overreaction?

Wait—do I have smelling salts? My first aid kit has to have them. I feel like that's a staple in any athlete's kit.

But...where is it? The bathroom? The mudroom? The—

The *Rocky* theme song interrupts my mental spiral and ends the most unhelpful thought process known to man. *Thank fuck.*

Pushing onto my knees, I slap my hand along the counter, pointedly ignoring the slice of Gemma's knife on my palm, and feel around for her phone. Finally, I make contact with the smooth rubber of her case, snatching the phone up and swiping to accept the call from her cousin before it can go to voice mail.

"Rocky," I croak, out of breath like I was on a penalty kill.

"Chance?" Confusion laces every bit of my friend's tone. "Umm...why are you answering Gem's phone? Oh my god"— she continues before I can get a word in edgewise—"*please* tell me you didn't actually end up killing her. That's not a good look fo—"

"Rocky!" I shout past the panic clogging my throat.

"What's wrong?" she asks, all the sass evaporating instantly, replaced with the serious professionalism Rocky is revered for.

"Gemma—she—she—she just..."

"She just what, Chance?" Rocky's voice is stern, not scolding, more controlled as if to guide me where she needs me to go to get whatever information I'm clearly failing to relay. She shouts something to someone on her end of the line, but based on the muted sound, she must have pulled the phone away from her mouth before returning to coach me through this. "I need you to take a breath and use your words to tell me what happened to my cousin."

"She passed out. One minute we're arguing about if she's wet for me, and the next, she just passes out." The words spew out of me in oversharing word vomit, tumbling over each other in panicked she-didn't-need-to-know-the-specifics detail.

Rocky puffs out a surprised breath, her silence only ramping up my fried nerves.

"Well…" she starts at long last, only to trail off for another hair-raising pause. "I guess I know the subject of the next Coven Conversation." My mental capacity is too busy overflowing with all the what-the-fuck-is-wrong-with-Gem questions to register the typical ball retreat those two words inspire. "But for now, I need to know what happened when Gem passed out. Did she hit her head as she fell? Is she bleeding? You don't see any blood, do you?"

"No, nothing like that." Still, I run my gaze over Gemma's prone body, searching for an injury I know isn't there but feel must be to explain what. The. Actual. Fuck? "I was right next to her when it happened and caught her before she could fall."

Rocky clucks her tongue, and I barely refrain from yelling, *What the hell does that mean?*

"Gemma's going to be okay."

My control snaps. "How the *fuck* can you know that?" Pain radiates through my palm as I grip the phone tight enough that it's a damn miracle the thing doesn't crack.

"Chance," Rocky cajoles. "Breathe." She repeats the command when I don't do what she says, waiting me out until I do. "Okay…now do your best to relax and listen for a minute. Can you do that? Can you give me sixty seconds?"

I nod despite her inability to see me, but she takes my silence as acquiescence.

"Gem texted me earlier saying she woke up with a migraine. That's actually why I was calling. I knew if it got bad enough, there was the possibility she would need a ride home."

A migraine? A migraine did this?

Plopping down beside Gemma, I cup a hand under her head, cradling it and stroking my thumb across the apple of her cheek.

"Does she usually pass out from migraines?"

"Not typically, but…it has happened in the rare instance when they've gotten bad enough."

I don't like it. I don't like it one bit.

"Isn't there anything she could take before it got to that point?"

"Yeah, but her meds were at home."

"Why the hell didn't she have them with her?" I ask Rocky

accusingly, as if she's responsible, like she reached inside Gemma's bag and took the medicine out.

"Chance..." I sigh at the return of Rocky's *Let's talk the grumpy animal off the ledge* voice. "She doesn't get them that often."

"This is still fucking unacceptable, Rock." I hit the speaker-phone button and place the phone on the floor, scooping Gemma into my arms and cradling her in my lap.

Nope, I don't like it. Not the holding Gemma part—no, that feels shockingly...natural.

I mean the rest of it: the migraine, the passing out, Rocky's casual nonchalance about the whole scenario.

None of it.

It makes me want to punch something—like a wall-type something.

# CHAPTER 9

*Gemma*

E *rmigah, my head is killing me.*
Ugh…migraines. These terrible motherfuckers are the worst. It's like a headache on steroids. Or, in my case, bath salts.

Never had one? Well, consider yourself lucky. Migraines are the devil's work.

Not even being on the tail end of one gives me relief. It literally feels like my dad decided to reach inside my skull, help himself to my brain, then let his fighters use my precious gray matter as their speed bag for the day before replacing it when they were done.

Also…

I can't…breathe.

That's new, but…

Something is…crushing me.

There's a snort.

A grunt.

A…growl?

Umm, none of those sounds came from me. That groan, though? Yeah, that was totally me.

*Holy guacamole.* Why is the bed starting to shake like we're having a flipping earthquake?

Uh, what the…

This is New Jersey. We may have the überrare tremor, but

nothing of a magnitude sufficient enough to churn my guts like my prized Ninja blender.

*Bleh!* This gives a whole new meaning to a migraine hangover.

Uh-oh. This is not going to end well.

I have no idea what's going on, but I feel like I need to hold on to something. With whatever measly strength lingers in my muscles, I fling out an arm, flopping my hand around like some sort of pathetic fish out of water, searching for my headboard.

Except…I can't find any of the cold metal bars that make up the diamond pattern I had custom welded. Nope, all I feel is smooth wood.

This isn't my bed.

Terrified by what I might find when I open my eyes, I carefully and painfully crack one crusted-over eyelid open and…

Realization slams into me, my morning replaying in vivid, totally has me squinting in pain Technicolor: waking up with the dull throb of a migraine simmering under the surface, only to discover my emergency stash of migraine meds wasn't in my purse.

Did I pack up and abandon my charges before their Dickhead Daddy arrived home? *Pfft.* No way. I'm a Steele, and stubbornness is woven into my DNA. I downed four ibuprofen and got to work batching their meals for the week.

I only had to last a few hours. I should have been fine.

Except…seeing as I'm now in bed, I wasn't fine.

Did Rocky end up coming to pick me up? I know I called her to warn her of the possibility, but…

Did the pain in my head get so bad I blacked out on the drive home? That's never happened before. So…then…

*Holy shiitake mushrooms.* This isn't my bed. What the—

How the hell did I end up in Chance Jenson's bed?

The pressure on my chest finally eases, and when the entire left side of my face gets covered in slobber, the pieces slowly start to fall into place as to what—or, more appropriately, who—was the source: Pebbles. Homegirl loves to impersonate a boulder any chance she gets.

With my eyes still pinched shut, I stretch my arm toward her and scratch at the underside of her neck. "If I wasn't certain of your love for me, baby girl, I would think your snuggles were an attempt to smother me in my sleep at your daddy's request."

"You wound me, Princess."

The unexpected deep voice causes me to jump like a sudden sound during a quiet scene in a horror movie.

"Ugh." I clutch my head against the stab of pain piercing my skull. "Stop shouting."

Chance's rumbly chuckle is far too sexy for its own good, not to mention the things it's doing to my overtaxed body. The brain is supposed to be the epicenter for all the things. How the hell is it able to tell my nipples to perk up and put on their best bra-free performance when it's busy feeling like taco filling itself?

And…

Wait…

Bra-free?

I may not have felt good this morning, but I know I had on a bra.

"I'm not shouting," Chance says around his annoyingly hot chuckle while considerably—irritably so in its consideration—lowering the volume of his voice.

"Shh." I limply wave a finger, too busy assessing my braless state to form a proper retort. Opening my eyes would certainly speed things along, but I'm not sure if there are any lights on, and I don't particularly want to feel like I'm being stabbed with ice picks if they are.

The quiet shish of sock-covered feet padding across the floor is the only warning I get before the bed dips and envelops me in that maddeningly alluring aroma of sandalwood and ice. I hate that he smells so good.

Calloused fingertips drag across the pinched skin of my fore-head, tracing along my hairline and brushing an errant wave off my face to gently tuck it behind my ear. "How are you feeling?"

"Where's my bra?" I blurt.

The fingers on the hand that never entirely left the side of my face tighten in my hair, tugging on the strands in a far-too-plea-surable-for-the-moment way. This time my moan isn't entirely pain-filled.

My god. I'm going to claim temporary insanity by way of migraine death march for my hussy-tastic reactions.

"I hung it up in the laundry room."

"Eww, you didn't jerk off in it or something, did you?"

"The fuck is wrong with you, Gem?" The snap in Chance's tone has me finally peeling one eyelid open.

*Shit.* I shouldn't have done that.

Not because of the eyeball ice picks. The lights are off, the room illuminated by the soft glow of the sun shining through the windows.

Nope, those bitches would have been preferable to seeing a slightly rumpled Chance Jenson. A backward navy Blizzards ball cap cuts across his bronzed forehead, highlighting the dark brows dipped in concern. His hate-him-more-for-having-such-perfect, thick lashes sweep along his high cheekbones as he scans me, his dark eyes swirling with something I can't quite read.

I swallow. Hard.

His annoyingly square jaw has the beginnings of a short beard, but there's no disguising his plump lips, pursed the slightest bit in what I'm sure is his standard Gemma Steele irritation.

Those stupidly broad shoulders of his stretch the limits of his white *Property of Blizzards Hockey* tee, the vibrancy of the fabric only highlighting the appeal of the dark ink spilling out from under it.

What the damn hell? The man just got off a cross-country flight—a red-eye, no less; where the hell does he get off still looking so...so...sexy?

A nonsensical "Huh" is all I manage in my dazed state.

And...*fuck me*, there go my panties. Just...buh-bye. I might as well add a wave for good measure because, damn, that upward tilt to Chance Jenson's mouth is lethal.

*Holy cannoli*, what is wrong with me?

I don't like Chance Jenson.

I repeat:

I.

Do.

Not.

Like.

Chance.

Jenson.

Because I don't like him, I refuse to be attracted to him, and being turned on by him? To borrow a line from one of my favorite movies, *The Princess Bride*, it's inconceivable.

Note to self: *Hey self, do not ever have a migraine around Chance Jenson ever again.* And before you ask, yes, both those evers were completely necessary. It's honestly the only thing I can think of that could be responsible for such an uncharacteristic response to the spawn of Satan.

*Keep telling yourself that.* If it didn't hurt so much to squint, I'd side-eye the hell out of that vexing whisper in the back of my mind.

"It's maddening how adorable you are when I want to be pissed at you." Chance's fingers skim down my neck before shifting to cup my nape.

You know what's maddening? How I lean into the touch, soaking up the possession.

Oh-kay, it's official: Gemma Steele has left this plane of existence and been replaced with some kind of pod person. What the hell kind of Roswell-type bullshit side effect is this?

"What reason would you have to be mad at me?" I attempt to scowl, but both the lingering pain of my fading migraine and the ginormous mutt sprawling out along my side and resting her way-too-heavy-to-be-resting-it-on-my-battered-brain head on top of mine kind of ruin the effect.

Chance's nostrils flare, as do those dark eyes staring at me before they narrow, the simmering depths making it hard to breathe.

"Oh…I don't know, Gem."

He throws both arms in the air, and I tell myself the whimper that escapes me is from him slightly yanking my hair with the jerking movement, not the loss of his touch. Or him calling me Gem—again.

Yup, that's my story, and I'm sticking to it.

"Maybe how you passed the fuck out in my arms."

"Your arms?" I parrot, racking my brain for any recollection of what he's talking about.

"Yeah. In. My. Arms." His words are clipped, as is each corresponding jerky head nod. "Thank fucking Christ I was next to you. Otherwise, you would have cracked that pretty little head of yours on the counter."

"You think I'm pretty?" I ask, my voice small, as if afraid he'll change his answer with the clarification.

"Jesus Christ." Chance rubs a hand over the hat covering his head, his large palm splayed over the polyester, gripping it like a lifeline—or maybe to prevent him from gripping my neck in a choke hold. The disbelief painting his features tells me it's a toss-up. "That's what you're focusing on?"

Oh yeah, it's definitely the latter of the two.

I glance away, concentrating hard on one of the gray splatters on Pebbles's coat.

"You scared the ever-loving shit out of me, Gem."

Why the hell is a part of me going melty like chocolate in a pan from him calling me Gem? He's flipping straight up yelling at me now.

"You act like I did it on purpose," I shout back, ignoring the wince of pain. Palms braced on the not-going-to-think-about-how-comfortable-it-is mattress, I wiggle around and push until I'm sitting up. I may have to lean back against the headboard for support, but I'll be damned if I'm going to take this argument lying down.

"What else do you call trying to cook a week's worth of food when you're having a migraine?" He cocks a brow. Just one, not both. Ugh, even his facial expressions are infuriating.

"Umm, a Tuesday," I deadpan, the duh implied in my tone.

"You're exasperating, you know that, right?"

"Hi, Pot." I extend a hand. "I'm Kettle."

Chance growls, ignoring my proffered hand.

Oh-kay then.

"Look"—I drop my hand to Chance's thigh, my own clenching at the strength in the flexing muscle—"I'm sorry, okay? Your couch is so comfy I never expected sleeping on it to trigger a migraine."

Chance's brows crash together, his dark gaze dropping to the bed before swinging around to the doorway and back again. His mouth opens, only to close again, the furrow between his eyebrows deepening. "You slept on the couch?" His disbelief is obvious.

"Yeah…"

"Like, you fell asleep while we were talking and just decided to stay there for the night?"

I nod because that part is true, but also…

"Shit. I'm sorry." Chance's unexpected and, let's face it, uncharacteristic apology causes me to lose my train of thought. "I shouldn't have bothered you that late. That's on me."

Wow.

There's another one of those dangerous chuckles. "Is it so hard to believe I can admit when I fuck up?"

"Huh?" I blink, then blink again, my thought process fuzzy.

Like he's moving in slow motion, I watch as Chance lifts one of his inked arms toward my face before he drags a crooked knuckle along the underside of my bottom lip.

*Dammit.* This time I can't blame my difficulty breathing on a canine. If I thought Chance's chuckles were dangerous to my hormones, a move like that is downright catastrophic.

"You mouthed the word wow."

"That's new." Suddenly, feeling unexplainably nervous, I start to chew on the corner of my thumb, a terrible habit I've had since I was a kid. "Usually, it's my face giving me away."

Chance reaches out, lazily scratching Pebbles between her ears. "Ain't that the truth."

My thumb falls from my mouth as my jaw drops in shock.

Chance shakes his head, a stupidly sexy smirk tugging up one side of his lips. "Don't act like this is new information."

He's not wrong. Dad always teased that if I didn't say how I was feeling, my face would give me away.

"I'm just surprised you noticed." I wince, rubbing where a dull throb is lingering at my temple like a party guest that refuses to leave no matter how many subtle *Hey, it's getting late*s you toss out.

"I notice more than you think," Chance mutters. It's said under his breath, so I think that's what he said, but I'm not quite sure.

"And because I'm making you feel guilty after accidentally scaring the shit out of you"—a giggle escapes before I can stop it, and oh my damn, that's a smoldery glare you have there, Mr. Jenson—"I would have slept on the couch regardless of our phone call."

"Why?"

"Uh…because that's where I slept all week?" I say it as more of a question than a statement.

There's another one of those comical pinging gazes, this one with bonus gesticulating arm motions.

"You"—Chance points to me—"slept on the couch"—he points in the direction of the living room—"when there's a perfectly good bed being unused in here?"

Perfectly good and ridiculously comfortable. I nod, choosing —wisely, I might add—not to voice those particular thoughts.

"That was stupid," he declares.

I shrug. "Or necessary."

Especially given the weird pull I've been feeling toward him lately. Sleeping in his bed would have been way too...intimate.

He springs up off the bed, stalking away, only to circle around at a clunky pace. He stops in his tracks, glaring the grumpiest glare to ever glare at me, ruining the last remaining bit of panties. "Why do you have to be the most stubborn person on the planet?"

Ooo, I'm shocked he was able to get the question out with how tightly he's clenching his teeth.

"Why would you sleep on a couch when you're prone to migraines?"

I roll my eyes, and he growls, which only causes me to giggle. "Prone is kind of a strong word."

"You have a prescription for migraine medicine—I think prone is the right fucking word here."

"Ehh."

"You could have died," he shouts.

"Pfft." I roll my eyes. "Not likely."

"Don't fucking roll your eyes at me, Gemma." The dropped octave in his timbre has my nipples dancing a jig.

"And what are you gonna do?" I roll my eyes again for good measure. "Spank me, Mr. Grey?"

Damn book club. It keeps my mind living in the gutter.

Chance stalks toward the bed, and I suddenly feel like prey under the predatory glare painting his expression. An *Oh shit* warning blares inside my head like a goal lap.

Hands balled into fists, he places them on either side of my hips, caging me in and pinning me down with the blankets covering my lap. His nose bumps against the tip of mine. He's so close that I can make out the slight ring of brown I've never noticed around his dark, almost black irises.

I lick my lips, squirming in my seat when his gaze falls to them, and attempt to swallow past the ball of lust that's leaped into my throat.

Minty fresh breath blows across the moisture lingering on my skin when he speaks.

"Don't fucking tempt me, Princess."

# CHAPTER 10

## *Chance*

*Fuck me,* I'm hard.

I'm sitting here, having the most infuriating conversation with the world's most exasperating woman—*after* having the shit scared out of me by her—and I'm fucking hard.

Three hours—that's how long I paced outside my bedroom door, Bamm-Bamm trailing in my wake step for step, waiting for Gemma to fully regain consciousness.

It's been a crapshoot.

She roused slightly when I used a damp cloth to clean away the worst of the dogs' venison from her skin then again when I changed her into a clean shirt, but for the most part, Little Miss Could Be Confused For A Disney Princess Herself did her best impersonation of Sleeping Beauty. For three. *Fucking.* Hours.

I've had it. My wits' end was passed almost eleven thousand seconds ago. The moment Gemma collapsed, I was done. As if that wasn't bad enough, I had to suffer through the live-action version of that damn selfie while taking care of the passed-out one.

Yeah, Kodak has *nothing* on Gemma Steele in the lingerie-covered flesh, and she's just casually teasing the idea of spanking her? *Holy shit,* now it's all I can think about.

If ever there was an ass made to be spanked, it was Gemma Steele's. It's round and full. My palm is downright itching to feel the burn of her skin turning a rosy pink under it, eyes yearning to watch how those curves would jiggle with each swat.

*Fuck.* Now I'm not just hard, but my erection is veering toward should-seek-medical-attention intensity.

"Don't fucking *tempt* me, Princess," I warn, a puff of air caressing my face with her shocked exhale, her knuckles brushing against my forearms as she grips my gray comforter in her fists. It takes a Herculean effort not to imagine all the ways I could make her clutch at my covers if given a chance.

Though I'd probably have to carry her ass out to the living room—if my bed wasn't good enough to sleep on (it is, it's like a damn cloud) then who's to say it would be good enough to fuck her on.

Wait...

What?

No. No. No.

*Stop fucking thinking about, well...fucking Gemma Steele.*

*Shit.* This is *all* her fault. She started it with her sexy selfie sending.

"You talk a big game, Rookie." Gemma feigns nonchalance, but she's not fooling me. I hear the waver in her voice and feel the quiver in her body. "But I know that's all you are—talk."

I have half a mind—and one fully ready and able dick—to show her just how actionable I could be with her.

I shove away from her, springing off the bed like my ass is on fire. Distance is imperative if I want to avoid proving precisely that.

"I'm not a fucking rookie," I bite out through gritted teeth. I fucking *hate* it when she calls me that. Because whether it's her intention or not, it only serves as a reminder of what I know to be true—that I'm beneath her.

She shrugs, utterly unconcerned with how vital my status with the Blizzards is to me. A rational man would most likely realize it's probably more unaware than unconcerned, but I'm far from feeling rational after the morning's emotional maelstrom.

"Nice to see that you're feeling better, but I could have done without the return of your bitchiness."

Gemma scoffs. "Look, I'm sorry for scaring you this morning, but it feels a *bit* convenient that you're forgetting how much of a dickhead you are to me on the reg."

"*Yeah*, I'm such a dickhead for making sure you didn't die and all that." I lay on some of the sarcasm she loves to favor.

"You're back to that?"

"Back to what?"

"The whole *you could have died* thing," she says, dropping the octave of her voice to mimic mine.

"Stop acting like that wasn't a possibility."

Pebbles whines at the brewing hostility, fidgeting until Gemma uses a comforting hand to place soothing strokes along her back.

"Possible?" Gemma nods. "Probable?" She shakes her head. "Not freaking likely."

"Erg!" I smack my thighs. This woman. "I'm so fucking frustrated with you."

"And that's different from any other day that ends in Y... how?" She waves a hand, palm facing the ceiling.

"Why didn't you just sleep in my bed? If you had, we could have avoided this entire situation."

There's no humor in the short laugh Gemma expels. "I don't get you. From the *day* we met, you've been all; you'll never get this hockey dick no matter how badly you want it."

"That's—" I try to cut in, but she barrels right over the interruption.

"One would think with a declaration like that, you wouldn't want me anywhere *near* your bedroom. And now you're *pissed* that I didn't *want* to sleep on your slutty sheets?"

"How the fuck are sheets slutty?"

Gemma's lips purse, her expression broadcasting how uninterested she is in entertaining my question with an answer.

"We're getting off topic here." Not that that surprises me. I've never met people who can squirrel brain like the Covenettes. It's why I constantly feel like we're having multiple conversations whenever Gemma and I speak. "What would have happened if I wasn't there when you passed out? If I wasn't there to catch you as you fell?"

I squeeze my eyes shut as each terrifying possibility plays out inside my head.

"Someone certainly thinks highly of himself." Her little chin tips up defiantly. "I never would have suspected you suffer from white knight syndrome."

My hands ball into fists when the brat rolls her eyes—again. Disbelief has me closing the distance between us, but instead of sitting, I plant my palms on the headboard and lean over to crowd her space.

"What if you hit your head? I could have come home to you bleeding out on my kitchen floor, or worse, you could have been lying there with a brain bleed, and I wouldn't know."

"Maybe lay off the *Grey's Anatomy* on road trips."

Why do I even bother?

That's it—I'm done.

Done worrying about her.

Done trying to take care of her.

Done waiting for her to acknowledge any of it.

Just fucking done.

"You know what?" I spin on my heel and head for the door. "Forget it."

"Seriously?" Gemma calls out, but I keep going.

Sheets rustle, and there's a muttered curse before the patter of hurried footsteps preludes dainty fingers wrapping around my wrist as I cross the threshold to the bedroom. I stop but don't turn around.

"You've spent the entire year we've known each other being the 'biggest dick to ever dick' to me, and now you're practically gaslighting me into feeling guilty about not falling all over myself in gratitude because, for once in your life, you were nice to me? Well…news flash." She tugs on my wrist. "It's hard to appreciate something you were too unconscious to witness."

She's right, and that realization finally has me spinning around, except the apology she's owed dies on my tongue the moment I'm fully facing her.

*Oh shit.* Talk about no good deed going unpunished. This is a karmic bitch slap if there ever was one. Her body is no longer obscured by bedsheets, and I'm hit with the full effect of one of the ways I took care of her—a wardrobe change.

Gemma may have only been aware of her missing bra, but her entire outfit was soiled by the dogs' food. So instead of standing in front of me wearing a scoop-necked tank and leggings, she's in one of my Blizzards Hockey tees.

*Sonofabitch.*

The sight of her wearing one of *my* shirts, *my* number proudly stamped across her chest, does fucked-up things to my head, causing me to think all kinds of things I have no business thinking. If that isn't bad enough, the added visual of her nipples tenting the fabric of the white material, the faintest shadow of areola tinting the well-worn cotton, and miles of long tanned leg on display only drive home the reminder that that's all she has on.

Neither of us says a word as we stare. The silence is not the only thing stretching between us as I start to do some tenting of my own, specifically in the below-the-belt region.

As if drawn by my gaze locked a few inches south of her face, Gemma glances down, shrieking and banding her arms across her chest.

"What the hell happened to my clothes?" she screeches.

"You got Bambi all over them."

Gemma's lips part with what I'm sure would have been a sassy retort, but nothing comes out. Instead, her expression stutters, her gaze bouncing from me to the shirt covering her body like a minidress then back again.

"We-well, I hope you got a good look when you stripped me down because I can guaran-damn-tee you'll *never* get to see me naked again." She punctuates the statement with a good old-fashioned hair flip before storming past me.

Capturing her wrist, I halt her escape, twirling her back around like a dancer. Then, with her arm still extended above her head, I use my hold to pin her to the wall, gently but purposefully maneuvering her until her back is flush with it.

Stepping a foot between hers, I kick her feet apart, hating that I notice how perfect the bright-teal polish painting her toes is. Shifting my weight, I feel the ball-tingling brush of Gemma's pebbled nipples against my chest as I press closer, my free hand gripping her waist when she squirms in my hold.

My palm glides along her rib cage, my knuckles skimming the jut of her collarbone before notching underneath her chin, tilting her gaze to meet mine. Storm clouds churn in the gray depths, and I'm studying every inch as I creep closer, Gemma's head tipping back, her bed head–rumpled waves messily pooling around her.

"If I wanted you naked, I sure as shit wouldn't need you to be unconscious to accomplish it." I pinch her chin between my thumb and forefinger when she tries to glance away with a scoff.

"But since you seem insistent on making me out to be some kind of predatory perv, let me clear a few things up for you, Princess."

Her jaw tics, but she remains silent.

"When I undressed you and *oh so gentlemanly* changed you into clean clothes—"

She mutters something that sounds suspiciously like *I wouldn't know what gentlemanly was if it bit me on the ass* under her breath, but I ignore it, continuing through the interruption.

"—I waited until I had my shirt on you before I removed your bra."

"Creeping on me in my underwear isn't the gentlemanly win you think it is, Pervy McPerverson."

A chuckle works its way up my throat, her eyes narrowing at the sound.

"Now who's being a hypocrite, Miss Kettle?"

"How the hell am *I* a hypocrite?" Gemma huffs, her voice rising at the end.

"Baby..." I drag my knuckles over her jaw, unfurling my fingers to cup her by the nape. "If you have a problem with me seeing you in your underwear, you probably shouldn't send out selfies of you in it."

Who knows how different things between us would be if she didn't?

" A lright, spill."

I squeeze my eyes shut at the sound of my cousin's voice.

*Dammit.* I should have known the first period was nothing more than my girls leading me into a false sense of security. Why did I think I could make it through an entire Blizzards game without them grilling me about what happened at Chance's the other day?

The fact that they didn't arrange to ambush me about it in the past two days is impressive for them, almost as much as Chance going all Florence Nightingale when I would have assumed he'd be more Nurse Ratched—at least in regard to me.

*Crap.* Why didn't I stay in the luxury suite our families have season tickets to in The Ice Box? Noooo. Instead, I was all, "Sure, let's go to our seats along the boards. You know I love feeling like I'm part of the action."

*Rookie mistake, Gem. Rookie, rookie mistake.*

My girls pounce before my ass even has enough time to fully make contact with the cushioned seat beneath it. *Annnnd* the inquisition begins.

I barely feel the chill being up against the boards usually entails. Nope, not when I'm warmed by the smothering weight of eight sets of expectant eyeballs trained on me. I do my best to ignore them, studying the controlled dance of the two Zambonis cleaning the ice in opposite coordinated circles as if there's going to be a quiz before the second period begins.

Does it work? *Yeah right.* There's no escaping. These bishes have their sights set on me from multiple directions. Still, like that *Hang in there* kitten, I stubbornly hold on to the hope that I'm wrong and slowly crack open a single eye.

*Shit.* No dice.

Rocky's steely gaze is locked onto me like a title bout, the side of my face burning from the intensity. I deflate into my seat with a sigh, chugging back half my cup of beer with a hearty swallow. I have a feeling I'm going to need a little liquid lubrication to help ease the discomfort of this conversation.

"Oh my god!" Maddey, who's still up from Virginia with her husband Dex while he's on short liberty from the SEALs, squeals, her long blonde curls flying about and smacking me in the face as she shifts around in her seat until her feet are propped on the cushion and her ass is perched on Jordan's armrest. "Spill the *damn* tea already, bitch."

Maddey's enthusiastic repositioning pulls Jordan from her conversation with the people in the row behind ours. She snakes between Maddey's elbow and side, the latter draping her arm around Jordan and tugging her into a tight snuggle. It's a running joke in our group that Maddey is Jordan and Jase's long-lost, someone-forgot-to-give-her-the-matching-piece-of-the-medallion triplet. Seeing them together like this is fun because it does make you do a double take.

"It is rude to keep things from your besties," Jordan agrees.

"For reals." There's no missing the enthusiastic bob of Becky's red head in front of me. "I've been feeling all kinds of neglected these last two days."

"Ain't that the truth," Holly deadpans.

Jaw unhinged, Becky whips around to face our roomie. "And how would *you* know?" She pokes Holly with an accusatory finger. "You've been spending all your time across the hall at the guys' place." Another poke. "I have half a mind to make a Shark Steamer Holly to go with Swiffer Gem just so I don't feel like I'm *living. By. Myself.*" Becky finishes with the type of dramatic flair only she's capable of pulling off.

"Can you *blame* the girl?" Skye jumps to our friend's defense, lifting Holly's left hand and folding the fingers on it to show off the sparkly new diamond adorning her ring finger. "I'd be getting in all the fiancé fuckery I could, too, if I were her."

"Ew, gross." Rocky points a finger toward her mouth with a gag.

"Seconded," I agree with a shudder. I can listen to stories about *all* the creative ways Gage bangs Rocky, but hearing about Vince's sex life is gross. I don't know what it is—and who knows, maybe it's borderline sexist in some way—but there's something about him being my male cousin that makes it hit differently.

"I promise we're normal." Jordan leans over the row in front of us toward Amara, Ryan's new and totally ah-may-zing girlfriend.

"Lies," Skye deadpans.

"But we're *awesome*," Becky singsongs with a *Breakfast Club* fist pump.

"Agreed," I cheer, along with seven other voices.

"Please don't break up with my brother," Jordan rushes out.

Amara cracks up, her white teeth flashing behind the stunning purple lipstick she chose to complete her look in honor of tonight's Hockey Fights Cancer night. You wouldn't think the unique color choice would work, but as a famed makeup artist and beauty vlogger—one with a follower count that puts all the professional athletes in our squad to shame—she knows her stuff.

It probably also helps that the half of the genetics she inherited from her former Bollywood actress mother are strong, both in her warm complexion complimenting the lip color perfectly and in how utterly gorgeous she is. I may have a tiny bit of a girl crush. Honestly, who wouldn't with how she slays the winged liner look?

"I love how you think a little thing like this would scare me off"—Amara waves off the idea, hooking a thumb behind us toward the family suite—"when I've lived with that fool for the past nine years."

One level up, Maverick, Amara's nine-year-old son, is dance battling from a distance with the Blizzards' mascot, Eddie the Yeti.

"Puh-lease"—Skye *V*'s her fingers at blonde one and two—"if you two didn't scare our girl off with your little ambush outside

Espresso Patronum, I don't think she's going anywhere." She finishes with a wink at Amara.

Maddey clasps her hands over her heart, a dreamy sigh of hopeless romantic bliss escaping. "Our Cap and his Whoa."

Beth, Rocky's cousin-in-law, groans, pulling all of our attention over her way like we're a school of fish. "Wyatt and I really need to up our pet name game if we're going to avoid being kicked out of the group."

"We would never." Rocky mock-gasps, clutching at her invisible pearls. "Plus, I think the nickname you routinely use for my husband qualifies you for Covenette membership on its own."

"Fact," Becky declares. "Anyone who can call a sitting UFC Heavyweight Champ Dumbass on the reg has the type of steel ovaries we look for in Coven recruits."

"Why do I feel like I need to snoop in your room for actual applications?" I ask, absolutely serious. We don't call her Trouble for nothing. The eyebrow waggle I get in return only causes that instinct to grow. Folding forward, I drape my arms over the back of Holly's seat, making *We're playing Nancy Drew next time Becky isn't home* eye contact with her.

"Jake and I don't have anything fun either," Jordan adds. "We're your boring babe and baby."

Beth *phew* wipes her brow playfully.

Skye nudges Jordan. "Don't act like you don't swoon so hard your panties fall off anytime Jake calls you baby."

Jordan's grin and single-shoulder pop are pure, unfettered satisfied woman.

Amara asks what some of our squad's other cutesy pet names are, and Maddey begins running down the list we've accumulated since Cupid started picking us off one by one.

"Wait, wait, wait." Becky waves her arms back and forth across her body. "All you colors, baked goods, and Disney characters are old news." My nipples shrivel up, ducking and covering under the lace of my purple bra when Becky's emerald eyes lock onto me like a heat-seeking missile. "The nickname I think we all need a little more information on is Dickhead Daddy."

*Shit. Shit. Shit.*

I was *really* hoping they forgot about that.

I should have known better.

"Ooo, can I join your conversation?" A light-brown-haired head pokes its way between Maddey and me. "It sounds like you guys are having a much more *interesting* conversation than us." Twinkling sky-blue eyes rise to meet mine, a dimpled grin practically *begging* me to answer with a yes.

*Sorry buddy, I don't even want to be a part of this conversation myself. I sure as shit don't need an audience for it,* I think, shaking my head—though his crestfallen, puppy-dog eyes have me *this* close to giving in, at least until Becky starts relentlessly knocking on my knee like it's a damn door.

"Umm..." I drag out the word, adding all the syllables I can think of to buy time, utterly clueless about how to get out of this conversation. "Chance has been a complete asshat to me since the day we met. Is it really all that shocking that I call him a dickhead?"

I watch in horror as Becky's trademark trouble smirk curls at the corners of her mouth, all "Grinch evil plan–like."

Her lips part, one of my eyes squeezing closed as if to prepare for the assault of her questioning. Then the crowd inside the arena roars as the home team retakes the ice for the start of the second period.

All hail the power of the Zamboni for the interruption.

Using the distraction to my advantage, I start to spin around to face our cute interrupter from moments ago, but I don't have to go far because he's still shamelessly hovering close.

"Eavesdrop much?" I tease, gaze roving over Mr. All-American Hot Stuff. He looks familiar, but I can't quite place him.

"Can you blame me?" He lays a hand over his heart, batting his typical beautiful-male-peacock-theory eyelashes at me.

"I can promise you would've been bored."

"I *highly* doubt that." The grin he shoots me is so damn infectious I can't help but return it with one of my own. "I'm Ben." He stretches a hand over the seat.

"Gemma." I lay my hand in his but feel nothing except the gentle pressure from the handshake.

Wait...that's weird.

Two days ago—in the midst of a migraine hangover, mind you—my body lit up like the ginormous Christmas tree Holly put up in our apartment when Chance touched me.

So...where's that spark? That thrill you get the first time a cute guy touches you? And this Ben guy? Let me tell you, he is cute with a capital *C*, not to mention hot with both a capital *H* and an extra *T*.

What the shit is this?

Hand still holding mine, Ben shifts back, leaning around the slightly bulkier and equally hot dirty-blond-haired dude sitting next to him, speaking instead to the bombshell on his other side. "Yo, Bette. Have you met—"

"Oh my god, Bette," I squeal, jumping to my feet to hug her. Bette Dennings, wife of the bigger dude, Eric Dennings, breakout star tight end for the Baltimore Crabs, is the hair magician—er, stylist we all faithfully use.

"Gem." Bette squeezes me tight before we reclaim our seats, Ben's gaze bouncing between us.

"You wound me, Bette." Ben mimes stabbing himself in the heart.

"Stop being dramatic, B."

"I'm not dramatic." Ben's flourishing lilt proves that statement to be false. "E, your wife's being mean to me."

Bette giggles, and Eric mumbles, "This should be good."

"You're both bad friends," Ben states.

"And how is that?" Bette asks with a smirk, clearly amused.

"You've known this beautiful woman and have been hiding her from me." Ben turns to me with a wink.

My cheeks heat from Ben's flirtation, but...that's it. Still no zing.

I don't get a chance to ponder how my husstastic hormones are mysteriously still on hiatus because Becky is over being ignored and spins around in her seat. I'm talking entirely around, any hope of nicknames being forgotten vanishing as she pulls her legs up to sit cross-legged, arms draping over the chairback separating us.

"So...this *daddy* stuff"—*oh great, Ben's leaning back in to listen, complete with a beefy arm around my shoulders*—"is Chance all strict and demanding like, insisting on you answering him with *Yes, Daddy* or *No, Daddy*? And does he reward you with the delectably delicious *Good girl* when you please him?" Becky asks, popping up onto her knees. If the chick gets any closer, she's going to tip over the seat and end up in my lap.

"What is *wrong* with you?" I deflect but can't help but laugh, doing my best to disguise it in the crook of Ben's elbow. Snuggled in close, I breathe in the delicious man scent enveloping me.

Except...

Where the hell are my damn sparks?

Knocking on the plexiglass pulls me from this strange spirally panic while also blessedly drawing any residual attention from the interrogation squad masquerading as my best friends off of me.

Oh look, it's the loveable captain we discussed earlier.

Captain America–printed mouth guard pinched between his far too perfectly straight and white for a hockey player's teeth, Ryan smirks devilishly at Amara, the promise twinkling in his baby blues naughty enough to have those of us in the vicinity fanning ourselves. Well...those of us who aren't related to him. Jordan? Yeah, Jordan is miming vomit coming out of her mouth. Her dramatics stop as Jake skates over and hip-checks Ryan out of the way, Jordan popping out of her seat to kiss her husband through the boards.

Maddey's dreamy sigh at their superstition playing out is almost a superstition in itself. She's been making that same contented sound since college when Jake and Jordan started their game-day ritual.

A sudden bolt of electricity shoots down, but a glance down at the thumb ghosting across my upper arm reconfirms the befuddling lack of sparks. So, where is...

"Don't you jackasses have a hockey game to play?" Skye's bellow pulls my attention back to the rink, and my gaze clashes with twin fiery pits of Mordor.

Chance?

Chance Jenson is why my body is suddenly lit up like the Blizzards' pregame light show?

*Are you squidding me?*

Disbelief wars with the unconscionable desire pulsing through my system, the sensation only intensifying as Chance slowly slides his gaze over Ben's arm draped around me before looping back with that stupidly sexy jaw clench of his.

I swallow thickly, doing my damnedest to keep from squirming in my seat. Why the fungi am I getting turned on by his accusatory glower? Though what he could be accusing me of, I have no idea. Even so, I can't stop the kernel of guilt growing in my gut, can't stop myself from easing away from Ben until his arm falls from my body.

Chance's dark eyes dance over the features of my face like a physical caress. It isn't until Ryan thumps him on the shoulder with a gloved fist that I'm able to break the strangely confusing connection.

What the fuck was that?

# CHAPTER 12

## Chance

Hockey.
Hockey.
Hockey.

The sport has been a part of my life for as long as I can remember. I've done the eat-sleep-repeat thing so much that it's woven into my DNA. So…

Why? Why has something that has become so ingrained in me it's an essential part of my identity suddenly become elusive?

*Shit.*

To make matters worse, hockey is also my fucking job, and I've been failing at it for the past period and a half.

Why you might ask? Because of Gemma fucking Steele, of course.

Or, I guess, more accurately, the goddamn quarterback having trouble keeping his fucking hands to himself while he flirts with her. Who the fuck does he think he is fucking touching her? Gemma Steele is fucking mine.

Wait…

What?

No, she's not.

She's the bane of my fucking existence.

What the hell is wrong with me?

I've been conditioned to ignore pesky things like feelings and override them with what really matters—hockey. So why can't I do that now?

You know what? This is all Gemma's fault. Yeah, that's it.

I mean…how is it she can go gifting that beaming smile of hers all willy-nilly to some hotshot football player she probably only just met since the asshole lives in fucking Baltimore? It doesn't seem fair when she couldn't even grace me with the barest of grins after I made sure she didn't fucking die.

*It's because you don't deserve someone as kind as her when you're an asshole.*

Stupid voice in my head and stupid charity weekend drawing all manner of professional athletes to the area. Why di—

The puck goes sailing by me as I miss yet another pass from Ryan.

*Pull your head out of your ass, Jenson,* my subconscious shouts, echoing what I'm sure Coach Watson must be thinking about my shitty gameplay. *Stop worrying about what is happening outside the rink and focus on the game being played inside it.*

Jumping into action, I chase after the puck, checking Diaz, the Winnipeg defenseman who's been glued to my ass all night, out of the way. I wouldn't be so annoyed—hell, I'd probably feel slightly honored he deemed me enough of a threat to dog me the way he has been—if my lack of focus wasn't allowing him to outplay me.

Back and forth, the puck is passed, Winnipeg regaining possession, their center flying up the ice on a breakaway, not a soul between him and Jake standing between the pipes of the Blizzards' goal.

My thighs shake as I dig my skates into the chopped ice harder, pushing harder, racing to break up the play, but it's too little too late. I fall short, still a full body length behind him as he dekes to the left before sending a beauty of a wrist shot toward the upper corner on Jake's glove side.

It feels as if the entire play happens in slow motion. The snow spraying off his skates. The wobble of the puck as it flies through the air. The scrape of Jake's skates and the thud of his body hitting the ice as he slides into a split, stretching his arm up high.

The wait for the buzzer and goal lamp is the worst delay of them all, but not even the cage covering his face is enough to disguise Jake's smile behind it, and that's when I know—he's just added another save to his stats for the night. No thanks to me.

The refs' whistles blow, and we reset for the next play.

Eight minutes. That's all that's left on the game clock, then I can stew in my obsessive thoughts without risking getting sent back down to the minors.

It's my turn to chase the puck as it bounces along the boards. Rotating my wrists, I'm angling the blade of my stick around the edge of vulcanized rubber when I'm rammed from behind.

"Looking a bit slow tonight, Jenson," Diaz chirps. "Did somebody forget to eat their Wheaties this morning?"

Gritting my teeth, I ignore the taunt, smacking his stick away from the puck, our battle reverberating through my gloves and up my arms. I'm shoved harder into the boards, my eyes falling closed as my helmet pings off the plexiglass and Diaz's stick digs into my back. But I barely notice any of it as I reopen my eyes and my gaze locks on the scene playing out on the other side of the glass.

Gemma, head thrown back in full-out laughter, that messy bun of hers listing to the side like always. A few dark tendrils have escaped the purple scrunchie I'd bet my salary from this game she chose in honor of the Hockey Fights Cancer weekend, one of the long waves curling against the graceful slope of her neck.

Why?

Why is she laughing with *him*?

Why can she laugh so easily with anyone *but* me?

Yes, I can admit I've *thoroughly* lived up to the dickhead name she calls me, but what will it take to earn the tiniest bit of grace, to give me a sliver of an opening to redeem myself?

*Are you actually redeemable?*

*Fuck.*

Whatever the case, it sure as shit wasn't taking care of her when she was sick. What the hell is up with that anyway? All those books foisted upon me at book club lied. Aren't girls supposed to swoon when the unexpected guy takes care of them?

As if she can feel the weight of my accusatory glower burning holes into the side of her face—well, into Ben's hand as it tucks that loose tendril behind her ear—Gemma shifts her gaze toward the ice.

Yeah, sure, *now* she looks up. It's not like there's a hockey game happening five feet away from her or anything.

Ben's lips move, spewing more douchebaggery and pulling

Gemma's attention back to him. Who the fuck does he think he is?

Hockey games—at least the ones where I'm playing and not sitting in the stands—have always been the one place where Gemma would forget she hates me. Now, this asshole is robbing me of that.

Yet another woman picking another man who isn't me.

Diaz's voice rumbles in my ear, but his words don't register over the cacophony of warring emotions filling my mind. Then Diaz drives his elbow into my kidney as Gemma lays her hand atop Ben's forearm, and that's it; my vision fades to black.

Whirling around, I immediately drop my gloves with a flick of my wrists and send a fist flying toward Diaz's face, my knuckles cracking against his hard jaw. Everything after that is a hazy flurry of activity.

Gripping the front of Diaz's jersey in my fist.

Yanking him in.

Holding him as close to me as our sliding skates will allow.

Landing punch after walloping punch until the refs intervene.

Not my finest moment.

Covenette

## CHAPTER 13

# Coven CONVERSATIONS

From the Group Message Thread of The Coven

YOU KNOW YOU WANNA: Okay, Gem...enough dancing around.

DANCING QUEEN: Yeah, that's my job, babes.

YOU KNOW YOU WANNA: Fact.

YOU KNOW YOU WANNA: Now spill your guts.

PROTEIN PRINCESS: I don't know why you keep INSISTING there's anything for me to spill.

MAKES BOYS CRY: Oh...I don't know...maybe it has something to do with this. *clip of Chance's fight in last night's game*

PROTEIN PRINCESS: Umm...Chance is an enforcer. Getting into fights is essentially in his job description.

MOTHER OF DRAGONS: Technically, "enforcer" is an unofficial role.

PROTEIN PRINCESS: Listen, Hockey Queen, there's no room for your technicalities in this conversation.

ALPHABET SOUP: Bahaha, nice try, Gem.

MOTHER OF DRAGONS: Oooo, Hockey Queen. I like it. Has a nice ring to it. *Can we change my text handle?*

QUEEN OF SMUT: Not a chance, Jor. You are the Mother of Dragons.

SANTA'S COOKIE SUPPLIER: **Khaleesi GIF**

BROADWAY BABY: **Wayne's World "We're not worthy" GIF**

MOTHER OF DRAGONS: Stop, guys. You're making me blush.

MAKE ME OVER GOOSE (Amara): I know I may be new here, but why don't I believe that to be true?

THE OG PITA: Umm...because you've met her?

FIDDLER ON THE ROOF: **She's got a point GIF**

BROADWAY BABY: **Fact GIF**

DANCING QUEEN: I don't know...Jordan is kind of my hero.

MAKES BOYS CRY: Great. Now I have to find a pin.

MAKE ME OVER GOOSE: Is that a typo? Did you mean pen?

ALPHABET SOUP: It's gotta be a typo. Why would she need a pin?

SANTA'S COOKIE SUPPLIER: OMG, are you crafting, Skye? Are you making stuff for the wedding?

QUEEN OF SMUT: No. Our super PR woman is borrowing the Girl Scouts' "Always be prepared" motto in case Jordan falls victim to the same affliction her twin suffers from.

BROADWAY BABY: Would that be big-headed-itis? Because I may love the crap out of Jason, but the ego on that boy…

ALPHABET SOUP: Uh-oh, she's full-naming Jase. Someone is in the doghouse.

DANCING QUEEN: You guys have NO idea.

PROTEIN PRINCESS: Sounds like there's a story there…

YOU KNOW YOU WANNA: Oh no you don't.

YOU KNOW YOU WANNA: **No, no, no finger shake GIF**

YOU KNOW YOU WANNA: If we're having story time, it's starting with you, Gemmy-Gem.

PROTEIN PRINCESS: THERE IS NO STORY.

THE OG PITA: Whoa, whoa, whoa. **Calm down GIF** Relax the shouty caps.

MAKE ME OVER GOOSE: Not to narc (as my charming offspring would say), but Gem, babes…I saw the look you and Chance shared when he got served with the major. Spoiler alert: it was hot enough to melt the ice.

ALPHABET SOUP: As a woman who had to replace a massage table because of it, I can say jealousy is a powerful motivator.

PROTEIN PRINCESS: OMG, I think my eyes fell out I just rolled them so hard.

SANTA'S COOKIE SUPPLIER: They didn't, but I am surprised they didn't get stuck in your skull because it was an EPIC eye roll.

MAKES BOYS CRY: Now, if only she gave in to the sexual tension with Chance. Maybe then her eyes would be rolling for a different reason.

DANCING QUEEN: **ba-dum-dum GIF**

QUEEN OF SMUT: **She's got a point GIF** Oh, and if you do get down with the hate fucking, I want ALL the details. You know you guys are one of my favorite tropes.

SANTA'S COOKIE SUPPLIER: Enemies-to-lovers for the win, baby!!!

YOU KNOW YOU WANNA: OOO

YOU KNOW YOU WANNA: OOO, OOO

YOU KNOW YOU WANNA: **rubbing hands together GIF**

MOTHER OF DRAGONS: Rock, can you translate? I think Beck broke in her excitement.

ALPHABET SOUP: I gotta see her in person for a proper assessment. Let me walk down the hall. Hold, please.

YOU KNOW YOU WANNA: No translator needed, boo. I was just thinking about how a certain football player will be at the charity event tonight.

YOU KNOW YOU WANNA: I can't WAIT to see what happens when Gemma is called to the auction block.

# CHAPTER 14

## Gemma

Purple uplighting guides my way down the tunnels of The Ice Box, adding a soft, almost intimate glow to the sporting venue. The purple color scheme of this Hockey Fights Cancer charity weekend continues through to the arena, the LED panels covering the ledges in front of each level lit up in matching purple. My heels sink into the plush purple carpet leading to the rink, but my attention is too focused on its revised setup to notice much.

It never ceases to amaze me how quickly the maintenance crew is able to completely transform the arena. You would never know two professional hockey teams were battling it out here less than twenty-four hours ago.

The whiteboards of the oval-shaped rink have been left in place, but the clear plexiglass that typically sits atop them is gone, opening up the space for the high-top tables surrounding the outer perimeter, allowing the guests gathered around them to feel included in conversations with those at the casino tables strategically placed on the hardwood flooring now covering the ice.

The team benches and penalty boxes have also been converted, each now full-service bars, and erected above the lower-level seats behind the goal Jake defends twice each home game is the stage for the charity auction. The circular Jumbotron hanging above the rink plays the video of a dancing Eddie the Yeti from last month's Blizzards For Boobies hair styling event on a loop. I still can't believe they were able to get a T-shirt big enough to fit Eddie's oversized body on such short notice. Though, with Jordan and Skye having undoubtedly been a part of the planning, it shouldn't surprise me the way it does.

A hip bump has me glancing to my right, finding the yeti-dressed man himself shimming his big beefy padded shoulders next to me. I may not be able to see inside his always-open eyes, but I can feel the playful wink he gives me before jumping into the stands to join the cluster of other mascots who have joined the Blizzards for their charity weekend.

A server carrying a silver tray loaded with champagne flutes walks by, and I do the polite thing of helping him lighten his load by accepting a glass. A moment later, the hairs on the back of my neck rise, and I wish I could blame the goose bumps blooming along the exposed skin of my arms on the giant, albeit covered sheet of ice in front of me.

But...

Nope.

I know better than to think that is the cause. Sadly, frustratingly so, there's only one thing—or, more accurately, one *person*—that makes my body come alive despite my best efforts.

"Wow." I close my eyes as Chance's deep voice rolls through me. "You look beautiful, Princess."

*Fuck a duck.* I hate it when he's nice. I don't know what to do with it.

"The words you're looking for are *Thank you.*" There's a far-too-pleased tease in his tone.

"Thank you." I bite my bottom lip, restraining the grin threatening to spread as I shift to face my nemesis. "And you look..." My gaze bounces over his far-too-hot-for-my-sanity ensemble, a pang of concern squeezing me at the bruise darkening his jaw. "Like Bamm-Bamm used you as his latest chew toy."

"You know"—Chance's hand covers mine, and not until his thumb strokes across the back of it do I realize I lifted it to trace the butterfly bandage bisecting his eyebrow—"I wouldn't have guessed a woman who grew up with a boxing legend for a dad would be squeamish at the sight of a few bruises."

"I'm not squeamish."

Chance shrugs, the shift of his custom-tailored suit only highlighting those dumb broad shoulders of his. "If you say so, Princess."

"Potato, vodka, Canada."

Chance's white teeth flash with a blinding smile. "Your cousin is so weird."

Any attempt to hide my amusement shits the bed with that simple sentence. Flipping Vince. Leave it to thoughts of him to make me feel like I'm having a moment with Captain Dick for Brains.

"GEM!" The booming bellow makes me jump and has me ripping my hand away from Chance.

*Must not think about how long I was voluntarily touching Chance Jenson.*

"GEM. GEM. GEMMA!" Speak of the man-child and he shall appear with wacky arm-waving. "Yo, Chance." Vince shifts his attention to the man beside me because I'm not giving him the attention he's seeking. "Get your sexy Canuck ass over here."

Chance starts toward the other side of the rink, reaching back for my hand when Vince tells him to bring me along.

He doesn't have to listen. Hell, I probably would have ignored my cousin's directive if the tables were turned.

So...why does he comply?

And why are his fingers threading through mine? More importantly, why do I like it so much?

# CHAPTER 15

## Chance

It shouldn't come as much of a surprise to you, but I'm typically not much of a fan of all the extra PR bullshit and charity events required of us. I also feel it will not shock you to hear that I once made the mistake of saying as much to Jordan and Skye. Yes, I can admit, not my brightest move. Damn, did those ladies pay me back by volunteering me for any and every event they could find. For example, being on the docket of the date auction portion of tonight's fundraising.

So why is it that I'm enjoying tonight's charity casino night?

*Maybe it has something to do with the curvy brunette who keeps getting pressed against you?*

As if the universe is in cahoots with my subconscious, the swell of Gemma's ass presses against my groin as she stretches across the roulette table to place her next round of bets. Arm extended, fingers still curled around the yellow chips hovering over the number thirty, she freezes. There's no hiding the very obvious hockey-stick-sized effect her nearness is having on me.

Fuck my life. I should have gone to a different table. Hell, I should have gone to a different table *three* tables ago.

So…why didn't I? Better yet, why did I grab her hand, going as far as linking our fingers together, when Vince called us over to join them at one of the blackjack tables an hour ago?

I'd like to say we managed to be civil with each other because we were alone; both her cousins and their significant others were with us. Plus, Jase Donnelly's enthusiastic cheering of Rocky raking in all her fake winnings was entertaining as hell.

But...why? *Why* did I follow Gemma when she left blackjack for roulette?

I blame the mind-boggling lack of attempted verbal murder from either of us. There's also the noticeable absence of a particular football player...

"Come on, one. Big money, big money, number one." The bellowing chant breaks me out of my confused spiral, drawing my attention to Tucker standing beside me. To most of the crowd here tonight, Tuck is a winger from Chicago, donating his time and himself to the auction portion of the evening.

But—and I can't believe I can say this, though I guess it's a testament to both their tenacity and how much things can change in a year—to those of us who make up the squad I've somehow serendipitously found myself a part of, he's the troublemaker with Golden Retriever energy, as evidenced by the way he is bouncing on the balls of his feet and rubbing his hands together as if praying to the roulette gods.

Usually, I like him. At least I do when we're at the beach house a bunch of them share in the summers and he's telling me stories and making me feel like I've always been a part of the group. But when I'm stuck watching Gemma smooth her palm down the front of his purple Oxford shirt, giggling with him around the shorthand of his manwhore nickname, not so much.

"Maybe take the intensity down a bit, M-Dubs."

"Where would be the fun in that, oh gorgeous Gemma?" Tucker slips his fingers around her hand, lifting it to kiss the back like the gallant gentleman he is not.

Gemma rolls her eyes, that sunny smile of hers radiating brighter as the overhead lights reflect off the pale gloss painting those lips of hers.

*Shit*. The last thing I need is something drawing *more* attention to the mouth I can't stop fantasizing about.

"Ugh. Where's Jordan?" Gemma asks, rising up on her toes to peer around Tucker's bulky frame. "I need someone to remind you that you're essentially playing with Monopoly money."

My vision tunnels onto the arm Tuck drapes around Gemma's shoulders, pulling her in close as he twists around to follow her line of sight. "I think Blondie and my boy snuck away for a little boom-boom in the Blizzards' dressing room."

"What the hell, Tuck?" Jase chucks a poker chip at Tucker, pinging it off his forehead with the same accuracy as he slips pucks inside the net.

"Sorry to tell you this, wonder twin..." Tucker's smirk belies his apology. "But those nieces and nephew of ours weren't delivered by the stork."

"I wonder if that would have made things more or less interesting when Jordan came to plead your case to me," Melody muses, looking up all moony-eyed at Jase.

I'm not saying she's one of my favorite Covenettes because she took Jase off the market, but I'm not saying she's not.

"True Covenette material right there." Tucker double finger guns Melody then lifts his gaze over her shoulder at Jase standing behind her. "But the adorable next gen who takes after yours truly"—he points at himself, adding a proud shoulder shimmy—"came from good ol'-fashioned *fucking*."

"There is something seriously wrong with you, Tuck." Jase collects his and Melody's chips with a headshake, readying to put literal distance between himself and the conversation about his twin's sex life. "And godfather or not, that's not how genetics work when there's no actual blood relation."

"Why you gotta do me like that?" Tucker shouts at Jase's retreating back, miming being stabbed in the heart.

The dealer at our table, patiently waiting out our ridiculousness and valiantly keeping her expression stoic while witnessing it, claps her hands together before waving her open palms over the felt, presenting the table for us to place our bets. This time when Gemma reaches to place hers, I move with her, intentionally pressing my body against her with an infinitesimal grind. Why? Because I've clearly lost my mind.

Gemma freezes again, her head swiveling around. Those gray eyes of hers are storm clouds of something I can't quite name as she glares at me over her shoulder before dropping her chips in place with an audible clink.

*Fuck.* I'm harder than hard now, my situation only growing more dire and obvious as Gemma straightens, the full length of her spine aligning with my front, the sexy-as-fuck strappy heels on her feet making her tall enough for me to breathe in her lemony scent without having to bend.

*Damn.* Why does she have to smell so good? It's heady and makes me do stupid shit, like placing a ghost of a kiss on the back of her head.

Gemma's entire body tightens with a stuttered inhale.

I cup her hip, instinct driving me to keep her close even as she dips her chin and arches her eyebrows—yes, I've studied her enough to know that even though I can see only one, both are lifted—at me, her voice pitching low.

"We really need to get you a dictionary, Canada."

"Is worrying about my vocabulary your love language, Princess?"

She scoffs, the sound rolling around in the back of her throat and reverberating through me. "Loathe language is more like it."

While I might have once believed her hatred for me, that belief has changed since she watched my babies. No, Gemma Steele does not hate me despite all her claims. Hell, I'd even go as far as to say she spars with me because she gets off on it.

"Whatever helps you sleep at night, sweetheart." I twirl one of her soft curls around the end of my finger before carefully tucking it behind the shell of her ear. The tip of my nose drags along the curve of her pinkening cheek as I lean in to whisper, "Was that supposed to be today's attempt at claiming you don't like me in your personal space?"

"It's not a claim. It's a statement of fact."

It's my turn to scoff. "Such a pretty little liar you are." The tulle of her tutu-style skirt crinkles in my flexing fingers resting on her hip. "But I'd be more inclined to believe you if you hadn't been grinding against me for the last twenty minutes."

The drop of her jaw and her little gasp of outrage makes my balls tingle, not in warning—but in anticipation. "I have *not* been grinding on you."

"Potato, vodka, Princess." I toss back one of her favorite borrowed phrases with a wink.

"If *anything*, I was trying to get your personal-space-invading ass to back the fuck up."

"Liar."

"I'm not lying." She forces the words out through clenched teeth.

"Then why didn't you jab me with your elbow like you've been so fond of doing in the past?"

"I was trying to show some self-restraint since we're in public." She casts her gaze around the charity event happening around us. We've barely paid any attention to it, nor our dealer dropping the ball into play and waving a hand over the table, calling an end to another round of betting we've missed.

"If that were true, why were you trying to measure the size of my cock with your ass?" I skim the shell of her ear, nipping it before whispering, "It's ten and a quarter inches, by the way."

"You're so fucking cocky."

I grind my pelvis into her with a grin. "I know. It's that extra quarter inch that puts me over the top."

"Will the two of you just fuck already?" Tucker's question is like a bucket of ice water. "I swear to Christ, the sexual tension pulsing off you guys is giving *me* blue balls."

"What sexual tension?" Gemma asks quickly.

"Umm..." Tucker stretches an arm between Gemma and me, making a sawing motion with his hand. "This stuff is thick enough to cut with a knife."

"You have to be attracted to someone for there to be sexual tension, Tuck," Gemma argues.

"Exactly," he confirms with an exaggerated eyebrow waggle.

"How much have you had to drink, M-Dubs?" Gemma tilts her head to the side, assessing Tucker for signs of sobriety. "Because I think beer goggles are making you see things."

"Bullshit, Gemma," he counters. "You wanna fuck Chance's sexy, broody self just as badly as I want to bend Skye over that poker table and remind her how *no one* will fuck her like I can." There's a possessive growl to Tucker's words as he points to the Texas Hold'em table where Skye is kicking the asses of the members of Birds of Prey.

Gemma steps out of my hold, squaring off with Tucker, her feet spreading hip-width apart, shoulders rolling back, a familiar glint in her eyes. I know that positioning. She's used it many times on me. It's her preparing-for-battle stance.

"Is that so?"

Tucker folds his arms across his chest. "It is." He's pure Tucker Hayes bravado.

"Well, Mr. Smarty-Pants." Gemma walks her fingers up his

chest. "If I want to bang Chance so badly, why did I say yes to Ben Turner when he asked me on a date for tomorrow night?"

# CHAPTER 16

# Gemma

"Y ou did what?" Chance barks the question out like an accusation. It doesn't matter that I moved far enough away that our bodies are no longer touching; I can still *feel* his reaction—bossy, angry, accusatory question notwithstanding.

And for some reason…it excites me.

Tucker, however…well, that colossal shit starter is beaming at me like I whipped my top off or something.

"Why are you looking at me like I grew a third boob?" I flick Tucker between the eyes.

His eyes shift down, locking dead center on my chest. "How cool would it be if you did?"

"You're such a child, Tuck."

He shrugs his broad shoulders, that charming, somehow boyish, while remaining stupidly sexy smirk pulling up the side of his mouth. That simple facial expression gets Tucker into as much trouble as it gets him out of. Skye hates that smirk, professionally *and* personally.

"I may not have that *crucial* extra quarter inch"—Tucker flicks his gaze toward Chance with an eyebrow waggle before bringing it back my way—"but if you give me your hand, I could show you just how much I'm *not* a child. Plus…" Tuck leans in like he's going to whisper a secret but doesn't lower his voice at all. "Mine is pierced."

I roll my eyes. I'm well versed in the knowledge of Tucker's piercing, except…

*Holy guacamole.* Is Chance growling?

And why are my nipples doing the cha-cha at the sound?

"I can't even with you, Tuck," I say, needing a redirection away from the confusion flooding my system.

"Is that why you're slumming it with the football set? I'm too much *man* for you to handle?" He flutters his hands down the length of his body, adding a body roll for good measure.

"Stop talking out of your ass, Tuck." Skye backhands him on the bicep, stepping into her typical *control Tucker* role.

Taking advantage of her finally moving into touching distance after purposefully staying out of reach most of the night, Tucker throws an arm around Skye's shoulders and pulls her in nice and tight against his body. "I have no idea what you mean," he says, feigning an innocence anyone with a social media account knows he doesn't possess.

Skye shoots me a *Does he really believe he's fooling me?* side-eye. "If you say so. But could you *maybe* explain how a Super Bowl champion qualifies as 'slumming it'?" She tacks on exaggerated air quotes.

"Uhhh, hockey players are better than football players." Tucker's face adds the *duh* he leaves off the sentence.

"Here we go again." I groan as the downside of being friends with professional athletes rears its ugly head. I've lost hours of my life listening to the guys bicker over which are superior: hockey players or fighters. We certainly don't need to add football into the mix.

"Says the man who doesn't have a ring yet," Skye challenges.

Tuck jerks away as if shot, leaning back *Matrix*-style. "Why you gotta do me like that, Bubble?"

Skye's expression darkens. "*Don't* call me *that*."

Tucker only shrugs, utterly unconcerned with Skye's ire. He's probably immune to it since he stokes it on the reg. "Don't try to make me think I'm not your favorite."

"You're *so* not my favorite."

"Looks like lying is contagious in the Covenettes," Tucker says to Chance, and I'm officially done with the conversation.

I push past my squabbling friends but only make it a handful of steps before calloused fingers wrap around my wrist and goose bumps bloom across my skin.

"We need to talk."

My spine straightens at the command in Chance's voice, and I give him my best *Who the hell do you think you are?* glare over my shoulder. "No thanks."

His eyebrows wing up his forehead, and I use his momentary shock to my advantage to shake off his hold. The sudden need for escape has my flight instincts flaring.

What is happening? Why? *Why* does Chance Jenson's touch make me feel like every cell in my body comes alive when Ben Turner's had zero effect?

None of it makes sense. Ben is just as hot as Chance. Yet…nothing.

*Ugh.*

I weave through the makeshift casino tables, my vision hazy around the edges. I dodge fashionably dressed attendees, side-stepping around purple-gloved servers holding silver platters filled with alcohol and hors-d'oeuvres.

Distance. I *need* distance.

I make it out of the rink and into the hallway the Zamboni comes out of before I'm caught. Chance's large hand grabs mine, stopping me with enough force that I stumble in my stilettos.

"I said we need to talk, Princess." His hard body presses against mine, his warm breath ghosting across my ear as he pulls me in tighter.

I start to respond but make the critical mistake of turning my head to face him. My lips brush along the stubble dotting his jaw, his scent invading my lungs, and the words get stuck in my throat. It takes two attempts for me to clear it.

"And I don't want to talk to you."

"You're such a fucking brat."

Ignoring the rumble rolling around in the broad chest dwarfing mine is one of the hardest things I've ever done in my life, but miracle of miracles, I manage, feigning boredom that could rival Melody's Tony award-winning acting ability.

"Is this the part where you threaten to spank me?"

"Fucking hell, Gemma," Chance growls before his arm bands around my middle, the fronts of his thighs pushing against the backs of mine, moving me until I'm pressed face-first against the wall.

I brace myself, flattening my palms and wiggling to make some space but finding none. I'm trapped.

"Wh-what are you doing?" Again I try to break free, but Chance's large frame behind me is as immovable as the wall in front of me.

His free arm rises, and he lays his forearm on the wall as he crowds me closer. "Why do you feel the need to test my patience all the *goddamn* time?"

"While I have found doing so brings me joy...what, pray tell, have I done to test your patience this time?"

"You mean besides breathing?"

"How homicidal of you." I take a step to move away, but Chance splays his palm over my abdomen, keeping me in place.

"Oh, Princess." He scoffs, bringing his mouth to my ear. "You think *that's* homicidal? You have *no* idea, do you?" His stubble scrapes the shell of my ear, and it takes everything in me to focus on the words he's speaking as goose bumps sprout across my skin.

"Wh-what?" Damn this stutter. I can't pretend he doesn't affect me when it's giving me away. "That you have a veritable Chucky doll living inside your skull?"

"Wait? So am I homicidal because I'm possessed by a serial killer, or because I'm possessed by a doll possessed by a serial killer?"

"I think you lost me two possessions ago." I awkwardly laugh and attempt to free myself again, only to fail.

"Let me simplify it for you, then." The fingers on my stomach flex, cool air caressing the bared skin of my upper thighs as the tulle of my skirt bunches and lifts in Chance's hold. "Last night's fight wasn't because Diaz was invading my personal space, as you would love to say." Any humor in Chance's voice vanishes with his next sentence. "It was because that *football player*"—he spits the last two words—"was invading yours."

My breathing hitches, my fingers curling into fists to keep from reaching for him, though that urge is pure insanity. Honestly, this whole scenario is a bit insane.

"Do you have *any* idea what seeing *his* hands on you did to me?" Lips skim down the side of my neck, his words and his mouth causing me to subconsciously tip my head to the side to allow him more access. "Seeing another man touch what's mine?"

# CHAPTER 17

## Chance

F *uck.* There I go again, thinking of Gemma as mine. What the fuck? When is this insanity going to stop?

Though…is it insanity?

Could we…? Would we…? Maybe…?

"I-I'm not yours."

Ah…there's that stutter that's been giving her away.

*Not as unaffected as we like to pretend, are we, Princess?* I think, grinning against the silky-soft skin of her neck.

First, it was seeing that asshat with his hands on her. Then, it was hearing that he has a fucking *date* with her. But it's her denial that finally breaks me, solidifying my resolve that she is, in fact, MINE.

It's time for me to accept that fact to be true—time for *her* to accept that fact to be true.

I hum into her throat, dragging my teeth over the vein fluttering under my lips. "Oh, that's where you're wrong, Princess."

Her moan is music to my fucking ears.

"Bu-but you ha-hate me."

No, I hated who she reminded me of.

"If only it were that easy," I admit glumly, not that I didn't try.

It didn't matter that our animosity was born of a triggery misunderstanding on my end or what I think Gemma would do if she *ever* found out why *she* triggered me. Any hatred I tried to harbor never stood a chance against Gemma Steele.

"You could have fooled me," she says, some of the sass creeping back into her tone.

I bark a humorless laugh, the abrasive sound echoing down the empty, cavernous hallway. "Hatred would be so much easier than what I feel for you."

Gemma trembles in my arms, and as if to prove the point I'm attempting to make, my dick strains against the zipper of my suit pants.

"Maybe if I hated you, I wouldn't be standing here, not sure what to think...or say."

I tug her tighter against me, my fingertips skimming the edge of her panties underneath her dress, my mind going fuzzy imagining what kind of lingerie she chose for the evening.

"You sure seem to have a lot of words for someone claiming to be speechless."

Her sassy retort earns her a bite on the shoulder, her hiss my reward.

"It's your fault, Princess."

"Ahh...there's that gaslighting blame you love so much."

Damn maddening woman. I really, *really* wish I could hate her.

Shifting, I push my elbow into the unforgiving painted cinder block and reach around to grab a fistful of Gemma's hair, wrapping the dark locks around my hand, tugging until her back arches, her ass nuzzled into my groin, her breasts pillowed against the wall.

"Wanna know why here, at this moment, it's your fault?"

My sassy Precious remains silent.

"Hmm?" I hum. "No? Not even a guess?"

Again she's silent—at least until I grind my hips into her and a whimper falls from her glossy lips.

"Well...let me tell you." A ball-churning whine escapes when I tighten my grip on her hair. "Ever since you said you were going on a date with that douchemonkey who thought he had the right to put his hands on you, there's only been *one* thing I know to be true."

"Th-this should be good." Her stutter makes her sass fall flat.

"All I know is right here, right now, I want to rip off this dress of yours." I flex my fingers again, gathering more of her skirt until the hem rises to an indecent height, living for the hitch in her breathing. "Then I'd drag you onto that auction stage and kiss every square inch of your body while everybody watched and wished they were me."

"Can I wish not to be the other half in this asinine delirium?"

Why this little...

I yank her around, slamming her back to the wall. I curl a hand around her rib cage, her tempting mouth forming the tiniest *O* as my thumb brushes the underside of her boob.

My temper flashes swift and fierce. There's zero chance I would *ever* hurt her, but Gemma Steele loves to push me until I'm riding that razor's edge. The proof is in the way she's biting her bottom lip.

Stepping a foot between hers, I move into her space until her tits brush my chest with her every ragged inhalation.

"Pretend all you want, but I'd have you *begging* to fill the role." I bury my face in the curve of her neck, licking a swirling path toward the soft spot behind her ear, luxuriating in her trembles as her sweet, salty taste coats my tongue. "And by the time I was done with you, any thought that you were *available* would be completely driven out of their minds."

"If this is your master plan, why do you sound so angry about it?"

I jerk back and glare at her. If only she knew what it's like to be at war with oneself, to want what drives you mad...to crave someone you could never deserve.

"Do you think I want to feel like this?" I lick my suddenly dry lips. And...*fuck me*. Her gaze just *had* to drop to my mouth.

Doubling down, I let my anger fully flip the switch on my attraction. "News flash, I don't—not about you, but fighting this pull between us is exhausting."

Gemma's expression shuts down, the fire blazing in her mercurial eyes doused as if miniature firefighters stood on her paling cheeks.

What the—

Pain knifes through my foot, and before I can ask why the fuck she tried to drive the point of her sexy-as-shit stiletto through my foot like a railroad spike, the infuriating woman is gone.

Tears burn the backs of my eyes as Chance's words about not wanting me because I'm not good enough have all those high school flashbacks and old insecurities surging to the surface.

*Shit.*

I hate this.

Therapy may have taught me healthier ways to cope with my trauma, but it's harder to control when I'm in the moment, and I hate, absolutely *hate* that the urge to flee is once again my prominent instinct.

But I can't leave.

*Dammit.* Why did I agree to be in the auction? It's one thing to dream about expanding my business outside my inner circle, but who is really going to bid on me, an unknown entity, at a charity auction?

Stupid, *stupid* decision.

Freaking Jordan. This is all her fault. She used that damn Donnelly charm on me and tricked me into accepting.

*What a bitch.*

I sigh at my inner voice because I know that's not true. Jordan adding me to the auction roster—and yes, she did so before I even agreed—was to give me a professional push. The evil genius in her knew putting my name and what I do out in a roomful of professional athletes—my ideal clientele—would give me an edge if I ever do finally pull the trigger on my business.

"Baby girl." The deep baritone of the best—at least in my eyes —fighter from The Steele Maker washes over me, comforting me like my well-loved fuzzy blanket.

Ray Howard has been one of my favorite people on earth since the first weekend Vince brought him home from BTU with him. Our Chicago transplant may have terrible taste in hockey teams—sorry, not sorry, Tuck—but he has exceptional taste when it comes to members of the Steele family, i.e., picking me as his favorite.

Wordlessly, I settle into the arm coiling around my shoulders, letting Ray chase away the negativity trying to infect me.

"What has you spinning?" he asks, reading me just as quickly now as he did back when I was in high school.

"I'll be fine. I just need a minute." Squeezing in one last hug, I release him to prove my words true.

Ray's brown eyes bounce along the features of my face, his eyebrows winging upward with a head-tilting chin jerk toward the area above my shoulder. Following his gesture, I glance down with a gasp. My carefully curled locks are now a tangled mess thanks to Mr. I Don't Want to Want You.

I don't know if I'm more annoyed by his treatment of a hairstyle I spent an hour burning the tips of my fingers to achieve or by the fact that his doing so destroyed my panties. It's a toss-up.

Ray continues to study me, and the longer he stares, the more I start to squirm. Holy intensity, Batman. This must be what his opponents feel like squaring off against him in the octagon.

"Fine." Ray releases a sigh, his bunched shoulders falling away from his diamond-studded ears. "I won't push if you promise me three things."

"Three?" I ask, my playfulness returning and bleeding into my tone. "What is this, some reverse-genie whatchamacallit?"

A smile steals across Ray's attractive face, far too pretty and perfectly toothpaste-commercial-worthy for a man who makes a living getting punched in the face, his white teeth a brilliant contrast against the rich dark brown of his skin.

"You're a nut, you know that, right?" Ray's hearty chuckle and resigned headshake are well-practiced in my company.

"But like a pistachio." I wink with a cheek click.

Ray bands an arm around his middle, hunching over in laughter. "My favorite kind, baby girl."

"And that's why you love me." I wave my hands out in front of me.

"You know it." He holds out a fist, and I bump it with mine. "Now, about my three wishes..." He taps his chin in contemplation.

"Oh, they're officially wishes now, are they?" I tease with a poke to his chest. "But I don't have a lamp for you to rub."

"Okay, smartass." Ray hooks an arm around my neck, pulling me in for a noogie.

"Watch the hair, watch the hair." I smack his hand away.

"Oh, *now* you're worried?" he singsongs, flicking one of the knots left from Chance. "Question: was this a preview of your big date tomorrow night, or did you finally give in to the bad influence of your fellow Covenettes and hate bang Jenson?"

"Ugh." The only banging that's happening is my head off Ray's chest. "Not you too."

"Sorry." His shrug is anything but apologetic. "I had to."

I roll my eyes and quickly cast my gaze out over the crowd, afraid if I were to make eye contact, Ray would easily figure out that while there was no banging...*something* did go down not that far away.

And because karma must not have seen the one white paw on the black cat I crossed paths with leaving Espresso Patronum this afternoon, Ben's blue-eyed gaze finds me from across the room.

I wave.

"Alright...tell me your conditions," I say to Ray as Ben starts in our direction.

Clearing his throat, Ray adjusts his tie and straightens his shoulders like he's about to get serious, but I know it's mock at best.

"One: you have to promise you'll come to me if you need me."

"Promise."

"I mean it, Gem. Even if it's the middle of the night, you walk those sushi-slippered feet across the hall and wake my ass up."

"They're *shoe*-shi slippers. You know, like shoes." I point to my feet. "But, yes, I still promise."

It's Ray's turn to roll his eyes. "Two," he continues with an indulgent grin, "even though I'm a world-class snuggler"—he tosses his arms open wide, emphasizing the impressive wingspan that does, in fact, add to his top-notch snuggle skills—"if at any point it gets to be too much, you have to promise to schedule an emergency session with Dr. Sonya."

Yes, Ray is on a first-name basis with my therapist. He was integral in helping me choose her.

Again, it's an easy acceptance, though the longer I stand here joking around with Ray, the more confident I am that it is a condition I won't need.

I check to see where Ben is, wondering why he hasn't made it to us already. I have my answer as soon as I spot him, watching as he gets stopped not once but twice with a backslapping handshake.

"And the third?"

"This one is different."

I arch a brow at the vague segue. Oh, wait, let's be real—both my brows go up. "How so?"

"This one you have to promise to do when we get home tonight."

"And if I don't?" I challenge, sassing him just because.

"Then I'll be borrowing your cousin's Superman slippers and walking my ass across the hall to knock incessantly on your bedroom door until you confirm you've complied."

A tiny—well, more like a *huge* part of me wants to say no just to see this scenario play out.

As if reading my mind, Ray adds, "And if it comes to that and you think you could put an end to the sick beat I'd be rapping on your door with my knuckles by lying, I'd send Becky in to make sure you're actually doing it."

Experience from years living in the same apartment as Becky and across the hall from the guys has taught me that isn't an idle threat.

"Spare me the Beck inquisition and tell me what you want me to do." I make a rolling motion with my hand, grinning at Ben when he joins us.

Ray and Ben exchange a round of those dude chin jerks, but I don't miss the way Ray's gaze flits between us. An extended beat passes before he finally says, "When we get home, you have to promise to do another naked time."

Ben's eyes alight with the type of boyish mischief guys seem to master when they are thirteen years old, going to a magazine rack and trying to sneak the plastic cellophane on *Playboy* open wide enough to get a peek at the inside. You know the one—that wide-eyed twinkle that screams *The possibility of seeing boobies is imminent.*

I point a finger at Ben. "Don't even start."

We may have only met yesterday, but during our time together, I could tell he has that same golden retriever man-child energy many of our guys have, and I can spot shit stirring from a mile away.

Undeterred by being called out, that playful smirk that charmed me into agreeing to a date with him comes out to play.

*Dammit.* Why aren't I going weak in the knees?

The music changes, and spotlights dance across the stage erected at one end of the rink in swirling beams of light. It must be time for the auction portion of the night.

*Oh goody.* I could use the distraction.

We move closer with the rest of the crowd, the three of us settling into an open pocket of space near the front of the audience. Eddie the Yeti moonwalks his way to center stage, popping and locking his padded shoulders with a precision only he can manage. Planting his sneaker-covered foot, Eddie Michael Jackson spins dreamily waving his arms to present Jordan and Skye, our auctioneers for the night, as they strut out to join him.

Both my friends look amazing under the twinkling lights. Jordan is a statement in her backless, sequined, eggplant-shaded dress, and Skye's curves and height take the sweetheart A-line cocktail dress to *dayum* levels. No wonder Tucker's been walking around with his tongue hanging out all night.

Jordan waves at the crowd and lifts a cordless microphone to her mouth. "Alright, all you wonderful, amazing—"

"And hopefully feeling super generous!"

Jordan nods her agreement with Skye's interjection then finishes her greeting. "Yes, and *generous* people sharing your evening with us tonight. It's time to put down the Monopoly money we've been gambling with and put up the real dough."

"It's time to make it rain." Skye shimmies around while sweeping the fingers coiled around her own microphone over the open palm of her free hand.

Jordan laughs, shoving her hand inside the bodice of her dress and pulling out a stack of what has to be actual Monopoly money, given the various colors, and tosses it to flutter around Skye.

The two of them yuck it up, their comedic antics warming up the crowd and, I'm sure, loosening more than a few pockets.

"Now, we have quite an array of items for you to bid on this evening." Jordan's wink is pure *You know you want this* tease, and I swear you can feel everyone in the arena shifting to sit on the edge of their seats—including those standing.

"But we're gonna kick things off with some of our hometown hotties." Skye grins as they continue their seamless back and forth.

"Eddie," Jordan calls, "bring out our boys."

# CHAPTER 19

## *Chance*

An oversized padded paw parts the curtains, Eddie the Yeti beckoning us to follow and leading us out like lambs to slaughter.

Slaughter, date auction…same thing.

Jake leads the charge, swaggering toward his wife, twirling her into a dip, and laying a completely not-suitable-for-public kiss on her lips. The crowd eats up the display, Eddie adding to their cheers by banging the portable drum he uses for our games.

"Okay then," Skye comments while Jordan swipes at the lipstick smeared under her mouth, the flush on her skin visible even from here. "I guess let's start the bidding with our formidable goalie."

Jake starts vamping for the bidders, but my attention drifts from the scene and snags on…*her*.

*Mother. Fucker.*

The football fuckhead has his arm around Gemma—again, and she's smiling and laughing with him—again. I'm sensing a pattern here, and it's one I don't fucking like.

Gemma ran to *him* when she ran from me? What the hell is it going to take to stop being relegated to the role of a spectator in her life?

"Twenty thousand."

"Twenty-five."

"Thirty."

The rapid-fire bidding draws my attention away from

Gemma and back to the auction. On and on, the bids roll in, Jordan growing more restless with each paddle raised in the air. She finally snaps somewhere around sixty thousand dollars, shouting her jaw-dropping bid of one hundred and fifty thousand.

"What?" She shrugs innocently to Jake. "I'll get you another endorsement deal."

"I thought the trope was touch *her* and die, not him," Jake says.

"I love how you pay attention to book club." Jordan cups his cheek.

"And I love when my wife is überpossessive." Jake hauls her against him, the two carrying on like they aren't standing in front of a literal crowd.

A few of my other teammates have their turns before it's finally mine. I walk to the end of the stage directly in front of Gemma, purposely making eye contact with her and daring her to bid on me.

Naturally, she doesn't. Instead, her paddle hangs limply by her side.

Up and up the bids go, our gazes ping-ponging between each other and the other paddles rising into the air. I love that no matter how hard Gemma tries, her gaze keeps returning to me.

"Fifty thousand."

I barely register the blonde extending her arm above her head or the extraordinary amount she's willing to pay for a simple dinner date with me. Or at least I don't until I realize Gemma is *still* staring at her.

The identity of the bidder remains unknown as her paddle rises higher and higher with each bid. Gemma's eyes follow it, but there's something different about her expression this time. With me as the obvious exception when I piss her off, I've never seen Gemma look at a person with such open disdain.

Ray leans over, speaking softly to Gemma while keeping his own gaze trained on the blonde.

Something is up, but what? Why?

What is different about this bidder compared to the others?

After fulfilling my obligation as a slab of man meat for sale and making arrangements with Cora for our private dinner date, I did my best to track down Gemma, but by the time I made it to where she had been standing, only the annoying football player remained.

Grabbing a drink from the bar, I take a beat to let my blood pressure settle—at least until Gemma's grouping is called to the stage for auction.

"Now, since my boo thang here decided to go all aggro female earlier, I'm going to start us off with my own selfish bid of fifteen thousand for my little Julia Child," Skye states boldly. "Don't look at me like that," she says when Jordan cuts her gaze over. "You bought your own husband."

"Touché," Jordan concedes while Gemma blushes, standing between her friends.

I'd say these two are the world's worst auctioneers, but given the amount of money they've already raised—not counting Jordan's ridiculous display of *Jake's my man*—their terrible lack of professionalism isn't affecting the loosening of the purse strings.

"Twenty thousand." Any amusement I felt drains when I see Ben's paddle in the air.

Fuck that.

"Thirty." I thrust my arm up.

Gemma's eyes flare wide when they land on me, her lips parting with a gasp.

"Thirty-five," Ben counters smoothly.

It's bad enough this asshat has scored a date with my girl for tomorrow night; there's not a chance in hell I'm letting him win any more time with her.

"Forty."

Gemma's gaze swings back to me with my bid, her hand going to her mouth to chew on the edge of her thumb. It means she's nervous.

Ben follows Gemma's line of sight, finding me in the crowd. He waves goofily with his paddle, giving me a big douchey grin, and says, "Forty-five."

*Dick.*

"Sixty." Gemma glares at me when I up the ante.

A slow, almost sinister smirk tugs at the side of my

mouth. *Run all you want, Princess. I'll always find a way to catch you.*

Ben hesitates, and Gemma tears her gaze away from mine when he does. The fact that she's checking on him feels like a blow to the heart.

"Sixty-five." Ben's voice has rage boiling in my gut.

I'm done playing games.

"Two hundred thousand dollars."

The room sucks in a collective gasp at the highest bid of the evening. *And I thought Jordan was being ridiculous, yet here I am, beating her bid by fifty grand.*

"Umm…" Skye trails off. Wow, rendering Skye Masters speechless is a feat in and of itself.

"Way to show me up, Jenson," Jordan jokes before calling out the last chances for bids, once, then twice, before finally, fucking *finally* declaring me the winner.

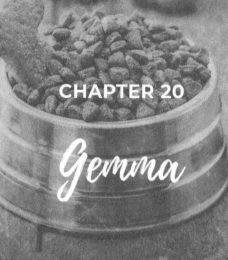

# CHAPTER 20

## *Gemma*

W hy is figuring out what to wear so goddamn hard? It should be simple, but instead, choosing an outfit for my date with Ben feels like a monumental feat reminiscent of climbing Everest.

*Maybe that's a sign you shouldn't be going on this date?*

Ugh. What's with the crisis of conscience?

Ben is hot. Ben is charming.

*Ben doesn't give you butterflies like Chance does.*

Son of a biscuit. Even when he's not around, that man drives me crazy.

*You know when he will be around, though, right?*

A string of unintelligible mutterings spills from my lips at the reminder. What the hell was that, anyway? What the fuck was he thinking? Why would Chance bid on me?

And *two hundred thousand dollars*? That's almost a quarter of his annual salary.

Seriously…what the hell was he thinking getting into a bidding war with Ben? Anyone with a Google browser knows that man makes forty times what he does. If Ben really wanted to challenge him, Chance wouldn't have—forgive the pun—stood a chance.

*Motherforking shirt balls.*

I *need* to stop thinking about Chance Jenson. I'm supposed to be preparing for a date with Ben Turner.

Okay, time to get ready.

But…what am I gonna wear?

Thankfully, wardrobe inspiration struck while I was in the shower, and waiting for me on my bed is a super cute, chunky knit cream sweater dress and camel-colored suede thigh-high boots.

Now all I need is the perfect lingerie set to give me that extra boost of confidence. Maybe if I treat this like any other first date, those annoyingly absent tingles will finally show up to the party.

*What to pick? What to pick?* I think, riffling through my drawer until a familiar swath of gray catches my eye. Hooking a finger under the straps, I pull the lingerie out and let my towel drop to the floor.

I love this set. It's always been one of my favorites. The unlined balconette bra is made in contrasting grays, the design mixing the delicate sheer dove gray with the bold storm cloud hue of the floral-embroidered cups and sexy cutout detailing.

Dancing my hips side to side, I pull on the corresponding matching panties, smoothing my palms over the wide lace band cradling my hips. Tucking my fingertips under the scalloped edge, I swivel to admire the way the cheeky cut highlights the fullness of the ass my mama gave me.

I can't help but giggle. Dr. Sonya would be so proud. While body dysmorphia was never a trigger for my eating disorder, keeping it from ever becoming one as we treated the other underlying causes has become one of the cornerstones of my treatment plan. It's how naked time was born. Every morning before I start my day, I stand in front of a full-length mirror and give myself one compliment—even if it's packed with humor—before reciting something I have control over and reminding myself it's okay that there are things I don't.

It's another tradition piggybacking off of naked time that has me reaching for my phone and snapping a mirror selfie to send to my girls. There are no better hype people than your best friends.

My phone pings as I'm shimmying into my dress, but the

notification banner waiting for me on the screen is not a welcome one.

> DICKHEAD DADDY: Like fuck you're gonna wear that for HIM.

Ex-fucking-*cuse* me?!

And what is he even talking about?

Thumbing through my text messages, my blood freezes in my veins when I realize what I did.

I sent him the texts I meant to send to the girls.

*Goddammit.*

This is all because I couldn't STOP. THINKING. ABOUT. CHANCE. JENSON.

*Shit. Shit. Shit.*

This stupid damn pull I feel toward him keeps growing stronger and is making me do dumb things.

> ME: Delete the message.

> DICKHEAD DADDY: Not a chance.

Stubborn asshole.

> DICKHEAD DADDY: Change your underwear.

I blink. Then blink again.

> ME: Excuse me?

> DICKHEAD DADDY: You heard me. CHANGE. YOUR. UNDERWEAR.

I love how he thinks his shouty caps have any effect on me.

> ME: Word of advice—being all growly like has more of an impact in voice memos than shouty caps.

> DICKHEAD DADDY: I'm not even going to bother asking you what you're going on about. Just do as you're told and change your fucking underwear.

A humorless chuckle leaves me as I sit on my bed, crossing one leg over the other, my fingers already flying across the screen of my phone. It's like this asshole doesn't know me at all.

> ME: Awww. You don't like them? Well...too bad, so sad for you.

> DICKHEAD DADDY: Like them? Of course I fucking LIKE them. I'll be damned if HE is going to see. TAKE. THEM. OFF.

> DICKHEAD DADDY: Better yet—cancel your date.

What? Oh, now things are just getting laughable.

> ME: No.

> DICKHEAD DADDY: I'm serious, Princess.

> ME: That's nice. So am I.

> DICKHEAD DADDY: This is your last warning.

> ME: Ooo. I'm shaking in my thigh-high boots.

> DICKHEAD DADDY: Cancel.

> DICKHEAD DADDY: Your.

> DICKHEAD DADDY: Date.

> ME: I.

> ME: Said.

> ME: No.

> DICKHEAD DADDY: I'm going to spank your ass
> so hard you won't be able to sit down for a
> week.

Oh shit. I need to wrap up this conversation before this infuriating man gets what he wants and I change my panties—not because he told me to but because his demands are about to ruin them.

Instead, I feign a nonchalance I'm far from feeling.

> ME: More empty threats. Maybe add that to the
> vocabulary lesson you undoubtedly need.

> DICKHEAD DADDY: Tell me where the football
> punk is taking you tonight, and I'll show you just
> how NOT empty my promise is.

> ME: That would be a no.

> DICKHEAD DADDY: Gemma.

> ME: Chance.

> DICKHEAD DADDY: I don't share, Gemma.

*That's* a shocker.

> ME: Good thing I don't belong to you. TTFN.

# CHAPTER 21

*Gemma*

"Y ou know..." Ben shifts, crossing an ankle over a knee and laying an arm across the back of the couch we're sitting on. "You're lucky I have a healthy ego."

Ben's grin is infectious, and I feel myself returning it as I tuck a leg underneath me, mirroring his position with an elbow propped on the cushion and sliding a hand into my hair. "Is that so?"

"Yup." He pops the *P*. "Otherwise, I'd be heartbroken over you friend-zoning me."

My cheeks heat from being called out. God, I'm such an asshole.

Ben planned a whole date for us at a swanky restaurant, but I was too busy obsessing over a text exchange that should have never happened to appreciate the effort. It's how we ended up at Rookies, a sports bar my squad has frequented since college.

"I'm sorry." I lay my hand on his forearm. "I suck."

"No, you don't." Ben rotates his arm around, linking our hands in a companionable hold and giving me an affectionate squeeze. "A bit crazy for not wanting all of this"—I giggle at the playful way he waves a hand over himself—"but no suckage." We both pull a face at his word choice. "That sounded better in my head."

"Ahh..." I bob my head. "I, too, have suffered from such an affliction before."

"Yeah…" Ben toys with the end of my fingers, those sparks I had been hoping would make an appearance still frustratingly absent. "But have you ever done it in a postgame interview?"

"I bet Jordan and Skye *loved* that."

"Enough to meme me into a viral TikTok," Ben deadpans.

I collapse forward in a fit of giggles, my head falling onto his shoulder. My friends may be the best sports publicists in the biz, but they do so enjoy humiliating their clients as a way of humanizing them to their fans.

"Don't you two look cozy."

I jackknife up, my head snapping around to search out the voice that should not be here.

*What the halibut?*

"What are you doing here?" I ask a brooding Chance Jenson.

Seriously…what is he doing here? And why the fig does he have to look so damn sexy with his arms crossed, his muscles all strain-y against his fitted black T-shirt?

"Correcting your mistake." The sheer confidence in his voice has shivers running down my spine. Oh, now those tingles wanna show up? *Wrong guy, assholes.*

"How is crashing my date going to unsend a text message?"

Chance's expression hardens—if that's even possible given the level of brood he started with.

Oh goody, Dickhead Daddy's bad mood is here in all its glory.

Chance uncrosses his arms and leans closer, his knuckles grazing my skin as he rests his fists on the back of the couch.

I make the mistake of sucking in a breath, getting a lungful of that delicious sandalwood-and-ice scent of his as he moves into my space. "I told you to cancel this date, Princess."

I turn to look at him, but he's so close I can only make out one of his eyes. "And I told you no."

"Actually, you told him ta-ta for now," Ben supplies helpfully, that same booming laugh he let out when I originally told him what happened with Chance breaking free.

And Chance? Well, he gives Ben the glariest glower of any glower there ever was.

I shouldn't like it so much. *Especially* when he opens his big dumb mouth and says, "And I told you I don't share."

"God, you sound like such a baby."

"You ever call me baby again"—Chance's lips skim the shell of my ear—"it better be to beg me to stop bringing you to repeated orgasmic bliss."

*Holy cannoli.*

His stubble grazes my cheek as he glances down, the back of my hand burning from his glare. "I suggest if Mr. Quarterback would like to keep his hand, he better fucking remove it from your body before I do it for him."

Okay…it's official. Chance Jenson has taken one too many pucks to the head.

"Excuse me," I say to Ben. I need a moment away from prying eyes to process my reaction to the insanity Chance is spewing.

"Sure." He nods. "Just let me know if you need me to defend your honor or whatever."

"I think I got it covered, but you're a doll for offering." I pat his arm.

Shoving up from the couch, I skirt around the bar, more grateful than ever that Jordan's aunt owns this place and I know where the break room is. Blessedly, I find the room empty and quickly step inside the small space.

"Gemma, Gemma, Gemma." Chance catches the wooden door before it can close behind me. "I'm getting tired of you running." He latches on to my wrist, spinning me around, the breath leaving me as he lifts my arm above my head and presses my back to the wall. "Though I can't say I mind catching you."

I swallow hard, resisting the urge to agree. Instead, I slam my free hand into his stupidly muscular chest, trying to shove him away. Chance smirks as if watching me struggle amuses him, deftly snagging my wrist and cuffing it with the other already above my head. Kicking my feet apart, he plants a booted foot between mine.

"You're cornered now, Princess." His chest pushes against mine. "There's nowhere left to run."

Unwilling to admit defeat, I desperately search for an escape route, but he catches my chin, pinching it between his thumb and forefinger, bringing my gaze back to his.

"Now." His dark eyes scan me like a physical caress. "What am I going to do with you?"

I narrow my eyes at his predatory gaze, trembling, not from

fear, but from the lust slamming into me. "Why are you looking at me like that?"

Chance drags a finger over the curve of my cheek. "What? Like you're my prey?" He tucks an errant strand of hair behind my ear, skimming his fingers down the line of my neck and taking me by the nape. "Maybe you are."

The fingers imprisoning my wrists flex, stretching my arms higher until my back arches away from the wall, my breaths stuttering as my nipples brush against his chest.

"Mmm…" Chance hums, his jaw working as he studies me.

He crowds me closer to the wall. With him looming in front of me, the corner of the room where the walls meet on my right, and the leather love seat to my left, I'm trapped, caged in on all sides. I track the fall of his free arm as he drops it down the length of my body, a gasp spilling free when his calloused fingers trace the edge of my thigh-high boots.

"Seriously, what are you doing here?" He doesn't answer, and I'm left to fill in the blanks. "Better yet—how did you find me?"

"I have my ways," he says, keeping his answer infuriatingly vague.

"Ugh." Again I try to buck him off me, but surprise, surprise, it doesn't work.

"Fuck, Gem." Chance buries his face in the curve of my neck, inhaling a labored breath. "You smell good enough to eat."

My eyes slide shut at the feel of his warm breath on my skin, my toes curling inside my boots, my sex clenching at his dark chuckle.

What is happening?

Against my leg, I feel his hand grasp, his knuckles dragging along my inner thigh, lifting the hem of my dress with the movement.

"Chance…" My voice is breathy and weak.

He jerks his head back to look at me, his heavy lids hooding his eyes before falling completely closed as he breathes deeply again. "Fuck."

My head falls back, thumping against the wall, anger and arousal swirling together in a confusing mix. "I can't believe you tracked me down just to fuck with me and ruin my date."

"You shouldn't have been on a date with that asshole in the first place."

I roll my eyes. "Unlike you, Ben is far from an asshole. Actually..." I pause, thinking back on the evening. "He's pretty sweet."

Chance growls, the sound so animalistic it makes my chest vibrate and my panties are drenched.

"If he's such a fucking dreamboat, why weren't you wet for him like you are for me?"

"God, you're delusional. Maybe you should get that ego of yours checked before you hurt yourself."

Chance's jaw tics, his dark eyes narrowing and pinning me in place. "You're wet for me, sweetheart. I can smell it."

I shake my head, even though there's a tiny voice whispering in the back of my head that he's telling the truth.

"You're *delusional*. I'm not wet for you."

The lace clinging uncomfortably to my sex proves that I'm a dirty, rotten liar.

"Oh yeah?" The promise behind Chance's question has me trembling in his arms. Unfurling his fingers, he grips my thigh with a squeeze, boldly taking my dress in his hand. "So you're saying if I were to check, there wouldn't be a wet spot on your panties?" His nostrils flare with his deepest inhalation yet. "Because I can smell how much of a lie that is, Princess."

His hand splays over my thigh, his fingertips close to the edge of my panties but not quite touching them. Thank god because, let's be honest, the dickhead is right and they are totally wet because of him.

I'm losing my mind.

His grip shifts, but he's still not trying to get under them, and I need to swallow down the plea for him to do so.

Seriously, I'm going out of my mind.

I swallow hard, my body reacting to his voice, mine only barely a decibel above a whisper. "No."

"Really?" A threatening and annoyingly sexy smile tips the corners of his mouth. "Prove it."

"Wh-what?"

Chance brings his mouth back to my ear. "I said prove it." He releases my wrists and steps back as if waiting for me to comply.

Why? Why does a part of me want to?

Instead, I go on the defensive.

"Is this your way of seducing me?" I ask with an unmistakable quiver in my voice. "Because, if so, you need to work on your technique."

He folds his arms over his chest, his muscles bulging, the ink decorating his arms dancing with his restraint. His forearms flex, his fingers twitching.

*Shit.*

*Shit.*

*Shit.*

I hate how tempting he is. I want to dig my fingers into his biceps, feel their terrain beneath his skin and trace the designs of the ink covering them with my tongue.

He's still looking at me when I lift my gaze back to his face, his gaze boring into me with a challenge.

"It's not my seduction techniques that need improving. It's your bullshit resistance, Princess." He stabs a hand through his hair, mussing the dark strands. "That's the only reason you're still dressed."

He's on me again without any hesitation, this time his lips crashing against mine in a bruising kiss.

At first, I'm too surprised to react, my mind too stuck on *Holy shit, Chance Jenson is kissing me* to do anything except let his mouth plunder mine.

I suddenly don't care that Chance is once again in my space. I don't care that he's imposing himself on me again. I don't care that I was in the middle of a date with another man five minutes ago. And I sure as shit don't care that there's nothing sweet or gentle about how he's kissing me.

No. Everything about the way Chance kisses me says he's in control, and fuck, does it feel good.

Passionate and hungry, Chance's lips move over mine, his tongue forcing its way past my lips to taste me, working against mine, our teeth clashing. A moan slips out of me, and Chance takes the opportunity to dart in deeper, all assertive and domi-nant, lapping at my top lip before moving down to suck my bottom lip into his mouth.

He's not trying to seduce me; he's making a point.

And you know what? I let him. All the fight drains out of me as I let him take, take, take.

I finally break out of the daze I've fallen into, blindly reaching for him, my hands clawing at his T-shirt, the soft fabric crumpling in my grip as I search for a way to steady myself because, holy hell, this man can kiss.

Biting Chance's bottom lip, my small teeth sink into the plump flesh, eliciting a growl from him that does wicked things to my senses. I'm not sure if it's a hum of approval or a warning of what's to come, but either way, it sends a shiver straight to my sex, leaving me even wetter.

He bucks against me, and I moan, my back arching to create the friction I desperately seek, but Chance has his hips canted too far back for me to grind on his erection. It certainly is on brand for him.

Instead, he grips the base of my skull, guiding the angle of my head and taking the kiss deeper. Just as I think I can't handle it anymore, he pulls back enough to allow me a breath, his mouth moving to my jaw, his tongue skimming over the pulse point behind my ear.

His eyes dart to where the slouchy collar of my dress has slipped down my arm, exposing the gray strap of my bra. My heart skips a beat at the feral look in his eyes when they rise back to mine.

His hand releases the back of my head, coming around to pin me in place with a palm splayed on my heaving cleavage. The heat from his skin leaches through mine, branding me with a single touch. His thumb sweeps down, pushing into the cup of my bra and brushing over my nipple. The contrast of his rough skin on my oversensitized nerve endings is electrifying, and I'm once again breaking out into goose bumps.

I'm not sure how he does it, but he evokes a response from me that I didn't know was possible. It's like he knows every inch of my body and how to make it sing with only his touch. More than a year spent doing my best to hate this man means nothing under the weight of his kiss.

Fuck me, I'm in trouble.

I tried to tell myself all his threats were empty but based on the feelings he's evoking inside me, I'm pretty sure he can do things to my body no one else has ever done. With how on edge I am already, I bet he could make me come in a way I never have before.

*Sonofabitch.*

This is why Ben did nothing for me. My body knew what my brain refused to acknowledge—Chance Jenson is the one I want.

*Shit.* This is *not* good.

Because I'm pretty sure Chance Jenson could be the most dangerous thing to ever happen to me.

# CHAPTER 22

*Gemma*

The tension in the room builds until it's borderline suffocating, Chance's intense glower only adding to the claustrophobic feeling.

"Fuck." Chance stares at the strap of my bra before fisting the top of my dress and yanking it down my other arm until my entire bra is exposed to his hungry gaze. "Fuck, fuck, fuck," he repeats, his words barely coherent, and yet I can't stop the pleasure that courses through me as I watch his eyes burn and his breathing hitch.

Despite all his claims about not wanting me, I've never felt more like a goddess in my life. It's an addicting feeling for someone like me.

"I can't believe you wore this on a date with *him*."

I love how he thinks he has any say in my wardrobe choices. "It's my favorite set. I've worn it on many dates." Not that any of those dates got to see it, but Chance doesn't need to know that.

His fingers dig into the flesh of my arms as he gives me the tiniest shake, the lusty growl rolling around in his throat chasing away any fear.

"Don't fucking tell me that when it's been haunting me for a year."

My brows knit in confusion. What is he talking about?

"Fuck, Gemma, fuck," he spits out before releasing me with a tiny shove.

I press my back to the wall for support, opening my mouth to offer a rebuke as he paces away, but he's back in my face in a single step, dropping to his knees and yanking my dress up to my waist until my panties are on full display.

"Fuck me, I fucking knew it." His warm breath fans out over my lace-covered pussy, and I smash my lips together to keep from panting.

I squirm, squeezing my legs together and twisting, attempting to hide the evidence. Chance's expression morphs into a scowl when I do, pinning me in place with a hand on my stomach and shouldering his way between my legs until there's no hiding in my spread stance. It's impossible to restrain my moan as he engages in a staring contest with my pussy, my head falling back on my shoulders to glance at the ceiling.

"No, no. Eyes on me, Princess," Chance demands.

Anticipation races through my veins at the sight of him kneeling between my legs. He holds my gaze for an extended beat before unceremoniously burying his face between my thighs, my knees buckling when his nose runs up my slit, scenting me like a wolf does his favorite cut of meat.

Umm…it may be time for me to lay off the shifter romances.

"Chance!" I squeal, my hands falling to his head and yanking at his hair, trying to press my thighs together again, but it's no use.

"God, you're such a fucking liar, Princess." Chance hooks a finger into the crotch of my panties, rubbing it between his fingers, pulling it away from clinging to my swollen pussy. "You're not just wet—you're soaked through for me."

"Again with the ego, thinking it's because of you," I challenge.

Chance surges to his feet, and I yelp when my panties, still in his grip, pull between my legs, smashing my swollen clit and sending a jolt of pleasure through me.

"Tell me your cunt is weeping for another man one more *fucking* time. I *dare* you."

I open my mouth, a denial ready on my tongue, only to die when he rotates his wrist, tugging my panties tighter until the lace scrapes my clit with pleasurable friction. I hiss through my teeth, writhing against the wall, but Chance's hands keep me in place, the hand on my belly curling up and around my rib cage.

"I told you not to fucking lie to me." He nips my jaw with a growling warning. "Guess I'll have to teach you a fucking lesson."

His body practically vibrates with a threatening promise that has me coating his fingers in further proof of the lie. Teeth bared in a menacing smile, he takes a step backward, bringing me with him via his hold on my underwear. I let out a startled shout, the room going topsy-turvy as he sits on the love seat, pulling me over and draping me across his lap, my stomach pressed to his thighs.

Blood rushes to my head as he maneuvers me around, tipping my head down, wedging one thigh in the bend at my waist, and tilting my hips high. I struggle reflexively, but he quickly snatches my wrists, binding them at my lower back with one of his large hands.

Fear and excitement war within me until his big hand descends in a hard smack to my right butt cheek, hitting the skin bared by the cheeky cut of my panties, filling the room with a loud echoing slap that resonates inside my ears, rattling my eardrums.

I gasp, pain lancing through me, but the pleasure radiating from the spot has my body begging my head to submit, to stop fighting. My hips lift, chasing the warmth lingering from the spank.

"That's my good girl." Chance smooths a palm over where he hit, squeezing the globe in a punishing grip. "I'm going to make it so you're very, *very* sorry for lying to me."

As much as I want to argue, want to tell him to fuck off and go to hell, I can't. A shiver runs through me as he traces a lazy figure eight on my warming skin before landing two more sure smacks on the same cheek.

"Fuck." Chance traces around the mark he's creating, heat pouring off it. "I knew your ass was made for this."

His hand connects with the spot he was petting, my skin already tender, the pain swirling with the tingles, creating a heady sense of arousal. I squeal, my hips bucking up and jerking away from the blow, but Chance keeps me trapped and still with a forearm banded across my upper back. His words roll around my skull, my mind desperate to keep up as a giant wave of lust breaks over me.

"These fucking panties," he mutters, his voice rough like he swallowed gravel. He plucks at the strings in the keyhole cutout at the top of my underwear, dragging the tip of one finger through the top of my crack.

I screw my eyes shut, flicking my tongue out to wet my suddenly dry lips, fighting the urge to press back and beg for more. Rational thought and common sense have no place here as Chance explores my prone body, his hold easily keeping me captive. He squeezes my hip, caressing the line of my spine and dancing down each of my ribs.

"Please," I beg, though I'm not sure what for.

"All in due time, Princess."

Usually, his condescension would set my teeth on edge, but his hand comes down on my left cheek, raining smacks again and again on the previously ignored skin, the pain and bliss warring until pleasure finally pulls ahead, the sting from his spanking fading, leaving me a breathless heap on his lap.

"Tell me you want me," he demands, his next smack landing directly on top of the previous one. "Tell me you sent me that text so I would show up and put an end to that date that should have never happened in the first place."

"It was an accident." I shake my head, my hair dragging across the floor. "I meant to text the girls, not you."

He responds by yanking my underwear down my legs, the cool air hitting my overheated center seconds before his hand swipes across it, gathering my arousal and smearing it over the abused flesh of my ass.

Chance tsks. "You just let me know when you're ready to be honest with me."

He stretches his hand, cupping my pussy from behind.

"Chance, please," I plead, raising my ass higher and offering myself up to his punishment if only to put an end to it before I completely break for him.

"You know what to do if you want me to stop." He thrusts two fingers into my pussy. "Though the way your cunt is strangling my fingers, I think stopping is the last thing you want me to do."

A keening cry escapes me, and much to my mortification, my pussy clenches around the fingers scissoring inside it. Chance makes a thoughtful noise, his hand leaving me, my body collapsing at the sudden loss.

"Tell me you're mine, Gemma."

I fight the command despite my body's willingness, my eyelids snapping shut when his hand connects with my tender skin, his palm squeezing and pulling until he opens enough to see my pussy and moisture coating my inner thighs.

"Tell me the only person you'll be sending pictures of you in your underwear to is me."

"I thought you didn't want me to lie to you."

"Such a fucking brat," he snarls, slamming his fingers back into my pussy, adding his thumb to my ass when I buck, the sharp burn from the sudden intrusion stealing my breath and making me go limp like a rag doll. "You don't get to pass this shit off as some sort of mistake."

His words filter through the fog in my brain, and I try in vain to stretch the fingers of my restrained hands, looking for a grounding touch.

"Please," I say, not sure what I'm pleading for, pleasure pushing me up the cliff and making me willing to do so anyway.

"Say it," he commands. "Say you're mine."

He buries his thumb in my ass down to the bottom knuckle, anchoring his hold on me, plunging his fingers in my pussy over and over, the squelching sound it makes obscene. It's also embarrassing because it's audible evidence of how much I want him, despite my less-than-vehement denials.

"Chance."

"Come on, Princess." He half laughs, driving into me harder, twisting his fingers and bringing me to the edge of an orgasm sure to ruin me. "Don't be scared."

"No, I'm not scared," I gasp, my voice breaking as he pulls out and does it again.

"But you are." He pinches his fingers, rubbing them together through the thin membrane separating them. "Scared of wanting me when you tell yourself you hate me. Scared of what I make you feel."

"I'm not," I shout, fighting his hold to no avail.

"You are," he coos. "The only thing you don't seem to be scared of is the pleasure you know I can give you." He rubs at my inner walls.

The muscles in my legs seize, going rigid, hanging off his,

stick straight. He's toying with me, tormenting me with rapture just out of reach.

"You're right," I admit, needing to come. "Pl-please, Chance. Make me come."

"Oh, I will," he promises. "I'm going to make your cunt so fucking hot, so fucking wet, so fucking swollen you'll be begging for me."

The weight of his words, the confidence in his tone, and the promise in them send a shiver down my spine.

"Ye-yes." I whimper, rocking my hips in small circles, desperate for more.

"You're so fucking wet for me." His voice is a rough growl. "You're practically screaming for my cock, begging me to fuck you."

"Yes. Yes. Fuck me. Make me come." I beg and plead, unable to hang on the edge of an orgasm a moment longer.

I cry out as he yanks his fingers out of me, my pussy clenching in protest at the sudden emptiness. Chance wastes no time, ripping my panties down and off my legs before hauling me around until I'm straddling his manspread legs.

"I'll make you come." He tugs me to him, rubbing my sex over the bulge tenting his jeans, not giving a single fuck that my juices are staining the denim.

"*Yesss*," I hiss.

"But not yet."

*No*, I scream inside my head.

Chance takes me by the hips, lifting me then bringing me back down, keeping me in place as he grinds up into me.

"First, admit you're mine."

# CHAPTER 23

# Chance

Watching Gemma unravel before my eyes is a thing of fucking beauty. With her disheveled hair and dress completely askew, the flush staining her skin is almost as alluring as the pink I turned her ass.

"I want to fuck you." I admit the simplest of truths, moving my hands along the silky skin of her back before grabbing her ass, relishing the heat radiating into my palms as I hold her firmly against me.

"Yes," she practically purrs, taking over rubbing herself against my erection.

"But I'm not giving you this dick until you give me the words I want."

What the fuck am I doing? I've gone from some kind of crazy stalker scouring social media for any mention of Ben Turner to figure out where he took Gemma on their date to complete psycho by not only showing up and crashing their date but also hauling Gemma away from it like some caveman.

I don't give a shit that she was on a date with another man. If she were really serious about him, she wouldn't have texted me a picture of her in her underwear hours before it.

I don't know what the hell is happening to me. I've never felt this urgency before, never felt this desperation with any other woman, but the one thing I know for certain is that Gemma Steele is mine.

I refuse to let another man have her anymore.

Her touch.

Her mouth.

Her pussy.

Mine. All mine.

I've claimed her, and I'm going to make sure she knows it.

Gemma's lips part, her mouth forming an *O* as her eyes roll back in her head.

"Admit it," I demand, my voice rough with need. "Be a good girl and admit you're mine."

She arches, her back bowing as she wars with indecision. When her gaze finally comes back to me, her big gray eyes are glazed with lust and desire, though that sassy spark of hers still blazes in the background. My Precious is always fighting me, though right now, I think she's fighting herself more.

"I'm yours," she huffs.

It doesn't matter that she sounds dejected; those words are still music to my ears.

"Again," I demand, my triumph short-lived when she doesn't repeat it, her body shaking as she tries to grind herself against me.

Oh, no, no, no. There will be no stealing orgasms not earned. Looks like somebody still needs to be taught a lesson.

Gripping her hair in my fist, I press my other hand to her spine, forcing her to still.

"*God.* You are the most *frustrating* man on the planet." She beats her hands against my chest.

"Yet you're still mine." I bury my face in the hollow of her throat. "Come on, My Precious, say it."

She gnaws on her bottom lip, and I know she's trying to think of a way to get out of this. Those spitfire eyes level me where I sit, and she whispers, "I'm yours."

It's not nearly enough given how swiftly she tried to take it back the first time, so I don't give her a chance to argue again. Instead, I whip her dress from her body, carelessly tossing it to the floor before doing the same with her bra.

My cock lurches at the sight of her naked before me while I remain fully clothed. Hastily undoing my belt, I yank open the zipper of my jeans, lifting my hips enough to free my leaking erection as another drop of precum rolls down my shaft.

"I need inside you," I beg, the heat from her pussy scorching as she hovers above me.

"*Please.*" She swivels her hips, the head of my cock dragging through her wetness.

"Good," I grunt, slamming her onto my cock in a single thrust.

"Fuck," we cry out in unison as I plunge into her.

I'm hard and hot, my cock buried inside the tightest, hottest cunt I've ever felt. How did I survive an entire year without doing this?

Cupping Gemma's throat, I pull her to me, slamming my mouth to hers. I lick at her lips, yearning for a taste. Done waiting for her to open, I force her lips apart with my tongue, using it to dominate her.

And dominate her I will. I'm going to make sure by the time she leaves this room, she knows exactly who she belongs to. And if she forgets, she's damn well going to be sore enough to be reminded of the fact for at least a week.

Her weight settles onto me, the slick walls of her pussy clinging to every ridge and vein of my dick. With my grip on her throat, I maneuver her back enough that I can stretch my thumb up to tip her chin down.

"See how good you take me, Princess?" I feel her swallow under my fingertips. "You're going to take all of me."

I thrust, giving her another inch.

"Yes," she moans, her hips rising slightly before lowering, her plump ass settling on my thighs with a wiggle.

*Oh fuck.*

My eyes roll back in my head. She's tight, so fucking tight I have to fight the urge to come.

"Goddamn." My head tips backward as I rock her back and forth over my cock.

"That's a good girl." I slide in more until I'm rooted to the hilt. "Take. Every. Inch."

Gemma shudders, mewling whimpers echoing every slap of skin on skin. Grabbing her tits, I let the soft flesh fill and overflow my palms as I smash them together, squeezing them and plucking at her nipples.

"Tell me I'm the only one who gets to touch you like this," I demand with a fervent need.

"Chance."

"Tell me I'm the only one you want to please."

I release her tits, fisting her hair at her nape with one hand, skirting the other down her quivering belly to the exposed nub of her swollen clit.

"I'm the only one who gets to see you spread out like this." I *V* my fingers around her clit, only the bounce of her body as I rut into her giving her the briefest touch where she wants me most.

"Tell me."

Thrust.

"Or I stop."

Thrust.

Thrust.

"No." She whimpers. "Don't." Her eyes and pussy plead with me to continue.

"Yes, that's right. You want this. You want to come on my cock."

A sharp crack rents the air, echoing through the room when my palm smacks down on her ass. Gemma gasps, her body stilling before squirming to chase the sting of my hand.

"Don't you fucking stop."

Thrust.

"Not for anything."

Smack.

"Not until I say so."

I suck her nipple into my mouth, biting down on the nub until she cries out.

"You are mine," I mumble around her tit. "Your body is mine to fuck."

Thrust. Thrust.

"Your pussy is mine to fuck." I slap her clit. "Your orgasms are mine. You come for me." I rub her clit furiously, and like a flipped switch, she comes. I hold her down onto me, her pussy clamping around my cock as I rock her back and forth again, dragging her clit along my belly. "Open your eyes, Princess."

Her heavy lids open, the gray of her eyes shaded by lust.

"I'm your only pleasure." I go back to her clit, rubbing it harder and harder. "Say it," I demand with a bellow, the desperation in my voice evident, my breath coming out in harsh pants.

"You're the only one who makes me feel this way," she admits with a scream, coming all over my dick for the second time.

"Damn straight."

I slam her down on my cock, drilling into her as I finger her clit.

"Chance."

I move against her, my fingers circling around and around.

"I want you to scream my name when you come this time because I'm going to make you come again and again. You're going to come until you forget you hate me."

Her heartbeat pounds against my chest, her breathing labored, face flushed, tits bouncing as she takes me, slamming onto my cock over and over.

"That's it." I tug her hair, angling her head to the side, exposing the long column of her neck and scraping my teeth along it, leaving a thin mark over the pulsing vein beating inside it.

"Oh god," she cries, her voice raspy.

"Let me hear you scream, baby." I circle her clit harder and harder, making her moan and squirm. "Come for me," I command, the hand on her throat flexing and relaxing.

"I'm too sensitive." She whimpers with a shake of her head, body trembling.

I flick her clit, making her shudder and cry out.

"Dammit, Chance."

"I want to feel you come again."

Her pussy walls tighten around my cock, her skin flushing as her body trembles and shakes.

"That's right," I grunt, my orgasm barreling toward the surface. "You're gonna come on my cock, and you know why?"

I grind my hips harder, my cock buried as deep as it can go, my fingers never stopping as I stroke her clit.

"Chance." Her nails rake down my forearms.

"You want it because you're mine." I wrap my hand around the column of her neck, squeezing her just enough to let her know I mean it. "I'm going to make you come so hard you scream like a little slut begging for more."

Her whimpers turn to moans, her body stiffening as she rides out yet another orgasm I've forced upon her.

"Good girl." I remove my fingers and grip her hips, holding her in place as I ram into her, my cock swelling. "You're gonna take it all."

I shove her back, holding her away from my body so I can get a clear view of her swollen, red pussy taking my cock over and over again. Her head falls back on her shoulders, her eyes rolling back as she comes once more. I feel my balls draw up, my throaty grunts ending with a shout, finally coming with one last thrust.

"Fuck," I mutter, sliding my hands along her sweat-coated skin as she collapses against me, utterly wrecked.

Knocking has Gemma jolting back to consciousness, her eyes flying wide in alarm, her hair a chaotic mess as she spins to look at the door. "Oh my god."

"You guys didn't kill each other, did you?" asks the jaunty voice of Ben fucking Turner through the thankfully still-closed door. "Because for as much as I pay Jordan and Skye, I don't know if their fee includes body disposal."

"We're fine. It's fine." Gemma scrambles off my lap in a panic, kneeing me in the side and hissing when my dick slips free from her heat.

Except...

That's not the only thing coming out of her cunt.

*Fuck.*

*Fuck.*

*Fuck.*

My gaze gets stuck on the cum—my cum—leaking from between Gemma's plump thighs.

A condom.

I fucking forgot to put on a condom.

"Motherfucker," I roar, tossing Gemma the rest of the way off of me, surging to my feet.

"What the hell?" Gemma sputters, shoving the hair out of her face.

I shouldn't have come inside her.

*Shit.*

I'm an idiot. An absolute fucking idiot.

Why didn't I use a condom? How the fuck could I forget?

*Chance, I'm pregnant.*

Three words that changed my life over a year ago.

"You better fucking be on birth control," I accuse, glaring at the pool of cum on the couch.

"I have an IUD," she snaps, snatching a handful of paper towels from the small folding table and wiping away the evidence with an indignant scowl. "And don't worry, I'm clean."

"It's not about that," I bark.

It doesn't matter if you always wrap it up. That doesn't mean it will stop you from hearing those three words.

"That wasn't supposed to happen." I scrub a hand over my face, trying to make sense of what just happened. "Fuck, this was a mistake."

"I... What?" Her lower lip trembles, her eyes welling with unshed tears.

"I can't believe I fucked you without a condom." My chest constricts, making it impossible to breathe as my heart pounds between my ears. I shake my head, trying to get rid of the image of my cum spilling from her reddened cunt.

"*God*, you're such an asshole." She cuts me a scorching glare, yanking her dress over her head without bothering to put on her bra.

"Oh, I'm sorry," I say, sarcasm dripping from my words, "but knocking up a bunny isn't part of my career path."

"Wow." Gemma's mouth remains partly open as the word hangs in the air. "Thanks for that."

"That's not what I meant." I take a step toward her, but she holds up a hand, stopping me.

"No." She gives a resigned shake of her head. "That's exactly what you meant." She tugs at her dress, stumbling in her heels. "After all...you don't *actually* want me. You just don't want anyone else to have me. How toxic of you."

"Gem—"

"Don't." She cuts me off, slashing her arm through the air.

Physically I freeze, but my mind is still spinning.

*No condom.*

*No condom.*

*No condom.*

I swore I would never come inside a woman without a condom on, and yet I did just that.

*Fuck.*

*Goddammit.*

I reach for her again, only to have her shrug me off and move around me. She pauses with a hand on the doorknob, cutting me a scathing glance over her shoulder.

"Don't worry, Dickhead," she sneers. "I know it was just sex. It didn't mean anything."

# CHAPTER 24

*Gemma*

The boisterous chatter of shit-talking man-children wars with Mariah Carey belting it out as said man-children strut into the apartment like they own the place. For the record, they don't, not that you would know it given the amount of time they spend here instead of at their place across the hall.

Usually, I ignore their antics, having learned long ago that's typically the best course of action to avoid encouraging them, but not today. No, today, I could use the distraction. Nay, I'm *desperate* for it.

*"Fuck, this was a mistake."*

Eighteen hours later, those words still echo inside my memory.

Setting my knife aside, I put the vegetable chopping on pause—no need to put any phalanges at risk—focusing instead on the spectacle that is my cousin Vince and his roommates, Declan and Ray, pantomiming the lyrics of Mariah's "Fantasy."

Yes. This is *exactly* what I need to drive out the memory of Chance declaring—vehemently, I might add—that us having sex was *never supposed to happen.* Seriously, talk about giving a person mental whiplash. Dickhead Daddy went from all *Tell me you're mine* to *We never should have happened* faster than sending a slap shot toward the goal.

So…why? Why is there still this tiny, *microscopic* part of me that longs for him? Or at least for how he made me feel before he made me feel like utter shit.

Vince snags one of my rubber spatulas out of the ceramic *All the shit I need to make you a fucking delicious meal* holder next to the stove, lifting it to his mouth and using it as a microphone to serenade Deck swaggering around the room, the latter winking at me as he strides in front of the island like a model down a catwalk, his workout shorts riding low on the trim hips rocking side to side with every purposeful step.

Then there's Ray, filming the entire scene for posterity—or more likely, for social media—shouting encouragement like he's directing their performance. As if he can sense his king-of-the-idiots crown slipping, Vince bobs and weaves, his free hand running through his hair like he's in front of a wind machine.

*Holy shiitake mushrooms.* Things like this seriously have me worrying about the gene pool that spawned me.

"Hey, boo." The singsonged greeting has me shifting my attention from bromance central to the gorgeous beauties settling onto the barstools across the counter—the people who actually live here, my roommates, Becky and Holly.

"Ooo, fajitas. Yum." Holly's excited clap as she wiggles in her seat is proof she's the perfect match for my numbnuts of a cousin. She's just whimsical enough to appreciate a man with superhero sheets on his bed.

"Fajitas? I thought we were ordering pizza?" Becky asks, contemplation twisting her brow, her green eyes falling to the counter, cataloging the feast's worth of ingredients I've prepped in an attempt to block out the memory of last night.

I'm stress cooking, and she knows it.

"This is bullshit," Vince bellows, momentarily interrupting the smack talk experience tells me I'm about to hear before skipping my way. I shit you not, the current UFC Light Heavyweight Champion skips, tall frame frolicking and muscly, tatted arms swinging to and fro like it's over the bridge and through the woods to grandmother's house he goes. You would never guess he's the oldest of our generation.

"What's bullshit?" I ask, indulging him as he leans across the island. "Oh shit." I pinch my nose. "You smell like a gym bag. We have showers at our family gym, you know."

"Maybe if you weren't leaving our texts unread, you'd know all about how the boys lost their shower privileges." Becky shoves Deck away when he comes at her with his arms wide open, the hug he intended to give her written clearly across his face.

"Could we—*maybe*—brainstorm punishments that don't affect us in the future?" Holly bounces a finger between the three of us. "I don't know about you"—she fans a hand under her nose—"but I'm not a fan of my olfactory system being collateral damage."

"For you, babes?" Becky hooks an arm around Holly's neck, placing a smacking kiss on her temple. "Anything."

"Suck-up," Ray cough-says into his fist, and Deck holds out his own for a knuckle bump.

"Whatever." Becky rolls her eyes before shifting them back to me. A sinking feeling settles in my gut as that saccharine smile makes an appearance, and I brace myself for the oncoming onslaught that is Becky Reese's brand of trouble. "So…"

"Nope." I slice a hand through the air, halting whatever prodding she plans on trying before it begins.

*I'm in control.*

I can choose who gets my mental bandwidth.

Chance Jenson is not in charge here.

Dropping to my haunches, I use the counter as a shield, yanking open the drawer we keep the pots and pans in, blindly reaching up to slam the cast-iron skillet onto the stovetop.

"You know…" *No, I don't want to know*, I think as I wait for Becky to continue anyway. "You wouldn't be taking your frustration out on our cookware if you listened to your best friends."

"*The Coven.*" Vince whispers the nickname he coined for our girl gang.

"Listening to you tends to land me in trouble," I grumble to Becky, ignoring Vince.

"Get your friends detained by the police one time"—she extends a single finger—"and you're labeled for life."

"It was twice." I extend and wiggle a pair of my own fingers for emphasis.

"Let's not forget about all those times we had to run from them to avoid being caught in the first place," Vince adds. However, the way his smile stretches into Joker mania-like territory, I'm pretty sure those are happy memories for him. Me? Well…okay, fine. I can admit they are for me too.

"Puh-lease." She waves us off. "Growing up would have been boring without me."

"It was how I discovered my love for handcuffs." Deck stretches his arms out in front of him, rotating his wrists to and fro. "Though I've learned quite a bit since then." He dances his eyebrows at Becky. "Wanna see?"

A spark of interest flares in her eyes, the green twinkling like the lights on the giant Christmas tree Holly erected to overtake half of our living room.

What is going on there?

"Now, you…"

I jump, rocking my hip off the beveled edge of the countertop and rubbing the tip of my nose. "Did you just flick me?"

"Yup." Becky pops the *P* with a proud flair that could give Ben's a run for its money.

*Oh shit. No, no, no, no.* I cannot think about Ben. Thinking about him is a slippery slope to thinking about how our date ended.

"Now tell me," Becky continues, completely unaware of the drift in my thoughts, "when are you finally going to bang the hockey player instead of the pots and pans?"

Whoop, there it is.

There it *flipping* is.

*If only she knew.*

"Wha—" I sputter, heat filling my cheeks.

Becky immediately notices my blush. "*Oooo.*" She circles a finger in front of my face. "Did something *happen*?"

No.

Nope.

Nothing happened.

That shiver shooting down my spine is from the screech of the barstool as Becky scoots in closer, definitely not from the memory of how Chance's body felt driving into mine. The goose bumps sprouting on my skin are from the intensity of Becky's stare down, not from the memory of Chance demanding I say I was his.

Nuh-uh.

Not a flipping chance I'll be thinking about that.

"I don't know what you're talking about, Beck," I say, playing dumb.

The winging of her eyebrows and the flat press of her lips tell me Becky's not buying what I'm selling. *Dammit.*

"*Suurrrre* you don't."

"Wait." Declan inserts himself into the conversation, helping himself to a handful of pepper slices and popping them into his mouth. "I thought you were on a date with the quarterback last night?"

Date turned platonic hangout turned crashed by that hockey player himself...

Yeah, I won't be explaining *any* of that.

"Oh, that's right." Becky perks up, drumming her fingers on the countertop. "Tell us all the things."

Yeah...

No.

"I don't think it went very well, Beck," Ray observes, his gaze tracking over my feed-the-entire-building spread.

Becky's jaw drops as she takes in the same thing Ray is. "Dammit. How did I miss that you're stress cooking?"

"Because you're easily distracted by Tex-Mex," Declan says, dropping an arm around her shoulders and tucking her against him.

"Ugh, you guys really need to go bathe." Becky slides Deck's arm off her shoulder.

"Maybe if you didn't punish us like we were *children*"—Vince singsongs the last word—"your noses wouldn't be suffering right now."

"Yeah." Deck adds a rebel yell, thumping his chest like Tarzan. "We're grown-ass men."

"Mm-hmm." Becky's lips press into an unimpressed flat line. "Because grown-ass men are known for their *Saran Wrapping the toilets in the locker room* skills."

I turn wide eyes on my cousin. "You *didn't*."

"They did," Holly answers with a resigned headshake.

"You sure you wanna marry him?" I ask my future cousin-in-law.

"Yeah, we can totally get you a better Christmas gift," Becky adds.

Vince slaps a hand over his heart, falling to his knees in his over-the-top dramatic fashion. "I'm totally writing you two traitors out of my will." He *V*'s his fingers at Becky and me.

"*Noooo.*" Becky clutches at the heavens. "My retirement plan!"

"Not my hand-me-down Batman sheets!" I lay the back of my hand over my forehead, feigning a silent-movie-star faint.

"Assholes," Vince curses.

"You *love* us," Becky and I chorus in unison.

"But until you can learn to treat my gym with respect, your smelly asses will stay grounded from using its amenities."

Laughter bubbles inside my belly.

This—this is what Dr. Sonya meant when she said to surround myself with what makes me feel whole. These people and this ridiculousness are what do that. Chance can call me a mistake every day that ends in *Y*, but as long as I have my people to go home to, I know I can keep from falling into bad habits again.

"Come on, Cupcake." Vince takes Holly's hand, helping her off her stool and twirling her around. "Help me wash my back."

"Good idea," Deck says a second before bending and hauling Becky over his shoulder in a fireman's carry. "Let's go, Beck."

"Put me down, you ass." Becky's squeals echo into the hall as Deck carries her out of our apartment, completely unfazed by her smacking his ass.

Becky won't be gone long since she won't actually be showering with our friend. Still, I inhale a deep breath, relishing the quiet that has befallen the kitchen.

"I take it things didn't go so well on your date with the quarterback?" Ray asks now that we're alone.

"I wouldn't say that," I hedge, picking up my knife and coring another pepper.

"Really?" He taps the jalapeño in my hand knowingly.

"Ben and I had a great time." I stab the tip of the blade into the cutting board. "At least we did until Chance showed up."

"Ahh." I hate the way Ray's eyes soften in understanding. "Guess his little display at the auction wasn't a fluke."

Ugh.

I totally forgot about the auction.

Chance winning cooking lessons with me is going to make it infinitely more difficult to avoid him like the plague he is.

But that doesn't mean I'm not going to give it the good ol' college try.

# CHAPTER 25

## Chance

A fter almost a year of being denied an acceptance to his proposal, Vince Steele is finally marrying Holly Vanderbilt. As crazy as it seems to me, I can't help but feel honored to be included in the small group of people invited to witness this special life event, though it's not the two people happily tying the knot under the twinkle lights strung from the beams of the small rustic barn that has me squirming on the edge of my seat with impatience.

Nope. That honor goes to the brunette sitting four rows in front of me.

One month.

It's been one fucking month since I last saw Gemma Steele in human form and not on social media.

*Holy shit.* Has it really been over a month since I saw her?

If it weren't for the fact that my fridge has continuously refilled with meals for my pups and that I've been staring at the back of her head for the entire ceremony, I would think Thanos had blipped her out of existence with how effectively she's avoided me.

*Can you blame her?* That annoying voice in the back of my head that's been hounding me since Gemma stormed out of the break room at Rookies chooses now to pipe up.

I'm over it.

A month is far too long to go without being able to talk to her, without hearing her carry on a nonsensical conversation with my dogs, without being able to touch her. A month since I kissed her —though it was the kissing that got me into this mess.

Well…that and me putting my big fucking foot in my mouth.

Essentially, it's been a month of pure fucking torture. My only saving grace is that it hasn't affected my playing, but that doesn't change the fact that I fucked up.

*Yup, calling her a bunny and a mistake were not your finest moments.*

Yeah, yeah, yeah. I get it. I fucked up bad.

But my biggest fuckup of all was forgetting to wear a condom. Gemma may not be the bunny I once believed her to be or what I accused her of that night, but I *know* better than to play rookie roulette with my dick.

My Gramps—the only person in my family who gave a crap about me outside of hockey—is probably spinning in his grave at my forgetting to suit up. If ever there was a motto he used more than his *Our actions have consequences* lesson, it was the *no-glove, no-love* one he hammered into my skull starting when my age was still in the single digits.

What the fuck am I going to do?

"And since you jerks were too impatient to wait and allow me the time to *properly* plan you a wedding…" Lyle, the world's great barista and owner of the world's greatest coffee shop, Espresso Patronum, casts a judgmental frown at the bride and groom standing before him.

"Not that you're bitter about that or anything…" The mic clipped to Holly's wedding gown allows all the guests filling the rustic farmhouse turned winter wonderland despite Lyle's complaints about lack of time to hear her chastisement, causing them to laugh.

"Hush, you." Lyle cuts her a glare.

"You can't hush the bride."

"Do you want to argue, or do you want me to finish marrying you to this sexy beefcake of a man?" Lyle winks at Vince, staying on brand by shamelessly flirting with the groom while he's in the middle of his nuptials.

Holly turns to the man dutifully holding her bouquet and standing behind her. "How about fulfilling your man of honor responsibilities by getting your husband in check?"

"Ly, babe," Kyle cajoles, a well-practiced affectionate smile on his lips, "they agreed to let you officiate, so don't be a vowblock."

"Vowblocking?" Lyle pauses in his monologue, his gregarious personality not caring that he's currently officiating this shindig. "Is that a thing?"

"Only when my best friend allows you to guilt-trip him into letting you perform his wedding ceremony," Jase comments from his best man spot.

"Whatever." Lyle runs a careful hand over the neon-green-and-hot-pink tips of his spiky hair before smoothing it over his green crushed velvet tuxedo jacket. "You guys still love me."

"That may be true." Vince claps him on the shoulder. "But if you don't pronounce my woman my wife in the next two seconds, I'm going to find a new coffee shop to frequent."

Lyle lets out a dramatic gasp, clutching at his chest. "You take that back *right now*, Vincent Steele." He shakes an aggressive finger in the groom's face.

"Tell me I can kiss my bride, and I'll consider it."

The two of them engage in a stare-off. Only with this group is ridiculousness like this considered normal, though everyone here knows they are both full of shit, a fact I can personally attest to after this past month. Because, yes, I've continued to hone my veritable stalker skills by spending way too much time in Espresso Patronum, hoping to catch even the briefest glimpse of Gemma coming and going from The Steele Maker across the street.

Too fucking bad that plan never panned out.

"You know what?" Vince's sure voice breaks into my moment of self-flagellation. "Screw this," he declares, then he hooks an arm around Holly, hauling her in and dipping her backward with a not-suitable-for-public-consumption kiss.

"Fine, fine, fine." Lyle tosses the notebook he was reading from. "I pronounce you man and wife and all that marital jazz. Merry Christmas."

Whoops and hollers continue to cheer on the display, though I can't tell if the loudest of the bunch comes from my section of fellow puck heads or the Covenettes sitting up front.

"Alright." Tucker grabs his lapels, straightening his suit jacket with cocky assurance. "Now that those two are finally hitched"—

he hooks a thumb at the still-making-out newlyweds—"it's time to boom-boom with the bridesmaids."

"I feel like, as your best friend"—Jake flattens a hand to his chest—"it's my duty to point out that Skye isn't technically a bridesmaid."

That's true. In order to have an actual guest list for their small wedding, Vince and Holly opted to only have Jase and Kyle—their bestest besties—stand up with them.

"I feel like you'd be better off pointing out how Skye shuts down *all* his attempts to get back into her pants," Ryan helpfully points out.

"*Ooo.*" Tucker lets out a long whistle. "Cap coming in with the burn."

"Why are we friends with you?" Ryan deadpans.

"Brothers." Tuck pulls Ryan in for a side hug. "Blondie declared me her BB3, remember? So that makes us framily."

Ah yes, the Big Brother 3 nickname. Hang around these crazies long enough and you'll learn all about their affinity for nicknames and their origins.

*Wonder if that's why Gemma calls you Canada and Rookie.*

I scoff at that insane thought from my mental nuisance. How easily it forgets she *loves* to call me Dickhead on the reg. Instead, I focus all my attention on a moonwalking, arm-dancing Tucker.

"You assholes doubt me all you want, but I have a good track record when it comes to weddings." With a jaunty salute, he takes off.

As I watch Tucker weave through the small cluster of wedding guests on his own made-up personal mission, I decide it's time for me to complete mine.

Getting Gemma Steele alone.

# CHAPTER 26

*Gemma*

Lyle may have bitched—*a lot*—about our friends' affinity for quickie weddings and elopements, but despite the quick turnaround from when Vince proposed last month, today can only be described as magical.

Twinkle lights drip from every beam, dangling like icicles and casting a mythical glow on this celebration of love as guests find their seats at their respective reindeer-named tables. The candy cane and poinsettia centerpieces adorning each one perfectly complement the holiday decor throughout the room, and the pièce de résistance is the massive Christmas tree in the corner that stretches all the way to the three-story ceiling. All we're missing are a few Rockettes in attendance to be able to officially declare this Vince and Holly's Christmas Wedding Spectacular.

As my cousin and his new bride make the rounds among their guests, I take the opportunity to duck into the venue's kitchen to check on the food preparation.

"Oh no you don't," calls out the boisterous voice of Hero, my mother's partner and co-chef at Prize Plates, the fusion restaurant they've owned for over a decade, as he swings a rubber spatula at me.

"I didn't do anything." I hold my arms up in a *Don't shoot* gesture.

Hero Papachristodoulopoulos has been one of my favorite adults for years. His name may be a mouthful—I'll spare you the dirty joke that goes along with that statement; let's just say it's vomit inducing when it comes from a parent-like figure—but it couldn't be more befitting for a man with his size personality.

"You Steele women really test my patience, you know." Hero's face morphs to one of his *I survived raising seven Greek daughters—I can smell the bullshit from a mile away* expressions, the spatula still waving to and fro with his frustration.

"You love us, and you know it, Hero," Mom says as she walks by, dropping a quick kiss on his ruddy cheek.

"Don't even get me started on you." Hero takes Mom's white chef's coat from her when she tries to slip it on, passing it off to one of their sous-chefs. "The only reason I agreed to this insane plan to have us cater your nephew's wedding was because you" —he slides a paring knife out of Mom's reach—"promised to actually attend it like a proper guest." Hazel eyes rimmed with the thickest, inkiest lashes rise to me with a leveling look. "*Both* of you."

"But—"

"Nope." Hero cuts me off before I can even form a sentence.

"I just—"

"Not a chance, our precious little Gem." Hero's headshake is finite, but it's his use of the term of endearment he coined for me as a teenager that has me freezing long enough for him to spin me around toward the door.

Chance called me My Precious in the break room.

*He also called you a mistake,* my temper reminds me.

Chance, who is out in the barn looking far too sexy for my sanity in a custom-tailored suit. I need to keep my ass in this kitchen and away from hot grumpy hockey players, especially when Mr. Grumpy Pants is bad for my self-esteem.

"But…" I spin in Hero's hold, deploying the puppiest puppy eyes in my arsenal.

"Not a chance." He boops me on the nose, still carefully maneuvering me backward.

"How come the bride was allowed to make her own wedding cake, but I'm being banished from helping cook?" I shout as the swinging doors close behind Hero.

"Because she was able to do that beforehand so it wouldn't keep her from actually enjoying herself the day of," he says, popping his head back through the doors. "Now get moving." He makes a shooing motion with his hands. "And go have fun."

I let out a defeated sigh. So much for hiding out in the kitchen.

I spin around to rejoin the festivities, faltering when I spot Chance standing less than five feet away. His black eyes zero in on me, tracking my movements, watching how I gather then lift the skirt of my gown to keep from tripping on it, his gaze not missing the way I clutch at the silk.

*Dammit.* There's that sensation of being his prey again, the race of my heart, the prickling under my skin. Why is it so hot?

No matter how much I wish to deny it, I crave the attention he gives me. But with the way our last interaction ended, I'm not sure how healthy it is for me. I do know I'm not going to put up with it.

Even so, it doesn't change the fact that he's dangerous to me. The dark-charcoal suit, the manicured stubble on his jaw, the crisp white shirt…it's all a siren's call to my hormones.

I peel my eyes from his in hopes of hiding the effect he has on me, staring instead at the ink decorating the back of his hand.

Yeah. Definitely not helping.

My gaze flicks back to his, and I watch as he watches me.

Back and forth. Back and forth.

What is he thinking? Why does the silence feel like he's edging me away from safety?

"You've been avoiding me," he says when my eyes meet his, his deep, rumbling voice caressing me all the way to my core.

*Shit, shit, shit.*

My mouth opens and shuts, purposefully swallowing down the immature *Duh* that jumps to my tongue.

"What?" He arches one of his stupid eyebrows. "Not going to deny it?"

"I'm surprised you even bothered to notice, seeing as I'm nothing more than a mistake to you."

"Shit, Gemma." He goes to rake a hand through his hair only to stop when he realizes it's styled and instead grips the back of his neck. I guess because I landed myself on Santa's naughty list —and not the fun one—I, of course, notice how sexy that particular move is.

*Gah!* I hate myself sometimes. Why can't I quit this man?

"Is that why you came over here?" I fold my arms over my chest, hating that I notice the way Chance's nostrils flare when his gaze dips to follow the movement. "To interrogate me about my whereabouts and not to, oh, I don't know…" I shrug. "Apologize for upping your dickheadedness to new Dickhead proportions the last time I saw you?"

Chance takes a step closer, and the space between us thickens with familiar tension. "We need to talk."

My pulse stutters when he draws near, as does my breath. I don't want to want him. I don't want to want the way he makes me feel. I try, like I always have, to ignore that annoying voice in the back of my head that asks why I'm fighting a battle with myself I'm sure to lose.

"No thanks." I need a distraction if I'm going to have any hope of keeping my temper in check.

He called me a mistake. He thinks I'm nothing more than a bunny.

But…*dammit*. There's still that pull drawing me to him, aching to feel the heat of his skin on mine again, to feel the strength of his body as he takes me without apology.

*Ermygah.*

I have to force myself forward and step around him so I can find my sanity.

"Gemma." Chance reaches for me, but I'm already halfway to the dance floor, hoping against hope that the fact that it's filled with couples slow dancing will help keep me from losing my shit.

My head says run.

My heart says stay.

My body—the traitorous bitch—says throw caution to the wind and just let it, whatever *it* is, happen.

"Princess, wait." Chance grabs my arm, his fingers sliding over the lace detailing of my sleeves, setting my skin ablaze as they curl around my biceps.

I can feel his gaze burning into the back of my head, my heart thumping wildly inside my chest as he crowds me, his body moving until there's the whisper of his suit jacket brushing against my dress.

"Stop running." His voice is all business, and a shiver of awareness crawls up my spine, followed by a flood of arousal.

"Why?" I pivot to face him, desperate to feel something other than want and confusion. "Because you're a hockey player, and you think I'm a puck bunny? Because you think my value is only in being a hockey groupie, so I'm supposed to just fall at your feet?"

"Oh, how much easier this would be if that were true."

God, I hate this man. He's so damn *frustrating*.

Chance glides his hand down the length of my arm, following the dip of my wrist to take my hand and thread his fingers with mine.

"Chance," I warn, my gaze dancing over the couples swaying to "I'll Be Home For Christmas" around us.

"Don't worry about them." He crooks a finger under my chin, bringing my attention back where he wants it—on him.

Despite his grip on me, I cast another furtive glance at the people surrounding us. This wouldn't be the first time we got into it in public, but I'll be damned if I cause a scene at my cousin's wedding. That's probably why I allow Chance to pull me into a dancer's pose, placing one of my hands on his shoulder and taking the other in his.

I suck in a breath at the possessive way he holds me around the rib cage, a lungful of his delicious scent surrounding me as he guides us in a slow circle.

"Give me one good reason why I shouldn't drive my heel into your foot right now."

Chance clucks his tongue. "You and I both know you wouldn't cause a scene at Vince and Holly's wedding."

I mutter a curse. It's infuriating that he knows me this well.

"But, in all seriousness, if you did that, I wouldn't be able to apologize."

"Really?" I side-eye him only to have him draw us closer together, the press of his hard chest against my breasts damn distracting.

"Really." The sincerity in his voice causes me to step on his foot, in the stumbling-dancer sort of way, not the maim-the-hockey-player one.

"Took you long enough."

"To be fair, I would have apologized sooner, but apparently you're a professional avoider as well as a professional chef."

"Hmm…" I dip my chin to hide the smile threatening to bloom on my lips. "That has a nice ring to it."

"Definitely something to add to your business card."

I stop dancing, my jaw dropping.

"Why are you looking at me like that?" Chance asks, and we begin dancing again.

"I'm not used to you having a sense of humor, but if I ever do end up getting business cards made, I'm totally putting that on them."

"You don't have business cards?"

"Never needed them." I shrug as if those little paper rectangles aren't a facet of my big-picture dream of owning my own boutique agency.

"Why—"

"You were trying to apologize?" I cut off his vein of unknowingly far-too-personal questioning. I'm already feeling extra vulnerable with him. The last thing he needs is a glimpse into my feelings about my side hustle.

He nods, and for some reason, I brace myself. "I'm sorry for how that night ended."

"Only for how it ended?" I tilt my head. "What about for crashing my date?"

"Not if you want my apology to be genuine."

I can't help but chuckle at the on-brand response.

"Damn." He twirls me away from him before bringing me back in closer until we're pressed cheek to cheek. "I would have thought you would lay into me for that one."

"I blame the Christmas spirit. It's making me soft."

"I like how you're soft." A shudder of need rolls through me at his words, his thumb stroking over my rib cage.

"I still think you're a dickhead."

An unexpected laugh rumbles up from his chest and pulls a smile out of me despite everything.

He pulls away, his expression sobering, his gaze intense. "I'm sorry," he says again, this time more earnestly than before.

Chance takes a step back and stares into my eyes, his apology still hanging between us. I want to push him away, want to run away, but I can't seem to move. His gaze drops to my lips, and my heart skips a beat.

He swallows hard before slowly reaching up to cup the side of my face. His thumb brushes gently over my cheekbone, sending little sparks of electricity shooting through me. "I'm sorry for what I said," he murmurs in a low voice, almost too softly for me to hear over the music. "It was wrong, and I didn't mean it."

Chance's eyes flicker with something closer to genuine emotion, and he gives me a small smile that seems almost shy before dropping his hand from my face.

"I know you're not a mistake," he says firmly, almost fiercely, as he takes another step back. He pauses for a moment before continuing in an urgent tone, "And you're definitely not some puck bunny looking for her next hockey player conquest."

My breath catches at his words.

"I was triggered, but it was my fault. I was the one who initiated everything without thinking about protection until afterward, and I took it out on you. Again, I'm sorry." He looks away briefly as if embarrassed by his passionate outburst before meeting my gaze again with determination burning in his black eyes. "You deserve better than what happened between us, but I refuse to be sorry about not liking the idea of you out with another guy."

"What?" I pull away from him, my face heating with a blush. "We're not together, Chance. If I want to date someone, who gives a crap?"

He leans in so close his breath fans over my lips, my pulse tripling as he whispers, "I do."

I feel his finger tracing the line of my jaw, down my neck, and over the jut of my collarbone, dragging the sleeve of my dress down my arm as he moves his mouth to follow, his stubble and lips grazing my skin along the way.

"That sounds like a you problem," I say, my breath catching in my throat.

"You're such a brat." His hand drifts south, inching closer and closer to my ass. "You're making my palm twitch, Princess."

Want slams into me as memories of how well he follows through on that threat crash over me. "People are watching," I admonish, hating that I can't disguise the waver in my voice.

Chance only pulls me closer, splaying his hand over my lower back. "And all they see is two people dancing."

I let out a muted gasp as he eliminates the last bit of space between us, confidently letting me feel the erection straining behind his zipper.

"But they don't know how your body reacts to mine." The

pressure of his palm as it moves over my ass makes me unconsciously grind against him. "Or how badly I need you." He follows the sloping neckline of my dress up my arm and across my chest. "Though I have to wonder…"

I swallow hard, my heart thudding under his touch as his thumb brushes over my nipple through my dress, feeling the texture of my lace bra underneath.

"If what you have on underneath is as sexy as this dress."

The hand on the small of my back slides up the long column of my spine, my back arching as his mouth descends toward mine.

"Well, isn't *this* an *interesting* development?" Becky's musing voice cuts into the moment like a bucket of cold water, and I jump out of Chance's embrace. Her way-too-observant gaze flickers between him and me, a small smile playing at the corners of her mouth. "You two certainly look cozy for two people who supposedly hate each other."

"We—" I dart my gaze from her to Chance and back again. "We were just dancing, that's all."

"I'm sure." Her smirk says otherwise. "But it does make a person wonder." She taps her chin, and I take another step away from Chance. I don't trust that chin tap for a second. "Did you guys finally bang the hate away?"

I choke on my spit, my mind blaring with a *Here comes trouble* warning.

"Leave the girl alone, Beck." Declan hooks an arm around her neck, coming to my rescue with a wink before throwing back the shot glass of quinoa salad. "*Armgah*," he mumbles around the mouthful. "Marry me, Gem," he says when he finally swallows.

I roll my eyes at Deck, ignoring the feel of Chance's body tensing beside me.

"I told you, Deck." I give his chest a pat. "Your proposals are meaningless when my cooking is involved."

"I can't help it." He snags a bacon-wrapped date from a passing server, groaning as he devours it in a single bite. "*Jesus.* How do you make the healthier things taste so *good*?" He draws out the last word, pulling a giggle from me.

"You made the food for the wedding?" Chance's shocked question pulls my attention back to him.

"Only some of it," I say, trying to keep my annoyance with

Hero kicking me out of my happy place from bleeding into my tone. "I curated the menu, too."

A playful glint I'm not used to seeing sparks behind Chance's dark gaze, holding me captive as he moves in closer, the air crackling with a new kind of tension.

"You'll have to excuse me then." He places a chaste kiss on my temple. "Because I have some of your goodies to taste." Then spins on his heel and walks away.

"What the fuck was that?" Becky's eyes are so wide I fear they might fall out of her head.

I shake my head, unable to form words.

I'm not sure what that was. Not the apology, not him owning up to his mistakes. Not the sincerity, not the flirting.

And I'm not sure how much longer I want to fight him anymore.

Covenette

## CHAPTER 27

# Coven CONVERSATIONS

<u>From the Group Message Thread of The Coven</u>

YOU KNOW YOU WANNA: Lookee, lookee *eyeball emoji*

YOU KNOW YOU WANNA: I almost forgot about this.

YOU KNOW YOU WANNA: **picture of Gemma and Chance dancing at the wedding**

MAKES BOYS CRY: Hold on **rubs eyes** are you and Chance dancing here?

MOTHER OF DRAGONS: Without any bloodshed?

ALPHABET SOUP: Impressive.

BROADWAY BABY: It was a Christmas miracle!

MOTHER OF DRAGONS: Damn, you're flipping perfect for my brother.

QUEEN OF SMUT: Yeah, yeah, yeah. Gemma and Chance danced all cutesy and such. But can we get to the GOOD stuff?

DANCING QUEEN: Give us all the dirty deets. **waggles eyebrows**

MAKE ME OVER GOOSE: Yes, I agree. You bishes have made me super invested in this little subplot of the group.

QUEEN OF SMUT: I swear to Cheesus, Ryan better marry you.

MOTHER OF DRAGONS: I would like the record to show I was NOT the person to say that.

THE OG PITA: And so it is noted.

FIDDLER ON THE ROOF: Can I just say how much I love us?

DANCING QUEEN: Same, same, but can we maybe do the whole we-are-so-awesome thing after Gemma tells us if she and Chance finally did the hippidy-dippidy?

MAKES BOYS CRY: Wait. The wedding was over a week ago—how are we only hearing about this now?

PROTEIN PRINCESS: OMG! It was just a dance.

YOU KNOW YOU WANNA: Just a dance, huh?

YOU KNOW YOU WANNA: Let's zoom in, shall we?

YOU KNOW YOU WANNA: **cropped and circled image of Chance's hand sitting dangerously low on Gemma's back**

ALPHABET SOUP: Oooo, I think someone likes you, cuz.

DANCING QUEEN: You don't need to like someone to fuck them.

QUEEN OF SMUT: True story.

PROTEIN PRINCESS: I think all of you need to make your New Year's resolution be learning how to mind your own business.

MOTHER OF DRAGONS: That'll never happen.

BROADWAY BABY: That's a fact.

SANTA'S COOKIE SUPPLIER: OMG, this being 6 hours behind you guys is NOT working for me. I'm missing ALL the things.

PROTEIN PRINCESS: You guys are RIDICULOUS. And Holly, you're on your honeymoon. As much as it makes me throw up in my mouth to say *puke emoji* shouldn't my cousin be keeping you too busy banging to text us?

SANTA'S COOKIE SUPPLIER: THANK YOU! THIS IS WHY YOU ARE MY FAVORITE COUSIN GEM!

PROTEIN PRINCESS: Hi, Vince.

SANTA'S COOKIE SUPPLIER: Don't you worry your pretty little head, cuz. I've been keeping my new wife VERY satisfied.

ALPHABET SOUP: Gross. **Clueless "I'm outie" GIF**

PROTEIN PRINCESS: ^^This. Byeeee.

# CHAPTER 28

## Chance

"So." Jake plops down on the cushioned bench beside me, unconcerned about only being clad in a towel. "Tonight's the big night."

"Huh?" I ask, drying my hair with a towel.

"Isn't it auction date night for you?"

"Oh. Right." I vaguely remember seeing it on my schedule. "It is."

"Why does it sound like you forgot?" Jake lets out a bellowing laugh when I cut him a telling glance. "Oh shit." He lifts a fist to his mouth. "How is that even possible with my wife as your publicist?"

It's my turn to laugh because, yes, Jordan Donovan has been blowing up my phone for the last two days about it.

Still…

I had other things on my mind.

Namely, a particular chef.

"*Sooo*…where are you going for your date?" Jake singsongs like a teenage girl at a slumber party.

"Bro—chill." Ryan claps him on the back as he reaches into his locker safe for his phone.

"I don't know." I step into a pair of boxer briefs with a shrug. "I'm curious to see if he'll burst into a rendition of 'Summer Nights' from *Grease*." I pinch my thumb and forefinger until there's only a sliver of space between them. "I feel like we're *this close* to seeing it happen."

"Ooo, funny man." Jake jumps to his feet, snatching my discarded towel from the bench, twisting it, and flicking it at me with a snap.

"I have my moments."

"You certainly have been having them more since Gemma stopped avoiding you."

One leg inside of my jeans, the other out, I freeze and slowly lift my gaze toward his smug-ass expression.

"What?" Jake holds his arms out wide. "I'm married to the head Covenette—I know *all* the things."

"It's gross how much you sound like her sometimes," Ryan grumbles with a disappointed headshake.

"Don't make it sound like I'm not all man," Jake counters.

"Mm-hmm," Ryan hums and starts for the door. "Sure you are." He laughs, the booming sound echoing off the walls as he strides out of the dressing room.

"Fucker," Jake growls at his brother-in-law's retreating form. "Anyway." He turns his attention back to me. "Give me the deets."

"I can't believe you just said deets."

Jake gives an unapologetic shrug. "I live in Coven Central, and the next gen has been spending hella time at my place. I pick up their vernacular."

"Fair," I concede, "but there are no deets."

"Give me the nondeet deets then." Jake slaps his hands onto his thighs and leans forward. "Let me live vicariously through your date."

"Why? Was yours not any good?"

Jake presses his mouth into an unimpressed *Don't be stupid* line. "My wife won me. Of *course*, it was good."

"Spare me the details." I hold up a hand then lean against the bench, toeing on my sneakers. "We're going to dinner at Prized Plates."

"Ahh…the chef's table with the Steele women. *Damn*, you're going to eat *good* tonight."

His pluralization has me straightening. "Women?"

Jake nods. "Hope lets Gemma use the kitchen whenever one of the fighters is camping for a fight. Gemma usually helps with the dinner rush first on the nights she uses the restaurant."

It sounds like something Gemma would do. Sweet, generous,

and thoughtful. I bet it's her way of giving back, even when it's unnecessary.

"You know what?" I push to my feet. "I think I'm actually looking forward to this date now."

"And why's that?" The appearance of Jake's dimples has me all kinds of suspicious.

"Because it'll give me another opportunity to taunt Gemma about me being able to eat her cooking."

From behind a carved black wooden podium, a pretty Middle Eastern woman in a classy black silk hijab and classic white button-down, black vest, and slacks marks my arrival with a bright smile.

I return the greeting, taking in how the black wood carries throughout the building, from the bar to the curved booths in various sizes, contrasting beautifully against the tan brick support pillars. Candlelight flickers from the center of each table, the Edison bulbs strung across the ceiling adding to the intimate glow.

I've never been to Prized Plates before, and damn, I gotta admit I'm digging the understated elegance of the place.

"Welcome to Prized Plates. I'm Farah. Can I have the name of your reservation, please?"

"Hi, thank you," I say, bringing my attention back to the welcoming hostess. "It's under Jenson."

She swipes a manicured finger over the tablet on her stand, and I know the moment she's found my name on her list because the wattage of her smile increases tenfold.

"Ah, the chef's table. You're in for a treat."

Farah's statement ramps up my excitement from Jake's earlier revelation. Thank god tonight isn't a real date because it would be a total dick move to be looking forward to seeing Gemma while on a date with another woman.

The heavy tempered glass doors part as if on cue, and Cora, my auction winner, steps through with a burst of frigid air.

"Hi, Chance." Her voice is breathless.

"Hi, Cora." My spine straightens from the assessing way she looks me over.

"Wonderful." Farah steps out from behind her podium, arms extended. "Shall I check your coats before taking you back to your table?"

I shrug out of my heavy wool coat as Cora does the same with the trench coat knotted around her waist, my eyes bugging out when I take in what she's wearing underneath. It's not that she doesn't look good, because she does—smoking hot, in fact—but the spaghetti-strapped silk slip of a dress is not at all what one would expect a person to wear to dinner at a classy restaurant, let alone when the forecast calls for snow. I feel cold just looking at her, and I say that as a Canadian raised playing hockey on a frozen pond.

Her only nod to the winter weather is her pair of black suede thigh-high boots. Sadly they have the unfortunate side effect of making me think of a similar camel-colored pair a certain Gemma Steele owns.

Thankfully, Farah instructs us to follow, guiding us through the restaurant and into the bustling kitchen.

"Chef," Farah says as she stops at a bar-height countertop. "I'd like to introduce the guests joining you this evening."

Dressed in your typical slouchy chef's hat and an atypical yellow chef's coat—yeah, there's no doubt this woman sired My Precious—Hope Steele works at the station directly connected to the countertop.

"Welcome to my kitchen." She greets us with a familiar-looking smile, Gemma evident in the curve of her lips. She gestures for us to sit, all while her hands never cease furiously chopping ingredients with impressive dexterity then seamlessly adding them to the sauté pan and giving them a toss.

"This isn't what I expected," I comment, pulling out one of the counter-height leather-back chairs and helping Cora into her seat before hanging my suit jacket over another and sitting down.

All around us, it's controlled chaos. Chefs—each of which I'm sure has a specific title I have no hope of knowing—man stations around the kitchen, moving around each other in a carefully choreographed dance. There's the heavy clank of cast iron hitting burners, and bursts of fire shoot high with splashes of wine. Music plays from speakers throughout the room, chorused by the slicing, dicing, and chopping of food preparation. There are shouted directions and muted conversations as the staff work as a cohesive unit. I've also seen more than one cook dancing along to their work.

No wonder Gemma likes to work out of here.

"Let me guess, a small table for two was more what you imagined?" There's a tease in Hope's tone I'm used to hearing her daughter use with my pups.

I nod. That's precisely what I was imagining.

"Well, you see…" Hope sets her knife aside, bracing her elbows on the counter and leaning onto it. "In my family, family dinner is a time-honored tradition. When I opened this place, I wanted a way to bring a little piece of that magic that comes from sharing a meal with those most important to us with the guests I'm fortunate to cook for personally. This"—she presses her palms to the counter—"is how I do that."

Hope pushes back then places a set of small gold plates in front of Cora and me.

"Tonight, we will serve you tapas style." Hope claps then waves her hands over the dishes, presenting them. "This way, you can sample a little of everything by the time your meal is over."

Cora picks up her fork, holding it over the plate. "I love tapas."

"This looks delicious," I comment, taking in the tiny cubes of watermelon topped with little round balls of feta cheese and finished with a zigzag drizzle of balsamic vinaigrette.

"Thank you, though I can't take full credit. This is my daughter's brainchild. It's one of her favorite snacks to prep for her clients." She pauses. "Though I guess you wouldn't have much experience with that, would you?" She hums like a mother well versed in all her daughter's secrets.

"No." An expected laugh pulls from my throat. "Gemma has made a point to cook *only* for my pups."

"I've heard all about your precious babies. Do you have pictures? My Gem has been traveling too much lately to show me any."

I spin to grab my phone out of my jacket pocket.

"Gemma shows you pictures of them?" I ask, swiping to the

shot I took of Pebbles and Bamm-Bamm snuggling with an Eddie the Yeti stuffy this morning.

"Oh my word, they are darling." Hope passes the phone to Cora, but she barely gives it a passing glance before handing it back to me.

If this were a real date, that would have been strike one.

Cora shifts in her seat as we dig into the first course, her knees brushing my thigh as she exaggeratedly crosses her legs, the already short hem of her dress sliding dangerously higher, exposing almost a full foot of toned thigh to my view.

Objectively, Cora is hot, but I seem to find myself partial to wavy brown hair and understated makeup that highlights a natural beauty as opposed to straight platinum locks and a face contoured within an inch of its life.

The conversation between us flows easily enough, but it's all surface-level bullshit and inane prodding about my life as a professional hockey player. If that isn't a kick in the sack...

Karma is laughing her ass off at me, paying me back for insulting Gemma by calling her a bunny by making me be stuck on a date with one, a date I can't fake an emergency to bail on because it was bought and paid for.

Joyful shouting rolls through the kitchen, and as the staff parts, I see her—Gemma.

Hope lets out an excited squeal and excuses herself to rush her daughter.

I know the instant Gemma spots me, the weight of her eyes heavy on the side of my face. I shift to see her over Cora's head and cough to cover a groan when the pink tip of her tongue darts out, catching a droplet of snow that's settled on her kissable lips.

Gemma's eyes are wide, but she's grinning as she smooths the hair that got mussed by removing her hat, a light flush creeping up her neck.

Before any greetings can be exchanged, Cora leans into me, pulling me out of my trance. She runs a hand down my chest, pressing her pushed-up chest into my arm, the neckline of her body-hugging dress dipping to the point I can see the dark shadowing of her nipples as she toys with the end of my tie.

The blatant display does nothing for me, my dick dormant, borderline bored and giving an *Is this chick for real?* yawn inside my pants.

At least until Gemma steps up to the sink in the chef's table area. Similar to the strangeness I picked up during the auction, Gemma angles her body in a way to minimize Cora in her line of sight, and when she speaks, it's only to me.

"Why does it feel like you chose tonight on purpose?"

I do a quick check on Cora, but that pull I always feel when Gemma is near, no matter how often I've fought it, is too strong to ignore.

"I swear I didn't." I hold my hands up. "I didn't even know you would be here until Jake tried to pump me for gossip like we were on a three-way call."

Gemma giggles, dipping her chin into her chest. "I take it you guys watched *Mean Girls* on your last road trip?"

"It's scary how you ladies seem to just know everything."

Gemma gifts me one of those sunshiny smiles of hers, and I can feel the warmth of it unfurl inside my chest.

"Oh my god, *Rusty!*" Cora interrupts with a girlish squeal, effectively bringing any possibility of ignoring her to an end. "I had *no* idea *you'd* be here."

Gemma's entire demeanor transforms into something I've never quite seen on her before.

"Did you just call her Rusty?" I question, utterly confused.

"Yeah." Cora bounces in her seat, the bubbliness of her personality turning up to eleven. "It's, like, her nickname from high school."

"Because being called *Rusty Steele* was *such* a compliment," Gemma's deadpan response and dark expression are all the clues I need to tell this isn't a happy reunion.

"Oh, stop being *so* dramatic." Cora rolls her eyes. "You'd think after all these years you'd have learned how to take a joke."

Gemma's hands ball into fists.

"Here you go, sweetie." Hope returns, interrupting the confusing tension and handing Gemma a hot-pink chef's coat.

She accepts it, and I'm not at all surprised to see the words *This shit is going to be delicious* printed on the front.

"How *cute* is it that you get to *play* chef, Rusty?" Cora coos, tracing shapes on the countertop with her finger.

"Play, earn a degree in nutritional sciences..." Gemma shrugs. "Yeah, *that's* the same thing."

Cora's eyes scan Gemma from head to toe. "I wouldn't have

guessed you had an affinity for food given that you were actually skinny in high school."

"Excuse me?" Hope asks, aghast.

"Don't worry about it, Mom," Gemma says, laying a hand on Hope's forearm.

My back straightens as Cora runs her gaze over Gemma in another pass, this one with a critical assessment. "Though I guess you certainly found a love for it. You should remember, Rusty, a moment on the lips is forever on the hips."

"The fuck?" I bark.

"You know what?" Gemma shakes her head at her mom and fumbles with the buttons on her chef's coat. "We aren't in high school anymore."

"Yet you still seem to be the lesser Steele." Cora taps at her chin with a hum. "One of you becomes a UFC champ, the other marries one, and you, what? Call yourself a chef because your family pities you enough to *hire*"—she puts air quotes around the word—"you."

I've had enough. I don't care that this woman paid fifty grand for a night out with me; I will not allow her to insult Gemma in my presence.

But before I can come to Gemma's defense, she shrugs out of the coat, places it on the counter, and turns a glare on Cora that puts any of the ones she's ever given me to shame.

"I don't have to stay here and be subjected to your bullying bullshit like I did back then." Gemma pulls her mom into a hug. "I'm sorry, Mom, but I can't stay. I need to be"—she glances to the heavens—"*anywhere* but here."

Hope nods, cupping Gemma's cheek affectionately.

"I'm done here too," I say, shoving my chair back and pushing to my feet.

Cora latches on to my arm, pleading with me to stay, empty phrases like "I'm sorry" and "I didn't mean it" spilling from her over-glossed lips.

Unfortunately for me, by the time I extract myself from her barnacle grip, Gemma is gone.

# CHAPTER 29

# Gemma

There's nothing like coming face-to-face with your high school bully on a date with a man you jilled off to in the shower that morning to *really* liven up a girl's Friday night.

Oh, you heard that sarcasm, did you?

"Jesus." Ray pinches the mitt on his right hand between his arm and side, removing it to shake out his hand.

I bounce on the balls of my feet, the adrenaline from the restaurant earlier pumping through my veins. "Try to keep up, big man." I make a taunting *Come and get it* gesture with my gloved hand.

"I'm ready for you, baby girl." Ray shoves his hand back into the mitt then lifts both arms, giving me back my targets. "Do your worst."

Punch after punch, I throw everything I have into my hits as Ray dances around the boxing ring with me, calling out different combinations to help me work out my frustrations.

"Take your time," he reminds me for the umpteenth time.

I narrow my eyes, pushing a sweaty flyaway out of my face with my forearm.

"Glare at me all you want, Gem, but we both know you crave control." He calls out another series of punches. "And when you forget to slow down and breathe"—he hides his hands behind his back, forcing me to pause—"your punches get sloppy."

I hate that he's right.

"Okay, again," Ray instructs.

Jab.

Jab.

Jab. Cross. Jab.

"Remember what Dr. Sonya taught you."

Jab.

Jab.

"We can't control how shitty people act."

Jab. Hook. Cross.

"But we can control how we react to it."

Punch after punch, I let Ray's words settle inside me. I've done the work. I've conquered my demons and come out the other side. I'm not afraid to keep doing the work when triggered.

Ray straightens, dropping his arms and looking at something behind me. I turn to follow his line of sight.

*Chance.*

He's here.

What is he doing here?

I blink rapidly, not daring to hope but praying my eyes aren't playing tricks on me. Snow coats his dark hair in a layer of white, but he pays it no mind as he locks his gaze on me, a desperation in his eyes I've never seen before.

Moving to the edge of the ring, I rest my forearms on the ropes, leaning forward and letting my gloved hands hang low. "What are you doing here?"

"I needed to see you."

His statement sparks an annoying little flutter behind my rib cage.

"Shouldn't you still be on your date? She paid good money for it, after all."

"I don't care how much she paid. She lost her right to my time the moment she started insulting you in front of me."

That spark blooms like a flower opening, wrapping around me like a hug.

"How did you find me?" I ask, feeling Ray move to stand beside me.

"Your mom said this is where you usually come when you're pissed." Chance crosses the gym until he's standing at the edge of the ring, tipping his head back to make eye contact with me. "And with the shit Tries-Too-Hard Barbie was spewing—"

I snort at the unexpectedly clever nickname coming from Chance.

"—even you happy, animals-help-you-dress-in-the-morning princesses would be pissed."

It's impossible to stop the giggles as I drop my head forward, the hasty ponytail I tossed my hair into falling with the movement and brushing my sweaty cheek.

A finger notches under my chin, lifting my face to see Chance, who's even closer. "There's that smile." He ghosts a thumb across my lower lip, sending a bolt of lust through me. "I missed it."

"I think I'm gonna head out," Ray says, pulling the sparring mitts from his hands and gathering them in front of him.

"You are?" A strange panic tinges my tone, but I couldn't tell you why.

"I think you'll be fine without me." Ray cuts a glance at Chance before bringing his gaze back to me, arching a brow with a knowing smirk.

Bubbles fill my belly.

"Thank you." I lay a hand on Ray's bicep, squeezing it to express all the things I don't need to bother voicing.

"Those promises work both ways, baby girl." Ray drops a kiss on the top of my head before moving past me. "Just don't go forgetting two and three because you were"—he lifts his chin at Chance—"*distracted*."

I groan. "You've been spending too much time with Becky."

Ray's grin is blinding. "Gemma." His attempt to scold falls flatter than a pancake.

"Yeah, yeah, yeah." I wave him off. "Dr. Sonya, naked time, rinse, and repeat when necessary."

Ray grabs his bag and heads out, leaving Chance and me as the only two people in the closed gym. Perks of your family owning the establishment.

The Eminem song currently playing from my "Pissed Off" playlist suddenly feels inordinately loud in Ray's absence.

What am I supposed to do?

What am I supposed to say?

*Ugh.* I still have too much adrenaline coursing through my system to deal with Chance's inevitable questions—and, let's be real, he's going to have questions. Who wouldn't after that little spectacle earlier? It's human nature to be curious.

*Shit.* Maybe letting Ray leave was a mistake, if for no other reason than because I still feel the urge to punch something.

"Are you okay?" Chance asks, resting his hands on the boxing ring by my feet.

"I'm fine."

"Now, why don't I believe you?"

"Because despite how often I've accused you of taking one too many hits to the head, you're not an idiot."

"You say the nicest things, Princess."

Damn, this new playfulness of his makes me weak in the knees.

Chance's dark eyes study me, dancing over my flushed cheeks, the corners of them crinkling at how my hot-pink zippered-front sports bra shoves my boobs toward my chin. His inspection continues downward, his tongue peeking out and wetting his lips as he stares at the dip of my waist and the exaggerated flare of my hips.

I don't typically work out in only a sports bra and a pair of leggings, but I wasn't necessarily planning on coming to the gym tonight, so I made do.

I gulp, closing my eyes.

What is he thinking? Why isn't he saying anything?

Then, without warning, Chance hoists himself into the boxing ring, and I turn to face him.

He looks damn good. In all the Cora drama, I didn't get to appreciate the suit he chose for the night. He always did know how to wear a suit—at least that's what all the bunnies say in their comments on the Blizzards' social media anytime there's a video of the guys arriving at the arena.

Chance moves in, crowding me against the ropes with an arm on either side of me.

*Grrr.* He even smells good, all sandalwood and ice and hot sexy *man.*

"I think"—Chance's warm breath blows across my ear as he leans in farther—"you still need to hit something."

"And what makes you say that?"

"Because listening to Cora's bullshit made me want to drop the metaphorical gloves." He chuckles, pulling back and taking my chin between his fingers. "Sadly, I was raised never to strike a lady."

"Why do I get the impression you've had that thought about me a time or two?"

"More like a thousand."

"Asshole." I laugh.

"Smartass." Chance's smirk is wicked and makes my panties wet. "Now, come on." He steps back, shrugging out of his suit jacket, tossing it to hang on the ropes.

"What are you doing?" I ask as he undoes his cuffs and loosens his tie.

"Getting ready to help you work out some of your frustration." He makes quick work of his buttons, my breath rushing from my lungs as his inked torso is revealed inch by inch.

"Is this your lame attempt at tempting me into sleeping with you again?"

"Let's get one thing straight, Princess." He's back in front of me in a single stride, his arm banded behind my back, his muscled chest pressed to mine. "What we did in that break room was fuck. Dirty, filthy, yes-I-promise-you-it-will-happen-again fucking."

"Is that what we're calling it?" I retort, refusing to let him get the last word despite the way my core clenches at his words.

"No." His grin is so full of arrogance I want to slap it right off his jaw. "I call it 'you and me, naked, my hands on your delectable ass, your pussy strangling my cock,' but that seemed like too much of a mouthful."

He releases me as quickly as he grabbed me, my feet stumbling, my tongue stuck to the roof of my mouth, and my brain completely incapable of processing his words.

"But right now..." He finishes removing his shirt, tossing it on top of his jacket where it's already hanging on the ropes. "You're gonna hit me until any thought of that cunt vanishes from your mind."

My mouth goes dry at the sight of him standing there in dress pants and bare-chested, every swirl and geometric shape decorating his olive skin on full display. I want to trace all of them with my tongue, from the grayscale maple leaf on the back of his right hand to the three-dimensional star on his left pec and every shaded inch in between.

"Are you crazy?" I take a step back, shaking myself out of my lustful stupor. "I'm not going to hit you. I'll end up breaking your nose or something."

"I don't doubt that for a second." Chance bends, scooping Ray's discarded mitts from the ground. "I watched you with Ray before you noticed I was here. Impressive, Princess."

His compliment is a salve to cracks I wasn't aware I had.

Chance moves to the center of the ring and smacks the mitts together. "Come on, baby. Do your worst."

I give him what he wants, throwing everything I have into my punches. I gotta give Chance credit; he's an excellent sparring partner.

"Tell me about this terrible Rusty nickname," he says, extending his left arm to move my target.

"Because Princess is so much more original?"

"Says the woman who calls the Canadian newbie on the team Canada and Rookie?" He lifts one of those damn eyebrows.

"Touché." I smirk and throw another combination of jabs and crosses.

"Spill." He points at me with a padded hand.

"Fine," I huff then explain how while being the youngest member of the Steele family came with a lot of perks, it also entailed a few pitfalls. "You've met my cousins," I say, stating the obvious. "It shouldn't come as much of a surprise to learn that Rocky and Vince honed their larger-than-life, confident personalities from a young age."

Chance nods, moving my targets in another combination. "An ego the size of Vince's does seem like it would take years to cultivate."

I giggle, pausing to catch my breath, then continue to tell the tale of how those personalities easily made my cousins the most popular people in school. But it was that popularity that put a target on my back years before I joined them at our high school.

"It wasn't like there was a rivalry or anything, but Cora and her minions didn't like how easily I folded into the popular set, garnering the invitations to parties and the like that they coveted."

"Guess my *Mean Girls* reference was more spot on than I thought."

I nod, appreciating the moment of levity before digging into the heavy.

"Nothing was different when Vin graduated because I still had Rocky, but that first year after she left—my junior year, that's when things started to change, and I became Rusty Steel, the less-than version of the family."

"And you believed that bullshit?" Chance growls.

"Not at first, but they were relentless. A whispered taunt here, a well-placed rumor there, and bit by bit, my day-to-day changed until finally, I wasn't even sure who my real friends were anymore."

I swallow the lump in my throat.

"Everything felt out of control, like my life was no longer my own. I tried retreating back into the comfort that was my bubble with my cousins, but they were in college. Rocky was on this accelerated genius brainiac degree program, and Vince had officially started to fight professionally."

"I find it hard to believe they wouldn't make time for you."

"They did," I agree. "But the time I was able to carve out with them wasn't enough to make up for the eight hours a day I spent feeling at the mercy of others."

I drop out of my fighting stance, rolling my shoulders back to ease the tension building between them. This is always the hardest part of my story to share, but it's strangely my favorite because I know the strength it took to overcome it.

"I needed a way to cope, to allow myself to feel a modicum of control in a world that had me spinning."

Chance tosses the mitts to the ground, giving up all pretense of our playful sparring as if he can sense the weight of my oncoming admission.

"How?"

The single word is all he speaks.

I glance away, unable to look him in the eye while answering. "I stopped eating."

"What?"

I inhale a steadying breath. "Anorexia became my coping mechanism. I found that restricting my intake of food provided me with the sense of security and structure I was desperately craving. That feeling of emptiness in my stomach was an accomplishment for making it through another day at school."

"Jesus, Gemma." Chance's eyes soften, not with pity—thank god—but with a need to just be there for me. "Are you…" He

till       g toward the ceiling as if searching for the right
 —         u okay now?"
 e,        covery if that's what you mean." Chance nods. "I'll
           -hundred-percent cured, but I'm vigilant where my
           concerned."

        m about how it was Ray who first noticed my disease,
        ecognized behaviors similar to those he witnessed his
        nibit with her eating disorder.

        pent part of the summer between my junior and senior in
        ient. It's where I discovered my passion for nutrition and
        ing and met my therapist, Dr. Sonya."

Recognition dawns on Chance's handsome face. "You
ntioned her name with Ray."

I nod.

"And what is naked time?"

A smile tugs at my lips. Naked time has become a running
joke with my friends. The guys—and Becky when she's feeling
feisty—have been known to hang outside my bedroom door and
shout creative affirmations to include in my ritual.

"Body dysmorphia was never a trigger in my disease, but to
help keep it from becoming one, Dr. Sonya suggested I start each
day standing in front of a full-length mirror—naked."

A moment of silence lapses between us, and I'm so caught up
in purging my greatest vulnerability to a man I used to think of
as my nemesis that I don't realize Chance is standing in front of
me until he's cupping my face between his large hands.

"And what is it you do while you stand there admiring this
sexy body of yours?" His thumbs glide over the apples of my
cheeks.

"Funny you should say that." He runs a knuckle along the
upward curve of my lips. "Because first I have to give myself at
least one compliment, then I recite something I have control over
and remind myself it's okay that there are things I can't control."

Chance glances at something over my shoulder, that
dangerous smirk of his tugging at the side of his mouth. "Now
that's something I can work with."

# CHAPTER 30

# Chance

R age unlike anything I've ever felt before builds inside me
like Lego blocks with every detail I learn about Gemma's
history with Cora. I've said my share of shitty things to Gemma
in my attempts to keep her at arm's length, but what Cora and
her bitch brigade did was vile.

"I am so fucking proud of you, Precious," I say, spinning her
around and pulling her in until her back is flush with my front.

"What?" Confusion mars her brow as she meets my gaze over
her shoulder.

"You not only overcame your demons, you bent them to your
will and fucking *thrived*."

"Chance," she murmurs, emotion strangling her tone.

"Can't you see how much of a badass you are?" I jerk my chin
at the wall of windows across from us, the one-way glass the
perfect reflective surface.

"You don't have to do this." Gemma looks away from our
reflection.

"Do what?"

"Handle me like I'm fragile because I used to be broken."

She's so far off base it's laughable. "You're anything but fragile, baby." I slide a hand around to cup her throat, stroking my
thumb along her silky skin. "If I've learned anything about you
in the year and a half I've known you, it's that you aren't made of
weak stuff like porcelain, where you can still see your cracks
even when put back together. No." I squeeze when she tries to

look away, keeping her eyes on me. "You're like bone, baby. A break only makes you grow back twice as strong."

Underneath my fingertips, I feel her swallow at my words. Still, she tries to look away from me, tries to hide herself from me.

This won't do.

With one step, I grab my necktie from where it hangs on the ropes, returning to my girl in a single stride. Gemma's gray eyes are wide, her long lashes brushing against her eyelids until I tug her back against me again, lifting her arms over her head and looping them behind my neck, binding them with my tie. With her bound to me, I take her chin between my fingers and move her gaze back to the windows.

"Now, about this naked time you talked about..." I drag my knuckles along her jaw and down her throat. "Why don't you show me how it works," I tease, slipping a finger into her sports bra and flicking the metal tab of her zipper pull.

"What makes you think I would share something so personal with you?"

Of course she's not going to make it easy on me. I wouldn't expect anything less.

I start to slide her zipper down then pause. "Stop me then."

Except no objection comes.

"Watch me, baby."

I pull again, another inch of tanned skin revealed as the zipper parts tooth by tooth until it's maxed out and hanging loosely from her shoulders. Pushing the hot-pink material aside, I cup her now bare breast, giving the nipple pebbling in the cool air a squeeze and rolling it between my thumb and forefinger. Gemma's eyes close, her head falling back on my shoulder, her lips parting with a gasp.

"Open your eyes."

I wait for her to comply, capturing her gaze in our reflection.

Dropping my mouth to her ear, I graze my teeth along her earlobe, flicking it with my tongue. "Let me know if I'm doing this right."

Releasing her breast, I place my hands on her rib cage, skimming them down her torso to the high-waisted band of her leggings. "These need to go."

Gemma sucks in a breath, her stomach hollowing out as I roll her tights over the enticing flare of her hips, not stopping until they are bunched around her thighs.

"Why am I not surprised these match?" I drag a finger over the scrap of lace covering her pussy, pushing the damp material between her lips. "But we're not going to need these," I say, ripping them from her body and discarding them carelessly onto the floor. "*Fuck.*" I nudge her feet wider, grabbing her waist with both hands. "Just look at you." I trail kisses over the curve of her shoulder and up the fluttering vein in her neck. "*Beautiful,*" I whisper into her skin.

The scent of Gemma's arousal hits me like a freight train.

Gathering my tie, I wrap it around my fist. "I kind of like having you on display like this." I give a tug, tightening her arms around my neck.

"Chance," Gemma moans, her body stretching along mine with an arch.

"I love when you say my name like that." It's all breathy and strained like she's fighting against her desire just to breathe.

I skim the backs of my fingers down her belly then cup her pussy.

"Fuck, Precious." I slip a finger along her wet slit and stroke her swollen clit. "Your pussy is so pretty." I hook two fingers inside her. "Just like the rest of you."

"Chance," she whispers, tightening around my finger.

I remove my hand, holding it up so she can watch as I rub her arousal between my digits. "Look at how wet you are."

Her hips roll as I plunge my fingers back inside her, a strangled whimper falling from her lips as I curl them against her G-spot.

"Stop closing your eyes, baby," I demand, letting go of my tie and threading my arm between her breasts. "How are you supposed to see how perfect you are with your eyes closed?"

Gemma's breaths come in pants. Her eyes are fixed on our reflection, a lusty glaze filling them as she takes in the easy way I've taken complete control of her body.

Damn, we are a sight.

My dick hardens to the point of pain at her flushed skin, her hard nipples, her tit overflowing the palm clutching it in a punishing grip, her plump thighs shiny from my hand working her sex.

"Just look at you, writhing in my arms, dripping down your legs…it's perfection."

Her head moves against my shoulder, her ponytail a wild mess. "You're torturing me, Chance." She sucks in a breath. "*Please.*"

I grind my erection into the swell of her ass where it's cradled against me and drag my thumb up the seam of her pussy to her clit, circling it lightly as I watch her in the windows. Her eyes close, and she moans, back bowing as she grinds down on my fingers.

"Please, what?" I repeat, rolling her nipple with my palm.

A breathy laugh escapes her lips. "I don't know."

"I think you do." I still my movements, my lips grazing her skin, my voice a rough whisper. "Tell me."

"Make me come," she begs.

"Oh, I'll make you come." I pump my fingers into her then slow to a stop that has her whimpering my name. "But you have to watch." I release her tit and cup her throat. "Watch me make you come apart. Watch how beautiful you are when you do."

Her breaths are ragged, her skin flushing a deep red, but her eyes remain pinched closed.

This won't do.

I slap her pussy, her eyes flying wide.

"That's better." I squeeze her throat, keeping her gaze captive. "Look at how wet you are." I drag my knuckles over one of her thighs. "You're dripping down your thighs, baby."

"Chance. Please, please, *please*," Gemma begs, her voice rising with desperation.

Done toying with her, I slam my fingers back inside her cunt, thrusting them in and out until Gemma screams, her pleasure echoing off the two-story ceiling of the gym.

"That's it, baby," I coo, holding her through her orgasm. "So gorgeous." Her body goes limp as I remove my fingers, a shuddering gasp spilling free as she watches me slip them into my mouth and suck, tasting her for the first time. "I could watch you come all day long and never get bored."

Unknotting my tie, I free her arms, keeping her body upright with an arm banded around her middle and removing the boxing gloves from her hands with the other.

"I'll never look at naked time the same way again." Gemma giggles.

"We're not done yet, baby." I lift her off her feet and move to the ropes, bending her over them with a hand between her shoulder blades.

Crouching behind Gemma, I work her leggings the rest of the way down her legs, removing her sneakers and tossing them and the leggings to join her previously discarded thong. Kneading up her legs, I spread them wider, making sure to pay special attention to her thick thighs, imagining how good it will feel when I finally have them clamping around my head like a vise.

Not tonight though.

Tonight is all about Gemma watching as I take her, as her body yields to mine, as I own her.

"Christ, you're breathtaking." I grip the backs of her thighs, cupping under the curve of her ass, pushing and lifting it, letting it fall with a jiggle. "Did you know your ass is perfect?" I grab each cheek, pulling them apart until I can see her pretty pink pussy, and I bury my face into it from behind.

"Oh my god." Gemma jerks against the ropes, a whimper of surprise spilling into the room.

"Fuck. I don't care if you never cook for me as long as you keep letting me taste this pussy."

"Please," she moans, wiggling her ass against my mouth.

"Stay still, baby." I smack her ass, pushing my tongue inside her, groaning at the musky sweetness of her inner walls. Thrusting deeper, I hold her hips still, not allowing her to push back against my face.

"Chance," she pleads, and I hear her hands searching for purchase on the ropes to anchor herself against my onslaught.

"Come on my tongue," I demand.

"Yes, please, just…" Then she moans an incoherent string of syllables.

"Say it, baby." I pinch her clit. "Get louder, Gemma. I want to hear you."

"Yes, fuck." She arches her back, pressing her ass into my face and grinding her pussy against my mouth. "I need…I need a minute," she says, voice hoarse when I pull away to stand.

"I don't think so." I slap her ass again, already digging into my pocket for my wallet.

She whimpers, and it's music to my ears.

Freeing my cock, I roll a condom on and glance at Gemma in the windows, nearly coming undone: head hanging low, ponytail obscuring part of her face, hands gripping the ropes as if terrified of letting go, and most importantly, all mine.

Bending my knees, I take my cock in hand, circling it around her entrance. With my free hand, I grab her ponytail, wrapping it around my fist, and lift her face to our reflection. Gemma's back arches, pushing her tits out and inadvertently lining my dick up perfectly with her entrance. The need to claim her pummels into me with a ferocity unlike anything I've ever felt before.

Leaning forward, I kiss the back of her neck, inhaling the intoxicating mixture of our combined scents, and whisper, "How hard do you want it, baby?"

"Do your worst, Rookie."

I still at her taunt, a surge of possessiveness rolling through me, every instinct readying to rise to the challenge.

"When you can't walk tomorrow, just remember you asked for it." I grip her hip, driving into her with a single thrust.

"Ah!" Gemma shouts, her pussy clutching my dick in a molten embrace.

I pull out, pushing back in as a growl tears out of my throat. "So tight."

I don't go easy, pounding into her with rough, skin-slapping pumps of my hips. Her knuckles turn white as she clutches at the ropes, her tits bouncing with every violent thrust. I slam into her again and again, reveling in the sounds of her pleasure.

"Ch-Chance." Gemma's body shivers as I yank her head back by her ponytail.

"I'm not done with you yet," I tell her, figuring out the exact moment to pull out and plunge back in, hitting a spot deep inside her that has her moaning louder than before.

"Oh god, oh god, oh god." She's chanting my name and rocking back into me with every stroke.

"Take it, baby," I growl. "Take my cock like your cunt was made for it."

"Yes," she squeals.

"There you go." I squeeze her ass and smack it. "Ride my dick."

"Chance."

I love that she says my name, love how it leaves zero doubt about her knowing precisely who owns her.

Keeping my hold on her hair, I bury my face in the curve of her neck, leaning over her and blanketing her body with mine. "Tell me what I want to hear."

"Wh-what?"

I take hold of her throat, squeezing. "You know what I want to hear. Say it, Precious. Say you're mine."

"I'm yours," she whimpers, riding the edge of the orgasm I'm withholding.

"Again."

"I'm yours."

"Louder." I rut into her.

"I'm yours. Fuck, Chance, I'm yours, I'm yours, I'm yours."

"That's right, baby."

As I pump into her frenetically, she comes apart in my arms with a guttural scream, the sound nearly swallowed by the roaring in my ears. Face buried in her neck, sweat dripping from my forehead, my balls slapping against her with every thrust, my teeth clench, and I let out a roar, following her over the edge.

I'm mesmerized by the look of utter ecstasy on her face. I can't get enough of it.

I did that.

I want to do it again.

I want her like this every day.

The question is, will she have me?

# CHAPTER 31

*Gemma*

T he buzzing of my phone wakes me before I'm ready, and I slap an annoyed hand around my nightstand, looking for the offending object. When I finally find it, an unexpected warmth fills my chest at the message waiting for me on the screen.

> DICKHEAD DADDY: Morning, beautiful.

> ME: Ugh, why did you have to be all sweet and shit. Now I can't even be mad at you for waking me up.

> DICKHEAD DADDY: You were still asleep? Don't you have athletes to nourish? Isn't breakfast the most important meal of the day?

> ME: It's my day off.

And a well-deserved one. It feels like I've been going nonstop since the auction back in November.

> DICKHEAD DADDY: Okay, I'll let you get back to sleep and dreaming about me.

> ME: You sound awfully sure of yourself, Rookie.

> DICKHEAD DADDY: Puh-lease. Don't play,
> Precious. My dick is practically bruised from
> how your cunt strangled it last night.

Oh-kay then. That's one way to wake a person up.

> ME: Why are you texting me? Don't you have a
> hockey game you should be getting ready for?

My text is nothing more than a lousy deflection. I know he has a game. It's a big one. It's the first time the Blizzards are playing Vegas, Coach Watson's old team.

> DICKHEAD DADDY: You and I both know my
> game isn't until tonight.

I check the time.

> ME: What about morning skate?

> DICKHEAD DADDY: I still have a few minutes
> before I have to be on the ice. I just wanted to
> check and see how my girl is doing. Your pussy
> did take quite a pounding last night.

I shift, the soreness between my legs flaring as if to prove his point.

> ME: God, you have to be the cockiest bastard I
> know.

> DICKHEAD DADDY: It's that extra quarter inch,
> baby. It makes all the difference. *wink emoji*

Ugh. I hate it when he's playful. Defending my heart against him when he's a dickhead? Easy-peasy. But like this? It just feels like I'm setting myself up for heartbreak.

DICKHEAD DADDY: Just so you know, I'm available to video chat should you need assistance with naked time while I'm on the road this week.

ME: I think you should be more concerned with your spiraling captain than my ability to handle something I've been doing just fine all by myself for years.

Ryan's ejection from last night's game for fighting has more than a few of us concerned, even when some of us—namely Jordan and Maddey—think he deserves a swift kick in the ass.

DICKHEAD DADDY: That may be true, but think of how much more fun it was when I lent a hand.

DICKHEAD DADDY: Umm, excuse me, Princess. Why the fuck are you in Baltimore??

ME: **Gemma's phone does not accept messages written in Who the fuck do you think you're talking to like that? tones**

Setting my phone on the counter, I glare at Chance's text, again thinking, *Who the fuck does he think he's talking to like that?*

The next time my phone buzzes, it's a FaceTime request instead of a text. I consider not answering for a second, but who am I kidding? We know I'm going to. There's no denying I want to talk to him despite his dickhead tone.

"I'm sorry." Chance rushes to get the apology out as soon as our call connects.

I stare at his handsome face filling the screen. Worry fills his dark eyes, and his hair looks like he spent the time between receiving my text message and me answering his call tugging at it.

"I didn't mean to snap at you like that." He thunks his head on the headboard he's propped against.

I press my lips together. "Then why did you?"

I can see him swallow while he thinks, the bobbing of his Adam's apple far sexier than it should be.

"Fuck, I don't know." He rakes his hand through his hair, confirming my earlier assumption. "It's been a week since I've seen you."

"And?" I shrug. "We've gone longer than that without seeing each other before." I hold up a finger when his mouth opens with a retort. "And before you try saying it's different because we slept together, let me remind you I didn't see you for over a month after the way you treated me the first time we did it."

"And that month almost drove me out of my motherfucking mind, Gemma," Chance growls, surging off the bed.

The video feed goes wonky as he stalks to the window of his hotel room, shoving the drapes open and resting his forehead on the glass, giving me the perfect view of his pained profile and the Philadelphia skyline.

"It's a goddamn miracle it didn't end up costing me my career," he says, more to the window than to me.

There's a sense of pained panic in his voice that has me softening my own when I ask, "What do you mean?"

Chance straightens, and now is not the time to notice how his muscles move beneath the cotton of his T-shirt, and it most certainly isn't the time to be considering asking him to take it off.

Slowly, Chance brings the phone back around, lifting his gaze, his eyes searching out mine.

"This is a contract year for me, Gem. I can't afford to play like shit."

My gut clenches as a startling realization hits me: Chance could end up playing anywhere next year.

What would that mean for us?

Not that there's even an *us* to worry about. But…still.

"But you've been playing great."

I would know. I haven't missed a game. Even when I wished I had a voodoo doll I could stab in the penis to curse him with limp-dick-itis for calling me a mistake, I still watched the games.

I tried to tell myself it was because I've been a Blizzards fan all my life. But…yeah…I can tell you don't believe that. Don't worry, Pebbles and Bamm-Bamm didn't either.

"I know, but I spent that entire month riding a razor's edge, one wrong word, one bad call, one…*anything* away from snapping and losing it all."

Chance gives me a smile that isn't actually a smile, but I don't know how else to describe it.

"My entire life has been working toward one goal—playing in the NHL. And yes, I know I've been doing that for three years, but that dream has shifted to playing for the Blizzards. *Continuing* to play for them—that's the only thing that matters."

Ouch. Talk about making a girl feel like she was punched in the tit.

"Wow, that sounds stressful," I say, full of sarcasm.

Chance's eyes blaze with a fiery intensity. "You want to know what's stressful?" His voice is full of accusations. "What's stressful is being stuck on the road with the team I'm trying to prove myself to, while the girl whose selfie of herself in sexy-as-fuck gray lingerie has haunted me my entire tenure with them is at the home of an asshole who wants to fuck her as badly as I do."

My mouth opens and closes three different times, and still, I'm at a loss for words. My head is a muddled mess.

The things he said…they don't make any sense. This is his second *season* with the Blizzards. I accidentally texted him *this* past November, which was two months ago, not over a year.

"Wow. I don't even know what to address first." I glance around Ben's kitchen, anger bubbling in my belly as I take in the carnage of the meal prep I've done for him. "Last I checked, *you* were the one who got into a pissing match with Ben because *you* were *jealous*."

"He asked you on a date, Gemma," Chance spits.

"So?" I narrow my eyes, shooting daggers at him.

"He *clearly* wanted to fuck you." Chance swings a frustrated arm out wide.

"Yeah, *wanted*—as in past tense."

Chance scoffs, ratcheting up my blood pressure another few points.

"And I can say that with certainty because Ben is also the same guy who, when we were on said date and he realized I was inexplicably stuck on your dickheaded self, put an end to the '*romantic*'"—I use my free hand to make air quotes around the word—"portion of our date."

Chance pulls up short. "He did?"

I roll my eyes. "Did you *really* think he took me to Rookies to woo me?"

Chance flops into the armchair in front of the window, the sunlight creating a halo not at all befitting his devilish nature.

"Honestly?" He leans forward, resting his elbows on his knees, steadying his phone in front of him.

I nod.

"I didn't even think about the *where* of where you were. You sent me that picture, and the only thing I could see was you on that date with someone who wasn't me, and I *needed* to put a stop to it."

I know...I *know* I should not be flattered by that statement, *especially* when he's being a total ass, but come. On. How can I not?

Don't be a Judgy Judy, mmkay?

"Speaking of that picture." I find the only clear space on Ben's gorgeous marble countertop and mirror Chance's position, leaning on my elbows. "In your little temper tantrum earlier—"

"I'm a grown-ass man—I don't have temper tantrums."

"Potato, vodka." I make a talking mouth with my hand. "Anyway...you said you've been haunted by my selfie the *entire* time you've been with the Blizzards. Explain how that's possible."

# CHAPTER 32

## *Chance*

I t's official: my dogs have spent far too much time with Gemma Steele.

Those two beasts have spent the last hour judging me like I've never been judged before. For a solid fifteen minutes, Bamm-Bamm dogged my every step, causing me to trip over his hulking frame at least a dozen times while I paced and straightened up things that did *not* need straightening.

Incessant squeaking pulls my attention back to Pebbles going to town on one of the giant googly-eyed plushies Gemma bought her and her brother. My pooch pauses her chomping, one of her furry eyebrows going up in a *You are so screwed* lift.

"Not helping, Pebs," I grumble and go back to pacing.

As much as I hate to admit it, my pup is right. There is no way Gemma is going to let this go.

I am such a dumbass.

I feel like my stupidity bears repeating.

I.

Am.

Such.

A.

Dumbass.

I mean, only a dumbass would casually out themselves for something they could have realistically gotten away with never revealing. But...*no*, I had to let it slip that I had seen *that* set of Gemma's lingerie *long* before she ever sent me a picture.

Fuck me, I'm a moron.

At least I'm not delusional on top of moronic, thinking she would let a nugget of information like that go. The reprieve I've had while everyone came together to help Amara and Maverick is officially over. It's time to face the music—and in front of an audience, no less, one made up of multiple Covenettes.

I'm fucking screwed.

My phone rings, startling me out of my thoughts.

"What?" I snap when I answer.

"Whoa, hey, calm down, buddy," Jake says without missing a beat. "I'm only calling to check in, make sure you're holding up alright given what's headed your way."

"Oh yeah, I'm great. Just peachy," I reply, deadpan.

I glance at my pups again. Pebbles's doggy cheek is scrunched around her plushy, her nose wrinkled up as she sniffs the air. Bamm-Bamm couldn't be more bored with me, having given up following me around half an hour ago, his face resting atop his front paws while he sleeps.

"Then why do you sound like you're about to pop a blood vessel? *Hmm?*"

It's times like this I wish I could hate Jake Donovan, but sadly, the bastard is too damn likable. Plus, he's one of the driving forces behind me finding the family I've never really had before.

"Because I am. This is so fucked."

"I love how scared you guys are of my wife." Jake's booming laugh has me pulling the phone away from my ear.

"She's not the one who has me worried," I mutter.

"Ooo." Jake's interest turns palpable. "I thought you and Gem were…wait, what *has* been going on with you and Gem?"

"Don't worry about it."

Pebbles lets out a disgruntled snort when I collapse onto the couch with her and scrub a hand over my face.

"That bad?" Jake's tone is full of humor, which I'm in no mood to appreciate.

"Why are you bugging me, anyway? Don't you have a brother-in-law in crisis? Shouldn't you be calling him?"

"Ahhh, deflection. Fine, fine." Relief has the knots in my shoulders loosening. "I'll just wait for Jordan to get home later. She'll fill me in."

I bark out a humorless laugh. I should have known that was too easy.

And when the doorbell rings less than a minute later, there's only one thought on my mind, one most appropriate given tonight I collect my auction winnings: I'm about to jump out of the frying pan and into the fire.

"I have a question," I ask, interrupting the trio of beautiful women gabbing on the other side of the counter. "When do we actually get to the part of tonight I paid a shit ton of money for?"

Jordan, Skye, and Gemma have been at my house for over an hour. They've overtaken my kitchen in that time but haven't let me do anything except "sit there and look pretty." That was literally the directive I was given by Skye.

A massive part of me bristled at being told what to do, but then Gemma sent me a sly wink when the others weren't looking, and suddenly sitting still while they filmed all kinds of social media content didn't seem so bad.

"*Some*body sounds impatient," Skye teases, impervious to my glower.

I shift my gaze back to where it wants to be—on Gemma.

Damn, she looks good. She's this perfect combination of sexy and cute. Sexy with her sheer black blouse showing off the lacy, cross-strapped bralette underneath and skinny jeans that I noticed when she arrived, hugging her ass in spectacular fashion, and cute with a *Don't mess with chefs, we get paid to chop things into little pieces* apron tied around her waist.

Gemma notices my assessment, her eyes capturing mine—again—and when she bites the corner of her lower lip, it takes a Herculean effort to remain on my barstool instead of leaping over the counter and taking her mouth with mine.

It's been ten days since I've tasted her. I'm not sure how much longer I'm going to last without rectifying that.

"Leave him alone, Skye," Jordan chides, moving to my side of the counter to check the ring light setup. "You know he's Gem's only client who doesn't get to eat her cooking."

"That's because my friends are my only clients," Gemma says, but it strangely feels more like self-doubt than a dig at me.

It's on the tip of my tongue to ask why she was cooking at Ben's if her friends are her only clients, but I think I put my foot in my mouth on that one enough the other day when she was at his house.

"That's right." Skye *Risky Business* slides over to where Bamm-Bamm is sprawled out in a sunny spot by the sliding glass doors. "Gemmy-Gem only cooks for you babies and not your dickhead daddy, right?" She lifts Bamm's massive head, scratching around both his ears, sending him into doggy bliss while cooing in an exaggerated baby voice.

With the other two finally distracted from my girl, I round the island, moving in behind Gemma, planting a hand next to her hip and breathing in that lemony scent I've grown addicted to. She stiffens when my chest brushes against her, and I can't stop my lips from twitching at the instant proof that I affect her as much as she affects me.

"I don't know." I bend, bringing my mouth to her ear. "You may not let me eat your cooking, but you let me eat your pussy."

She sucks in a breath, her fingers curling against the countertop. She turns, and I'm treated to a profile of her perky breasts. She's so close all I would need to do is shift slightly, and I could wrap my arm around her waist, slide my hand right under her shirt, and palm her soft flesh.

"Chance," she murmurs, and heat rushes through me at the sound of my name falling from her lips in that same pleading tone she used when I withheld her orgasm.

My cock throbs, pressing against the zipper of my jeans at the memory. The situation only grows worse when Gemma oscillates her hips, dragging the swell of her ass against my eager organ.

"Alright." Jordan claps her hands, interrupting the game of sexual chicken Gemma and I are playing. "Enough teasing the man."

I drop my head to hide my laugh. Jordan has no idea how right she is.

"You mean it's time for me to finally let him"—Gemma's eyelashes flutter as she runs her gaze over me in a quick pass—"ea*t*?"

Oh, it's on.

The second Jordan and Skye are out of here, I'm throwing Gemma on the counter and devouring her pussy.

"Why do I always feel like I'm watching your foreplay when you two are together?" Skye *V*'s her fingers at Gemma and me as she joins Jordan holding an iPad.

"You mean kinda like how the rest of us feel when you and Tucker are together?" Gemma tosses back, causing Skye's cheeks to burn a bright pink.

The deflection also has the added benefit of getting us back on track. The sooner we get through this cooking lesson I couldn't care less about anymore, the sooner I get Gemma alone and under me.

Gemma clears her throat and steps away from my crowding stance. "You think you can handle this, Rookie?" she asks, picking up a chef's knife identical to hers and holding it out to me, handle side first.

"I can handle anything you throw at me, Princess," I say, taking the knife from her.

"Just don't cut off a finger, okay? I don't need Coach Watson firing me for landing one of his players on the injured list because I let him play with sharp objects."

Jordan and Skye shamelessly giggle but thankfully keep any colorful commentary to themselves.

"Okay, first things first." Gemma angles her body to face me more directly. "On a scale from 'can't boil water without burning it' to 'can cook an entire Thanksgiving meal by yourself,' how adept are you in the kitchen?"

"I'd say I'm solidly in the middle."

A loose tendril of hair falls from her messy bun, and I reach out, tucking it behind her ear, reveling in the way her eyes flutter closed at my touch.

She swallows thickly then says, "Good."

"Good?" I press my lips together to restrain a grin. "More like necessary. Otherwise, I'd have starved since my dogs are the only Jensons you will cook for."

Gemma lifts her chin defiantly. "You know the whole *You catch more flies with honey* saying?"

I nod. "Ryan has spoken on it before."

"Well, the same can be said about chefs. Being a dick to one means you can feed yourself by eating a bag of them, mmkay?"

Gemma's sass and how she's never once cowered away from me—in fact, she's always given it back twice as hard—have always been my favorite things about her.

"Is it wrong that I'm having a proud mama bear moment?" Skye says with feigned emotion choking her words.

Jordan tilts her head, leaning it against Skye's shoulder. "They just grow up so fast."

Gemma giggles, shaking a resigned head while muttering under her breath. "I hate being the baby of the group."

"Shut up. You love us," Jordan and Skye say in unison.

"Alright. Let's do this." Gemma takes control, having me wash my hands while pointing out the various ingredients she has set out in clusters around the island countertop.

"Wait." I hold up a hand as she pulls out two packs of ground venison she had stored in my fridge. "Are you teaching me how to make your mom's famous chili?"

A teasing grin plays on Gemma's kissable lips. "It was her suggestion."

I drop an arm around her shoulders, tucking her against me. "I guess hating me isn't genetic, huh, Princess?"

"Hush, you." She hip-checks me and hands me a tomato to dice.

We work together side by side, and all the while, I'm hyper-aware of her, her heat soaking into me, her scent mingling with mine. Every time she leans toward me, her soft tits brush my arm. She's so close it's a wonder I'm able to slice any vegetables without doing exactly what she warned me about and slicing off a finger or two.

Gemma occasionally adjusts my hold on the vegetables or the angle of my knife. At first, I tease her for correcting me for the sake of correcting me, but even I can't deny that any change she makes yields better outcomes.

Out of the corner of my eye, I see Jordan and Skye watching us with poorly disguised amusement. I know Ryan has had his own shit to deal with recently and seeing as I haven't gotten the third degree from the busybodies I call teammates, I'm going to assume I haven't been a topic in a Coven Conversation.

Chaos ensues when we start to brown the venison and my two beasts barrel into the kitchen. Gemma handles it all in stride, dropping onto her knees—giving me all kinds of *ideas*—wrapping an arm around each of them and putting her body between them like a Gemma sandwich.

After loving them up properly, she rises to stand and crosses her arms.

"Listen." Immediately, my two obedience school valedictorians sit, giving Gemma all their attention. "I know this *smells* like it's for you"—Gemma's messy bun lists to the side as she shakes her head—"but it's not."

Pebbles and Bamm-Bamm howl.

"I know, I know." Gemma holds up placating hands. "Weird, right? But don't worry, babies, I have treats for you, but you have to wait until your daddy and I are done."

Is it weird that I'm popping a boner watching her bond with my fur babies?

My dogs whine pitifully, but Gemma holds her ground, pointing toward the living room until they both settle in with their googly-eyed plushies. With the furry distractions taken care of, Gemma returns to the task at hand, passing me a package of ground venison to add to the saucepan heating on the stove. Gemma's passion for cooking is adorable, and I find myself getting lost in her stories about how she started personal cheffing.

"Have you ever thought about doing it for more than just your friends?" I ask, moving the venison around in the pan.

"You mean adding grumpopotamuses to my roster?" Gemma nudges me with an elbow.

I tap the tip of her nose with the spatula. "Among others."

"She has the plans." Jordan sends Gemma a pointed look from across the counter. "She just needs to finally pull the trigger."

"We are *not* talking about that right now," Gemma declares.

"I don't know." Skye drums her fingers on the counter. "I think if you were waiting for a sign, the auction was it. You had the people fighting for your services."

"Oh yeah. A best friend, a charming football player, and a jealous dickhead—I'm *really* in demand."

"Why does he get called charming, but I'm still considered a dickhead?" I ask.

"Just calling it like I see it, Canada." Gemma shrugs.

"You're a brat."

"I know," Gemma says, an obvious flare of heat entering her gaze.

When the meat is finished browning and the designated spices are added, we combine all the ingredients into a Crock-Pot to complete the final step. Jordan and Skye blessedly take their leave while Gemma and I are straightening up the disaster zone that is my kitchen.

"I missed you," I mumble into Gemma's ear, coming up behind her at the sink.

"Did you?"

"Yup." I nod, undoing the ties on her apron and sliding my hands up her waist, under her blouse, and right up to her breasts.

Gemma's breath hitches as I squeeze each of her tits through her bra, loving the way her skin feels beneath my fingers.

"And why is that?" she asks through clenched teeth when I pluck at her nipples through the fabric.

"Because I can't do this"—I roll her nipples between my fingers—"over FaceTime." I pull her against me, letting her feel just how hard I am for her.

Her back arches, pushing her tits into my hands and her ass into my groin as she grinds herself against me with a strangled moan.

"I knew you missed me too."

Gemma's head drops to my shoulder as my fingers make quick work of her buttons, my hands curling over the curves of her shoulders, slipping her blouse down her arms.

I curse when I get my first unobstructed view of her bra. "This one is sexy as hell." I trace the straps riding the swells of her cleavage with my thumbs. "It might even replace the gray one as my favorite."

Gemma stiffens in my arms, and all I can think is, *Oh shit.*

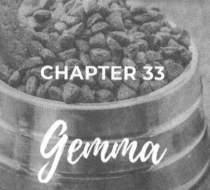

# CHAPTER 33

# *Gemma*

The craziness of the last few days made it easy to forget that Chance dropped this weird sorta bomb nugget of information and then claimed he needed to leave to catch the team bus to the arena. I say claimed because I certainly didn't hear the knock Chance magically seemed to hear two seconds after I asked for time line clarification.

This man is a master of distraction, saying sweet words while trying to use my own body against me.

No more. I want answers.

Knocking his hands off my boobs, I spin around and face him. I can't think straight when he's touching me, but looking into his handsome face, especially when he's looking at me with *that* look, is just as dangerous. It's the only excuse I have for why he's able to take my face between his hands and kiss me.

Chance's tongue is warm and wet, his fingers digging into my jaw, coaxing my mouth open to taste me, to do everything to me. I'm not sure how long we stay like that. The only thing my brain is capable of processing is the warmth of his hands, the feel of his skin caressing mine, the minty taste on his tongue dueling with mine.

I've missed this. It's crazy to have missed it since I'm not actually sure what *it* is, but I can't seem to stop myself.

When Chance finally does pull back, it's to rest his forehead against mine, his breathing just as ragged as mine, his broad chest brushing my nipples, which are begging for his attention with every inhalation.

"Hi," he says, the side of his mouth hitching into that lethal smirk.

"Hi," I respond, steadying myself by grasping his forearms, my head swimming with all things Chance Jenson. "Wait." I shake my head. "No." I place my hands on his chest and shove him back two much-needed-for-my-ability-to-think-straight steps.

"Are you playing hard to get, Precious?" He takes a step closer, but I throw my hands up to stop his approach. "You know what happens when I catch you."

My entire body goes molten.

*Gah! No, no, no, no.*

Answers. I want answers.

"Stop trying to distract me."

"I have no idea what you're talking about." The divot forming in his cheek from his biting it proves that's anything but true.

"Stop. Stalling." I fold my arms over my traitorously hard nipples and square my shoulders, trying to make it clear that under no uncertain terms will I be distracted again.

"Who says I was—"

"No." I brace my arms behind me, my hands curling over the edge of the sink. "We have a time line issue, you and I, and I want answers."

"Baby..."

"Don't," I warn.

He raises an eyebrow and his mouth opens, but he stops himself before whatever he was going to say comes out. "Fine," he says, throwing his hands up in surrender. "But keep in mind it was an accident."

I dig my fingers into the stainless steel of the sink, the luke-warm water soaking my knuckles. "*What* was an accident?"

Chance grips the back of his neck, and I don't think I've ever seen him this insecure. "You know your predate ritual that broke my brain?"

I try to look mad, but a smile threatens to break free. I still can't believe I told him my mistext to his phone is part of one of my rituals. Though I did tell him about naked time, so I guess I shouldn't be so shocked.

"Well…that wasn't the first time I saw one of those texts."

"What?" My mind spins. "When?"

He doesn't say anything, sparking the fuse on my temper.

"When, Chance."

He swallows, licking his lips. "The day I moved in with Ryan."

I blink. Then blink again.

That was…

That was a year and a half ago…before he even met me.

Is that why he was a dick to me the first time we met?

"How? How, Chance?"

Seriously, I can't think of how he could have seen one.

"Jordan's phone was on the counter when you sent your text to the girls."

"And you looked because…" I make a rolling motion with my hand.

"I don't know." He stabs a hand into his hair, causing it to stick out wildly. "The screen lit up, and my eyes were instinctively drawn to it."

I try to make sense of what he's saying, but it just doesn't add up.

"It was an accident, Gemma. I swear. I didn't mean to look, but once I did, I couldn't tear myself away from you."

I don't know why, but that comforts me. I mean, it doesn't excuse his behavior, but it does show it wasn't intentional, and a part of me can't help but feel complimented by it.

"Precious."

God. That nickname.

Why couldn't he call me Princess? I know how to handle when he calls me that, but Precious? It disarms me, especially when he says it in that soft voice I've only ever heard him use with me.

I swallow, trying to work through the onslaught of emotions that have my stomach churning. I turn my head to avoid the kiss I see coming, but his fingers are already at the nape of my neck, his fingertips branding my skin, his every movement leading mine to follow his directives. His fingers slide into my hair as he whispers my name, my breath catching as they slip down to my neck.

My back arches and I lean back farther, my fingertips brushing against the squishy material of the sponge I used to wash the dishes. His tongue licks my lips, and that's when I snap.

This motherfrankfurter is trying to dickmatize me into forgetting there's still so much more he needs to apologize for.

Wrapping my fingers around the sponge, I lift it from the sink and wring it out over Chance's head, soaking him in soapy water.

"The fuck?" he sputters, water dripping off his hairline, drenching the front of his T-shirt, the cotton clinging to his abs.

"What? You needed to cool off." I hold the sponge out like I'm keeping it out of reach, but he has way too big of a height advantage on me for that to ever be true.

Chance's obsidian eyes track from the water soaking his shirt to the electric-blue rectangle squished in my grip, realization of what I did dawning.

"Cool off?" He grins at me, shaking the water droplets from his head.

I roll my eyes, the smirk on his face pissing me off. "Yeah, you know, like when Bamm-Bamm starts looking at the lounge chair outside in that special kind of way, and we have to spray him with the hose?"

"But you like what happens when I start looking at you that way." Chance slides a hand over my hip, dipping his fingers into the band of my jeans.

"I do," I concede because there's no denying it.

"Then maybe you need to cool off too." He reaches behind me, and I understand his plan a split second before he can execute it.

I yelp, ducking under his arm and taking off down the hall while he gives chase with a glassful of soapy sink water. Never ones to miss out on fun, Pebbles and Bamm-Bamm immediately join in, adding a much-appreciated buffer between their dad and me when I end up dead-ending in Chance's bedroom.

"I got you now, Princess."

"No, you don't." I'm all bluster as I use Pebbles as a shield.

Chance leans against the doorjamb, letting the glass dangle

from his fingers in a casual taunt, his dark gaze studying me with that cocky confidence.

I cut a glance at the open door to his en suite, mentally calculating the distance and if I can make it before Chance catches me.

Of course, he notices this, bringing his fingers to his mouth and bleating out a whistle. "Dogs, out," he commands, and the obedient babies trot out of the room, completely unaware they are leaving me defenseless against their daddy when he closes the door behind them.

With my escape routes disappearing, I jump onto the bed, scrambling across the mattress, only to have a hand snag my ankle and trip me down to the memory foam, yanking me until my legs hang off the edge.

Chance bends a knee onto the mattress, planting his free hand next to the side of my head, pinning me in place while dancing the glass over me, letting the water tip over the edge and onto my skin with each waving pass he makes.

"Let me go." I try to squirm away with no luck.

"What's wrong, baby?" Chance teases, spilling a line of water from my throat to my belly button.

"You're getting the bed all wet." I screech when a cold droplet slides into my armpit.

Chance tosses the cup behind him, the plastic pinging off the wall with a clatter.

"Not as wet as you're about to make it." He takes my mouth in a hot and demanding kiss, and I give myself over to it, to him.

His fingers dig into my jaw, holding my mouth open for his tongue to tangle with mine. My hands find their way up into his hair, making a mockery of my earlier protest as I clutch at the wet strands.

Chance shifts his weight back, towering over me on the bed. It's both thrilling and overwhelming at the same time. He reaches behind his back, removing his shirt in that ridiculously hot one-handed way guys seem to master at the same time we women learn the remove-our-bra-under-the-shirt thing.

His skin is still damp from earlier, but it looks darker now, almost bronzed in a way that makes my insides melt with a single glance.

"Like what you see, baby?" he asks when my gaze lingers a little too long on the cut of muscle tapering into his Adonis belt. "You do," he answers for me. "And you hate it, don't you?"

I run my tongue over my teeth in an effort to hide a smile, but his smug grin tells me I'm not as successful as I would like. That seems to be all the answer he needs, my core tightening when his fingers work the button on my jeans, the slow drag of the zipper the only sound in the room, save the harshness of our breathing. My jeans are peeled from my skin, and I can feel the heat radiating off Chance's body, suddenly aware of every inch of my skin that's not covered by clothing.

I want this so bad.

So, so bad.

I want him over me, and in me, and under me, and all around me.

I need him to take me.

We still have so much left to discuss, but right now, I need him to make me forget everything my brain is trying to throw at me.

Chance brackets my rib cage, sliding his thumbs underneath my bralette while lifting my torso off the mattress with his other digits, the easy display of strength so damn hot as he tosses my bra to the side. He keeps me upright with a palm splayed between my shoulder blades then unwinds my scrunchie from my hair, freeing my messy bun.

The kiss he gives me is as quick as it is fierce, leaving me breathless and desperate for more as he lays me down and removes my panties.

"Fuck, you're so goddamn beautiful." The sheer reverence in his voice brings an embarrassing heat to the backs of my eyes.

"I want you," I whisper, not caring if my desperation is showing.

I'm done fighting.

I need this.

I need him.

Desperate to touch, I reach for him, my hands moving up his chest as his slide up my legs, hitching them around his waist. He growls, his eyes darkening with lust, not once looking away from my face as he grips my nape.

I hold my breath, anxiously waiting for him to do…something…anything.

"What are you doing?" I ask when he still hasn't done anything but stare.

"Just looking at my girl."

His words make my heart skip two beats. We haven't discussed what we are, and after his revelations earlier, we have even more to discuss than *What are we?*

My back bows off the mattress as he toys with my nipple then drags his free hand down the length of my body to thumb my clit, my wetness easing his path, dragging out the action for an agonizing amount of time before soothing the pressure away.

"I want to take my time with you." His voice is a deep timbre above me, his words full of promise and want.

I groan when his thumb flicks over me again, my hips bucking into his touch, egging him on to give me more.

"Nuh-uh." He clucks his tongue. "We're going to do this my way," he says, eyes narrowing to slits as they lock with mine.

Chance's words make my body heat up even more. He's always so dominating, but I'm not sure how much more of this I can take before I completely lose it. I want to tell him to hurry, to give me what I need, but I know those pleas will only fall on deaf ears.

Chance drops to a kneel, pulling my legs over his broad shoulders. His tongue licks a path over my rib cage and down the freckles dotting my torso until his mouth finally covers my pussy.

"You're so damn soft and wet, baby." He drags a finger down my slit. "Always so wet for me."

My hands claw at the sheets beneath us.

It's not enough.

I need more.

"Chance…more," I plead.

He chuckles against my clit, the vibrations shooting through my body, sending a new wave of need coursing through me.

"I have so much more planned for you, Precious. Patience."

He kisses my core and lifts his head, running his tongue over the wetness clinging to his lips before sitting up, his eyes shining with something I can't decipher.

He leans down, his lips brushing over my collarbone, his hot breath making the delicate hairs on my arms stand up and take notice. "I'll take care of you, baby," he rasps.

The shivers in my body reach all the way down to my toes, and my hands fist the sheets again. Chance's lips find mine, and I can taste myself on his tongue. Though it's erotic as hell, it's not enough for me. My fingers push into his hair, my legs wrapping around his waist, pulling him tighter against me. He's hard against my inner thigh, the denim of his jeans keeping him from me.

I want him inside me.

I need him inside me.

As if reading my mind, he straightens, undoing his belt and pushing his jeans down his legs, kicking them and his underwear to the side. I'm acutely aware that this is the first time we've both been completely naked with each other as he rolls on a condom. He comes back over me, a rush of awareness flaring over my skin when he takes his dick and traces it around my entrance.

"Chance," I whine when he stops, resting his weight on the elbows he has braced on either side of my head.

"Shh, baby. This is going to be good."

So, so good.

He takes a second to catch my eyes, but they close a second later, and I release a shaky exhalation as he pushes inside of me, stretching me. Chance stills, then his hips rock against me, making my toes curl. His hands cup my skull, tilting my face and kissing me with something that feels like more than desire.

I moan into his mouth as electricity courses through me from his touch, and I'm filled with warmth that quickly turns to heat. My body tightens around him, the pleasure so intense it borders on pain.

He gently breaks away from the kiss but doesn't shy away from my eyes, instead looking into them deeply. His touch is tender yet firm, exploring with an expertise that sets my entire being alight with need.

"Look at me." He holds me still as he pumps into me with measured strokes. "I want to see you."

I dig my nails into his back, my legs riding his waist. "Chance…" I'm breathless, unsure what I'm even asking for. I move my hips to meet him, our bodies moving in sync as he kisses me again deeply, moaning into my mouth.

A whimper escapes my lips when he stills, pulling back to stare down at me. "Do you feel me, baby?"

I nod, incapable of words as he thrusts in and out, my walls tightening around his cock.

"Fuck. It's like you were made for me."

I throw my arms around his neck, pulling him to me, needing his weight because I fear the same might be true about him, fear he was made for me. All of this feels like a dream: his muscular body on top of me, his voice in my ear, his hips grinding against mine.

When he dips his head to kiss me, it's impossible to hold back the low rumble of his name that comes out of my throat. Chance hooks an arm around me, maneuvering us onto the bed correctly, my hair fanning out over his pillow. He takes both my hands in his, threading our fingers together and pinning them to the pillow. His rhythm quickens, driving into me with quick, deep strokes.

"How close are you, baby?"

"Close." My pussy clenches around his dick, signaling my impending orgasm.

I moan into his neck as I shake, my body splintering into a thousand pieces. Chance slams into me, his movements jagged and erratic as he falls apart. His lips fall to my shoulder, his teeth sinking into my skin.

"I can't get enough of you, Gem." One last thrust and he grinds against me as he comes, his muscles clenching and quivering as his cock pulses inside me.

My body trembles with pleasure, my eyes fluttering shut as his hips meet mine again and again. Chance collapses beside me, bringing me to snuggle against him, my head resting on his chest, his heart pounding erratically beneath my ear. We lie there, entwined in each other's arms as we catch our breath.

He kisses the side of my head, and I hate to ruin the moment, but there are things I need to know…things I deserve to know.

"There's something I don't get," I say, tracing the ridges of his six-pack with my finger.

Chance captures my hand, kissing my fingertips. "What's that?"

"Why were you such a dick to me when you met me?" I ask into his chest, unable to meet his gaze, afraid of what I might see in it.

He places a finger under my chin, not having it. "I thought I was protecting myself."

His words stab me in the chest, and I try to pull away, but his grip tightens.

"You didn't even know me," I challenge.

"True, but you had me triggered."

"Because you invaded my privacy?"

"Can't say I regret that part."

I pinch him when he waggles his eyebrows at me, holding my breath when his expression turns serious.

"What do you know about the why of me getting traded?"

"Just that you went all Hulk smash on your old captain."

"Fuck, Precious." Chance huffs out a laugh, hugging me to him, his hand skimming up and down my spine. "Only you can make me laugh about one of the worst days of my life."

"What can I say?" I drop a kiss on his pec. "I have a gift."

"You do." He pulls me in close, wrapping me in his arms and burying his face in my hair. "If it's any consolation, it makes me feel like an even bigger ass when I think about how I treated you, and I'm sorry."

"You don't have to apologize. It's in the past."

Chance exhales a loud sigh, his chest rumbling beneath me. "I do, though. My behavior was inexcusable."

I press my lips against the soft skin of his chest, and he groans, his arm coming up to wrap around me.

"To be fair, I may not have acted as my most mature self with you either."

"Truce?" He holds out a hand for me to shake.

"Truce," I agree, slipping my hand in his.

We lapse into silence, chuckling at the dogs whining on the other side of the door.

I prop my chin on his chest. "Can I ask you another question without risking our newfound peace treaty?"

He tucks a strand of hair behind my ear, his touch lingering on my face. "Shoot."

"What did you mean I had you triggered?"

"Well...the reason I went all Hulk smash, as you so eloquently put it"—he tweaks the end of my nose—"was we were..." He pauses as if searching for the right word. "Ugh...*dating* the same bunny."

I push myself off Chance, holding the sheet to my chest. This conversation has turned, making me feel all kinds of vulnerable; I need some sort of protection for my nakedness.

"I know you're not a bunny." Chance sits up, resting against his headboard.

I give him an *Uh-huh, sure you do* face that has him reaching for me, but I knock his hands away. His narrowed eyes tell me he's not pleased with my rebuff, but I can't seem to find it in me to give a fuck.

"Oh-kay, I know you're not a bunny *now*." His concession falls a little flat.

And because he knows me enough to know I'm trying desperately to hold on to my mad, he growls and yanks me to him, tucking my body tight to his.

"But that day?" Chance cups the side of my face. "I was *convinced* you were just like Wendy, happy to bounce from one hockey player's bed to another."

"Why? Because I sent a picture of me in my underwear to my friends? My *girlfriends*?" I add the last part for emphasis.

"I know, okay, and I get it. This shouldn't have even been an issue in the first place, but yes, I invaded your privacy, and…"

"And what?" I prod when his words trail off.

"And I may know now that it was *Jordan's* phone I saw the text on, but that day…I thought it was Jase's."

My eyes go wide. "*What?!*"

Chance hangs his head. "I know."

"Wrong Steele woman where that's concerned."

"I know," he says on a sigh. "But in my defense, you also sent a *Would this make you show me your hockey stick?* joke shortly after the selfie."

"Ugh." I drop my head, beating it against Chance's chest. "I wish I could hate you for hating me because of my bad puns."

He pinches my chin to halt my head banging. "Why don't you?" The sincerity in his tone has the poorly crafted wall I attempted to erect crumbling.

"The hell if I know. You seem to be annoying like that."

Chance strokes his thumb over my cheek, and I find myself leaning into the touch. "Only you, Precious."

"I still don't get why thinking I was a bunny would trigger you."

Chance swallows, looking down before returning his gaze to me. "You and Wendy…umm…you look a lot alike."

"Wow." I rear back. "Just…wow." I'm not sure how else to respond to that.

"Fuck." Chance jerks upright as if realizing what he said. "Shit." He reaches for me, taking me by the nape. "You two may have similar features, but *that's* where the similarities *end*."

I try to look away, but his fingers squeeze me tighter.

"You are so different from her," he murmurs, brushing the pad of his thumb across my bottom lip. "She used men like they were disposable, while you…you give every ounce of yourself to others, even to those of us who don't deserve it."

My heart thuds against my chest as his words wash over me like a soothing balm.

"I still don't get why dating the same woman would make you Hulk-smash your captain. Like it got you *traded*, Chance."

"Thanks for the reminder," he says dryly.

"It's what I'm here for."

"Brat."

I poke him. "Seriously, what happened?"

Yes, he has a temper, but he's not violent without cause.

"My…*whatever* I had going on with Wendy ended because she told me she was pregnant."

"But it wasn't yours?" I ask, filling in the blanks.

"Yup."

"Why don't you sound sure if dating is what you were doing when you talk about her?"

His uncertainty is kind of adorable, and I trace the shapes decorating his skin.

"I don't know." He rakes a hand through his messy hair. "Things were casual"—he waves a hand between us—"kinda like how they are with us."

A vise grips my heart. I know we haven't labeled anything, but given some of the things we've shared with each other—especially on my end—I thought we were more than casual.

# CHAPTER 34

## Gemma

"Go pee on this," Rocky demands, bouncing a babbling seven-month-old Ronnie on her hip and slapping a pregnancy test down on the counter.

I use the tip of my chef's knife to move the box she placed in my workspace out of the way.

How rude.

I go back to my chopping as three other sets of eyes ping-pong between each other.

Still…

Nobody says a word.

Unable to stand the silence any longer—seriously, it's thick enough it's drowning out Ms. Lauren Hill telling me why us ladies need to watch out—I shout, "Oh my god, Holly, go pee on the damn stick."

My beautiful cousin-in-law's jaw drops. "What? Why me?"

"Oh no." Becky brings the back of her hand to her forehead, feigning fainting on her barstool and onto the counter. "The pregnancy brain is already setting in. Quick, someone AirTag her keys so we can find them when she inevitably leaves them in the fridge."

"What are you talking about?" Holly asks, though I gotta admit, she is still looking a tad bit green underneath her newlywed glow.

"Do you remember how a mere, oh, I don't know"—Becky looks at her wrist as if checking the time, except she lifts the one without her watch—"four minutes ago you ran down the hall and tossed what I'm sure was some of your beautifully decorated cookies in Gem's toilet?"

"You have such a way with words, Beck." Rocky takes the hand Ronnie's waving in her face and hides her laugh behind it.

"Ohemgee." Becky flattens her palm to her chest. "I could totally help Madz with her books."

"Madz is gonna *kill* you, Rock." Unlike my cousin, I don't bother to hide my laughter, letting my giggles fly free.

"Over-under, how many *You should unalive this person* or *surprise baby* plot suggestion texts do you think it would take for Madz to block her?" Holly asks, smothering a burp that has her eyes flying wide behind her fist.

Uh-oh. Maybe we should take an over-under on how many times she pukes before we leave for the Blizzards game.

"Come on, Hol." I lift the test box from the counter, take her hand in mine, and guide her back to my bathroom. "Time for you to pee on a stick."

"But I'm scared."

I stop, turning to pull her into a hug. "Scared of what?"

Holly glances away, her voice small when she answers. "What if Vince is mad?"

"Mad?" My question comes out as a bark, and I double over, laughing at the sheer audacity. "You can't be serious, Hol."

"I don't know." She flops her arms out. "We've only been married a *month*. I mean…" She flops them twice more, looking like a penguin attempting to take flight. "Who gets knocked up on their honeymoon?"

"Jordan," I deadpan.

"Dammit. I knew I spent too much time with that fertile bitch."

"Come on, Myrtle." I nudge her into my en suite. "Pee-pee time." I dance the box in front of her face.

Holly still looks queasy, though now I'm not sure if it's nausea or the possibility that she's probably, most likely, preggers.

"Would it make you feel better if I took a test with you?"

"You think you're *pregnant*?" Holly latches on to my forearms with a screech.

"Not unless my IUD suddenly failed." I shake my head. "But

we're family, and you're *kinda*"—I pinch my thumb and fore-finger until there is only a sliver of space between them—"freaking out, and it's freaking *me* out."

I slip my thumb under the cardboard flap and rip open the box before tossing it in the wastebasket next to the toilet. With a plastic-wrapped test in each hand, I wave them in the air.

"Are you sure?" Holly asks, tentatively taking one of the tests.

"Duh." I spin her around and give her a nudge. "What's the harm in peeing on a stick for one of my babes?"

# CHAPTER 35

## Chance

ME: Did you get the gift I left on the counter for you?

PRECIOUS GEM: I did. But you do know I have a whole section of my closet dedicated to Blizzards gear, right?

ME: Yeah, but I'd bet good money none of it has Jenson on the back.

PRECIOUS GEM: OMG. Really? *shocked face emoji* It's almost like that was intentional or something.

ME: You're making my palm itch, Princess.

PRECIOUS GEM: That sounds like something you should have the team doctor check out. You never know what kind of fungus can grow inside those hockey gloves. I've smelled Jase's before —those things get rank.

ME: Do I even wanna know?

PRECIOUS GEM: Probably not. Let's just say I wouldn't suggest playing truth or dare with that particular Donnelly twin. Like EVER.

ME: Now, stop trying to change the subject. Are you wearing my jersey to the game tonight or not?

PRECIOUS GEM: I don't know *shrug emoji*

ME: What's not to know? It's a yes or no question, Princess.

PRECIOUS GEM: Eh. I'm not sure if you've earned it yet or not, Rookie.

ME: I don't know, baby. I think all those orgasms I've given you this last month have earned me the right to see my name on your back where it belongs.

PRECIOUS GEM: Who said I wasn't faking it?

ME: If you're gonna lie to me, at least do it to my face so I can put you over my knee and spank the urge out of you.

PRECIOUS GEM: It's annoying that I find your stupid cockiness hot.

ME: You also think my cock is hot.

PRECIOUS GEM: I'm hanging up now.

ME: You can't hang up. We're texting, and I swear to god, Princess, if you decide to leave me on read, I'm going to start withholding your orgasms.

And because Gemma wouldn't be Gemma without giving me a hard time, she makes me wait until Ryan and Jake are finished with their pregame Ping-Pong game before texting me back.

PRECIOUS GEM: I'm not seeing how that's much of a threat, seeing as I've been faking them, remember?

ME: I can't wait to remind you of this conversation the next time you're coming all over my cock.

PRECIOUS GEM: That's a bold claim, Rookie.

ME: Wear my jersey tonight, and I'll show you how bold I can be.

PRECIOUS GEM: **picture of Gemma wearing Chance's jersey**

ME: Good girl.

PRECIOUS GEM: You like that, do you?

ME: Very much.

PRECIOUS GEM: What about this?

PRECIOUS GEM: **picture of Gemma lifting the jersey to show off her matching Blizzards-colored lingerie set**

ME: Fuck.

PRECIOUS GEM: What's wrong?

ME: Nothing, baby, you're perfect.

PRECIOUS GEM: *preens* Then why are you cursing?

ME: Because now I have to figure out how I'm supposed to play hockey with a boner.

This isn't the first time we've played my old team since I was traded; it's actually the third, but the frequency hasn't seemed to lessen the animosity between Stanton and me, at least not if the way my old captain is glaring at me from across the ice is anything to go by.

"You straight?" Ryan asks, his skates spraying me with snow as he joins me.

I force my gaze away from a man who doesn't deserve my attention—let alone the C on his chest—and glance at a man who has become so much more to me than just my captain. "I'm fine."

"You sure?" Jake asks after kissing his girls through the glass for his pregame ritual. "Because you *kinda* have this murder-y thing going on"—he pokes a gloved hand between my eyes—"right here."

I smack his hand away and skate away from him backward, heading for the plexiglass and, more specifically, my woman sitting on the other side of it.

All the Covenettes look up when I knock on the glass, but it's Gemma I crook a finger at. The ladies *ooo* and playfully nudge her as she pushes out of her seat to join me at the boards, her nephew Ronnie propped on her hip.

"You *rang*?" Gemma drawls in her best Lurch impression.

"Always so sarcastic."

She gives me one of those sunshiny smiles I'm growing addicted to. "It's my most authentic self."

Ronnie reaches out to smack the glass, but Gemma snags his hand before he can make contact, kissing all over his palm and fingertips when the baby pouts.

"Show me." I circle a finger, directing her to spin.

"Show you what?" Her mock ignorance has me grinding my molars.

"Don't play with me, woman. You know what I want to see."

The pink tip of Gemma's tongue peeks out between her teeth when she grins at me. I purposely arch a brow, biting back a laugh when her nose wrinkles at me, showing off a facial expression she recently admitted to being jealous of.

Finally, her gorgeous gray eyes sparkle with mischief, and she obliges, pulling her hair to the side and turning around slowly so I can admire the way my name looks stamped between her shoulder blades. It's a sight that makes my heart stammer in my chest.

"My name looks good on you, Precious."

"Eh." She rubs Ronnie's back in gentle circles as he coos

against that spot on her neck I love to nibble on. "I didn't have anything else to wear." She pops a shoulder. "Laundry day."

I run my tongue over my teeth, meeting Gemma's challenging stare with one of my own as I tap the glass barrier between us. "You're gonna pay for that tonight."

"Why? Are you planning on prank calling me about how I need to catch my running fridge all night?"

"The fuck you going on about?"

"Earmuffs," Gemma mock gasps, covering one of Ronnie's already-wearing-noise-canceling-headphones ears.

"You're coming home with me tonight, smartass, and I'm going to spank some of that sass out of you."

"Sorry, Rookie." Her singsongy tone tells me she's anything but apologetic. "I didn't pack an overnight bag."

"Don't worry, Canada," Becky calls out, utterly unconcerned about giving her shameless eavesdropping away.

"We'll make sure she's ready when you pick her up later," Rocky tacks on, seamlessly finishing her best friend's sentence.

"Though I honestly don't see why she needs more than a toothbrush if she's just going to be naked with you," Becky finishes.

"Oh my god." Gemma thunks her head against the plexiglass. "I need new friends."

"We're your family." Rocky cups her hands around her mouth. "There's no getting rid of us."

"I like the way they think." I waggle my eyebrows at Gemma.

"Don't you have a hockey game to play?" she retorts, cocking her hip out.

"Yup." I start to skate away backward. "But your ass is mine after we get this win."

A whistle gets blown, and I readjust my helmet in time to see the referee closest to me put his hands out and pull them across his body in an inward tugging motion.

"Four, blue, hooking." He calls the penalty, sending me to the box for two minutes.

I skate that way, even though it's a crap call. That seems to be the theme for the night. Stanton and I have been trading cheap shots and penalties for most of the game.

I take a seat on the bench inside the box, removing my helmet and wiping away the sweat dripping down my face. And just like every other time I've ended up in the sin bin tonight, I find my gaze drifting to the right and the brunette holding an almost-one-year-old wearing a Stanton jersey in her lap.

*Wendy.*

Nothing like having your past stare you in the face all night —literally.

The last time I saw her, I was holding her hand in the obstetrician's office as the ultrasound tech confirmed that the baby she told me was mine—the same baby she's currently holding—wasn't.

*It's not yours.*

Fuck me if that set of three words didn't rock my world more than when she said, *Chance, I'm pregnant.*

I can still feel the secondhand embarrassment from the poor ultrasound technician who was stuck sitting awkwardly by while tears streamed down her face, snot bubbles clinging to the tip of Wendy's nose as she admitted she knew the baby wasn't mine but panicked after she was rejected by the real bio dad.

We had an on-again, off-again type of relationship, but she was also the only bunny who warmed my bed with any regularity. We may have always used protection because I knew better than to play fast and loose with an empty net—unlike a certain sassy brunette who makes me lose my mind—but that doesn't stop condom failure from happening.

Now before you start sharpening your pitchforks, I didn't try to skirt my responsibilities, but I did ask for proof—I am a professional athlete, after all. Plus, I'm sure my agent would have my pecker pudding producers if I didn't.

I don't know what Wendy's plan was for when the paternity results came back from having my cheek swabbed, but there was no faking the math when the tech confirmed the baby's gestational age meant the date of conception didn't fall into one of our "on-again" periods.

The details of why losing something I didn't think I wanted in the first place hurt worse than when I had a skate slice through my calf aren't important. No, I've been conditioned to ignore pesky things like feelings and override them with what really matters—hockey.

But, alas, I wasn't able to remember that lesson in the heat of the moment. Why, you ask? Well…would you like to venture a guess on who supplied the baby batter for the bun in Wendy's oven?

Yes? No?

Yeah…well, remember how I was traded for punching my old captain?

*Fuck.*

I don't want to be thinking about this. Not tonight. Not when Gemma is sitting on the other side of the rink. Not when Stanton has been chirping me all night. Not when my team is down by one.

Not…ever.

I turn back to the ice, determined to refocus my attention back on the game, needing to be prepared for my next shift.

For two minutes, Minnesota pounds on my team. For two minutes, they take shot after shot at Jake in goal. For two minutes, my teammates work their asses off on a penalty kill. For two minutes, I'm stuck sitting and watching it all play out.

The time clock for my penalty counts down under fifteen seconds, and the penalty box official gives me a warning.

At ten seconds, I stand, readying to retake the ice.

*Five.*

I click the strap on my helmet.

*Four.*

I shove my mouth guard back in place.

*Three.*

I work my stick between my gloved hands.

*Two.*

I shift on my skates as the official knocks on the glass.

*One.*

He opens the door, and I explode out of the box, legs pumping, eating up every inch of ice, trying to get in position to help defend our zone.

"The rookie is back," Stanton mutters as I pass him along the board, shoulder-checking him into the plexiglass with a satisfying smack.

The puck gets knocked loose in front of the net, and I scoop it up, passing it to Ryan and flying down the ice to keep any overzealous Minnesota players away from my captain. We're down a goal, but the game is still close because all it takes is a split second for that to change, and the crowd knows it, the energy in the arena palpable. With less than a minute left in the third period, it's essential we keep the puck out of our zone if we want to have any hope of tying this game to send us into overtime.

Ryan drives through Minnesota's forwards, passing the puck to Parsons, who gets off a quick wrist shot that pings off the crossbar. I chase the puck, battling against the boards with Stanton for possession. My skates slide and swerve, my edges cutting into the ice as I twist and turn with him until we're nearly parallel, pads colliding, bodies shoving against each other as our sticks jostle for control.

Stanton smirks as he edges the nose of his stick's blade under the puck a split second before mine. I reach for it, but I'm too late, and he dumps it off to one of his teammates.

"Still too slow, Jenson." He sneers at me, pushing away from the boards.

My breath rages in my chest as I glare at him, wanting to lunge after him but knowing my team needs me out here more than they need a fight right now. "Fuck you, Stanton." I shove him into the boards for good measure before reclaiming my position on defense.

Time keeps ticking by with Minnesota's forwards driving toward our net with a vigor like they're the ones down by one. They maintain possession, circling in our zone, the puck bouncing to and fro between their sticks as they work to find a hole in our defense. Jake remains confident in the net, his focus on the puck unwavering as he continues to shut down Minnesota's offensive attack, blocking shot after shot.

Unfortunately, defending our zone comes at a cost, and when the buzzer sounds seconds later, it's official: we've lost.

"Nice job showing the Blizzards they didn't trade up when they got you," Stanton says, skating by.

"Not worth it." Ryan stays me with a hand on my chest.

Reporters from ESPN make their way onto the rugs being rolled out on the ice for their interviews while our on-ice commentators call other players over to where they broadcast from between the penalty boxes.

I stay out there long after everyone else has started to head back to the dressing room. I don't know why I can't bring myself to leave. Maybe it's because Ryan and Jake are among the players being interviewed, or maybe it's because I feel a need to torture myself over our loss longer.

Whatever it is, it doesn't matter when the consequence of my actions is having to watch Stanton give his interview, playing up the doting father role that feels like a farce, spewing his drivel about how having his family in the stands supporting him makes all the difference.

Standing there watching as he talks about how proud he is of his team and how glad he is that they brought home a win sends my blood boiling. I want nothing more than to walk up to him, shove him into the boards, and let him know that no amount of postgame punditry will make me forget what kind of player he is off the ice.

Instead, I just stand there simmering in my anger until Jake claps me on the back and drags me away from a past I need to stop infecting my present.

# CHAPTER 36

*Gemma*

Trudging into my room, I flop onto my bed in a graceless swan dive as the adrenaline from that nail-biter of a game flows out of my body through my toes.

"No, no, no," Becky declares, walking into my bedroom like she owns it. "Get that sexy ass up." She smacks me on said ass. "I promised that grumpy boy toy of yours you'd be packed when he picks you up."

"Why did I tell you guys about Chance?" I mumble into my pillow.

"It's hilarious that you think you could have kept it a secret." She riffles through my lingerie drawer, holding one of my thongs in front of her as if modeling it before tossing it back.

"I could have."

"Uh-huh."

"Ugh!" I chuck a pillow at Her Royal Annoyingness, but Becky deftly catches it and starts hitting me with it.

"Why do I feel like I walked into one of Jase's fantasies?" Rocky asks, leaning against the doorframe, taking in the impromptu pillow fight.

Becky pauses, hugging her pillow to her chest. "Nuh-huh. If we were *really* in your bestie's fantasies, we'd be wearing unicorn onesies or something."

I bring my legs around to sit cross-legged and shove my hair out of my face. "If we're going for accuracy, it would be something with potatoes on it."

"Melody got them matching Mr. and Mrs. Potato Head onesies for Christmas." Rocky holds out her phone, a selfie of Jase and Melody wearing their new getups on the screen.

"Okay, but why do I need a fun onesie now?" I reach for my phone, Becky dropping beside me to lend her finger to my scrolling.

"Ooo, you could totally be a pineapple." Becky taps away on the screen, completely taking over like it's her phone, not mine. "*Oooo, no*—an avocado. One hundred percent be an avocado. So healthy, boo-boo."

I look at my cousin, grinning at us from her perch against the doorjamb. "Can you come handle this, please?" I say, hooking a thumb at Becky.

Rocky holds up both hands, looking like a live-action version of the shrug emoji. "What do you want me to do?"

"I don't know." I throw my arms up. "She's your best friend."

"And she's your roommate."

"Ugh." I flop over, starfishing on my mattress. "Why did you and Holly have to go off and get all married, leaving me alone with Trouble?"

"*Somebody* is in a mood," Becky singsongs, going back to my underwear drawer and slingshotting a thong at me. "And don't act like you aren't going to be the next one to abandon me to matrimonial bliss, Gemmy Gem."

"Oh my god, Beck. Slow your roll. I've been dating Chance for all of two weeks." I hold up peace fingers, wiggling them.

"Shit." Becky gives an *aw-shucks* snap of her fingers. "I better get started on the pool. I'm already behind on taking bets."

I turn to my cousin, needing someone to translate for me. "You speak fluent Beck—what is she going on about?"

"Do you remember how you jerks placed bets on when I would push the Butterball turkey I call a son out of my hoo-ha?" Rocky's face may be placid, but her *payback's a bitch* tone has an itch forming between my shoulders.

"Yeah?" It's more of a question than a statement.

"Well…" Rocky does something on her phone that causes Becky's to ping three seconds later.

"And that right there"—Becky mic drops—"is why you're my *beh-est fraaand.*"

I narrow my eyes. "What did you do?"

"*Nothing.*" There's nothing innocent about Rocky's tone or the pop of her shoulder.

"She just dropped a Benji that you will become Mrs. Grumpy Pants before the year is out."

"Oh. Em. Gee. I can't even with you bitches." I bury my face in my hands, the three of us collapsing onto each other in a fit of giggles.

And that's precisely how Chance finds us, a mass of giggling females in the center of my king-size bed. I squint an eye under the bend of Becky's arm and sneak a peek at my sexy man leaning against my bedroom doorframe, looking like Maddey's next book cover. Arms crossed, muscles testing the limits of the Blizzards hoodie he's wearing, he arches one of those stupid, stupid brows.

"Do I even wanna know?" he asks.

That makes us dissolve into a fresh wave of laughter, but it breaks apart when Chance takes a step forward. The air in the room thickens as he strides toward us and perches on the edge of my mattress. Even with the three of us piled together on top of it, his presence commands every bit of my attention.

Rocky is the first to compose herself, pushing up and reaching a hand out to Becky. "Come on, Beck."

"But I don't wanna," she whines with a pout.

Rocky wiggles her fingers. "But you get me *all to yourself* for the night."

"Eep." Becky springs from the bed, jumping on Rocky's back, piggyback style. "Double Trouble, bestie boo-boo time." She lassos her arm in the air. "Let's go."

Chance rests a heavy hand on my hip, drawing circles with his thumb that match the ones going round and round in my stomach. "What were you ladies talking about?"

I look up into those midnight eyes that make everything else —even other people—fade into obscurity. "Covenette things," I hedge.

Chance snorts out a laugh that sends vibrations down to where his hand still moves over me. "Covenette things? That sounds pretty dangerous." He says it with a wink, but his good humor quickly fades, a weight seeming to fall on his shoulders.

Chance shakes off the sudden shift in his demeanor, but it's too late—I feel the darkness emanating off him like a cloud.

"What's wrong?" I ask, lifting my hand to his face, the slight five-o'clock shadow abrading my fingers.

He presses a kiss to my forehead and withdraws his hand from my hip, tucking a lock of hair behind my ear. "Nothing, Precious."

My shoulders relax at his words, but I can see the shadows lingering in his eyes, so I press again. "I'm sorry you lost."

"Thanks, baby, but it's okay." Chance drags his thumb along his bottom lip, hesitating before finally admitting, "I just always feel a bit off when we play Minnesota."

"Because they traded you?"

"Yeah." He rubs at the back of his neck. "It doesn't help that we lost tonight, and Stanton was in my fucking ear all night."

He's right about that. I watched his old captain chirp him nonstop.

Chance shakes his head as if shaking off the memory of the game. "Ready to come home with me?"

"I still need to pack a bag."

He mock-gasps. "You mean Becky didn't make good on her promise?"

I shake my head. "She was too busy playing in my underwear drawer to make it to my bathroom for that toothbrush she promised you."

"That won't do." Chance pushes off the bed and holds out his hand. "Let's rectify that, shall we?" He pulls me up in one swift motion.

I go to my closet and pull out my taco-printed duffel, Chance eyeing it when I set it on top of my dresser. "That seems like an *awfully big* bag for just a toothbrush."

I skip over to him, pushing up onto my toes and wrapping my arms around his neck. "I promise to only use the toothbrush tonight, but I need clothes for work tomorrow."

Chance loops his arms around behind my back, tucking me against him tighter. "One of these days, Precious, you're gonna add me to your list of clients."

"What do you mean?" I tilt my head in mock innocence. "You're on my client roster."

His teeth bite into his bottom lip, his eyes going all smolder-y on me. "Your *human* roster, smartass."

"*Ahhh.*" I tap my chin. "I'll consider it."

He gives my ass a quick slap that has me smothering my giggles in his chest.

"Who are you cooking for?"

I chew on the edge of my thumb, hesitant to answer. It's not that I have anything to hide—I don't, but I know how Chance tends to react when I say the name of this particular client, my first nonfriend client.

Blowing out a breath, I say, "Ben."

Chance's smolder turns homicidal, his scruffy jaw tensing so hard I worry he might crack a tooth.

"Is it wrong to hope the Crabs lose so you can be done cooking for that jackass two weeks sooner?"

I roll my eyes at his immaturity. I've only been cooking for Ben for the playoffs. Honestly, making the drive to Baltimore every week is not a sustainable long-term goal. Now, if I ever pulled the trigger on starting my boutique agency, it would be, but until I can find the time to put all my plans into motion, I need to keep the clients more than three hours away on short-term contracts.

"Isn't wishing ill of another team's championship prospects bad juju or something?" I ask, folding an outfit into my bag.

"Shh. It'll be our little secret."

"You're ridiculous." I push him toward my bathroom. "Now go get my toothbrush so I can see my babies."

Chance spins to face me and walks backward. "You remember they're *my* dogs, right?"

"Yeah, but it's me their collars claim as their favorite *hooman*."

Chance's muttered curses about canine betrayal have me cracking up, at least until an entirely different version of Chance comes out of my bathroom than went into it.

"Just tell me this…is it even mine?" he accuses.

"Is what yours?" I ask, utterly confused by his complete one-eighty attitude.

"The baby."

"What baby?"

He's not making any sense. The only baby I know of is the one growing in Holly's womb. Why is Chance suddenly asking about babies?

Then it hits me like a frying pan to the face—Holly's test.

My gaze flies to the wastebasket in my bathroom, the same one Chance is glaring at like he's never glared before.

"Did you lie about having an IUD? Or are you not sure if it's mine or Ben Turner's?"

"Ben?" My brows slam together. "What the fuck are you talking about, Chance? I'm not sleeping with Ben."

"Are you saying you're not sleeping with him in the same way you claim you have an IUD?"

I fold my arms over my chest. "There is so much wrong with that sentence I don't even know where to start."

"I can't believe this is happening again."

"Chance, you're not making any sense." I reach for him, but he backs away before I can make contact. "How could you think I'd cheat on you?" Disbelief colors my tone. I can't believe he would think something like that about me.

"Cheat on me?" He laughs, but there's no humor in it. "We'd have to be a couple for you to cheat on me."

Pain stabs me right in the heart. Is that really how he views our relationship? I know we haven't put a label on things, but to be so casually dismissed hurts in a way I can't describe.

"So much for not being a bunny, *hmm*?" He grabs his chin in mock contemplation. "Oh, wait...what are they called in football? Cleat chasers? Or I guess maybe we should use the catchall —jersey chaser?"

Each accusation feels like a slap to the face.

"You're a dick."

"I've never pretended to be something I'm not." Chance levels me with a look full of venom. "Unlike you."

"I don't have to stand here and listen to you spew your toxic jealousy." I point aggressively at my bedroom door. "Get out."

"Fine." He slaps his hands against his thighs, but instead of leaving, he steps back inside my bathroom.

"What are you doing?" I ask.

Chance ignores me and keeps rummaging through my bathroom cabinets.

"I said get the fuck out."

"I will. But first..." His words trail off, and I guess he finds what he's looking for because he stops slamming drawers and holds up a Q-tip.

What does he need that for?

He brings the cotton swab to his mouth, rubbing the inside of his cheek before holding it out to me. "Here."

Instinct has me taking the tiny stick from him. "What do I need this for?"

"So you can let me know if the baby is mine."

"What are you talking about?" I ask, meeting his gaze with a defiant one of my own.

Chance huffs out an impatient breath. "I want to know if the baby is mine or Ben Turner's."

My mouth drops open in shock. "Are you crazy? We just established that I'm not sleeping with Ben."

Chance scoffs and shakes his head. "And I thought we established you have an IUD and I wouldn't have to worry about knocking you up that *one time* I forgot to put on a condom—yet here we are."

When he forgot a condom? What is he talking about? The only time we didn't was—

"Are you talking about that night at Rookies?"

All the jerk does is quirk a brow at me.

"You're such a dumbass. That was *months* ago. I've had my period like *three* times since then."

I don't bother waiting for him to comment and instead start moving toward the door to my bedroom. If he won't leave, I guess I will.

"But since you're having trouble figuring out the math"—I stop with one foot on either side of the threshold—"the test isn't mine. It's Holly's."

"What?" Chance glances back at the wastebasket, the white plastic test glaring at us through the wire mesh.

"So congratulations, Dickhead, you are not the father."

"Gem—"

"Nope." I shake my head. "You're also no longer my boyfriend—though I guess you never considered yourself to be, so not much is changing for you in that regard."

# CHAPTER 37

## Chance

The lamp lights with another goal from the Storm, another goal that came off of a bad turnaround by yours truly.

"Jenson, you're done for the night," Coach Watson says, pulling me off the ice when our line returns to the bench.

*Fuck.* I'm playing like dog shit and have been for the last week. It's a goddamn miracle I haven't been sent down to the minors.

I spend the rest of the third period riding the bench, watching as my teammates try to dig us out of the hole I created for us. But their efforts are in vain, and when the final buzzer sounds, we fall to the Storm 3-2.

The weight of tonight's loss is heavy on my shoulders, but none of it compares to the loss I've been carrying since I wedged my foot so far into my mouth with Gemma I'm going to need to have it surgically removed. I've left at least a dozen voice mails and countless texts since she walked out of her own apartment to get away from me. They've all gone unreturned, and we're back to her avoiding me.

Not that I blame her. I was a complete ass.

I've looked for her at both our home games since that night, and each time I've seen her empty seat, my chest hasn't just ached, it's fucking screamed as if my heart was being ripped right out of it.

It doesn't make any fucking sense. With the things I accused

Gemma of, I should be relieved. I never thought we were a couple, at least that's what I said, so why am I suffering like this?

The trek to the dressing room is a blur, the questions from reporters and my teammates' chatter fading into background noise as I go through the motions. When Jake and Ryan sit down, bookending me on the bench, I couldn't tell you how long I've been sitting here, stewing in my turmoil.

"Okay, buttercup." Jake loops an arm around my neck. "Time to spill your guts."

"There's nothing to spill," I say, shoving him away from me when he starts to *There, there* pat me on the head.

Jake sighs, looking over my head at Ryan on the other side of me. "Can you"—he bounces a hand back and forth—"captain him or something?"

Ryan rolls his eyes. "Captain is a noun, not a verb."

"Not the way you do it," Jake retorts.

"He's not wrong," I say dryly, latching on to any topic that has the potential to keep the conversation off of me.

"Fine." Ryan shifts, angling himself better on the bench. "You want me to *captain*?" He crosses his arms over his chest. "How's this? You're playing like shit, Jenson."

"*Ooo.*" Jake whistles through his teeth. "Careful—he's cursing. He's überserious."

Ryan narrows his eyes at Jake. "I really wish my sister would divorce you."

"Puh-lease." Jake waves him off and flubs his lips. "You love me, and you know it."

I glance around the empty dressing room, wondering how I got left alone with these two bickering ninnies. Then as if my thoughts make the universe perk up and say *Hold my beer*, the doors to the locker room swing open, and the most ridiculous member of this brotherly brother-in-law-love conglomerate, Jase Donnelly, enters.

"You lost, bro?" Jake asks. "The away team's locker room is thataway." He points to the left.

"I *love* how you think I'd miss this." Jase claps his hands and rubs them together.

"What?" I bounce a finger between Jake and Ryan. "Them ragging on me for playing like shit?"

"Aww, look, Cap—he admitted it," Jake says proudly.

Ryan claps me on the back. "Good. The first step is admitting you have a problem."

"Nah." Jase waves off the notion. "Why would I give him shit for it when his brokenhearted gameplay gives my team the *W*?" He shimmies his way-too-broad-to-be-shimmied shoulders. For real, the guy is an enforcer like me, as wide as he is tall.

"I'm not brokenhearted," I argue.

"Pee-ew." Jase waves a hand under his nose.

"What are you doing?" Ryan asks his brother when he pinches the end of his nose.

"Protecting myself from Canada's bullshit. He's laying it on so thick you can't tell me you don't smell it." He pauses for a beat and glances at Jake and Ryan, who both end up nodding in agreement.

"Look." Jase crouches into a squat in front of me. "We get it, dude. We've been there. You fuck up with the woman you love, and your game suffers."

My stomach clenches at his words. "I don't love Gemma."

Jase rolls his eyes so hard it's a miracle they don't fall out of his head. "That's what all us dumbasses say before we have our *aha* moment."

"Umm…" Jake leans forward, raising his hand. "I would like to point out for the record that *I* never had this issue."

"Those who date a teammate's sister in secret need not comment." Jase makes a lip-zipping motion in front of Jake's mouth.

"I *married* her," Jake shouts with the same exasperated tone I've heard him use every time he's made that same statement.

"And that's why we haven't murdered you in your sleep," Ryan deadpans.

Jase holds up a hand for a high five. "That's my favorite big brother."

"I'm your only big brother, stupid."

"I'm just gonna leave you guys to your little brotherly love powwow." I rise from the bench, only to be met with two different hands pushing me back into my seat.

Jake levels me with a hard stare. "You're not going anywhere until we figure out how to fix your love life."

I scrub both hands over my face and groan. "I don't have a love life."

"You do." Ryan nod. "You just fucked it up for a bit."

"Wh—" I start then stop, realization slamming into me.

I love Gemma Steele.

*Fuck.* When did this happen? When did the occasional check-in text about my dogs when I'm on the road turn into a need to talk to her, just her? When did her messages, no matter how sassy and sarcastic they may be, change into the thing that brightens up my day? When did I start to crave the way she finds joy in the simplest things?

"Fuck," I shout.

"There it is." Jase Cheshire grins. "There it *fucking* is."

Jake joins in, making a picture frame around me with his fingers. "Who doesn't love a good *He finally realized he's in love* moment."

I scowl, but these assholes are right. I'm in fucking love with Gemma Steele.

*Shit.* There's no more denying it.

Everything I've done on the ice lately has been dictated by my thoughts of her. My too-hard hits happen when I'm trying to punish myself for the things I've said to her. When I'm too slow off the line or miss a puck, letting it sail by, it's because I'm weighed down by the sadness I felt bleeding off her. When I miss a shot on goal, it's because visions of her crestfallen expression blind me to anything else.

"Don't worry, bro." Jase slaps a hand on my knee, breaking me out of my mental freak-out. "We're experts at planning epic grovels. We got you."

"I fucked up," I admit.

"Yeah, you did," Jake says, and the other two nod in agreement.

I let my head hang low. "I'd ask how you know, but even I know the answer."

"*The Coven*," Jase whispers.

"You should be happy we gave you as long as we did." Jake shrugs.

Yeah, because a week is an eternity. Well…I guess in Coven time, it is. It's kind of like dog years—each day is more like a month where they are concerned.

"Alright." Jase jumps to his feet, making a beeline for Coach's dry-erase board on the far wall. "Let's workshop this shit." He uncaps a marker, turning to look at his brother. "Your future father-in-law isn't gonna kick my ass for this, is he?"

Ryan shrugs. "He's not typically prone to bouts of violence—"

"Unless you break his daughter's heart," Jake interrupts.

"Shut it." Ryan glares at his brother-in-law. "Anyway." He brings his attention back to Jase. "If he does wanna kick your ass, I'll hold you down for him."

"Suck-up," Jake cough-says into his fist.

"Can you ladies bicker later?" Jase props his fists on his hips. "We have a grovel plan to draft."

I make a rolling motion with my hand to Jase.

"Step one."

"Step one?" I hold up a finger. "As in, there's more than one step?"

"Oh, young grasshopper." Jake claps me on the back. "You have so much to learn."

"Why do I feel like I'm going to regret this?" I mumble and gesture for them to go on.

Ryan and Jake start shouting ideas for how I can grovel to Gemma. Jase bobs his head along, writing any of the suggestions he thinks hold promise on the dry-erase board.

I sit back and watch them plan, feeling my stomach twist in knots as they come up with ideas ranging from the benign to the progressively more outrageous ways to apologize.

"I never knew you fools were fairy godparents under your hockey sweaters."

"Nah." Jake waves me off. "We're just big on the love and romance shit."

For the first time in a week, I feel marginally better. At the very least, I don't feel alone anymore.

The truth is I don't know if anything I do is going to be enough. What I do know is this: there's only one woman I want, and that woman scares the shit out of me. I shouldn't want her because I'm nowhere near good enough for her, but I can't seem to stop thinking about her.

Gemma consumes my thoughts. I want to be with her. I want to breathe in the scent of her shampoo and feel the softness of her body against mine. I want to kiss her senseless and spend hours making her come until she can't come anymore. I want to take back every single word I said so I can tell her I'll never let her walk away from me again.

She's everything I never knew I always wanted, and it's time for me to show her.

# CHAPTER 38

## Gemma

I glare at my full-length mirror, not because of my reflection but because of the fifty sets of googly eyes now surrounding the perimeter.

Okay, maybe it has a little to do with my reflection and the stupid smile threatening to appear on my lips. Nothing like having the evidence of your own amusement staring you in the face.

I don't know how Chance did it, and yes, I know it was him because he also left a note, but I suspect my don't-know-how-to-mind-their-own-business framily had a hand in this particular gesture. Our squad never did know how to butt out of each other's love life. Just ask Melody the lengths Jordan went to when she and Jase broke up.

Ugh. Stupid Chance Jenson.

I hate him.

Except...I don't.

I love him.

Now, if I could fall out of love with him, that would be great. It's been over two weeks; surely that's enough time to get over a relationship that was never actually a relationship to begin with.

So why? Why can't I get past this feeling that I made a mistake by walking away from him?

I shake my head and force my gaze away from the mirror, only to have my eyes land on the Ben Turner football jersey spilling out of my suitcase.

"Dammit, Canada." I wad up the purple material into a ball and toss it into my closet. I can't stand looking at it when it only makes me think about Chance.

"I see we're going for the out-of-sight, out-of-mind approach to heartbreak."

Letting out a screech worthy of a B-level slasher film, I jump a solid foot in the air and slap a hand to my chest.

"Holy guacamole, you scared the bejesus out of me." I glare at the cousin responsible for causing my mini heart attack, irked by how Rocky seems entirely without care, casually leaning against my doorjamb.

"I knocked, but you were too busy having a staring contest with your new *friends* to hear it."

It wasn't so much a staring contest as it was replaying the words on the note that accompanied those new friends.

**As much as I wish I could take back the deplorable things I said, I can't. All I can do is say I'm sorry and hope our little friends here can help you see what I always knew but was too afraid to admit.**

**You, Gemma Steele, have the most beautiful soul of any person I have ever had the privilege to know.**

**-X-**

**Dickhead Daddy**

"Oh," Rocky says, pushing off the wall and heading straight for my mirror. "I stand corrected." She removes the Post-it stuck to the glass, fanning it in front of her. "You're obsessing and hating yourself for wanting to forgive him."

"I hate him, not myself." I bite the side of my thumb.

"Liar." Rocky perches on my dresser, eyeing the finger in my mouth. "You love him."

I open my mouth to argue again but stop, knowing there's no use. My cousin is right. I'm lying.

"He's a dick."

Rocky hums thoughtfully. "So? He's been a dick since you met him. That didn't stop you from falling for him."

"God, I'm toxic."

"Don't do that." Rocky pushes off the dresser, taking me by the shoulders. "Don't diminish your worth because your relationship isn't storybook perfect. You guys are human. You know better than anyone how fallible we can be."

I stab a hand into my hair, tugging on the strands. "He hurt me, Rock."

She slides her hands up and down my arms. "I know he did, honey. But—and don't hate me for saying this—I think he knows it, and he's trying, Gem."

Rocky turns, picking up the other Post-it I haven't had it in me to throw away, the one that came with the Ben Turner jersey.

*I'm sorry for being a jealous prick.*
*I heard from the annoying birdies I call teammates that you and*
*the Covenettes are going to the Super Bowl. I got you this so*
*you can cheer on your friend properly. And...okay...maybe so*
*you'll still end up thinking of me while you're hanging with him.*
*Not sorry for that. Miss you.*
*-X-*
*Dickhead Daddy*

"Grr." I snatch the note from her and stick it in my pocket, still unable to destroy it. "I wish he'd stop."

He's making it extremely difficult to forget about him when he keeps blowing up my phone with calls and texts and leaving me sweet notes where he owns up to assness.

Rocky rolls her eyes at me. "No, you don't."

I groan, balling my hands into fists. "Why won't he stop, Rock?"

"I think you know the answer to that."

Gray eyes the same as mine bore into me, daring me to deny it, and I do because it hurts too much to hope.

"That man loves you, Gem."

"No, he doesn't."

Rocky grabs my hand, squeezing it tightly in hers. "Yes. He does."

My chest aches with the possibility.

"But how do you know?" I ask in a strangled voice.

"Because..." Rocky steps around me and moves to my bedside table, sliding open the top drawer and lifting out the tiny rectangular Fujifilm instant picture hidden inside. "Only a man hopelessly in love cross-dresses."

I stare helplessly at the image, my eyes burning with tears, though I'm not sure if it's sadness or amusement that's the cause. Probably a little bit of both.

Rocky offers me the photo, and I accept it with trembling fingers, barely able to believe it's real, barely able to believe Chance would do something so outrageous for me. But there it is, in full CMYK glory: Chance Jenson rocking a killer dove-gray balconette bra and matching hipster panties.

"I know you're hurt, and I know you're mad because of that hurt, which, hello"—Rocky puts her hand out, palm facing up—"is *totally* understandable given that Chance was a complete asshat."

I sputter out a giggle that's more of a choked sob.

"But I implore you, my beautiful-souled cousin." Rocky cups my cheek, thumbing away the single tear that managed to slip free. "Don't let that hurt and mad make you miss out on the grovel."

My brow furrows. "The grovel?"

"Come on, cuz." Rocky gives my shoulder a playful shove. "Have you not been paying attention at book club? The grovel is one of the best parts. Let that man prove he deserves your love."

I tried so hard not to fall for him, and when I did, he hurt me. Can I risk it happening again?

I really wish the swooping in my gut was indigestion.

"And if he doesn't?" I ask, my voice small as if too afraid to put the possibility out in the universe.

"Then we let Vince break his face."

# CHAPTER 39

*Gemma*

**M**y cousin is a brilliant woman.

Hell, I'd probably go as far as to say she's the smartest person I know, at least that's what the gajillion degrees she has make me want to believe.

But…

That doesn't mean I always take her advice. Or, in this case, I don't take it right away and instead choose to wait until I know Chance is at practice before heading to his house to cook for the pups. My stubbornness runs deep like that.

Coffee cup in hand and shoulders weighed down with enough groceries to feed two horse-sized dogs—which is a damn lot, trust me—I'm greeted by my two favorite canines as soon as I let myself inside their daddy's house.

"Hi, my babies." I blow kisses as Pebbles and Bamm-Bamm circle around me. Thankfully, I've learned how to properly two-step with them to avoid suffering any more coffee casualties.

I go to place the bags on the counter, but the island is covered in papers, so I set them on the floor instead and kneel to get my doggy kisses. Except I'm not just slobbered on—I'm scratched by something poking me from their collars. I pull back, and sure enough, there's a folded piece of paper taped to each of their tags.

My breath catches at the sight.

I know what they are without having to read what's on them. I've been getting the Post-it note versions for the last week.

"Oh, this is low, even for you, Dickhead," I say, thumbing the paper attached to Pebbles's collar.

"I thought it was a good way to make sure you actually saw them," a voice answers.

A *human* voice.

A human voice that is *not* supposed to be here.

A human voice that is *supposed* to be at *hockey practice*.

I yelp, pain radiating through my tailbone and up my spine when I fall on my ass.

Chance is in front of me in a flash. "Shit. I'm sorry, Precious."

I push his hands away from my face, blinking to bring him into focus, trying to make sense of why. He's. Here.

"What are you doing here? You're not supposed to be here."

"I needed to see you."

*Gah!* Why does that make my belly do loop the loops?

"You're supposed to be at practice."

"I'm aware."

"It's your job, Chance."

"The fine was worth it to see you."

His words hang in the air, and I'm left speechless.

He's here. Here for me.

And even though the thought of that warms my heart, I can't ignore the fact that he hurt me, that he accused me of things I would *never* do.

I push off the floor, scrambling to get away from him. I can't think when he's near, can't breathe. Pebbles and Bamm-Bamm don't leave my side, following me wherever I go, their tails beating against my legs.

"Can we talk?" Chance asks, shoving his hands into the pockets of his joggers—his gray joggers, I might add. The asshole is not playing fair.

"Do we have to?"

He takes a step forward, and I take one back, the defeated slump of his shoulders squeezing a vise around my heart. The silence hangs heavy, neither of us ready to break it first until Bamm-Bamm barks, demanding attention.

Chance grins, scratching him behind the ears, and it's like everything else fades away for a moment. The hurt, the anger—all of it evaporates for just a few seconds until he lifts his gaze back to me, showing me all that pain swimming in it.

"When I first met you, I was so fucked up from everything that happened with Wendy—"

"That you held whatever her sins were against me and took it out on me?" I snap.

I didn't mean to say it, but I can't help myself. I've been holding on to those words since they left his mouth weeks ago, and they still sting as if he just said them yesterday.

He winces and opens his mouth to speak, but no words come out before he shuts it again. It's like he doesn't know what to say or how to make it right without breaking himself in half, and that's our problem in a nutshell.

"I didn't tell you because that's not what I do. I was raised to be an island unto myself. I don't open up to people."

It breaks my heart to hear him say that, especially when I don't know where I would be today—if I *would* be here today— without my support system.

"Fine. But what about after *I* opened up to *you*? After I bared my soul about the shit I went through in high school? I trusted you with the most vulnerable parts of me, but when you finally opened up to me, it was with only half-truths."

Chance takes a step closer and wipes away the tear that sneaks down my cheek with his thumb before dropping his hand back by his side. My breath hitches at the tenderness of the gesture, and my heart speeds up as I finally gather enough courage to meet his gaze again.

"I was scared," he finally says. "I wanted to tell you so much more than what I did, but with everything that happened with Wendy…it felt like it was too much."

The sincerity in his voice brings a fresh wave of tears cascading down my cheeks, and all I want is to wrap my arms around him and tell him everything will be okay, tell him we'll make it through this together—but just as the thought enters my mind, reality sets in.

We still have so many issues to work through if we want any chance at a future together, and any words beyond that feel empty against the heavy air between us.

"Did you ever think if you trusted me with the truth of what happened in Minnesota, maybe we could have had an open dialogue, and I could have had a basic understanding?"

"I didn't want to think about it. I didn't want to taint what we had with what happened with her."

He can't even bring himself to tell me what happened with Wendy, so how could I ever expect him to open up to me about his feelings?

"And what did we have, Chance?" I swallow hard, willing myself not to cry again, but it doesn't work. "Because I thought we were a couple. I thought we were building a relationship, but that's not what you thought."

"That's not true."

"That is *literally* what you said to me. I couldn't believe you would think I would cheat on you, and you said—and I quote— *'We'd have to be a couple for you to cheat on me.'*"

God, those words have haunted me.

I swipe at my face, squaring my shoulders. "So, why, *why* would you worry about tainting something you didn't even believe we had?"

Chance takes a deep breath, his eyes holding so much pain it nearly breaks my heart.

"I felt like I was getting too close to you, too quickly, and I…" His words trail off, and when he still hasn't said anything a full minute later, all the emotions I've tried to suppress these past weeks churn together inside me, pulsing under the surface like magma, ready to erupt until I can't contain them anymore.

"I loved you, you idiot," I finally shout.

"Why the fuck are you speaking in the past tense?" His voice is low, but there's a spark of temper there that makes me want to strangle him.

"Because it's too fucking hard to love you," I turn on my heel, needing…to be anywhere but here.

Chance snags my wrist, spinning me back so quickly I bump into his chest as he steps closer. "I don't accept that," he says firmly, his gaze never leaving mine.

"Too fucking bad." I beat the side of my fist against his chest.

Chance wraps his hand around mine, unfurling my fingers and laying the flat of my palm over his heart, sliding his other hand into my hair. "I love you, Precious."

I'm momentarily stunned by his proclamation, my breath catching in my throat as I try to process what he's just said. I want to believe him. I want to believe him on a visceral level, but my heart is too busy trying to protect itself from rejection to even acknowledge the possibility.

"No, you don't." I refuse to accept his declaration so easily.

"How can you say that?" His voice is incredulous, and there's a hurt in his tone that makes me want to take it all back.

"Because…if you loved me, you wouldn't have held me in one arm while pushing me away with the other."

He brings his free hand up to cup my face, his thumb caressing away a tear I didn't even realize had escaped down my cheek. "I fell in love with you, Gemma," he whispers softly, his gaze locked with mine. "Head over skates in love with you."

My heart jumps into my throat, my mind desperately trying to process the words that just came out of his mouth.

# CHAPTER 40

## *Chance*

Gemma has never been one of those people capable of keeping their feelings from showing on their face, and never have I been more grateful for that fact than I am right now. While her words are telling me she doesn't love me, that's not what her expression is conveying.

My heart aches as I watch her struggle to make sense of how she feels. She loves me; she's just too scared to admit it. That's my fault, but I'm going to fix this.

"I fell in love with you, baby, but I was too fucking terrified to tell you."

Tears cling to her lashes as she blinks up at me. "Terrified of what?"

"That if I told you, you would finally realize how much better than me you are, and you would leave me. And guess what? You did."

Gemma shakes her head, her messy bun coming undone from the ferocity. "That's not fair."

"Am I wrong?"

My gut tightens, waiting for her answer.

"No, but the problem is you didn't trust me to begin with, and I get that. I didn't trust you, either. Hell, I didn't even like you for a solid year."

I don't bother restraining my chuckle. Leave it to my girl to call me out on my shit.

"But, Chance…" Gemma pushes against my stomach, trying

to create distance between us, but I'm not having it. "The difference between you and me is you never *started* to trust me. How can you expect me to believe you love me when you never trusted me?"

I take a deep breath and slowly let it out, searching for the right words to explain what I'm feeling. I don't want to make excuses or blame her. All I want is for her to understand.

"I can't love you anymore, Chance. It hurts too much."

The tears that have been threatening to spill over finally do. I brush them away gently with my thumb and cup her face in my hands.

"No. I don't accept that. You love me. You *know* you love me."

"It doesn't matter."

"The fuck it doesn't, Gemma."

"It does when you're so consumed by worrying about your past repeating itself that you forget to live in the present."

Fuck this shit.

I love her, and she loves me. We've already wasted a year because I was too afraid to let her in. There's no fucking way I'm going to let her stubbornness keep us apart any longer. I'm fighting for my woman, even if it means I have to flay myself open and let her see every ugly part of me.

"You're right," I finally admit. "I was scared of being hurt, so I didn't give us a real chance. I was defensive with my heart." I brush my fingertips across her cheek, wiping away the remaining tears. "But that doesn't mean I don't love you, Gemma. It doesn't mean I don't want this. All it means is that it's taken me a while to get here."

"I-I don't know…"

A ball of pain lodges in my throat, making it hard to swallow.

"I love you, and I'm done being scared. I'm done letting my past dictate my future. I'm sorry I ever held what went down with Wendy against you. It wasn't fair to you. It wasn't fair to *us*."

Gemma's expression softens as she looks into my eyes and sees the truth there. She may still have questions and doubts, but she knows what I'm saying is real and these feelings are genuine.

"When she told you she was pregnant, she told you it was yours, didn't she?"

I may hate this story, but Gemma deserves to know the truth.

"She did. But it wasn't mine." I swallow the puck-sized lump in my throat. "It was Stanton's."

Gemma's eyes grow wide, her mouth hanging open. "Shut the front door."

"Fuck, I love you so much it hurts." I grab a handful of her hair and pull her mouth to mine, quickly deepening the kiss to show her just how perfect, just how *Gemma* that reaction was.

I pull back, but only enough to rest my forehead against hers. "That whole situation made me feel like I was cursed. My world kept getting rocked by three little words."

Gemma never breaks eye contact, listening intently to every word.

"First, it was *Chance, I'm pregnant*. It didn't make sense—Wendy and I always used protection."

Realization dawns, and Gemma's lashes flutter closed. "That's why you freaked that night at Rookies."

I nod, our noses bumping together. "I've always been fastidious about protection. Never, *never* have I not used it."

"Until that night," Gemma whispers.

"Until that night," I confirm.

"Why?"

"Why what, baby?"

Gemma shakes her head, pulling back enough to see me without having to cross her eyes but not actually moving away from me. "Why did you believe her if you've always used protection? Why did you forget to use protection with me when you've always been anal-retentive about it?"

"I believed her because, contrary to what *I* made *you* believe, I'm not a complete asshole. And I forgot *with* you because you make me lose my head, Gemma Steele." Her eyes narrow, and I kiss the tip of her nose. "In the best way, baby."

Gemma purses her lips, not all that impressed with my smooth line attempts. "You said first, so what was the second?"

"When she told me the baby wasn't mine."

"Ouch."

"No. The ouch came from not hearing the words until we were in the middle of her ultrasound, and it became obvious that the math you told me I'm bad at didn't work out in my favor."

Gemma's eyes soften, her lip curling in disgust. "Damn."

I drag a knuckle across her cheek and along her jaw. Then I

tell her about how that's when Wendy broke down, admitting that she was also sleeping with Stanton and she knew the baby was really his, but when she told him about it, he wanted nothing to do with either of them.

"Is that why you punched him?" she asks, but the glint in her eyes tells me not only does she know the answer, she also approves.

Despite the circumstances, the corner of my mouth rises in a half grin. "Yup. And then I got the final set: *You've been traded*."

Gemma gives a low whistle and shakes her head. "Oof, three strikes and you're out."

"Can you not use a baseball metaphor? Hockey is the superior sport."

She rolls her eyes. She's used to the superior-sport debate.

"Guess the joke's on me." I let out a humorless laugh. "Because what I wouldn't *give* for three little words from your pretty mouth, Precious."

Gemma searches my eyes before finally bringing her lips up to mine in an almost chaste kiss. When she pulls away, she murmurs the three words that set my heart soaring: "I love you."

My breath catches in my throat as I stare at her in disbelief for a moment before crushing her body against mine and whispering fervently into her ear, "Present tense—thank fuck."

# CHAPTER 41

## Gemma

The scariest thing I've ever done in my life was falling in love with Chance Jenson.

The second scariest, telling him.

But the craziest thing, the absolute *craziest* thing, is that he loves me back.

"Now kiss me, baby, and tell me you're mine," Chase demands, dragging open-mouthed kisses down my throat.

"I'm yours," I groan, pulling his lips to mine.

I just can't get enough of him. I'm dizzy with it, breathless.

A dark laugh rumbles up from his chest, sending a shudder of need through me. "I'll never tire of hearing you say that, Precious."

I run my hands down his muscular torso, feeling my way over all his peaks and valleys then slipping beneath the hem of his Blizzards T-shirt. Chance's breath hitches as I trace patterns over his toned stomach, counting each of his abdominals. He bends, his large hands cupping the backs of my thighs, lifting me in the air. I instinctively wrap my legs around his waist, giddy with how effortlessly he carries me around.

The dogs dance around our feet, and Chance mutters a curse when Pebbles almost takes us out.

"Dogs, go lie down," Chance growls.

They scamper off to whatever mischief they have planned for the day. I can't help but giggle. This is my life.

We move through the kitchen, me clinging to Chance while

our mouths battle for dominance before he finally sets me down on the counter. Something crumples under my ass, and I break our kiss, remembering the papers that had been covering the entire surface of the countertop.

"Wh—" I pick the small business card out of the pile—the small business card with *my* business name and the logo I dreamed up for it on it. "Chance? What is this?"

His chest expands with a deep inhalation, his eyes meeting mine. "It's a business card."

"Yes. I can see that." I flick the premium card stock. "But why does it have my logo on it?"

He reaches up, sweeping my hair back, his fingers moving over the shell of my ear, sending shivers over my skin. "I know this is your dream." He takes the card out of my hand, framing it between his fingers.

"How?"

"Because I listen even when you're being cagey about the topic."

I struggle not to smile because he's not wrong.

"But from everything I keep hearing, you keep putting off putting your plans into motion."

I nod, still feeling a little perplexed by the whole thing.

"So I called Rocky."

"Smart choice, given Vince kinda wants to break your face," I say offhandedly.

"What?" Chance pulls up short. "Why?"

"Umm…you made me cry?" I say with a *Duh* tone.

"Awesome. You Steeles are going to be the death of me."

I loop my arms around his neck, using my heels to nudge him closer to me. "But what a way to go." I give him my sunniest smile.

"Do you want to hear the rest of my story, or do you want to give me a hard time?"

I toy with the hairs on Chance's nape. "Can't I do both?"

He chuckles, pressing a kiss on my forehead. "You're such a smartass. Why did I have to go and fall in love with you?"

"Don't know." I lift a shoulder, floating on the bubbles of happiness hearing he loves me makes me feel. "But if you figure it out, can you let me know? I feel like the same can be said about falling in love with grumpy dickheads."

"Brat." He cups my throat, hauling me in for a soul-searing, panty-ruining kiss.

We break apart, and he tells me how he had Rocky give him all the materials I compiled in my planning process and how he found my Pinterest board with other ideas. He did all the legwork for my business, from taking my sketches of a logo to a graphic designer to filing my LLC and setting up my website. He even went as far as having the app I wanted to use for a client portal developed.

By the time he's finished talking, my heart is pounding with excitement, possibility, and, okay, a fair amount of nausea from nerves.

Chance watches me carefully as if trying to gauge my reaction. "Are you mad?"

I shake my head automatically. "Why did you do this?"

"So you'll finally cook for me." He smirks that devilish smirk.

"Shut up." I shove him playfully.

Chance bands his arm behind my back, hauling me to the edge of the counter, letting me feel just how much he likes me before his expression turns serious.

"Because it's your dream, and if anyone deserves to have their dreams come true, it's you."

"Why?"

"Because, baby." He runs his thumb over my jawline before tipping my chin up so I have no choice but to look him in the eye. "You have one of the kindest souls of anyone I've ever met."

I lean into his touch as my eyes brim with tears before I shift forward to press a kiss against his lips and whisper, "That feels like an exaggeration."

"Do I need to remind you how you took care of my dogs even when you hated me?"

I look over my shoulder, watching Pebbles and Bamm-Bamm chomping away on the plushies I gave them. "Well...I always liked them."

"Shit, babe," he murmurs against my mouth as he kisses me. "I love you."

"I love you too."

# EPILOGUE

## Chance

**Two months later**

Not being greeted by my pups when I get home has become a fact of life I've needed to come to terms with, but when the reason behind their increased neglect is because a certain chef has been spending more and more time at my place...well, I guess I can't be too upset about being knocked down on the man's best friend list of favorites.

Except...that doesn't mean I'm going to go down without a fight. My girl's Etsy game may be strong, but my sheer stubbornness to spoil is stronger. It's why after dumping my bags in the mudroom, I make sure to grab the two new Eddie the Yeti plushies I got to replace the ones they decimated last week.

"Who wants presents?" I call out, brandishing a plushy in each hand as I round the corner into the kitchen and stop in my tracks.

The scene in front of me is not at all what I expected to find. Yes, my girl is at the counter, slicing and dicing, but the dogs I expected to be by her side—Pebbles dancing around her, begging for scraps, Bamm-Bamm obediently and obtrusively lying at her feet—are nowhere to be seen.

And my girl?

*Holy shit.*

I rub my eyes to ensure they aren't playing tricks on me.

They aren't.

She's cooking, wearing her apron. *Only* her apron.

My jaw drops, and it takes me a moment to realize I'm standing there, gawking like an idiot. I shake my head and give myself a mental kick, willing my dick to stop throbbing so my brain can come back online.

I take a beat to savor the sight before me, thinking of all the ways I'm going to take her before I need to leave for The Ice Box later. Who needs a pregame nap when sex with your girlfriend is on the table? Or, in this case, the kitchen counter.

But before I can move, Gemma glances up, giving me that sunshiny smile of hers that always makes my heart flip-flop in my chest. "Hey, babe."

I bite the inside of my cheek. Two months of officially being an official couple—Gemma's phrasing, not mine—and greetings like this are still strange. That's not to say my girl doesn't still sass me—she does and excels at it, too—but nothing compares to being the recipient of her lovey side.

As if she can read my thoughts—a distinct possibility—Gemma's nose scrunches adorably. She gives me a ball-tightening wink then spins to fill a measuring cup with water from the sink.

Holy mother of all things hockey.

Gemma's ass has always been one of my favorite things, but *damn*, it is something else seeing it all out for me with nothing but the neatly tied bow of the apron's strings resting above it.

"You're staring, Canada," she singsongs, not bothering to turn around.

She's right. My eyes are glued to her ass, tracking down her long, toned legs then back up again, devouring every inch of the delectable curves on display for my viewing pleasure. I'm transfixed by her every movement, following the dip of her lower back as she arches ever so slightly. It's such a small movement, one that could seem instinctive, but I know her; she did it on purpose to drive me insane.

It works, and I'm across the kitchen and standing behind her in seconds, pinning her against the counter. Gripping her hip, I yank her to me, cupping her throat and tilting her head back to bring my mouth to her ear.

"You're an evil, evil woman, Gemma Steele."

Her laugh is low and sultry as she shifts enough for her lips to drag along my jaw. "I thought you liked it when I cook for you."

My hands trail around to her waist, curling into the natural dip of her body and up the flare of her rib cage before slipping beneath the apron to cup her breasts, pulling and tweaking her nipples until they're tight, hard buds.

"I do." I bite her earlobe, drawing it into my mouth and grazing it with my teeth. "But when you cook like this, the only thing I'm interested in eating is you."

She moans a little, shivering beneath my touch as her head falls back to rest on my shoulder. Her hands press against the counter, fingertips digging into the granite and turning white.

Blood roars in my ears, my pulse pounding in my head as I let a hand travel down the soft contours of her body, slipping one between her legs, cupping her pussy.

"Chance," she moans, her breath coming in short, shallow pants as I tease her with my fingers. She arches against me, a silent plea for more, and I'm quick to deliver.

"You know what I want to hear, baby," I coax, moving my hand faster, pressing into her harder, and grinding my palm against her clit while continuing to thrust in and out of her depths.

"I'm yours, baby."

"Fuck." I thumb her clit. "Three of my favorite words." I press a kiss to that soft spot behind her ear. "Now give me my other three."

Gemma loops an arm up around my neck, pulling me closer to nuzzle her neck as she whispers back shakily, "I love you."

My heart flutters in response to those three little words, and I bite down hard on the soft skin of Gemma's shoulder with a satisfied groan before muttering back gruffly into the crook of her neck, "I fucking love you too, Precious."

She sighs dreamily, not erotically. "I love when you call me that."

I kiss my way up to her ear, swirling the tip of my tongue around the shell then nibbling on the lobe. "I know, baby."

Taking her hips in my hands, I spin her around and hoist her onto the counter, chuckling at her yelp of surprise. Moving into her space, I push against her body until there's no distance left between us. Gemma's long legs wrap around my waist as I lean down and press my lips against hers in a deep, passionate kiss that leaves us both breathless.

Breaking away, I drag my lips down her neck, scraping my teeth across her collarbone.

"More," she begs, stripping me out of my T-shirt.

Reaching behind her, I deftly work the apron strings, untying the bow and easing it over her head, exposing the little bit of her that was hidden from me. The heat between us is palpable as I slide my palms up her legs, her skin smooth and soft. She shivers beneath my touch, her body trembling as I knead and trace along her curves.

"Chance," she murmurs, gripping my shoulders as if fearing I'll disappear.

But that won't happen. I have no intention of leaving this spot until we've both gotten what we need.

Cupping her tits, I test their weight, squeezing and teasing the supple flesh. Gemma squirms against me, moaning softly as I suck a nipple into my mouth, nibbling around the tight bud and flicking it with my tongue. She hisses in a breath, arching into me as I roll the other one between my fingers, pinching and pulling it just like she likes.

"You're so fucking perfect," I murmur against her skin, my lips tracing along the valley between.

Her hand curls into my hair, holding me to her as I nip and lick my way to her other breast. My cock jumps in my sweats, and I groan, grinding into the unforgiving countertop. Releasing her tit with a pop, I pull back and slide a hand into her hair, cupping the base of her skull.

Gemma's eyes are still half-closed with pleasure when she finally looks up at me and touches a hand to my cheek with an adoring smile on her face.

"Fuck, Precious, you shouldn't look so innocent while you're writhing against me like this."

"It's your fault." She pouts, and I nip at her bottom lip.

"You ain't seen nothing yet, baby."

I feel my way back down her body before settling between her thighs. Gemma gasps as my fingers start their exploration, playing and teasing until she's panting for more. I slide two fingers inside her delicious warmth, curling them toward me as I rub circles against that sweet spot deep inside her. Gemma moves with me, riding my hand as I drive her closer and closer toward pleasure-filled oblivion.

"Give it to me, baby," I murmur against her lips as I work her into a frenzy, my hand moving faster, my rhythm stuttering. "Come all over my fingers, Gemma, and I'll give you all of me."

"Chance," she whimpers, her fingers pressing into my skin and gripping tight as her body begins to shudder.

"That's it, baby," I whisper, rubbing circles on her clit with the pad of my thumb. "Come for me."

A scream, long and guttural, rips from Gemma's throat as her whole body jerks and shakes, her pussy clenching around my fingers. I love the way she looks when she comes undone, the way her eyes flutter shut, her mouth forms a perfect O, and her body starts to tremble.

I don't let up until I've wrung every last bit of pleasure out of her, until she's sobbing and pleading with me to stop.

"Oh god." She moans, and I know she's close.

Taking my free hand, I run the tip of my finger up the length of the seam of her pussy. "I want to hear you say it again."

"Chance," she whimpers.

"Say it, baby." Teasing her more, I continue to press into her, slow and gentle.

"I love you." She hiccups as I build her up again.

"Again." I nip at her bottom lip.

Her eyes flutter open, and she stares hungrily at me. "I love you."

Gemma whimpers in protest when I drag my hand from between her legs, bringing them to my mouth and sucking them clean.

"Fuck me, Chance," she pleads.

"Here?" I ask, lifting a brow, chuckling at how she narrows her eyes as if my eyebrow personally offended her. In her case, that's exactly what my crazy girl believes. It's one of the many reasons why I love her.

"Right here, baby." She nudges me closer with her heels. "I ache for you."

Damn, she slays me.

"Lean back and open those pretty little thighs of yours," I

whisper in her ear before pulling back and lowering my joggers enough to free my straining erection.

"*Yesss*," she hisses through her teeth, her head thunking against the cabinets.

A slow groan of approval turned growl rumbles in my chest as I press the head of my cock against her wetness, her heat searing me without any barriers between us. There is certainly something to be said about being with someone you can trust enough to be with like this.

"Fuck, baby." I grit my teeth. She's still so tight after coming, and I know I won't last long. "You're so tight, Precious." I groan, flexing my hips harder into her, desperate to get closer.

"I love the way you feel inside me." Gemma's eyes slide shut, her head falling back as she arches up, pushing her tits into the air. She's an offering, a sacrifice to be ravished and worshipped, and I'm more than willing to comply.

I plunge into her soft wetness with a guttural growl that rakes from the back of my throat. Her breath hitches as I thrust into her again and again and again, harder and deeper, until we're coming together in a wave of pleasure that leaves us both trembling and spent.

Pulling away reluctantly, I stare down into her heavy-lidded eyes, and she grins, her cheeks flushed, messy bun completely undone. I bury my face against her neck, breathing in the sweet lemon scent of her skin mixed with mine before I whisper, "I'm never letting you go, Gem."

I feel her smile against my cheek, and her hand slides up my arm to my bicep. "Good, because I kinda wanna keep you too."

"Smartass." I nip at her cheek.

"You love me." She lazily drags her nails through the hair at the base of my skull.

"Lord help me, I do."

# Gemma

I never knew a king-size bed could feel small until I started staying over at Chance's. Then again, I never knew Chance Jenson, of all people, would kill it as a boyfriend, yet here we are more than two months into finally being an officially official couple.

I used to tease my hot hockey player boyfriend about not knowing the definition of personal space, but I guess the joke's on me because it's his dogs who struggle to grasp the concept. Pebbles is sprawled out on what should have been my side of the bed, and Bamm-Bamm has decided since I'm not as tall as his daddy, it's okay for him to take over the entire bottom of the bed.

The mattress dips, and an arm bands around my middle, pulling me in to spoon with a warm, nonfurry body. "Mmm." Chance dots kisses across the bare skin of my upper back. "I love coming home to you in my bed."

"I'm surprised you could find me among these bed hogs," I mumble into my pillow, not ready to fully give up on the last vestiges of sleep.

"Not so fun being their favorite *hooman* now, is it?" Chance's rumbly chuckle has all my lady bits standing up and taking notice.

"I love how salty you still are about it."

"Brat."

I hiss, pressing my ass into him when he bites my shoulder.

Jostled by our movements, Pebbles cranes her neck, flopping

her massive head onto my shoulder, darting out her long tongue to lick her daddy on the nose.

"You trying to steal my woman, Pebs?" Chance asks, scratching along her floppy ear.

If dogs can roll their eyes, that's precisely what Pebbles does before letting out a disgruntled huff and settling back alongside me.

"*Really* feeling the love." Chance trails kisses up the side of my neck. "The females in my life are so mean to me."

I yawn, wiggling around to snuggle against my man more. "I feel like I should be saying something about karma and all that jazz."

Chance chuckles, running his hand down my spine before nipping at my earlobe playfully. "Don't hold back on me now, baby."

Spinning in his arms, I lazily drape mine around his neck and stretch, letting my curves mold to his hard muscles. "Do I ever?"

Chance's smirk is pure temptation, but the thing that makes my heart pitter-patter inside my chest is the ease with which it comes for him nowadays.

"No." He dips his head, brushing his lips against mine before deepening the connection into pure possession. "It's one of the reasons why I love you."

Rubbing my nose against his, I tease, "Keep saying sweet things like that, and we'll never make it to The Steele Maker."

Chance's eyes darken, his hands slipping under the hem of my tank top. "*Yeah*, because *that's* going to get me out of this bed."

My skin is on fire wherever he touches me, my brain going foggy with desire.

Chance's lips move against mine, the way he kisses me leaving no doubt that I'm his and his alone.

Yeah…we're going to be late.

# *Becky*

My last name may be Reese, but The Steele Maker is in my blood as much as those it's named after. Being the manager of an MMA gym may not be all that glamorous, but what I've helped this place evolve into is incredibly fulfilling.

And it does come with a few perks.

Perk number one: getting to stare at a bunch of half-naked men in their professional fighting prime. *Hubba-hubba, mama likey.*

"Hey there, babycakes," Lyle says, sashaying up to the large semicircular welcome desk I use as my command station, a giant to-go cup of coffee extended in one hand.

I make *gimme* hands, wiggling all ten fingers with extra emphasis because we all know that speeds up the process of getting what I know is a red velvet latte into my possession.

Gotta love perk number two: hand deliveries of the world's best cup of coffee (don't worry, Buddy the Elf, this is a factual claim) from the greatest barista in all the land. I don't even care that Lyle only does it because of perk number one. I can't judge. Perk number one is my favorite too.

"Have I told you lately you're my favorite?" I lean across the desk, placing a lip-smacking kiss on Lyle's upturned cheek.

"Nope." He drapes his body across the desk, looking up at me upside down. "And I'm feeling *so* neglected because of it."

I give him a *There, there* pat then bend to give him another lip-smacking kiss, this one on his forehead, because I know my needy friend needs it.

"There ya go, an extra dose of some Beck lovin'."

Lyle's face lights up, and he hoists himself onto my desk, perching on the edge like my very own punk Troll doll—complete with neon-tipped spiky hair. "That's more like it."

I blow across the plastic lid and take a cautious sip of the best stuff on earth, sighing as the sweet, semichocolaty goodness rolls over my tongue. "Ah. It's like you're my own personal coffee genie because I was totally wishing for this."

Lyle gives me a wink. "I did take a class in customer service, you know."

I snort. "Maybe you should take a class in sexual harassment."

Lyle's jaw drops, and he flattens a palm to his chest. "I do no such thing."

"Oh *really*?" I poke him in the side. "And how many men have you asked to take their shirts off so far today?"

"Maybe I should be asking *you* the same thing, Trouble." He arches a brow at Deck and Gage—both shirtless—sparring under the watchful eye of my bestie boo-boo, Rocky, and a handful of Hollywood types.

I mime zipping my lips and throwing the key over my shoulder. When your nickname is Trouble, you learn pretty early on never to admit to anything that can't be proven.

"So..." Lyle crosses his legs, folding his hands at the wrists over his knee. "How *are* things in the land of the buff and athletic?"

I eye the hunky men sparring again. "Can't complain."

Just then, the door to the gym opens, and in walks my pseudo-cousin and roommate, Gemma—though I don't know how much longer the latter label will be accurate given the epic postorgasmic bliss she seems to walk around in any time she sleeps at the hunky hockey player's place instead of at home.

"Hey, boo." I greet her, propping my chin on my fist. "You might wanna fix the sex hair before coming into work next time."

Gemma squeaks, smoothing a frantic hand over her messy hair and burying her face in her boyfriend's side—a boyfriend I feel it's important to point out is smiling like he hasn't spent most of the time we've known him being the grumpiest person to ever grump before.

"*Ooo*, watching you spar with Vinny Boy is going to be *so* much more fun now." I clap excitedly.

"On that note." Chance turns for the door, only to turn back and lay a scorcher of a kiss on Gemma.

"I really need to start carrying around a fire extinguisher." Lyle fans his face.

"Oh my god, I forgot today is *that* day." Gemma slides under Lyle's outstretched arm, leaning around him to watch the scene unfolding on the mats. "Oof, how *hot* is Christian Court in person?"

"Careful, Precious," Chance growls, tugging Gemma back into him.

"Oh, hush." She swats him.

"So hot," I agree, my mouth tugging into a grin at Chance being all possessively jealous. Gemma tries to act like she hates it, but the smug smile she's failing spectacularly to hide proves otherwise.

"How's it going?" Gemma tugs on the hand Chance is trying to cover her eyes with, peering over his palm to spy on our friend working his charm.

"I think good."

The crew has been here for close to an hour, checking out the gym and evaluating Deck to see if he's a good fit to be the fight choreographer for their next big superhero blockbuster.

From what I've observed, Deck and Christian—one of the hottest superheroes to grace the silver screen—have had an easy rapport, and Serenity Black, his leading lady, *certainly* seems to approve if the way she keeps being all touchy-feely with him is anything to go by.

Not that I'm jealous or anything. I'm not. Deck and I are just friends and have been most of our lives. But I've seen her sex tape—as has most of the world—with the franchise's last fight choreographer. It's hard not to feel a certain way when someone who looks as fuck-hot as she does and has the *moves* she does is flirting with my...friend.

What the?

*Jeez.* Thank god Lyle brought me coffee because, *obviously*, I need the caffeine.

As if he can hear my wildly confusing thought spiral, Deck

chooses that moment to look up and call me over. "Beck, I need you for a sec."

"Duty calls." I excuse myself from my friends with a half bow and skip to join the La-La-Landers.

"What's up, handsome?" I slip an arm around Deck's waist as he drops one around my shoulders. We may just be friends, but we're both shameless flirts.

Deck stares at me for a beat, an inscrutable expression tugging between his brows.

I arch one of my own at him, not at all sure why the hell he's looking at me like that. It's weird. When he finally clears his throat, he pulls me to him tighter—also weird—and then drops the weirdest bomb of them all.

"I know a bunch of the crew met Beck here when you were making arrangements for today, but for the rest of you, I'd love to introduce you to Becky Reese, my girlfriend."

*Ex-fucking-cuse me?*

**Want to know what the pups really think about their dad and Gemma finally getting together? Or just how helpful Chance is with naked time?** Get you bonus epilogues here.

**Are you one of the cool people who writes reviews?** *Defensive Hearts can be found on Goodreads, BookBub, and Amazon.*

And if you liked seeing a peek at Vince and Holly's wedding, you'll love the story I'm writing for the Wild and Windy *Sexy Bedtime Stories Anthology*. Preorder here.

**The BTU Alumni Squad will be back.** *Add Caged Love to your* TBR here.

*Did you like meeting Ben Turner? He's also a side character in my # UofJ Series. Start it today with Looking To Score in Kindle Unlimited.*

# RANDOMNESS FOR MY READERS

Ahh, welcome back to the BTU Alumni world!

2022 was a rough one for me. I felt very broken in the fundamentals, where I felt I didn't know how to string a sentence together. I was actually working on a different book when I broke, so Gemma and Chance were what helped unbreak me when my friends wouldn't let me retire.

When I first introduced Gemma and Chance's enemies-to-lovers tension in Sweet Victory I didn't know why they hated each other.

But…man…let me tell you, Chance Jenson? He took me a bit by surprise. And he, dare I say, might rival Jasper Noble as my most possessive and jealous book boyfriend to date.

At least for now…

And if you liked seeing a peek at Vince and Holly's wedding, you'll love the story I'm writing for the Wild and Windy *Sexy Bedtime Stories Anthology*. Preorder here.

If my rambling hasn't turned you off and you are like "This chick is my kind of crazy," feel free to reach out!

Lots of Love,

Alley

# ACKNOWLEDGMENTS

This is where I get to say thank you; hopefully, I don't miss anyone. If I do, I'm sorry, and I still love you and blame mommy brain.

I always start with Mr. Alley, who still bitches about not having a book dedicated to him yet. I try to tell him I always mention him first in the acknowledgments lol.

Also, I'm sure he would want me to make sure I say thanks for all the hero inspiration, but it is true (even if he has no ink *winking emoji*)

To the Team Alley Wranglers for being the best team a girl could ask for and putting up with my crazy and me being the worst professional ever. I love you ladies!

To my favorite necklace of author besties. I joke saying you refused to let me retire, but I'm also serious about it. 2022 may have sucked, but I beyond grateful that the internet allowed me to force my friendship on you all and for book signings allowing me to meet most of you in human.

Julia, Laura, Cora, Jenny, and Amanda...thank you for not blocking me and still being my friend after all our insane voice memos trying to get this beast done.

To Jules and Kate my cover designers for letting me torture you both for these gorgeous covers, and James my illustrator for pretty much the same.

To Jess my editor, not only are you always pushing me to make the story better and giving such evil inspiration that leads to shouty capitals from readers, you were the real MVP for this book with your flexibility.

To Caitlin my other editor who helps clean up the mess I send her while at the same time totally getting my crazy.

To Rosa and Britt for giving my books their final spit shine.

To my street team for being the best pimps ever. Seriously, you guys rock my socks.

To my ARC team for giving my books some early love and getting the word out there.

To every blogger and bookstagrammer that takes a chance and reads my words and writes about them.

To my fellow Covenettes for making my reader group one of my happy places. Whenever you guys post things that you know belong there I squeal a little.

And, of course, to you my fabulous reader, for picking up my book and giving me a chance. Without you I wouldn't be able to live my dream of bringing to life the stories the voices in my head tell me.

Lots of Love,

Alley

# FOR A GOOD TIME CALL

Do you want to stay up-to-date on releases, be the first to see cover reveals, excerpts from upcoming books, deleted scenes, sales, freebies, and all sorts of insider information you can't get anywhere else?

If you're like "Duh! Come on Alley." Make sure you sign up for my newsletter.

**Ask yourself this:**

&ast; Are you a Romance Junkie?

&ast; Do you like book boyfriends and book besties? (yes this is a thing)

&ast; Is your GIF game strong?

&ast; Want to get inside the crazy world of Alley Ciz?

If any of your answers are yes, maybe you should join my Facebook reader group, Romance Junkie's Coven

**Stalk Alley**
Master Blogger List
Join The Coven
Get the Newsletter
Like Alley on Facebook
Follow Alley on Instagram
Follow Alley on TikTok
Hang with Alley on Goodreads
Follow Alley on Amazon
Follow Alley on BookBub
Subscribe on YouTube for Book Trailers
Follow Alley's inspiration boards on Pinterest
All the Swag
Book Playlists
All Things Alley

# ABOUT THE AUTHOR

Alley Ciz is an internationally bestselling indie author of sassy heroines and the alpha men that fall on their knees for them. She is a romance junkie whose love for books turned into her telling the stories of the crazies who live in her head…even if they don't know how to stay in their lane.

This Potterhead can typically be found in the wild wearing a funny T-shirt, connected to an IV drip of coffee, stuffing her face with pizza and tacos, chasing behind her 3 minis, all while her 95lb yellow lab—the best behaved child—watches on in amusement.

- facebook.com/AlleyCizAuthor
- instagram.com/alley.ciz
- pinterest.com/alleyciz
- goodreads.com/alleyciz
- bookbub.com/authors/alley-ciz
- amazon.com/author/alleyciz

CPSIA information can be obtained
at www.ICGtesting.com
Printed in the USA
BVHW061737170223
658742BV00029B/1006